KYNHAVEN

GEN-HEIRS: THE GUARDIANS OF SZIVERIA

SARAH WESTILL

KYNHAVEN

Gen-Heirs: The Guardians of Sziveria – Book 3

Copyright 2021 by Sarah Westill

ISBN 978-1-955293-06-8

Cover Design by For the Muse Designs

fully restrained passion and the ongoing threats surrounding them."

Indies Today

"Wow, this series just keeps getting better! ... I read this book from beginning to end, losing myself in their world."

Archaeolibrarian Book Reviews

"The suspense, espionage, and intensity of the story kept me from putting this 5-star fantasy story down."

Reader's Favorite

Praise for Kynhaven –

"…emotional and heart-breaking while still having elements of mystery that keep you hooked and wanting more. Overall, Kynhaven is an amazing book to read."

Miche Ardense for Readers' Favorite

"…a brilliant addition to the series and highly recommended…"

Merissa for Archaeolibrarian

"Another captivating story in the world of the Gen-Heirs… Kynhaven is a must read, part of a great series that you'll want to get hooked on!"

Nicky Flowers for Indies Today

Praise for Wintersfall –

"Very rarely do I read books like this that rise above the romance elements and actually deliver in terms of storyline."

Alex the Shadow Girl Reviews

"The chemistry between Sean and Katria is so steamy and intense."

Blessing of Blessing's Book Reviews

"…beautifully crafted and filled with vivid imagery…"

Julia from Literary Lotte Reviews

Praise for Raiventon –

"…Kevin and Raina dominate the pages with their care-

OTHER TITLES BY SARAH WESTILL

Levkaseon – A Prequel

Wintersfall

Raiventon

Kynhaven

Asherwick (June 2nd 2022)

Ericksen - A Wintervail Special (Nov. 2022)

Survaine (Feb. 2023)

For world maps and to stay up-to-date on the latest information, be sure to visit www.sarahwestill.com

Dedication and Acknowledgement

For every woman whose scars can't be seen…

CONTENT WARNING:
This book contains mature content, including but not limited
to –
Consensual sex (non-graphic)
Action violence
Character with a past of torture and rape
Attempted rape
Loss of a sibling

Reader discretion is advised.

WELCOME TO THE GEN-HEIRS WORLD

In the distant future, a major cataclysmic event not only reshaped the world as humanity knew it, but left entire lands uninhabitable. As generations of survivors struggled to endure a fight for territory and resources, humanity regressed into what became known as The Primal Years. A dark and dangerous time that lasted for centuries.

Slowly, civilizations formed in the new nations. Limited means of transportation and communication began to develop in a resource-poor world. Powerful countries arose known as Sziveria, Ruthenia, Italyssa, Westica, and Cairo. New cultures, with their own standards of honor, became global powerhouses.

By 830 Post-Cataclysmic Event (PCE), strong talents are now inherited traits, passed down through genetics. The recipients of an unavoidable hereditary legacy are known as Gen-Heirs. Trains, ships, carriages and if one can afford them, small magnetically powered vehicles move people. Radios are the only means of quick communication besides handwritten messages. Heated water is a luxury. Extreme drops in temperature and harsh arctic winds have forced most food growth indoors, in greenhouses. A dangerously lethal virus known as Human Rabies Syndrome (HRS) plagues the globe. The inhabited world is growing at a slow rate, each unique country striving to exist in harsher, cold climates, and those who survive have become ruthless in their quest to thrive in this new, forsaken world...

THE RANKING SYSTEM:

Guardians of Sziveria

Queen/King Elect
    Prince/Princess Elect
    Arch Guardian
    Prince/Princess
    Shield Guardian
    Master Guardian
    Primary Guardian
    Key Guardian
    Guardian (anyone who serves the realm)

Other Key Terms –

First Intelligence Office (FIO)
    Sziverian National Investigative Division (SNID)
    Haven City Enforcement Services (HCES)
    Medical Science Officer (MSO)
    Medical Science Investigator (MSI)
    Uninhabited Zones (UZ)
    Human Rabies Syndrome (HRS)

PROLOGUE

Haven City, Sziveria
August 13, 835 P.C.E (Post-Cataclysmic Event)

A notification for the family of Cora Dandridge from the Senate Office of Uconnland Region, Westica: We regret to inform you that the body of Ms. Dandridge was found…

The thin, yellow slip of paper with typed out words from a radio message shook in Mason Dandridge's hand. Someone said something to him, but all he heard was a strange, distant buzzing sound.

…near the city of Rhode Haven. Our investigators have determined the cause of death to be…

Mason didn't remember sinking to the ground, yet the cold marble beneath his legs told him he must have. A hand slid along his shoulder. Another grabbed his bicep. The same person? He wasn't sure. The inky letters stabbed at his heart until he wasn't certain how it still beat within him.

…multiple knife wounds to the chest. If more information is desired on the investigation, please contact transmission codes…

No, no, no, this wasn't happening.

His twin was not dead.

Not his Cora, the literal other biological half of his person. Despite being opposite genders, they were identical. Until they were around four, no one had known the two of them apart without one of them being naked. Then Mason had begun to gain mass, while Cora remained slender and light.

...For release of the life remains for burial or transportation, please contact transmission codes...

A tear splattered on the paper, shocking him into blinking. "I never should have..." He swallowed against the sting of bile rising in his throat. "I never should have let her go."

The message slipped from his fingers before he could stop whoever took it from him, the last words he'd ever know about his sister. No, that wasn't true. He would read the investigation report, no matter what it cost him. And of course, there'd be an article about her death, along with words from the family, which his mother would expect him to write.

"I never should have let her go," he whispered again, not caring about the tears soaking his cheeks.

"Mason, look at me," a soft, female voice urged. A light touch feathered along his jaw and forced his face to turn. Vibrant blue eyes filled with unshed tears stared at him with concern. Katria Blackbain smoothed her palms along his cheeks and into his long, black hair. "This is not your fault. Do you understand? Nothing you did, or didn't do, caused this to happen."

He shook his head in disagreement. There were lots of things he could have done, like tie her to a chair, lock her in her room, send her to Kynhaven for their mother... *their mother*. How was he going to tell their Matriarch about the death of her only daughter? Another wave of horror washed through him.

"My mother." The adrenaline from the loss finally hit his

system. Mason stood so swiftly, Katria fell back in surprise. "She... I..."

"I'll tell her," Sean Blackbain offered, taking hold of Mason's forearm to steady him when he swayed on his heels.

"No, it has to come from me," Mason said more to himself than to his friend and team leader.

"All right, you can tell her, but you aren't going alone." Sean still held tight, taking a step closer.

The words chaffed at Mason's already raw nerves. He fisted his hands and glared. "I'm not going to do anything stupid, and I'm not a child to be overseen."

Sean took a slow, calm breath. "I didn't say you were. But you're hurting, and don't even try attempting to lie to me. We're your friends. Cora was our sister, too. We aren't leaving your side."

Mason knew better than to lie to his friend, who as a Sympath, was capable of feeling all the emotions swirling through Mason at the moment. The endeavor would be useless. So he stayed silent, and for the first time since the wretched yellow slip of paper had been handed to him by Jonathon Hunter, an investigator with Haven City Enforcement Services, Mason looked around.

Katria had stood, her focus on her husband, her beautiful, pale face drawn tight. Jonathon leaned against a wall, his hands on his knees, eyes closed. By the exaggerated rise and fall of his back, Mason assumed he was either trying to keep from panicking, crying, or not throwing up. Maybe all three, since Mason had the same urge. Jonathon had been Cora's latest crush and attempted conquest. Perhaps his sister had succeeded, perhaps she hadn't. Either way, the enforcer wasn't taking her death any easier than the rest of them.

A faint movement from his left drew his attention to the small, pixie woman sheltered under Kevin Merrick's arm. Kevin's wife Raina held him tightly around the waist, her face buried in his side. Kevin was normally the calmest and collected of the group, only now he wore his emotional pain openly. The message, a beacon of color that Mason quickly hated, trembled in his hand.

This strong Guardian Team had been brought to their knees by the murder of one their own.

And for what?

Taking a deep, shuddering breath, Mason lifted his face to the faint rays of light sweeping down from the high windows in the foyer. He couldn't stomach to see anymore. The pain mirrored on each of their faces.

The agony of loss.

Along with every color, every pastel, floral painting hanging on the wall, every statue or vase overflowing with flowers, was what Cora wanted. All of it suddenly became too much. While the house had been passed to him, his twin had made the space hers since he traveled so much. He only used his study and bedroom when home for a few days. The last few months they'd spent in Sziveria was the first long stretch in his near ten years as Primary Guardian Kynhaven.

"We leave now," Mason said.

PART I

-WESTICA-

1
____

THREE WEEKS LATER
   Rhode Haven
   Uconnland Region
   Westica

A COOL, CALM BREEZE DRIFTED BETWEEN THE THIN PINE TREES surrounding a small, rundown house. Mason stood outside, while inside, the panicked screams of Cora's murderer were barely muffled by the clapboard walls. Finding him had been surprisingly easy, considering the Westican officials had sworn he was a ghost, wanted for at least a dozen rapes and murders, likely more. The serial killer had outsmarted them at every opportunity.

The Guardian Team had found him in three days.

Weak and pathetic, the murderer hadn't posed a challenge. Either the Westican government didn't care about the ravaged bodies he left behind, or they didn't have very talented investigators. He'd put up no fight when they'd busted through his door, screaming like someone had his balls in a vice. A quick flash of Mason's blade had sent words tumbling out his mouth. But none of them had mattered.

Mason was fairly proud of his reserve. He'd managed to keep himself together for Sean to ask three questions. And then he'd emasculated the crazy scab, and barely kept from shoving the body part in his mouth before sinking the knife to hilt in the man's thigh. Sean had thrown Mason out then. Now, they were trying to get answers before the sadist bled to death. Even though as a Medical Science Officer, Sean could maybe save the man's life, he wouldn't.

The outer door slapped against the frame. Mason took a deep breath and continued staring through the rows of trees. Katria stopped beside him. The black folds of her simple dress fluttered around her ankles in the breeze. Long tendrils of midnight hair brushed her cheeks and danced in the wind.

"A woman escaped him," she said softly, crossing her arms over her chest.

"When?"

"Five years ago."

Mason glanced down at her. "Why is that significant?"

Katria took a slow, deep breath. "He claims the same man who hired him to kill her, hired him to murder your sister."

Shocked, Mason's jaw dropped open. "What? She wasn't part of a serial obsession?"

"Turns out the scab isn't a serial killer. He's an opportunistic assassin. If he takes a liking to his marks, he plays with them a little before he kills them. Since no one has seemed to care, and he gets the job done, he's continued to bring in contracts. In fact, some have even taken his violence as a bonus."

A knot formed in his gut. Taking a deep breath, he turned his focus to the puffy clouds drifting across a blue sky between swaying tree branches. "Cora hadn't even been here two weeks, and nothing was found in her room to indicate she'd made any progress on her investigation into the rail systems."

"I know, but she must have found something."

As a journalist, his twin had taken to finding information on a ghost rail line associated with a secret group threatening their nation as a challenge. She'd departed on the next ship to Westica, leaving a note of her intentions behind so no one could talk her out of the dangerous, insane plan. Mason had known though. She'd voiced her desire to go and he'd voiced his displeasure with the idea. Grinding his teeth, he pushed away the guilt. He should have done or said more.

"Someone may have gone through her room before the officials did," Mason surmised.

"Yes. Was anything noted in the report?"

Mason considered the question and then shook his head. "No. Everything looked as if she'd be returning. Her room was paid for another week. Interviews with housekeeping at the inn said they'd found nothing suspicious. Her bed was unmade, a towel was on the floor, and a few papers were on the desk. The investigators had made a note of the documents and I read them on the way up here. Mostly menus from local eateries, and a few clothing boutiques. Nothing incriminating. I don't think she'd had time to find anything out."

"Then someone wanted to make sure she didn't," Katria said.

Mason let loose a deep, uneven breath. A sharp twinge of pain clenched around his heart. Someone had hired a vicious maniac to silence Cora, and Mason didn't even know why.

A distant bird cry mingled with the rustle of leaves and branches on the wind. Silence emanated from the house. Mason resisted the urge to return inside. Katria turned when the door opened and slammed into the exterior wall.

"Well?" she asked impatiently before Mason could.

Sean grimaced and rubbed the knuckle of his thumb across his forehead. "I'm not really sure I want to tell you."

"Did he have more to say about the girl?" Katria asked, eyes wide.

"Yes, but…"

"But what? Either we have a thread to follow or we don't, which is it?"

Sean cast his wife a heated glare. "If you'll be patient, I will tell you."

Pressing her hands together, Katria took a deep breath. She opened her palms. Sean remained calm, his expression questioning. She nodded, giving a sheepish smile. "Okay."

Mason glanced between the two of them. "What did I miss?"

"I'm trying to teach Katria patience when she's away from a scope, not just behind one. It's an on-going struggle."

"Ah."

A delicate, pink flush crept up Katria's cheeks. "Not my fault my peaceful place happens to be with a rifle in my hands."

"No, I blame your father," Sean stated and then crossed his arms over his broad chest and faced Mason. "All right, yes, we have a thread. Her name was Jessalyn Silverna…"

When both Mason and Katria opened their mouths to interrupt, Sean held up his hand, cutting them off.

"However, from what he was able to get before he bled to death," Sean glared at Mason, "I have no idea what condition she'll be in *if* she in fact did survive. There's a chance she died shortly after escaping him."

"What do you mean condition? Kat said it was five years ago."

"Yes. But he had her for nine days."

Mason sucked in a sharp breath. According to the reports, Cora had been in the murderer's custody for three days before she'd succumbed to her wounds and died. Naked, her body had been dumped like trash outside a town thirty miles from where they stood. What were the chances someone had not only managed to escape, but *survive* nine days of brutal torture?

"Do you think she had help?" Mason asked, his gaze going from the house to the long, narrow, leaf covered path that eventually led to a dirt road.

"She must have. I don't see how she'd have been able to walk away on her own," Sean surmised, his gaze following the same path as Mason's.

"Did he give you any information about her?" Katria asked, smoothing wisps of hair from her face when the wind picked up.

Sean helped, pulling the long, thick mass behind her back. "A little."

When he failed to continue, she glanced over her shoulder. "Are you going to enlighten us?"

"I'm working myself up to it," he muttered, securing her hair with a long strand of leather he'd pulled from his pocket.

Mason braced himself for more disturbing news.

"She was young, between fifteen and seventeen. An innocent. He said her build was similar to Katria's. She has red hair and green eyes. He was told to kidnap her first and take her as far from her home city as possible before completing the contract."

"What was her home city?"

Sean shrugged. "That he couldn't remember, but he didn't take her farther than this. Since he can't remember, I don't know if this was far enough or not. And that's all I was able to get out of him before he passed out."

Mason stiffened. "But he's dead?"

Sean sighed. "Yes, he dead. I didn't walk outside until I checked."

A little weight lifted from Mason's shoulders. He closed his eyes from the fluttering sensation. "Thank you."

Surprisingly, Sean didn't lecture him on the merits of keeping the enemy alive, or how it'd have been nice to take him back to Sziveria to see if his face spurred any recognition or caused any ripples. His team leader stayed silent, his amber eyes watchful. Mason drifted on the edge of something terrible. A darkness encroaching that if he weren't careful, would consume. He didn't attempt to deny the simple fact, or make excuses for it.

"We'll check in with Kevin at the next city we come to with a radio center," Sean said, taking the lead to head down the path back to their waiting horses.

With Raina being pregnant, Kevin hadn't felt comfortable leaving his wife. If his father-in-law, the Arch Guardian Synintel who oversaw all the elite Guardian teams in the First Intelligence Office, ordered their departure, he'd have no choice. Jonathon had wanted to help, but an unpleasant case landed on his desk and he'd had to back out. Since Sean and Katria had shown up with bags packed, Mason had simply been thankful he hadn't had to go alone, period. He was grateful to Sean, especially, for helping him maintain a semblance of sanity on the ocean voyage over.

Having lost her own sibling to murder, Katria had been too distressed to stay long with Mason during his more painful episodes. His ever calm and rational Sympathic friend, had no such qualms. A veteran to grief and betrayal, Sean kept Mason grounded with rational purpose. They would find out what happened, and they would make the killer pay. And they had.

The now familiar constricting of his chest and sudden pounding of his heart made his steps falter. Katria's hand slipped around his forearm.

"Breathe," she whispered, her soft voice carried on the wind to him. "In, out, like I told you."

Pausing mid-step, he closed his eyes, his hands fisting, and took slow, centering breaths. "How did you do it?"

"Well," she began, pulling on his forearm to get him moving again. "I didn't lose a twin, and I had a gun, so I shot a lot of trees for months and basically ignored what happened. I wouldn't recommend the ignoring part. Shooting targets however, is oddly soothing."

Mason couldn't stop the twitch of a smile at the whimsical tone in her voice. The action died before it could fully form. "I'll keep that in mind."

2

———

TUSCINGHAM, CAROLINA REGION
   One week later

SWEAT SLID DOWN JESSI'S TEMPLES AND INTO HER EYES. PAUSING to stretch out the ache in her back, she wiped her forearm across her forehead and surveyed her progress. How could she only be six posts in? Sighing with aggravation, she yanked up the leather gloves sagging on her sweaty hands.

"I should just let the bears eat you," she grumbled, glaring at the two-dozen honey bee hives buzzing with life within the shell of the beehouse. "Like you'll thank me for my blood, sweat, and tears."

Ah, but they provided for her with their hard-earned life's work. The least she could do was protect them from aggressive intruders. Which, with another long sigh, she did, unrolling a long stretch of barbed wire fencing.

Normally a task for two or more, she'd been relegated to single duty this morning. Wilson had woken up coughing too badly to be of any use. She'd been shocked blood hadn't appeared on his thin lips. She'd sent him straight back to bed, ignoring his mumbling about not being some feeble old fogey. Well, he was an *old fogey*, and he'd kill himself if he didn't learn to recognize his limitations. Tears swelled in Jessi's eyes at the mere thought of losing her crotchety guardian.

Without him, *she'd* be dead.

A soft whine drew her attention to the huge wolf-dog laying a few feet away. She gave a small smile. "It's okay, Sesay, I can handle it."

If the old man couldn't be on the front porch keeping a personal eye on her, then Sesay was within literal reach. His tongue flopped out of his mouth on a pant, his warm, golden eyes attentive. Thick, silvery fur gleamed in the high blaze of the sun, ruffling gently on the occasional breeze. A draft that kept teasing her with a coolness that never delivered.

Of course, they'd be in the middle of a hot streak, if eighty degrees could be considered hot. She knew once upon a time, almost a millennia ago, eighty would have been temperate. Now, with temperatures averaging in the fifties for summer, and twenty-below for winter, unless the country was located around the equator, eighty was downright sweltering. The bees agreed. Their fuzzy little bodies coated the outside of each box-built hive.

Like all living life in the inhabited world, they'd adapted to a much cooler climate. Anything above the comfort of sixty was hot. All the glass panels had been removed from their house for the summer months, until only the frame remained, hence the backbreaking labor she found herself in.

Without the shelter of the beehouse, the hives were much too vulnerable. A week ago, she'd noted bear sign, and had been vigilantly stalking the forest's edge since, making noise and being a general nuisance to nature. But she knew eventually the lure of sweet, sticky honey would be too great. The fleeting wisps of desire she'd caught, left behind by the animal as it'd brushed against a tree in an effort to figure out how to get to her hives, had told her more than anything else she worked on a clock.

Being an inexperienced fool, Jessi figured sinking the posts would be the hardest part. How wrong she'd been. With a fierce tug, she tightened the wire between two posts using the claw side of a hammer. When the wire was taut enough, she hammered in a stay. Cautiously she released the hammer, thankful when the strand remained tight and fixed.

For the next several hours, she tugged, grunted, and shook from the strain of affixing the perimeter. Jessi almost quit after every blood-inducing nick from the sharp points she seemed unable to avoid. Twice she went in to check on the old man, and twice she found him snoring in his rocker, the paper on the floor in sections. She'd chugged water, ate some fruit and cheese, and headed back out with Sesay padding quietly after her.

Back at the naked posts, she counted how many more remained. Too many. But, she'd managed to secure one side, and almost a second. Another day, maybe two, and she'd have accomplished a difficult task. Ignoring the burning in her shoulders and biceps, she pulled free one of the hammers from a loop in her pants and uncoiled a strand of wire.

Sesay let loose a deep, doggy whine and laid heavily in the dirt near her feet. Jessi cast him a sideways glance. "Yeah, yeah, things are so hard for you aren't they, Sesay?"

His head popped up at his name, his fluffy tail swishing lines on the dusty ground. Shaking her head at the silly beast, she secured the length of wire into the hammer end and then pulled tight from one post to the next. In a flash of a second the wire snapped. She tumbled backward as metal barbs whipped around her left arm and shoulder, gouging into flesh. Crying out, she landed hard on her rear. The wire tangled further along her torso, catching on fabric and skin.

The moment Jessi attempted to move, the snarled mess tightened, making her a prisoner. Trembles danced through every tensed muscle in her body. Tears of fear and frustration fell unheeded down her burning cheeks. Oh no... what was she going to do?

Even attempting to turn her head caused excoriating pain to lance through her arm, shoulder and across the side of her neck. Ugly memories threatened to make her panic, something she *definitely* couldn't afford to have happen. Taking slow, calming breaths, she waited until she was certain she could speak coherently.

"Sesay, *vae'ny*," she ordered softly, barely remembering the handful of commands Wilson had taught her for the wolf. When he responded with a curious whine, Jessi took another deep inhale and put more authority behind the words. "Sesay, *vae'ny!*"

After a short, sharp bark in response, he took off for the house. Alone, shaking in terror, Jessi burst into choking sobs.

Rock crunched beneath Mason's boots. With each step, small plumes of dust swirled, coating the black leather in a layer of grime. Readjusting the backpack slung over his left shoulder, Mason wondered if any part of Westica had brick or stone roads. So far, despite traveling nearly the entire distance of the country, none did, even the busy city streets.

The entire country seemed to be stuck four hundred years in the past where its travel was concerned. With the exception of new rail lines. A house path didn't seem to warrant any type of civilized construction either. Not even pebbles. Only dirt and more dirt.

Mason had traded his horse for information in town, learning an old man lived with his redheaded granddaughter on the outskirts of civilization. Whether or not the relationship was correct, Mason hadn't a clue. The description he'd managed to acquire on his journey south to find the fiery-haired woman matched. He was so close to possibly finding a clue, he didn't care how inaccurate the information was, providing the woman turned out to be *the one*.

A scream echoed through the trees. Birds fluttered and squawked into the sky. Mason froze, listening, waiting for something to sound again. When nothing but insect droning and frog calling filled the air around him, he shook his head and continued on.

Three steps forward, a massive beast barreled down the path toward him. Stopping inches away, the huge dog bared its canines in a snarl. Golden eyes challenged. Black tipped silver fur quivered along the ridges of his muscled back and shoulders. Mason stayed calm, holding his palms out. All their investigating had told them the old man who'd rescued Jessalyn Silverna traveled with a large dog. A Ruthenarc Wolf was the last dog Mason had expected to encounter. The almost terrified reports made sense now.

Wracking his brain back to his training days with the First Intelligence Office, he tried to remember the group command to render the dog obedient to him and lead Mason to its master. *Sesay* something… Keeping from snapping his fingers to jog his memory, Mason kept his attention on the wolf that refused to back down.

"*Sesay vae'ny,*" Mason said firmly. The dog sat and stared at him. Mason leaned forward and repeated the command.

The wolf gave a short, impatient bark and then turned with a swish of his tail and headed back down the path at a lope. Mason jogged to keep up. The dog glanced back, making sure to only get ahead by a few feet. Fiercely loyal to their owner, and highly intelligent, the Ruthenarc Wolves were a national treasure to Ruthenia.

Trained by the nation and only offered for adoption by a direct proven lineage to Ruthenia, they were a rare breed. In Sziveria, they used them for tracking and scenting in all aspects of security, from fugitive recovery, to drug detection.

Mason frowned. To find one outside of a government program was unheard of.

The wolf burst into a clearing. Low horizon sun glared over the tree line with blinding brightness. Mason shielded his eyes, pausing for a moment to glance around. The footpath branched off, leading to a small, two-story house with a sagging porch to the right, and to a tight grouping of greenhouse shells to the left. Straight ahead the wider trail went to a barn.

His guide let out an annoyed yip. Tongue hanging out, the dog stared until Mason began walking again. Naked fence posts surrounded the last greenhouse. As they neared, the terrified sobs of a woman joined insect buzzing. Mason picked up his pace. The wolf disappeared between two greenhouses where rows of corn blocked the view. The source of near deafening insect droning became clear when the corn gave way to the rows upon rows of beehives. He stopped midstride.

An old man fought a losing battle with yards of barbed fencing wrapped around a small, trembling woman. The dying sun cast her bound red hair in a warm golden light, making the strands seem alive with an inner fire. Blood ran in rivulets down her exposed forearm, small patches formed on what he could see of her light brown shirt from the back. The wire twisted around her bicep, shoulder and tangled in the fabric around her hip.

"Stop, just stop!" the woman sobbed. "You're making it worse, not better. I c-can't anymore… just g-give me a second. Please."

The old man muttered a curse. His thin skin had been no match for the vicious fencing. He bled as much as the woman. When the old man reached for the wire again, Mason rushed forward. Clearly, the elderly man had never dealt with the chaos caused by loose barbed wire.

"No, don't do that," he ordered quickly. "The coils unwind further and the barbs dig in."

"Who is that?" the woman asked breathlessly.

The old man surveyed Mason with wary, aged eyes. Short tufts of white hair stuck out at odd angles around his head, likely from dragging his fingers through the mess in anxiety. Dust coated his baggy, black wool pants and dark blue shirt. "I don't know. Who are you?"

Mason glanced around, taking in the tools they had available. "Do you have any metal sheers?"

"I-in a box a couple p-posts away," the woman said.

Mason followed the line of completed fencing until he spotted the small wooden toolbox. After dropping his bag, he found what he needed and returned. He shooed the old man away and sat on the dirt ground far enough from the wire to keep from getting it tangled around himself while he worked. Tear swollen, smoky green eyes met his. Fear shining in her gaze, she looked him over before quickly focusing on the ground. Muddy streaks tracked her reddened cheeks. She attempted to wipe snot from under her nose, but the movement caused her to cry out and Mason shook his head.

"Don't worry about messy tears on my account. I grew up with a sister who cried to get her way, bubbles out her nose and everything if whining didn't work." Carefully, Mason reached for the wire away from her body. Cutting it from the main coil, he winced when the pressure changed around the section wrapped around her, knowing the shift likely hurt. "Sorry."

"You c-can get me out of this?" The green of her eyes blazed against the redness from crying.

"Sure can." He snipped another section, pulling it away from her forearm.

A soft sigh of relief rewarded his efforts. "Th-thank you."

Tremors continued to wrack her body with each small piece he cut and pulled away. "What's your name?"

"J-jessi," she answered, giving him another shy glimpse of her beautiful eyes.

"Jessi," he repeated. "Is that short for anything?"

She took a slow, deep breath. "Used to be, once upon a time."

"Yeah?" Gently, he unstuck a nasty barb from her bicep, amazed when she barely flinched. "What was it once upon a time?"

Sniffling, she surveyed his progress. "Jessalyn."

Mason kept from showing any reaction, though inside he wanted to shout with relief. Finally, a possible thread that could lead to somewhere useful. He wanted to start questioning her immediately. However, now wasn't the time, or the place, nor was she in any condition for them. "Pretty name. Fits you."

She snorted. "I don't think so. You're just trying to distract me."

Mason smiled, untangling a barb from the shirt at her back. "Am I succeeding?"

"Maybe. What's your name?"

"Mason." He dropped another small section on the ground near his thigh.

"Why are you here?"

Shocked, he met her stare. While the question shouldn't have surprised him, he found he wasn't ready to answer. He had a plan, and it wasn't getting kicked off the property right away for asking questions neither of them were likely ready, or willing, to answer. "Someone in town said the old man always has a room to rent."

"Oh? So far from town?"

"Does he or doesn't he?"

"He does," the old man's gruff voice said from behind.

Mason uncurled a nasty bit of wire from around her shoulder, snipping above her breast, careful not to touch even her shirt's fabric. He noted the way her breathing changed and the color faded from her previously flushed skin. "Are the bees yours?"

"W-what?"

"The bees, are they yours?"

She blinked and then frowned. "Who else's would they be? The dogs?"

A smile twitched his lips, but he only shook his head at her rude quip. "You'd give my mother a heart attack with those manners."

"Good thing I don't have to meet your mother." She regarded him again. "Unless you want her to have a heart attack?"

Straight-faced, Mason asked, "Would you meet her for me if I said yes?"

Jessi laughed. The sound was so musical and carefree, Mason found himself staring. "Consider me distracted. I might, since you've done the impossible. I didn't think I'd ever be free of that wire."

Mason tugged the last piece free from her shirt. "Done."

Jessi tried to rise, only to collapse back to the ground. The old man rushed forward to help Mason lift her. Once he was sure the old man's strength was enough, he stepped back. Despite having rescued her, he was still a stranger. A large stranger. While his size served him well for most things, seeming harmless wasn't one of them. He retrieved his bag and followed them.

The walk to the modest, two-story house was slow. Jessi held her injured arm to her stomach with her good hand. Every now and again she'd glance over her shoulder at Mason, as if assuring herself he wasn't imaginary. At least he figured that's what she did, since her gaze seemed to travel the entire length of his person each time.

Mason forced himself not to do the same, not wanting to see the way her rear filled in the work pants she wore. Or how the loose shirt brushed against the promise of curves with each step. She was the last woman he needed to be looking at with any sort of interest.

The dog ambled beside the old man. When he seemed to get bored, he'd circle around all of them and then settle back in near his owner. Watching the regal canine, Mason asked, "What's the wolf's name?"

The old man paused, turning enough to see Mason over Jessi's shoulder. "Pardon?"

Mason motioned at the dog sitting loyally beside the man's leg. "Your dog, what's his name?"

"Oh, doesn't much matter, he won't respond."

Ruthenarc Wolves only responded by name to their masters. Which was why the group moniker and associated commands were so important to memorize if one found themselves on a mission with wolves. "I know that. I'd still like to know what to call him."

Jessi sighed. "His name is Sesay. And he does respond."

Mason lifted a brow. "His name is the—"

"Sesay works just fine," the old man bit out with a glare.

"Okay then," Mason muttered and decided to change the subject from the dog. For whatever reason, the old man didn't want Jessi to know the wolf's true name. "What is your name?"

"They didn't tell you in town?"

"No, they just called you Old Man."

He harrumphed. "Sounds about right."

"Do you have another name?"

"Sure. Wilson."

Mason narrowed his gaze on the backs of the two people meandering ahead of him. He figured Wilson's acerbic attitude must have rubbed off some on Jessi. Rude people weren't something he was used to. In Sziveria, people made an effort to be polite. Even if they intended on killing you, they'd be apologizing the entire time while doing so. Then again, perhaps the woman had always been surly and the two happened to complement each other.

Wilson assisted Jessi up the steps. At least at first that's how it appeared. After watching a bit closer, Mason realized the roles were reversed. Despite being injured, the young woman helped her much older companion tackle the six, wide stairs to the porch in desperate need of repair. Mason rushed ahead and grabbed the door.

Before entering, the old man met his stare. "How long you needing to stay?"

Mason shrugged. "I'm not sure. How long am I welcome?"

Wilson smiled, showing off a few missing teeth while nodding toward Jessi. "As long as she lets you."

3

JESSI HAD ONE BASIC RULE FOR HERSELF. STAY AWAY FROM GOOD looking men. Eventually, she figured, any male who could lure a woman with nothing more than a smile, would think they could catch *her*. Since she was far too broken to be any man's romance, let alone conquest, staying clear of them seemed the safer, saner, option. And now the hottest of the hot was standing on her porch, waiting for approval to sleep under the same roof as her.

Wonderful.

Matters weren't helped when said male stood almost a full foot taller than her own five-foot-five height, and was at least twice her size. This man named Mason was huge. When they brushed past him at the door, she couldn't stop herself from staring at the long length of straight, black hair tied behind his back, or wondering if the strands were silky. They looked silky. His hair fell past his shoulders and appeared in better condition than her own had ever been. On a good day, untamed frizz best described hers.

A long and shiny mane wasn't the most startling thing about the man. The pale, silver of his eyes set against light olive skin, and thick, black lashes had made her almost gasp when she'd first seen them. Had she not been in immense pain, she knew she wouldn't have been able to stop the reaction. Not even the bushy beard he sported seemed to detract from a good bone structure underneath all the fuzz. He was an attractive, bear of a man.

Now she just needed to know if he'd bite like one.

Frowning, Jessi focused on getting Wilson somewhere to sit. All the excitement was bound to catch up to him any moment, and once his body decided to go down, she had a hard time getting him back up. Injured, the task would be impossible. Doing anything less would require her to admit she now seemed to have the help of a strong, capable man around the decaying house. Since she wasn't ready to acknowledge his presence, she ignored him and any assistance he'd likely provide.

Wilson stumbled into his rocker. The chair swung wildly back with a creak before righting. "There, the old man is safely contained." He waved as a coughing wheeze escaped between his thin, pale lips. "Go get those cuts tended. The young man can help."

Jessi froze. Oh no, the *young man* would most certainly not be helping. "I can handle it myself, you know that."

She picked the paper off the floor and placed it on his skinny legs. The familiar sense of panic at his declining state of health threatened to surface. No matter the amount of food she placed in front of him, he picked at it like a chicken. She didn't know how much weight he'd lost in the past few months since the cough started, but she knew the wool pants hadn't always drooped from his thighs.

Cold, wrinkled fingers touched her wrist. The only physical contact he'd dare. "Jess." He didn't say anything more until her gaze met his. "You know we can't afford for you to get an infection. If he hadn't come along…"

She'd still be tangled in wire, cut worse and wishing for the second time in her life death would claim her. And Wilson spoke the truth. If an infection took her down, no one would be able to care for their small farm. Though meager, the little they had provided. The chickens produced eggs, the cow milk, and the bees the honey and wax that supported them. Until Wilson's health improved, without her, they'd lose everything.

Taking a slow breath, Jessi tried to keep tears from betraying her fear. "What about… you know?"

Wilson glanced past her to Mason, who'd closed the door and stood in the small alcove looking around. The house wasn't large. A kitchen and eating area to the left, the sitting room to the right. A small hall to the left of narrow stairs led to Wilson's room. Two additional bedrooms were upstairs, across from each other.

"He doesn't seem the sort to care about such things. He has scars of his own."

Jessi wasn't so sure, but what choice did she have? "All right. Do you need anything first?"

"You're bleeding all over my floor, but can you get me something?"

Glaring, Jessi stood. "Fine. I'll check on you in a bit."

"Shine is above the sink."

"I know where you keep your shine," she bit out in annoyance. Not that he drank the clear, fiery liquid any longer. His throat couldn't stand the burn, and hers never could. The only reason she kept the nasty stuff around was for first aid.

Grunting in reply, he snapped his fingers. Sesay ambled over. With a whine, the hulking dog folded at Wilson's feet. Content to leave the old man to his rest, Jessi crossed the short distance to the kitchen.

"Sink is in here, it's the only running water we have in the house." Pausing at the wide entry into the eating area, Jessi realized she hadn't bothered to ask the stranger if he'd assist her. Then again, she didn't really want his help. Curling her fingers into her palms, she took a soft, calming breath. "I could use help with some of my cuts."

When she went to the sink and looked back, Mason hadn't moved. His arms were crossed over his broad chest. A frown pinched his face.

"Were you raised by the wolf dog?" he asked with complete sincerity.

Jessi blinked. "What?"

"Where I come from the words *please, thank you* or even *I'd appreciate it if,* are all part of our vocabulary. Important parts. You don't seem to know them, so I'm thinking maybe no one taught you. Since any self-respecting mother knows to teach basic manners, I won't insult your mother, she must not have raised you."

So much heat burst into Jessi's cheeks she was shocked her face didn't spontaneously combust. Had being around Wilson's gruff nature really rubbed off on her so drastically? More than a little embarrassed, she turned her back to him and reached with her good arm above the sink to retrieve the quart jar of moonshine.

"I'm sorry, I'll understand if you don't want to—"

The jar disappeared from her fingers before she could pull it down. The warmth of his presence made her stiffen. Despite being near enough to sense, no part of him touched her physically.

"I never said I wouldn't help."

The mere whisper of his deep voice near her ear caused a strange reaction in her stomach. Breath caught in Jessi's throat. Lowering her hand to the sink, she tried to make sense of the fluttering sensation along with the desire to hear his voice hum so close again.

He didn't disappoint. "I only pointed out your manners could use some work."

Trying to keep from giving away her flustered state, she cleared her throat. "I'll remember that."

"Since your shirt is already ruined, do you mind if I cut away the sleeve to get to your back?"

Her back. No! He couldn't see her back… no one could. Ever. Panicked, Jessi tried to find a way to recant his assistance. All she managed was a pitiful, "Um."

"I promise I won't touch you." A tenderness in the soft spoken words almost made her turn around. How did he know she didn't like to be touched? Had she been so transparent?

"It's not that." Then after careful thought, she rephrased, "Well it is, but, it's also, well, I… I have a lot of, um…"

Tears stung her eyes. She tried to block out every painful dig of a blade into her skin that had left her mutilated. A disfigurement no one could stand to look at, or her, if they happened to catch a glimpse. After the third time of being treated like a pariah, she'd taken to wearing long or half sleeves. If the fabric didn't reach her elbows, she didn't wear the shirt. For some reason, Mason looking at her with revulsion and pity made her queasy.

"You know, I can handle this on my own," she said softly.

"You can?" The hint of shock in his voice almost made her smile.

"Sure."

"Show me."

Blinking, Jessi went to turn and face him, only to realize if she did so, she'd be chest to chest with him. A cool sensation swept across her back as he stepped away, giving her room to maneuver. Straightening her spine, she reached around with her right hand. Slicing pain tore through her shoulder. She gasped and clutched at the sinks edge until her nailbeds turned white from the force.

"You handled that very well," he said into her ear again.

When he leaned forward to test the water from the faucet, his long hair brushed against her forearm. She couldn't stop her fingers from touching the strands. They were softer than she imagined. Like silk, the inky black mass flowed across her hand without a single tangle.

Mesmerized, she wound a piece around her index finger. "I've never seen hair like yours before."

"I can tell." There was a gruff edge to his voice that hadn't been present before.

Jessi's heart fluttered and she released the lock and took hold of the sink again. "Sorry."

He wetted a cloth. "Feel free to explore any part of me you find curious. I won't stop you."

Wide-eyed, Jessi glanced over her shoulder to find his silver eyes dancing with merriment, even if the expression didn't fully reach his mouth to form a smile. Once again, he managed to render her speechless. While she'd always feared male interest, for some reason the reality intrigued rather than alarmed.

Unsure of what to do, she figured she wouldn't have to worry about the dilemma for long. Once he saw her back, his curiosity would vanish. Maybe he would too. Holding on to that thought, she worked up the courage to warn him.

"You may remove my sleeve. However, don't freak out over what you see."

"I've seen worse injuries than what that barbed wire managed."

Jessi chewed on her bottom lip. "I'm not talking about the barbed wire. My back is… it's…" She took a deep breath. "It's not pretty."

"I know."

The words were so quiet, she almost wondered if she imagined them. "You know what?"

"Where are your scissors?"

"In the last drawer, over by the window."

Metal objects clanked together as he dug around. His ponytail flopped over his shoulder again, making Jessi's fingers tingle. How silly. She'd never cared about a man before, why was he so enthralling now? Because everything about him was different. New. From his size to his mannerisms, he intrigued her.

Well too bad, you know you can't have anything to do with him, so don't even think about it.

Having found scissors and washcloths, Mason returned, setting everything beside the sink. Jessi stared out the small window into the early evening. Shadowy blue light made details hard to discern. An anxious jumble of nerves tightened her muscles. She wasn't ready for someone, especially a handsome stranger, to see her deepest shame. Tears strung her eyes. What choice did she really have? The insidious monster known as infection didn't care about her modesty or past, only the future it could steal without prejudice.

She shouldn't care anyway, he'd never see more, so why did it matter what he *did* see? The faint tug of fabric was her only warning before he stripped away the sleeve and portion of the back, exposing her past and present injuries. Breath held, she waited for his reaction.

Fabric dropped onto the counter by the sink a second before his hand reached around and turned on the water. "I have to clean away some of the blood before I disinfect."

Blinking, Jessi turned her head and took in his unconcerned expression. "Okay."

He ran a washcloth under the water and then rang it out. Jessi turned off the tap out of habit before he could. Distracted over his lack of a reaction, she barely noticed the cold cloth running across her ravaged skin. Then she remembered his earlier words. *I know.*

"What exactly do you know? What did you mean?" she asked, trying to keep her words calm but knowing she probably failed.

He let out a long sigh that teased the edges of her hair, and continued to slide the cool washrag across her skin in gentle strokes. "I know what happened to you."

Jessi processed his words in a haze of denial and fear. No one could know what happened to her unless... She swallowed against the sting of bile in her throat. Injured or not, no one would lay a hand on her again unless she was dead at their feet. Then she didn't care what he did.

Snatching an iron skillet off the drying wrack, she spun away from him, holding the heavy metal with both hands. Pain throbbed in her injured shoulder and bicep. The pan trembled in her grasp. If he made one wrong move, she'd call for Sesay and smack the man upside the head while the dog kept him distracted.

"How? How do you know?"

Unfazed by her outburst, he leaned his hip on the edge of the counter and regarded her with those cool, silver eyes. Jessi clenched her teeth, wishing she knew more about men. She'd trusted two in her life, good men. And a stranger, like the one standing before her, had taught her in the worst way not all men were decent. Some were downright evil. Desperately she wanted Mason to be one of the good ones. However, she couldn't afford to be wrong.

"The man who hurt you, hurt my sister, too." The statement was given without emotion. Not even his face revealed how he felt about the matter. "Unlike you though, she didn't survive."

EVERY CELL IN MASON'S BODY RAGED. BLOOD POUNDED FURIOUSLY in his ears. He'd managed to remain centered while he'd helped her, focusing on a task, and the beautiful woman. Once he spoke the truth, voiced the reminder of why he really stood in her kitchen, all the rampant emotions returned with a vengeance.

On the outside he remained composed, motionless. The frightened woman standing before him didn't need to know about his inner struggle. If the fury and guilt tearing him up inside showed, she'd likely see him the way he imagined she already did. A crazed lunatic better dead at her feet than left to freely roam her house.

The thick metal pot shook in her clenched hands. Her muscles and injuries had to be burning, and yet she refused to back down. She hadn't called the dog, which meant her mind wasn't made up fully about him yet.

Staying calm when he'd seen the scarring on her back had been difficult. From her upper arm, to the back of her neck, and beyond where he could see, had been covered in ribbons of white. Some thick, some thread thin, they crisscrossed over every inch of visible skin. Evidence of a blade slicing without care across her once beautiful flesh.

Anger and shock had assailed him. Reading about the atrocities committed against Cora had been bad enough, seeing the healed reality had hit hard. But he'd known before even removing the fabric she was afraid to reveal her skin. She deserved better than to feel inferior over a situation in which she'd had no control. Forever she'd carry the reminder of something precious stolen from her. An innocence lost that could never be returned.

Their little exchange had revealed another surprise. Jessi was a woman interested in a man. More specifically, him. Mason wasn't sure how he felt about the revelation, but he knew from her retreats, she wasn't sure either. Both of them stood on uncertain ground. Only he was the one who needed to tread carefully. She didn't deserve to be hurt, nor could her already fragile confidence afford a broken heart. If Mason were perfectly honest, his brittle state couldn't take on anymore guilt. He had nothing to offer her at the moment, and likely for a long time. His heart was busted enough for the both of them.

Her smoky, green eyes stayed locked on him, the thoughtful depths seeming to process his confession. Keeping his movement slow, he pulled the trembling pot from her hands. "I'm not here to hurt you, I swear."

Unarmed, she took a weary step away from him, but didn't reach for a new weapon. "Then why are you here? How did you find out about me? No one knew, no one except Wilson, and I know he didn't tell you."

"Someone knew." Mason set the pan on the small woodstove.

She shook her head. Anger flared in her eyes. "No. I've not told a single soul, and neither has he."

Annoyed, Mason crossed his arms over his chest. "I'm not lying to you, Jessalyn. I know because I killed the man who hurt you, who murdered my sister. And before he died, he confessed some information I thought you should know."

The hard glint remained in her gaze. "My name is Jessi. *Jess-e.*"

Mason regarded her. In the dying light filtering in through the few small windows in the room, he couldn't make out much. When he delivered the life-altering news, he wanted to see her. At least, that was the reason he forced himself to acknowledge. Not because a certain desperation to get a good look at her had taken hold. "Where are the lamps and matches?"

"What?"

"It's getting dark."

A low growl sounded from her throat, mixed with a sigh of exasperation. "You're... weird."

"I've been called worse."

She muttered something while turning. Seconds later a match flared, chasing away shadows. "There's another one right by the kitchen entry."

Mason crossed the short distance. Matches were on a small shelf underneath the lamp. After removing the thin glass globe, he lit the match and touched the delicate flame to the wick. A warm glow encompassed the room between the two lamps. Satisfied, he shook the match out and replaced the glass. He dropped the spent stick in a little metal box next to the lamp.

Basked in soft light, not even the dirt streaking her skin could detract from the porcelain smoothness. She tucked a strand of hair behind her ear, her attention on the floor. Cut crudely to just above her shoulders, the fiery waves sprouted little flyways in all directions. The tip of her tongue swept from her top to bottom lip, coating her full mouth in a seductive glossy sheen. The smooth shadows swept across her high cheekbones and accented the curve of her jaw. Her perfect, straight nose wrinkled slightly in a sniff.

Everything about Jessalyn Silverna was striking, and she didn't even know it. Her confidence should be a constant, an inborn knowledge of her beauty and her desire to keep it to herself, or show others what she wanted. Not just present when she was scared and needed a weapon to make herself believe she was strong. Anger once again had Mason fisting his hands at his thighs. Too much had been stolen from her. But not ever again. He'd made sure the scab would never touch another human.

The reminder soothed him enough to relax his hands. "If I told you I'd never lie to you, would you believe me?"

Her gaze shot up. His breath caught in his throat as the light accentuated the exotic, green hue of her eyes. Once he'd seen that shade in a necklace around a dignitary's throat. Never having seen it before, he'd been told the precious stone was named jade. A unique pale, smoky green.

She licked her lips again. Unexpected desire seized his body, clenching his stomach. Would her lips be as soft as they looked? If only he weren't a hollowed-out shell, and she wouldn't likely panic. She was nowhere near ready for a kiss. Neither was he.

"I'm not sure," she answered cautiously. "I don't know

you. But, so far, you've done nothing to make me think you're untrustworthy."

"Fair enough." Mason decided on a different approach. "In my country, where I'm from, we serve in Guardianship positions. I'm on a team and my leader is a Sympath. Do you know what that is?"

She shook her head, her mop of hair sliding along her neck.

Mason continued. "Sean, my leader, is known as one. They can detect emotions, and with a touch, can actually feel them. I can't lie to him. Not even a little one. He's been our team leader for almost six years now. Since lying is useless, I've basically been trained to be honest in all my dealings."

A small frown played at her mouth. "I can tell."

"Before I reveal what I need to, I have to know you believe I'm not lying, that I won't lie to you."

She rubbed her hand along her uninjured arm. "All right."

Mason motioned and took a step closer to the sink. "Do you want me to continue taking care of your injuries while we talk?"

Her frown deepened. "That depends. Are you going to say something upsetting?"

Without hesitating, he replied, "Yes."

A huff of air blew from her lips. Her hands fell to her side. "Well, you *are* honest, aren't you?"

Before returning to the sink, Mason reached into his backpack he'd set on the table. After searching around, he found the jar of wound cream Sean made all of them keep on hand. "I try to be."

"Very well. I guess being a little distracted won't hurt anything."

Mason set the cream next to the jar of moonshine. "As long as you're paying attention."

"I'll hang on your every word," she said, returning to her spot in front of the sink.

A smile twitched at his lips. She seemed to have a remarkable ability to almost coax one out of him. But Cora's smile, a duplicate to his own, shimmered into memory and all semblance of cheer faded. He rewetted the washcloth and angled his body so the light behind him fell across her injuries. "Why are you putting up a barbed fence by yourself?"

He touched the damp cloth to a cut on her upper arm and she inhaled sharply. "There's a bear."

Mason paused and stared at her face. "A bear? A real bear?"

Laughing, she looked at him. Her teeth were perfect, and a little dimple appeared in her left cheek. The entire demeanor of her face changed, taking on a youthful glow. He thought her beautiful before... He almost dropped the washcloth.

"It's not a stuffed one like Mr. Danner has at the General Store in town, that's for sure." The smile faded and she sighed. "It's after my honeybees."

Mason tried to wrap his head around such a dangerous predator being so near. "We don't have bears in Sziveria. The only predator we have is a white leopard beyond the Northern Boundary."

Her eyes widened. "You're from Sziveria?"

"Yes, why?"

She looked down, her fingers smoothing along the edge of the sink. "My father was from there."

"Who's your father?" he asked as casually as he could manage. This could be the clue he needed to find out who had wanted her and Cora dead. He slid the cut fabric away from her back, careful not to touch her skin. A thick scar caught his attention, disappearing at both the top and bottom edges of the fabric. Resisting the urge to lift up her shirt to see how long it was, he wiped dried blood away.

"I only ever knew his first name."

"You don't have his surname?" Mason somehow managed to keep his disappointment from his voice.

She shook her head. "No, I have my mother's. My father was very paranoid, I think. Since he wasn't always with us, he preferred that no one could identify us as his family."

Mason continued to carefully cleanse her skin, rinsing the cloth when needed. After a few silent moments, he said, "I think perhaps he wasn't so paranoid. What do you know about him?"

She swallowed audibly. "Not much, really."

A little tremor raced along her spine. Mason lifted the cloth away and waited for her to collect herself before reaching for the moonshine.

"I remember he loved us," she said on a whisper he had to strain to hear. "I always wondered..." She swallowed again and sniffled. "I always wondered if he knew, knows, I went missing."

Mason's chest tightened at the defeated state of her words. Like a little lost girl. He wanted to pull her into his arms, sink his fingers into her hair and assure her the father who loved her, still did. Instead, he took a deep breath and unscrewed the lid to the moonshine jar. "It's been five years. I imagine he knows."

She nodded faintly. "Perhaps. I suppose I'll never know."

"Move around so you're over the sink."

Without a word, she obeyed. She even pulled the shirt tight across her back to try and keep it from getting in the way. Mason did his best, but alcohol flowed down her back and side. A high squeak was the only noise she made when the stinging liquid touched the open wounds.

Finished, Mason set the jar on the counter and stepped away. "I'm impressed, barely a sound. I usually carry on like a two-year-old."

She fanned the damp shirt away from her body. A small

smile tugged at her lips. "Yeah, well, a little liquor burn isn't much really."

No, Mason supposed it wasn't. Not after what she'd been through. He propped his hip against the counter and crossed his arms. "You really don't know anything about your father? You're sure?"

She copied his stance, raising her chin a fraction. "I'm sure. Why is that so important?"

For a moment he considered playing down what he had to say. He didn't want to scare her, or take away the safe bubble she had formed in the small house with the old man and his wolf. But Mason had never been one for sheltering, and if a danger was present, she had the right to know.

"The man who abducted you was hired by the same one who paid him to kill my sister." She stared at him, her mouth gaping. "Who would want you dead?"

4

"WHAT ARE YOU TALKING ABOUT?" JESSI ASKED, THINKING FOR sure the man in front of her was crazy.

Handsome or not, he *had* to be insane. Why else would he think someone had paid to have her kidnapped, tortured, and raped? And he figured the eventual outcome would have been her death. No. She refused to believe that.

Well, fine, yes, she admitted she'd known she was going to die. After the second day, with at least a dozen knife slices across her back, the wretched memories of the victims before her leaching from the mattress, distorting her sanity and playing further havoc on her will to live, death had been an inevitable conclusion. She'd always assumed she'd been a random victim like those she'd been unable to avoid witnessing, but certainly not a hired mark. In none of the flashes of chaotic fear and pain, had she been given the impression the other victims felt the same. She swallowed against the rise of bile and old fear.

"I thought he was a serial killer too, but turns out he wasn't," Mason said softly. "He was a hit man who occasionally took a liking to his targets."

The silver of his eyes flared in the dim light and Jessi had

40

the sudden urge to take a step back. His words were too raw, to painfilled to be a joke or misunderstanding. What if he were right? "And someone hired him to kill your sister?"

"Yes, the same person who paid him to kill you. They must have figured he succeeded since they were a repeat client." His jaw worked under his beard. "Is that why you changed your name?"

Jessi looked away in discomfort. How could she ever explain Jessalyn Silverna had died a terrified teenager, tied to a bed in a small room? Broken, Jessi hadn't been able to face the brutality any other way than to leave the shell of a girl Wilson had dragged to freedom behind. To know the decision may have also saved her life for another reason all together further frayed her already tense nerves.

Perhaps she could ignore the question. "I didn't know anyone might be looking for me."

"I'm not sure anyone is. *He* certainly didn't disclose the failure."

Jessi wasn't so sure of the failure, if her murder was the end goal. After all, she *had* disappeared as if gone from the inhabited world. She rubbed her arm to ward away a sudden chill. "I suppose when I didn't turn up, he didn't need to. I must have played right into his reputation."

"I know I've already asked, but can you think of anyone or any reason why someone would want you dead?"

"No. I was seventeen, a kid. My mother was a bookkeeper." By that point in her life, her *gift* of seeing powerful, emotional memories by touch had revealed little except for the occasional excited flash of a cat after successfully stalking a mouse. Nothing she'd *seen* could account for someone wanting her dead. Up until the horror of being pinned to the mattress, she'd figured her imagination had played tricks on her.

"What area did you live in?" he asked.

"What region you mean?"

"Region and city."

"New Maine, Lewista. Where was your sister?"

Mason took a deep breath. "Outside of Rhode Haven, in Unconnland."

"Yes, that's near where he… kept me. Where was she taken?"

"I'm not sure. She paid for a room a month in advance, she still had two weeks left on her reservation in York, New Maine."

Jessi considered the information. "That's pretty far inland, less than a day from the UZ in that region."

"Do you know if your father had anything to do with the bordering UZ there?"

"No, Lewista is a port city. The main port city for the region actually. It's also the seat of that region's Senate office. We lived on the outskirts, my mother never appreciated large city life. Whenever he came to visit, he conducted whatever business he was there for within the city itself." Jessi tried to recall all her father's visits. They had been many throughout her life, but not for very long. She shook her head, wishing she could be more helpful, for both their sakes. "I'm sorry. My mother likely knows."

"You haven't tried to reach out to her?" The question held no condemnation, only curiosity.

Guilt reared an ugly head at his inquiry. She bit on the inside of her bottom lip. "I didn't…" She took a deep breath. Not once since her abduction had she spoken about it. Mason had pulled the past into the light, and she was about done with the discussion. "No."

Confusion flitted across his face and for a moment she thought he'd ask more. To her relief, he didn't. Instead, he said something more shocking. "You could return with me."

Jessi stared at him. "What? To Sziveria? Why would I want to do that?"

"You can possibly find answers," he said, his face softened in compassion.

She balked. "I could also find myself dead. If you're right, then whoever wanted me gone thinks they've succeeded. Why in the inhabited world would I challenge their assumption? No thank you."

When she went to walk past him, he reached out. She quickly sidestepped to avoid his touch. A sliver of regret caught her by surprise. Somehow, deep inside, she knew he'd be different. While her heart made the safe declaration, her mind refused to accept. In the end, his brute strength matched to her small frame would lead to disaster. She wasn't willing to take the chance. Ever.

"I haven't finished dressing your wounds yet." His words made her stop before she left the kitchen.

She looked over her shoulder at him. A small jar was poised between his thumb and index finger, a question in his eyes.

"What is that?" she asked, nodding her chin at the jar.

"Cream, to help keep away infection and pain."

He had her at *keep away pain*. The scrapes, tears and gouges burned like crazy anytime she moved. Uncertain though if she wanted to subject herself to another round of reliving the worst memories of her life, she narrowed her gaze on him. External pain was much easier to deal with than the internal. "Are you done with your questions?"

"For now." He removed the top of the jar and motioned to where she'd been standing. "The light is better here, between the two lamps."

At the mercy of his promise to ease her discomfort, she took slow steps to fill the gap between them. "I'm not going to Sziveria, so you can drop that subject, too."

"Noted."

Placated by his response, Jessi returned to her spot before the sink. She grimaced at the grubby faced woman reflected in the window. Mud streaked her cheeks to her jaw. Her curls had given way to frizz. Good grief, did she really look like that? Looking deeper into the reflection to Mason's, she drew her brows together when she noticed he hesitated. Had the scars finally become more than he could tolerate?

He glanced up and met her out-of-focus stare reflected in the glass. "I have to touch you," he began, and then added in a rush when she stiffened, "barely though, only enough to apply the salve."

Too surprised to do much more than nod, Jessi watched in the window while he feathered the medicine onto her skin. His touch was so light, if she hadn't been observing in the mirrored window, she would have sworn he wasn't doing anything.

The delicate way he handled her, since the moment he'd first stepped forward to untangle her from deadly fencing, once again forced Jessi to acknowledge his difference. Like Wilson, he seemed to be a distinct sort of male. One who gave and protected, instead of hurting. As with her earlier thoughts about him, this one wasn't any easier to accept. She clenched her teeth. No, she wasn't going to trust a man in her presence for mere hours simply because he was *nice* to her. She wasn't so desperate to redeem his gender.

Finished, he stepped away, closing the jar. He held it out for her. "If you can't reach, ask and I'll help in the morning. I suggest you put on a sleeveless shirt so it doesn't rub off before it can work."

"Okay, thank you." She took the small glass container, careful not to touch his fingers. "If you want to follow me up, I'll show you your room."

A deep, wheezing cough echoed from the living area on the way up the stairs. Jessi's hand tightened on the banister. She resisted the urge to look behind or rush back down the steps to check on the old man. "Wilson sleeps downstairs. Sesay will wander between rooms if you leave your door open. If you don't want a dog in your bed, make sure you close yours."

"Good to know." When they reached the top of the stairs he asked, "How long has he been sick?"

Jessi crossed the short distance to the vacant room. "The cough started a little over four months ago."

She pushed open the door and revealed a small space. One curtain-less window would fill the room with light upon sunrise, cutting across the narrow bed. Stepping aside, she frowned, wondering if the bed would hold his large body. A little chest under the window and a small stand next to the bed with a lamp finished out the room. When he stepped in, the area shrunk.

He dropped his backpack on the chest before braving the bed. The old wooden frame groaned in protest and shuddered under the force of his weight when he bounced. "Well, it didn't break. That's good."

Jessi couldn't help but laugh. She motioned toward a door in the right wall. "That's your closet. It's almost the same size of the room. I use it for storage, but half of it's empty."

"I don't have anything but what I walked in with, no worries there." He looked around. "Where's the bathroom? I only saw one other door up here. Is it downstairs?"

"Um, sort of, yes." She retreated to outside the door. "Let me change my shirt and I'll meet you downstairs to show you everything else."

She couldn't help the secret smile or the little tingle of mischief in her chest. Maybe once he saw how primitive they lived, he'd change his mind and leave, taking with him all the crazy notions about someone wanting her dead.

For close to five minutes, Jessi stared down at the maroon tank top on her bed. Fear of pain, and a deeper fear of Mason's reaction, kept her from taking off her ruined shirt and putting on the clean, far skimpier article of clothing. At one time, wearing the cooler top hadn't bothered her. No one was around to see her ravaged skin.

Then she'd made the mistake of going into town with Wilson on their monthly supply run wearing one.

Hushed whispered and averted gazes had plagued her every place they'd had to stop. Considering they were the only honey distributors in the area, they made many. After that disastrous experience, she'd sworn to only expose her back when she slept. Absolutely no one would ever see a single scar then. She'd managed to keep her little self-proclaimed promise until tonight.

A far too handsome stranger, who caused a shadow of anxiety to flit in chest because he knew how she came by each scar, and appeared unbothered by their presence, had managed to make her consider poking out of her shell. If she obeyed his request to wear something to keep the medicine from rubbing off, a really big *if*, he'd see even more than he had cutting the fabric away.

Scoffing in disgust, she swept the ruined shirt aside and let it flutter to the floor. Why did she care? That's right, she didn't. Perhaps if she reminded herself over and over, she'd remember. Let him get an eyeful. She'd show him around and then return to her room the moment she knew he wouldn't use one of her empty flower pots as a toilet.

Realizing she'd be alone, outside, in the dark with him, prompted a new wave of panic. What if he had a complete change of personality? Not that she'd had enough time to be a good judge of *who* he was. Maybe she could give instructions from the kitchen and wait until morning to show him the shower.

Plan in mind, Jessi pulled the top over her head, surprised at how little pain the action caused. The cream had begun to work. Letting out a breath of relief, she shimmied the fabric over her breasts and helped it settle around her hips.

Downstairs the murmur of conversation made her pause. They spoke so low she couldn't make out their words. For a moment she considered listening in, but Mason's earlier words about her lack of manners changed her mind. She didn't need another lecture from him.

At the entry, she cleared her throat and waited to be noticed. Mason's attention flitted to her, then back to Wilson, only to immediately returned to her. A flush spread across Jessi's cheeks as he looked her over. Somehow his gaze felt like a physical caress. He didn't even have the decency to hide his interest, the dim light showing his masculine approval.

"Are you ready to finish the tour?" she asked, shifting her weight to her other foot.

"Sure." He rose and then reached down to grasp Wilson's elbow. "Let me help him first, as I said I would."

"Stop treating me like some old man. I can get to my room on my own," Wilson fussed through strained words.

"I know," Mason patronized. "I'm more concerned about the how. While on your knees counts, I think both feet are better."

Wilson snorted and Jessi smiled, stepping out of their way. Sesay lifted his head and then decided the bedroom shuffle wasn't worth his attention. With a doggy groan, he resumed his lounging. Jessi observed the men. On one hand she was thankful Mason had taken over handling what was often uncomfortable for both Jessi and Wilson. On another, she tried to ignore feeling resentful about the same said help. How could she be both thankful *and* jealous?

Minutes later, Mason emerged, leaving the door open enough for Sesay to enter if he chose. Nervous now that they were truly alone, Jessi crossed an arm over her chest and tucked stray hair behind her ear.

Mason stopped a few feet from her and sighed. "I won't hurt you, or even touch you without permission."

Jessi straightened her spine. Had she been so transparent? "I know."

His eyes searched hers. "Do you?"

When she didn't answer, he shook his head.

He slipped past her and stopped in the living room entry way and pointed sternly at Jessi. *"Sesay Custrazva."* The dog stood and went to Jessi's side. "There, now you aren't unaccompanied with me."

Jessi's fingers slid into the warm, soft fur between Sesay's ears. "What did you say to him?"

"I told him to guard you."

She glanced down at the wolf and let his words sink in. How did he know that? What language had he spoken? Wilson often muttered what she considered gibberish around Sesay, now she wondered if they weren't similar commands. And if he issued one command, surely he could counter it. "But you could tell him to stop too, couldn't you?"

"Doesn't work like that. I do anything bad, your wolf dog will make sure I don't walk again." He swept his arm in an arc. "So, where to? I think I've seen the entire house, haven't I?"

"Yes, mostly."

Jessi showed him around the kitchen so he could find firewood, the pantry and the stairs to the small root cellar. A side door from the kitchen led to a modest sunroom. Off the sunroom, a wooden stall with a brick laid floor made up their outdoor shower. She showed him how to use the simple water heater, warning him he needed to start the process at least two hours before he planned to bathe.

Next, she led him to the outhouse. He entered and exited the small commode at least three times, as if convincing himself of the reality of an outdoor toilet. The barn was the last stop, though she doubted he'd venture there, she wanted him to know since she spent a large part of her morning doing chores in the building.

At the side door back into the house, Jessi paused. The silvery moonlight cast enough light to see, but not well. "So, still want to rent a room?"

"Yes."

Jessi crossed her arms over her chest and leaned against the closed door. "Why?"

Several seconds passed before he answered, his voice soft. "I know I have people back home who love me, who care. But right now, it feels like I have nothing, no one. Cora…"

His voice broke and Jessi's heart clenched. Before now, he hadn't spoken a woman's name. She knew saying his sister's name out loud hurt.

He took a deep breath and continued. "She was my twin. For my entire existence she's been there, sharing every second. Even if I wasn't in our country, I knew *she* was, aggravating someone in a way only she knew how, living her life to upset our mother as much as humanly possible. I don't… know how I'll go back. Since you're the closest thread I have to knowing why someone would steal her from us, this is where I need to be."

Jessi wanted to argue again that she knew nothing, and therefore was of no help. But the tortured confession and pain in his voice had her nodding in acceptance. Fine, if he wanted to spend his grieving period on their humble farm, she wouldn't stop him. After all, she'd handled her own tragedy the exact same way, and never left.

Frowning at the thought of Mason becoming a somewhat permanent fixture on their property, and her lack of concern over the prospect, Jessi went back into the house. Sesay stayed on her heels, his long nails clicking on the hardwood. The wolf followed her up the stairs and then sat in front of her door, his long pink tongue flopped out of his mouth. Jessi hesitated when Mason paused a couple steps below. He was barely shorter than her and she had the urge to put space between them.

"If you're hungry—"

"I'm fine. You showed me where everything is. If I get hungry later, I can grab some cheese and bread or something."

Mason's independence was a welcome relief. Once she'd been healed enough to take over the domestic aspects of the house, Wilson had gladly handed them over. Since he'd never asked for her to earn her keep beyond chores and cooking, Jessi never complained. She quickly learned to cook and care for the animals. With the onset of Wilson's illness, almost everything fell to Jessi now.

"Okay, good. Do you cook?" she asked, resting her hand on the railing near her hip.

"No, and trust me, you don't want me to. I've never had a desire to learn. If it can't be eaten as is, I don't eat."

All right then, maybe not as independent as she first assumed. "I usually see how Wilson is doing to determine when I cook, but I'll make sure to get you something hot at least once a day."

He rose a step, placing him at eye level with her. "You don't need to do that."

She inhaled through her nose and stepped back. A sharp, clean woodsy scent filled her senses. How had she not noticed how good he smelled earlier? *Maybe because you were bleeding everywhere?* Hand still on the banister, she shook her head, both to clear her thoughts and disagree with him. "You're paying to stay here. A hotel would provide the same service."

"I'm not asking for anything more than somewhere to sleep. Promise." He took another step up.

Jessi frowned, except he was asking more of her, or at least he already had. "Are you going to try to convince me to go to Sziveria with you again?"

Another step. Only one stair between them now, and once again he nearly towered over her. He stood with his mouth level to her gaze and she couldn't stop herself from staring. Despite the rather ragged beard hiding his face from view, his full lips weren't obscured. She wondered if they'd be forceful in a kiss, or soft and gentle. Then she frowned, shoving the thought away. Kisses led to other *things*, none of which interested her.

"Probably," he finally answered, his silvery eyes turning smoky.

Her breath caught. She didn't know eyes could do that. Did hers? She quickly blinked and looked away. "You'll be disappointed again, then. My answer will always be no."

"Never disappointed," he said gently. He closed the small space between them.

Having nowhere to go, Jessi shifted and bumped into the wall next to her bedroom door. Her fingers splayed along the smooth wood. Flecks of paint brushed onto her hands. The strange texture allowed her to focus on something else besides his closeness. The heat from his enormous frame surrounded her, carrying his unique, masculine scent. Jessi tried not to breathe in deeply. She also tried to ignore the unfamiliar flutter of her heart and flip of her stomach.

"Can I touch you?" he whispered, his hands bracing on the wall above her.

"No." The answer was so immediate, an instant rejection, that her voice took her by surprise, as did the desire to take the word back. She stared up at him, eyes wide. A little tremor of fear raced up her spine. Men didn't handle dismissal well.

"Goodnight, Jessalyn." He pushed off the wall with a wink and then disappeared into his room, his broad back taking up the doorway before he closed it with a soft click.

Sesay yawned, whining with the flex of his powerful jaw. Jessi let out a heavy breath. Her mind tried to make sense of Mason's calm departure. No anger, no frustration, he'd just… walked away. What did that mean?

She eased from the wall, brushing her fingers on her pants. With a sigh to match Sesay's, she touched the disintegrating paint. Time to focus on something she *could* control. "I guess I need to add paint to our list of fixes."

The list was never ending. A sagging porch, bear threatened hives, chipping walls, and she was positive they had a leak in their roof. If it rained while Mason was with them, she'd know for sure. With her luck, the water would drip right onto his face while he slept.

5

———————

JESSI PULLED BLUEBERRY MUFFINS FROM THE OVEN, CHECKING TO make sure they were set before placing them on top of the woodstove. Their sweet scent drifted around the room, mingling with the bacon sizzling in a pan at the rear. She flipped the thick slices before removing the mitt. Wilson's ragged cough entered the room before he did. Breathless, he sat in a chair at the table nearest to the entryway. He coughed again.

"Bad morning?" Jessi asked, glancing over her shoulder.

"It'll get better, always does." He scratched between Sesay's ears when the big dog laid his head on Wilson's knees. "Where's that man of yours?"

Jessi blinked and returned her attention to breakfast. "He isn't mine."

"Where is he?"

Jessi shrugged. "His door was closed. I guess he's still in bed."

"You didn't check?"

"Why would I wake him?"

"Will you wake him when food is done?"

She pondered the question for a moment and then

53

shrugged again. "I don't know. Should I? Seems rude to wake him. We don't know how long he'd been traveling."

"Almost a month."

Jessi turned and stared at him, spatula in hand. "A month?"

The old man nodded, eyes sad. "Yes."

"Is that why you let him stay? So he didn't have to travel anymore?"

Wilson shook his head, resting his forearms on the table. "He saved you. He could have walked away, but instead he took on barbed wire. And I knew the moment he spoke he was Sziverian. Not just a national either, but from an old Guardian family. Man like that could be real handy around here, especially right now."

Jessi didn't argue the validity of help at the moment. She did recall Mason telling her he was a Guardian. "What exactly does an old Guardian family mean?"

"His family has been faithfully serving their country for generations. There's a lot of pride in that. He likely has an awarded rank."

She leaned against the counter, crossing her arms over her chest, ignoring the drip of grease from the spatula. "How do you figure?"

"The way he speaks, and holds himself. Only a handful of nations have awarded social or nobility positions. Sziveria is one of them."

She worked her bottom lip between her teeth, returning to the bacon. "Did he tell you why he's here?"

"Yes."

Jessi spun around. "What did you tell him?"

He coughed again. When he spoke, his words were hoarse. "Absolutely nothing. Your story isn't mine to tell, and what I know isn't mine to share. You know that."

Yes, she did know. To every frustrating end. Wilson had promised whoever sent him to save her not to reveal any details of their identity. Regardless of the circumstances. After a year, Jessi had given up.

Jessi finished up the bacon, placing the slices on a plate next to the muffins. She poured a steaming cup of coffee for Wilson. After placing everything on the table along with plates, she sat beside him. The empty chair across from her made her heave a guilty sigh.

"Fine," she muttered, shoving away from the table. "I'll go up and see if he wants a hot breakfast."

Only she didn't find him upstairs. A knock went unanswered. She pushed the door open and found an empty room. The bed was made. His backpack lay crumpled beneath the window, as if half the contents had been removed. Jessi frowned. Where had he gone?

Back downstairs, she fixed a plate, ignoring Wilson's watchful gaze. Sesay followed her out in search of their missing guest. Now she wished she knew more of those fancy commands Wilson had tried to teach her years ago. Only one had mattered, making sure the dog knew when she needed help. She figured the intelligent wolf knew how to follow a scent and would find Mason with little effort.

The echo of a hammer against wood offered a direction. Jessi shielded her eyes from the brilliant morning sun. A faint wind teased her messy hair, piled up in a loose knot on top of her head. Already the air was thick with humidity, promising another hot day. She followed the trail of noise, finding herself near her bees. She came to a stop when she noticed only three posts remained. Mason had finished stringing the wire on the rest.

He rose from hammering in a bottom stay. The thick length of his braid hung over his shoulder. Sweat soaked the navy t-shirt clinging to his muscular arms and chest. Jessi's breath stuck in her throat. A man shouldn't look that good.

His gaze traveled the length of her body while he

scratched at his bearded jaw. "You didn't have to bring me anything."

A faint flush crept into her cheeks and she forced her attention to the near completed fence line. "And you didn't have to finish my work."

He took the plate from her outstretched hand and then sat on a stack of wooden planks she used to repair her hives when needed. Jessi surveyed his work, noting where she'd failed to consider needing a gate to gain entry. She groaned in frustration. "I forgot about a gate."

"I noticed. Bears are smart, aren't they?"

"Yes. In fact, this fence will only be a deterrent. I might still lose my hives if it's able to figure out a way around, or even through, my fence."

The plate sat on his thighs. He leaned forward to rest an elbow on his knee, chewing bacon. "We could take turns scaring the thing off if it becomes too big of a nuisance. A little pain goes a long way to discourage."

"Yes, I've thought of that. All we have is a pellet gun, though."

"Do you have hinges for the gate?"

"I think so. If not, I'll be making a run into town in two days to make a delivery. I haven't seen my new friend the bear since I last rushed it off. Maybe I'll get lucky and can wait that long."

Bits of the muffin floated down to the plate when he took a bite. He regarded the buzzing hives. "Where are the hinges?"

"If I have any, in the barn."

He set the plate on the wood beside him and stood. Sweeping his arm toward the barn, he said, "After you."

Jessi hesitated for a moment. Once again, he'd made himself seem harmless enough. Then he stood, and reminded her of how small she was compared to him. While she wanted to believe if in an emergency she hid in the stall with their old mare, the docile beast would protect her, Mildred was currently out to pasture with, Berne, the cow. They'd be alone in the barn, and she'd have limited places to run.

Mason heaved a long-suffering sigh and with an exaggerated head flop, looked down at Sesay, dutifully at Jessi's side. *"Sesay Custrazva"*

The dog's ears perked up and his spine straightened.

With the same annoying toss of his head, Mason looked at her. "Happy?"

Suddenly Jessi felt foolish for her fears. They were unwarranted concerning him. She took a bracing breath, her palms facing the ground. "I'm sorry, I'm not used to being around anyone but Wilson. I get nervous."

He locked his hands behind his back and took a small step toward her. "I understand, and I don't want you to be. If Sesay helps you feel safer, I don't mind. I'm just not used to being viewed as a predator by those I don't wish to be."

Jessi couldn't help but ask, "Do you often wish to be viewed as one?"

"Only when absolutely necessary. I handle most situations behind the scenes."

They approached the barn. Dirt crunching under their shoes and the chirping of birds and crickets filled the air. Small beads of sweat tingled along Jessi's scalp from the sun shining brightly onto her from above. "What sort of situations?"

"Hostage recovery, supplying an insurgent force that will align to our countries benefit if they succeed in their rebellion, rapid evac of a high-profile target in a hostile environment, that sort of thing."

Jessi stopped at stared at him. "What exactly do you do?"

"I'm a strategist."

His declaration did little to help her understand. "I've never heard of that." She resumed leading him into the barn.

An odd clicking sound made her look over her shoulder at him. "Ah, that's right, Westica doesn't focus on Gen-Heirs."

"What is that?"

"Short or long version?"

The inside of the barn was considerably cooler, still retaining the low temperature of night within the shaded walls. Jessi stopped at the corner with the all their supplies. Pegs, shelves and wooden drawers helped keep some semblance of organization. She picked a random drawer and began her search.

"Short, I guess."

"Some people are born with a natural ability that never has to be taught, simply honed," he said. "They're born with the capability already imprinted. They are genetic heirs."

Jessi stopped searching and stared at him. Her heart made an uncomfortable turn in her chest. "Like being able to touch something and see a memory?"

His gaze searched her face. "Can you do that?"

An unexplainable urge to deny and hide had her digging around in the drawer again. Why had she said anything? She'd never spoken of her odd ability before. Not even to her parents. Then again, she'd never known she might not be weird, or seeing things without explanation. "Sometimes," she hedged.

"Can you tell me about it? What happens?" he asked, his voice calm, almost gentle.

Jessi took a deep breath and shrugged. "I'm not sure really. Most of the time, when it happens, there's a really strong emotion, like anger, fear or..."

She flushed and dug further into the drawer. "Or something like desire, for me to see anything. The bear was very excited about the honey," Jessi quickly gave as an example, not wanting the word *desire* hanging in the air between them.

When he remained silent, Jessi chanced a look at him. Focused and intent, he watched her, brows drawn. Then he snapped his fingers, the crack of sound making her jump. "You're an Emorypath."

Jessi blinked. "A what?"

"Emotional Memory Empath. You're a touch-based talent."

She gripped the edges of the drawer and met his gaze once again. "I don't understand."

"There are two types of Gen-Heir talents. Touch-based, like yours, and my team leader, Sean's. Remember me telling you about him being a Sympath?" She nodded and he continued, "Right, well, for them work, you have to touch something. I'm a logic-based talent. I had to be tested to ensure I was a genetic heir for my mother, and what my specific inherited ability happened to be."

"And you're a strategist," she said slowly, remembering what he said earlier.

"Yes."

"And you don't have to touch anything for your... skill... to work," she said, her mind whirling, trying to make sense of everything.

"Correct. You however, have to touch something, as you know."

"How is this possible? Where do the gifts come from?"

"Your genetics, passed on by your parents from somewhere in your family line," he explained. "Someone, at some point, was also an Emorypath."

Jessi considered her parents. Neither had ever spoken of genetic abilities, or asked if she'd ever experienced anything odd. Did they know? She looked Mason over. Her father at least, must have, since he came from a land where such things mattered. She swallowed. "Where did they come from, to start? Have people always had such gifts?"

He crossed his arms over his chest and leaned against the wall next to a rake. "No, I don't think so. History books are vague on preternatural talents in humans. As for where?

There are many theories, my favorite is runaways from Ruthenia."

"Why?"

"They were the first to record natural genetic heir abilities. In fact, the next country to record a Gen-Heir wasn't until almost five hundred years later. By that point, Ruthenia hadn't recorded a non-genetic heir citizen in their entire history. To be common is almost a crime in their society."

Jessi turned her attention back to the hinge search. "And every civilization has people like that? Who just *know* how to do certain things?"

"I think so, though we aren't sure because some countries, like this one, never check."

"What's the genetic skill to strike someone first?" she muttered, shoving a drawer closed and opening another.

"An interceptor."

Startled, Jessi stopped and snapped her attention to him. "What?"

"The skill to kick someone's ass before they can kick yours. They're called interceptors."

"Oh." She sighed and went back to her search. "Is there any to make the ability go away?"

"No. Like your hair or eye color, it's part of you, a gift you're born with."

Rough objects and cold metals shifted underneath her fingers. She squeezed her eyes closed. "What if you don't see it as a gift?"

"Jessalyn," he said in a calm, yet forceful tone, making her look at him. "What you are able to do is so incredible, and very rare. In my country, you'd be a ranked Guardian, helping solve crimes and bring justice to families desperate for answers, if you wanted. You *do* have a gift, something remarkable and special."

Jessi didn't know what to say, or how to take his declaration. Most times, *special* wasn't a word she'd use when a memory she hadn't asked for skated across her vision. None of the drawers yielded results. She growled in annoyance and went back to one she'd already searched. They were so full of junk she wondered if she missed seeing one. Though a single hinge would be useless, it would save a little money if she had to buy more.

The strength of his presence, and the scent of sunshine and man reached her before his arm snaked around and opened a drawer above her. If she took a step back, she'd bump into his chest. Despite his proximity, the only part of him touching her was his braid brushing along her shoulder when he leaned forward enough to search the contents.

Jessi remained still, afraid to move or else she'd touch him. Annoyed because she wanted to. He'd told her last night she could explore him however she wished. She wondered what he'd do if she tested his words. If she leaned back into his solid chest and slid her fingers along the corded muscles of his forearms. Would his skin be warm and smooth? Would his muscles flex under her caress?

She licked her lips, dry from the vivid imagery playing in her mind. Jessi had never fantasized before, and she didn't know what to do with it now. The drawer closed, and instead of opening a higher one, he opened one near her hips, forcing her to step back. To her shock, he stepped back too, keeping the same maddening sliver of space between them.

Mason's arms formed a cage, locking her in place. And yet, regardless of her earlier misgivings about being alone with him, she wasn't scared. She had to slide her drawer closed to provide enough light for him to search through the lower one. Jessi did so slowly, afraid to accidently bump him and embarrass herself by giving into temptation. To make sure she didn't, she kept her hands planted on the face of the drawer.

"Can I touch you?" he whispered, teasing the curls around her ear and forcing a shiver up her spine.

A strange warmth curled in her stomach. Jessi closed her eyes and focused on the curious, pleasant sensation. She'd had the same one last night. She wondered if it'd change at his touch. Would fear block whatever effect he had over her, or was the feeling stronger?

"Where?"

"Where am I allowed?"

Her breath hitched. What would be mundane and safe? She opened her eyes and blinked, considering her options. Not her shoulders, one was still a bit sore, and she couldn't stomach him touching her back anyway. She doubted he'd be able to either. Not her hips, too intimate. Or her neck, too close to... other areas. Her breasts tightened at the mere thought of his touch at her neck and collarbone. What was that about?

She should say no. Her thoughts were out of control and he'd likely make things worse. But her curiosity had been sparked. A smile curved her lips when she wiggled her fingers.

"My hands."

"Only your hands?"

Jessi bit her lip in thought. "To my wrists, but nothing else."

The pads of Mason's fingers whispered along the outside edge of her palms up to her pinky. Jessi forgot to breathe. He slid his much larger hands under hers. Starting at the tops of her fingers, he caressed down, creating a trail of sensation along the sensitive nerve endings. Maybe her hands hadn't been such a good idea either...

"Not so bad, is it?" he murmured, his mouth almost touching her ear.

She had the distinct impression, if she'd let him, he'd kiss her neck. A sliver of anticipation tightened in her chest. His fingers teased up and down her palms, to her wrists and then back. Little arcs of lightning sizzled through her, awakening a woman Jessi didn't know existed.

The echo of her pulse in her ears mirrored an aching throb at her core. In subtle, slow motions, he traced the line of her thumb, across her palm and around to the inside of her wrist.

Somehow Jessi managed to swallow a whimper and keep from pressing her legs together. If he was aware of his current power over her, he'd ask for more. She wasn't certain she could deny him anything at the moment. The short, shallow depth of his breathing near her ear told her he wasn't unaffected either. For some odd reason, the knowledge added to her blossoming desire.

His fingers laced between her smaller ones. Jessi took in the neatly trimmed nails with a little dirt from working outside under them, and the darker tone of his skin against hers. The simple, yet intimate act of his palms pressed to hers intensified the fluttering in her stomach. He could wrap his arms around her with her hands held hostage and she'd be helpless. Yet he made no move to step closer. Slowly, his fingers uncurled and he slid them away, leaving cold behind.

Without another word, he strode from the barn.

MASON WAS IN DEEP TROUBLE. CURSING HIS STUPIDITY, HE stalked back to his self-appointed chore. He snatched the thick gloves he'd dropped when he spotted Jessi with breakfast and tugged them on.

You had to touch her, didn't you?

Yes, yes he did. Now he regretted the decision. If she'd shifted any at all, she'd have known how deeply his little stunt to crack the wall she'd built around herself had affected him. The evidence still tented his trousers.

Fantastic.

Thankfully she hadn't followed him out, and the old man still seemed content to stay inside. No one else knew of his embarrassing predicament, nor did he have to deal with a razor thin level of control. Who knew caressing a woman's hands could be so erotic? Mason blamed the years of celibacy he'd endured, along with the knowledge no one else had likely managed to get Jessi's pulse racing the way he had.

Knowing she responded to him turned out to be the biggest aphrodisiac he'd ever experienced. What had he wanted to prove? Mason took a shuddering breath. He closed his eyes and breathed again through his nose. Still his heart pounded, his blood on fire for a broken woman. While he knew breaching all her barriers would prove a worthy distraction, she deserved so much more.

Mason jerked the fencing tight with more force than necessary. On a sigh, he loosened the wire enough to keep it from snapping. Jessi didn't need to unravel him from a tangled mess... at least not a barbed wire one. He took another moment to calm his raging hormones. Jeez, he'd have thought himself sixteen, not twenty-eight, the way his body carried on.

He finished the remaining posts, leaving space between two for the eventual gate. Jessi hadn't reappeared. Either he'd spooked her, or she'd had other things to handle on the small farm. Mason hoped chores beat out avoidance.

Hot and covered in sweat, Mason went to the barn to put away the tools and gloves. The outbuilding was empty. A quick search around didn't reveal Jessi. Sighing, Mason went to the shower. He'd heated up water before starting the day, but the temperature outside made him choose cold water over hot.

Next to the shower, a small stall had been built for changing and drying. With no one around, Mason figured Wilson had constructed it solely for Jessi's need of privacy. Both the shower and stall were constructed of simple wood walls, a brick floor, and a tin roof. A bench seat made of brick lined one wall in the shower, being used as both a seat and a shelf for soap. Mason had set his shampoo and conditioner next to the lone bar. No wonder Jessi's hair was a wild mess, she had nothing to keep it controlled.

The cool water washed away the sweat and dirt from not only his travels, but the morning work as well. With a wary shake of his head, he ran the bar of soap over his chest and wondered how Jessi had stomached him being so close, smelling the way he did.

Once finished, Mason pulled on a loose pair of pants, buttoning them up, before donning a gray cotton t-shirt over his head. He left his hair unbound to dry, his towel draped over his shoulders. He went inside, toweling the lengths of his hair.

Wilson's watery brown eyes grew wide when Mason stepped into the kitchen. When he sagged in relief, Mason lifted a brow.

"Everything okay, old man?"

Wilson's focus shifted to his hands. Translucent wrinkled skin showed off every pronounced vein with each twist of his fingers. "I'm afraid I need a little help."

The only one who didn't need his help on the dilapidated farm seemed to be the wolf. Where Wilson sat came fully into view and Mason kept his shock internal when he noted the puddle beneath the old man's seat.

For a moment he wasn't sure how to handle what was an embarrassing circumstance for the man. However, ignoring it was out of the question, so Mason opted to go with how he always handled situations – as is. "To your room, or the shower?"

"Shower, if you don't mind. And I'll clean up."

Mason didn't know how he'd manage the task when he couldn't seem to even rise from his seat to get to the bathroom outside. He stayed silent however. "You're in luck, there's hot water in the tank. Come on."

Wilson held his arm out for Mason to grasp on a

thankful smile. With little effort, Mason helped get the ailing man who weighed probably half what he should outside and situated in the shower. After ensuring he could handle the rest on his own, Mason went back inside to clean up.

Jessi had beat him to it. She was on her hands and knees scrubbing the floor. The sight of her round butt swinging in rhythm to each sideways swipe of her brush left him mesmerized. His gut tightened and he took a step back before he succumbed to the temptation to sink onto the floor behind her and sample all her lush curves.

She stopped and glanced over her shoulder. On a startled gasp, she toppled onto her side, half sitting. The brush clattered out of her hand. "I didn't hear you come in."

"I helped Wilson into the shower." He looked around. "Where's the dog?"

"Out chasing birds, I'm sure."

Mason frowned. "Did you release him?"

She picked up the brush and dropped it in a small bowl. "Released him from what?"

"The order to guard you."

"I don't know. It doesn't wear off after a while?"

Mason opened his mouth to say he didn't think so, but then realized he wasn't sure. "I guess maybe so."

She rose in slow motions, and Mason went to help, only to realize she'd balk at his sudden touch. Only her hands. Right. Instead, he closed the distance between them and relieved her of the brush and soapy bowl.

"How are you feeling?" He set the dirty items in the sink.

"The salve helped a lot, thank you." She glanced at him and then away, her teeth working her bottom lip. "I... I can't help but realize how fortunate we are you stumbled across us when you did. Between my getting stuck in barb wire, and Wilson this morning..."

Mason looked out the window in the direction of the

shower. The bathing area wasn't visible from the kitchen. Worry nagged at him. "I should go check on him real quick."

"He's fine. Give him a little longer. The water helps soothe his cough."

"Is this a normal thing?"

A faint flush tinged her cheeks. "No, no he's never had an accident before. I'm actually not sure what to do."

Mason was thankful she didn't misunderstand his inquiry for something else. He considered the problem, not having much experience with caregiving or the day to day of handling a household. "Could you hire someone to help out?"

Startled, she blinked a few times and shook her head. "No." The pink spread further across her cheeks and she took a long breath. "Sorry. I mean no, we couldn't. Maybe a woman, but I doubt if Wilson would allow a woman to help. He barely allows me. And a man is out of the question. And that's *if* we could get one to agree. They'd likely want more than we could afford."

A female being the only option, and one which wouldn't work well, he understood. Between Jessi's obvious reluctance toward men, and Wilson's need to remain seen as a man to a woman, their problem did indeed appear unsolvable. "Aside from you not liking men, why would any not want to help?"

Jessi turned on the water, casting him a shielded glance from beneath her long, dark lashes. "Between Sesay's massive size, and Wilson's glowering and holding his pellet rifle everywhere we go, no one usually comes near us. If anyone bothered to walk up our drive for friendship or sales, they received the same."

Mason kept near on purpose, invading her space without touching. A sliver of satisfaction raced through him when she didn't try to expand the distance between them. He knew he played with fire. The closer he was to her, the more he wanted her to accept his presence. Since he had nothing to offer but the chance of answers, and a hollowed husk of a heart, he shouldn't push for more than what he'd already managed.

Yet, he couldn't seem to help himself.

Something about Jessalyn Silverna pulled at his very being. A sort of desperation to know how she'd taste, how her body would soften under his touch, how she'd react to a new world of sensations he'd offer. Even in a baggy shirt and loose-fitting slacks women in his country wouldn't dare wear, she was beautiful. He could only imagine how she'd look with her hair styled and her shapely body clothed in feminine elegance.

"Come back to Sziveria with me."

She stilled from washing the scrubbing bowl out. "I already told you to give up on that."

Clasping his hands behind his back to resist grasping her hips to pull her to his aching body, where he could savor all her soft curves, he leaned forward enough to whisper into her ear, "I don't *give up*. On anything."

Her shoulders stiffened and her spine straightened. She scrubbed at the soap covered bowl with more force than necessary, splashing water. "Well, then this will be a first for you, I'm sorry to say."

A smile tried to break free. He shook his head instead. "But not too sorry."

She rinsed the bowl. "Nope."

Mason had to step back when she placed the bowl under the sink, along with the rinsed-out brush. She washed her hands and turned to face him holding a towel. Sadness shone in her beautiful smoky green eyes. A frown tugged at her full lips.

"I'm not sure what to do. What happens if he needs someone in the middle of the night now? Neither of us will hear him. He's getting weaker and…" She tossed the towel aside and toyed with a stray lock of hair over her shoulder. "I wasn't prepared for this."

"I don't think anyone can be prepared for the rapid decline of health in a loved one. My father had the withering cough. He lasted six months before he couldn't even get out of bed any longer."

Horror filled her wide eyes. "Is that what will happen to him?"

"I'm not sure. Is that what he has?"

Jessi looked away, toward the side door leading outside. "I don't know, we've never had a Clinician come look him over."

"A Clinician, that's like our Medical Scientists, right?

"Yes, I believe so. They're trained to work solely at medical clinics. In large cities some are able to specialize. Out here however, they handle everything they're able with what they have available in their clinics."

"Why didn't he want to see one?"

"He said it was just a cough, nothing to worry about."

Pride. Sean had always told them keeping a wound or sickness hidden from him would lead to their death, they had to put the pesky emotion aside and let him do his job if something ever happened. Seemed no one had been around to give Wilson the same lecture, or the old man didn't care.

Mason flexed his jaw and sighed. "Do you think he'd allow one now? You said you had to go to town in two days. If I go with, I can make sure one visits. I'll pay for it."

Jessi crossed her arms over her chest and leaned back against the counter. She narrowed her gaze on him. "If you keep fixing up the farm and taking care of us, they'll be no need to pay for a room. You'll be like me, working to earn your keep."

Mason shrugged. "Whatever you two want to do, let me know, I'm good with whatever works. The labor keeps me busy, and right now, I don't want to sit alone with my thoughts for too long."

She nodded. "I understand, that's why I have my bees."

Of course, she understood. Mason realized she was probably the only person who truly did. Once again, the urge to kiss her became unbearable. He took a hasty step away and pointed to the door. "I'm going to go check on the old man. It's been long enough."

A strange expression scrunched up her face. "All right."

Mason fled before he could give into temptation and contemplate all the ways to convince Jessi a kiss wouldn't end her world.

6

——————

Confused, Jessi resisted the urge to chase after Mason and ask if she'd said something wrong. Although he hadn't exactly run from the room, he'd definitely fled. Then she realized of course she'd done something wrong. She'd said no to leaving with him again. Maybe he'd accepted her answer this time, and instead of hounding, he'd walked away. Jessi gave a quick nod of agreement toward her own thought process. Yes. That's what'd happened.

With a heavy heart, she sighed and glanced at the still damp spot on the floor near the table. When she'd noticed Mason helping Wilson to the showers, she'd had a sinking feeling. Her self-appointed guardian hadn't needed much help, except the stairs and *maybe* getting into bed at night. Managing the two stairs to the shower or the outhouse, let alone getting up from a chair, had never been an issue before today. That he hadn't even been able to stand to make it to the door was more than concerning.

Faced with the evidence of such frailty had been difficult. She'd breathed slowly in an attempt not to cry. Needing to take her mind off the already emotional day, she focused on cleaning the remainder of the kitchen from breakfast. But the chore didn't stop her mind from replaying the memory of Mason's fingers sliding along hers, or the anxiety of Wilson's physical decline. The two opposite emotions warred within her until the swell of a panic attack ached in her chest.

She took a deep, calming breath. No… she hadn't had one in over a year and she wasn't about to relapse now. The creak of the door opening made her sniffle and pull herself together. Wilson was tucked underneath Mason's large arm. From the shuffling way he moved one foot in front of the other, she noted Mason did most of the walking, supporting the older man's weight around his ribcage.

Jessi made herself busy again, pretending nothing out of the ordinary was happening. She fixed a cup of sweet tea for Wilson, along with some fresh fruit and thin slices of cheese. Mason helped him settle in a chair, and Jessi set the items down. She went in search of a favorite book of his. The likelihood of the book being read was slim, but he'd appreciate the gesture and someone thinking he was doing something other than sleeping. A deep cough wracked his thin body. Mason grabbed a folded handkerchief from a stack on the table and handed it to Wilson.

Sesay barked at the side door. Jessi went and let the big dog in, slipping out once he was clear of the door. Birds sang high in the trees. Insects droned in a steady hum of high-pitched noise. Jessi inhaled the humid air, thankful for the soft breeze sweeping across her skin. The anxiety from earlier threatened to consume her once more. Shaking her hands at her side in an attempt to subdue the tingling in her fingertips from the still threatening panic, she strode to the hives.

Tomorrow, she'd begin the long task of harvesting and packaging honey for distribution in town. She had a lot to do in preparation. Enough to keep her mind focused on something other than the unfamiliar tightening in her belly when a certain man came to mind, or the scary prospects of Wilson's health.

Hours later, the sun scorching down on her, sweat running along the sides of her face, back and between her breasts, soaking her shirt, she opened the top of her last hive. The little workers investigated her presence, but didn't do much more than settle on her clothes before flitting away again. Jessi inspected the frames inside, checking for completely sealed combs. Only three. She eased the lid back on. Once secure, she fished blue chalk from her pocket and wrote the number on the upper left corner.

As she walked to the opening in the newly constructed fence, the bees lost interest all together until only a few confused strays meandered on her. Jessi gently shooed them on their way. So absorbed in making sure she didn't house any *friends*, she failed to notice the giant of a man observing at the fence edge.

The deep sound of his voice breaking through the constant buzz and symphony of bird song made her gasp and jump. "Do you ever get stung?"

Jessi froze in place and stared at Mason. He made no effort to shift from where he stood outside the fence. The gentle, on again, off again, breeze tugged at the wispy edges of his long, unbound hair, brushing them across his chest and biceps. Rich warm light from the setting sun glinted off the midnight strands, making Jessi's breath catch. Even from where she stood, the pale silver of his eyes captured her. She wondered if he'd stick around long enough for her to get used to his striking features.

Giving a little shake of her head, she turned her attention back to the hives, her gaze flickering over each number written in the upper left corners. "I was stung a few times when I first started, because I was nervous. Staying calm is essential."

"What were you doing?"

"I collect honey tomorrow, I needed to know how many frames were ready."

"Can I help?"

Jessi glanced over her shoulder. His dark brows were raised in question. Curiosity shone in his eyes. She'd never had help with the bees. When the professor from the local school arrived a couple years ago, almost begging her to take a queen and her swarm, Wilson had said yes on the condition the chore was hers alone. She'd been the professor's last stop, the farthest he could venture from the school in one day. The added bonus of income from the honey and wax turned out to be a blessing.

"Sure, I guess, if you want."

Mason cleared his throat and motioned at the collection of hives. "But not with the actual bees themselves. Just the honey part."

Jessi laughed. "A man your size is scared of tiny little insects?"

He didn't join in her laughter. "They sting. It hurts."

"Right." She shook her head and continued to chuckle.

When she came through the opening, he took a step back and then fell in beside her. "Do you process everything in the house?"

"No, I have a small out building. I'm heading there now."

Jessi provided a quick tour of the building she used to construct new frames and collected honey. Empty jars lined the entire left wall. A work table took up the right. Collection buckets were arranged in the center of the room, enough to work ten frames at a time. She'd be doing around four rotations in all tomorrow. Her little hives had been busy.

Mason seemed genuinely interested, which made Jessi talk way too much about her passion. To his credit, his expression didn't begin to glaze until she started in with the specifics of frame building and honey collection. Laughing, she slapped his arm and waved at the door.

"Why have you let me carry on like this?" Air breezed past into the building as she stepped outside.

He shrugged, closing the door. "It's the first time I've seen you, I don't know, look happy." His pale eyes met hers. "I liked it."

"Oh." A little breathless, Jessi turned and headed for the house.

No one cared about much of anything concerning her, least of all her happiness. Once upon a lot of years ago someone had. The trauma of her abduction and the agony of healing had left the memory a distant dream. Wilson's only goal was making sure she stayed alive. Beyond that, Jessi had to find her own way. The bees were her claim to sanity. They kept her focused.

A strong gust of wind swirled around her. Between yesterday's excitement and today's work, Jessi hadn't managed a shower and the stiff breeze reminded her. Mortified, she quickened her pace to the house.

"Would you mind checking on Wilson? I really need to wash up before I cook us dinner."

"Of course. And feel free to use anything I left in there."

Intrigued, she wondered how different could his soap be from hers. Turned out *very* different. For a good long while Jessi stood under the warm spray, eyes closed, inhaling a scent so deep, so Mason. She couldn't stop the tiny tremors quivering in her belly, or the delicious tingles throughout her body. The thick white bar smelled crisp, clean, of woods in the early morning after rain. She carefully set the bar down, not sure what being surrounded by his scent all night would do to her.

A bottle of thick cream drew her attention and she read the label. Conditioner. Jessi followed the directions after shampooing. The soft texture of her hair after she rinsed astounded her. She was still combing her fingers through the damp silky length when she walked into the kitchen.

Mason sat at the table. His jaw flexed and she was sure for

a moment she'd actually witnessed a smile. "You used the conditioner."

"Yes. It's amazing. My hair is… soft. Is yours this soft?"

His long fingers drummed on the table. "I never really thought about it."

Jessi stared at his long, glossy hair. Her fingers twitched. What she'd felt yesterday when he'd helped her had counted as soft. Before she realized her intentions, she'd crossed the room to him.

A feathery sensation along her wrist made her jump. She glanced down at Mason's hand sliding along hers. Slowly he brought her hand to his hair. Without thought, Jessi sank her fingers into the silken length, brushing through the weight from his scalp to past his ear. His eyes closed and he leaned into her touch.

Jessi's heart skipped and then beat too fast. She was touching a man… And she wanted to do more. She wanted to slid across his lap, sink her other hand into his hair and find out what he tasted like. She wanted to know if he'd crush her with all his strength, or be gentle, like their moment in the barn. Which would she even want?

But then he'd want more.

She'd *feel* that he'd want more. The sudden flash of a man slamming painfully into her made her gasp and jump away. Silken strands flowed through her fingers like water until she was left empty.

Mason's fingers wound through hers, preventing her from moving too far away. "I won't hurt you."

Tightness squeezed Jessi's lungs. She licked her dry lips. "You wouldn't mean to, but…"

"No." His hand tightened around hers. "I wouldn't. You do know you're in complete control of yourself, don't you? And that includes from me."

Jessi tugged her hand free and pulled in a shaky breath. Anger rose at the raw memories threatening to surface, to pull her under if she allowed. Of course he'd believe it'd be so simple. "Yeah, well, I wish that were the case. If *no* was all it took for me to remain in control, it wouldn't have been ignored a thousand times while I screamed."

Sesay's long nails clicked on the wood. The long sweep of his tail brushed the doorway. Oblivious to the interruption, he sat beside Mason, and stared at him with a *pet me* plea. Mason's jaw flexed and he looked away. His fist beat a soft rhythm on the table. Jessi rubbed her nose and sighed. The horror of her past was hers to handle.

Unable to stand the mortification of an event he not only had nothing to do with, but now had to see in her, thanks to her big mouth, Jessi went to work on dinner. "I'm sorry."

"You have nothing to be sorry about," he said softly.

"You didn't deserve to be dragged through my bad moment."

Mason's deep exhale made her glance over her shoulder. A shadowy expression she could only think of as pain-filled darkened his face. "I hear you... I hear her... and there's no one to stop it. Just screams."

Jessi's heart clenched. He was up and out of the room before she could say anything. Sesay whined. She tried to ignore the realization of the hurt her words must have caused. They hadn't opened a gap in heart alone, but his too, reminding him of the helplessness his sister must have experienced. Only his twin wasn't around to complain about them. She'd died at the merciless hands of the fiend, while Jessi hadn't. Another reminder. As she cut up an onion, she had to wonder how Mason could stand to look at her at all.

7

"NO, LIKE THIS." JESSI TOOK THE KNIFE SHAPED TOOL FROM Mason and demonstrated for the third time how to properly uncap honeycombs with a swift downward scrape. "You have to be gentle, or you'll ruin the comb."

Rich golden fluid dribbled from the scraped sections, sliding down the wax and into the bucket below. When Jessi flipped the tool to hand it back, Mason hesitated. "Maybe you should do this part, I'll keep stacking them for you."

"You'll get it," she assured him, pressing the blade in his direction.

Still, he shook his head and moved away. "No, these are too valuable to be ruined on training. I'll keep watching you, and if next time you want me to try again, I will."

A little flutter tingled in Jessi's chest. Next time? The thought of him being around for the next collection excited her far more than she cared to admit.

She'd spent most of the previous evening by herself, and she'd discovered, much to her shock, she'd been hoping to spend it with Mason. No longer did she fear being alone with him. Another surprise. Though she hadn't decided if it was pleasant, or worrisome. Trust given to a man could be a dangerous thing.

Yet, Jessi wanted to know more about the stranger named Mason Dandridge. She wanted to know about his home, his family... about his twin if he'd talk about her. But the moment Wilson announced he needed help to bed, Mason had assisted and then disappeared upstairs. Sesay kept Jessi company until she'd been too bored to read and went to bed.

Come morning, Mason was already outside doing whatever he seemed to do in the early hours. Jessi found him after she had everything ready in the honey house.

Now, he did what he could with little instruction and the least amount of chance to fail on his part. She found the efficiency of his decisions humbling and practical. The few men she'd known in her life would never admit to failure. Not only did he raise his hands when he didn't seem to catch on, he went to a simpler task, freeing her to continue with the challenges. It made for a smooth workflow and streamlined the entire process, cutting an all-day affair to mere hours.

"Are you always this agreeable about what you can and can't do?"

He lifted a honey-filled frame with minimal effort over a bucket, situating how she'd need it for processing. "I'm a visual learner. The more I watch, the easier I can duplicate. I've only watched you the three times before I attempted what you can do. Three times wasn't enough, so I will do more helpful things."

Jessi ran the blade down the comb, releasing the next row of honey. She completed the side before shifting to the back of the frame and finishing the process. Mason watched her silently, his forearm braced on a frame two buckets away. Jessi tried not to be self-conscious each time he stopped to observe her work. However, she couldn't seem to stop from tucking a stray lock of hair, getting the strands sticky, or adjusting her dark green tank top to try to hide as much of her back as possible. The little shed had to be kept warm to make sure the honey flowed. Wearing long sleeves would have been sweltering torture.

After the last frame was scraped, Jessi went to check on the first one and found it halfway done. They had a bit longer to wait until she could start straining into jars. Unable to resist, she allowed some honey to drip onto her finger. Sampling the batches was always her favorite part. Sweet yet balanced, the flowery honey warmed her taste buds and made her smile.

Mason joined her, interest shining in his gaze. "Good?"

Jessi pulled her lips into her mouth and nodded. "Always. The clover is blooming. I love clover honey."

She let more drip onto her finger. Mason leaned forward, peering over the ribbons of liquid amber streaming down. "Can I try?"

"Of course."

Before she could bring the taste to her mouth, he captured it and brought it to his. Jessi's breath lodged in her throat. Eyes wide, she watched his mouth envelop her honey tipped finger. Wet and impossibly warm, his tongue wrapped around her finger, his gaze locked with hers. Heat flashed in his eyes. Her body answered with an intensity deep inside she never thought she'd be able to have. Gasping, her focus shifted back to his lips. Slowly, he pulled her hand away, sucking as he did so. Jessi had to fight not to whimper at the sliver of pleasure the action caused.

"Delicious," he whispered. Hyper focused, his gaze rattled her senses and caused another rousing tremble in her belly. "Can I kiss you?"

Jessi forgot her words. She looked at his mouth again. Her body screamed *yes* while her mind froze. But oh, summer sun, she wanted to know what being kissed by this man would feel like. Somehow, she managed to nod, unable to speak.

Not sure if she could remain bold, Jessi closed her eyes

and tried to remember she needed oxygen to survive. Or at least to be able to experience the impending kiss. Jessi figured passing out would ruin things. The pounding of her heart echoed in her ears. She wondered if he could hear it. Then all rational thought fled her mind.

In a tender brush, his firm lips feathered across hers. The faint tickle of his beard teased her chin. Jessi's mouth parted on an inhale. His tongue glided along her bottom lip and she opened. The sweet floral notes of honey burst within her mouth as his tongue slid along hers. Unhurried and undemanding, his lips moved over hers. His tongue explored and savored. Her knees weakened. He made no effort to crowd her space or pull her against his body. His mouth slanted and his fingers slid between hers, but he didn't touch her further. Only, she noticed, where she'd given him permission.

Jessi realized with a little tremor of fear laced desire, *she* wanted more. She wanted his body pressed to hers, to know what his muscles felt like under her hands. More than anything, she wanted to be held by him. Her hands tightened around his. Emboldened by his restraint, she stepped closer until her breasts brushed his chest. The sexy little groan he made let her know he liked what she did. Desire thrummed at her center and made sensible thought flitter away. Before she could chicken out, Jessi brought his hands to her hips.

Kissing Jessi was everything Mason imagined it'd be, and dangerously more. He knew then he could get lost in her glorious body. For a few wonderful moments, his world would be right and okay again. Only the two of them lost in sensation and pleasure. But he'd be using her as an escape, and Jessalyn Silverna deserved so much more. She deserved to be treasured, explored in agonizing detail. Loved.

The fullness of her hips filled his hands. Her breasts pushed against his chest. All soft curves and lovely enticement. If he took a small step forward, he'd know how well they'd fit together. In short, massaging motions, her fingers kneaded his biceps as she deepened their kiss. He let her take over, let the blossoming confidence of the moment sweep her away.

No matter how much he ached to discover more of this woman, Mason knew he couldn't. Not yet anyway, and maybe never. For some reason she'd trusted him enough to allow a thorough kiss. He wouldn't betray the decision by making further demands, nor would he let her think she was ready for more.

She wasn't.

Once a little coherent thought crept in, she'd panic as she'd done yesterday in the kitchen. He didn't want that to happen. Fear ruined memory, tainted the experience and diminished the likelihood of another. Mason had every intention of a repeat.

Easing away from her, he gave a few soft, gentle pulling kisses. With a sigh he broke their embrace and stepped far enough away that she had to either follow, or straighten. A slightly confused, yet desire-filled look swam in her striking green eyes. Smokier colored than green now, he noted.

He slid the pad of his thumb along her glossy bottom lip, tugging at the pouty fullness. With a tsk, he let his hand drop. "You are a beautiful temptation."

Blinking, she took a step away, reaching for the work surface behind her. Doubt replaced the haze of desire clouding her eyes. "What are you talking about?"

Mason didn't dare speak aloud the emotional turmoil raging inside him. That in his mind he tore her pants off, lifted her onto the worktable, spread her legs and sank deep into her liquid heat. Saying something like that would doubtless send her screaming for the house, and within seconds his backpack would be thrown out a window. So instead, he crossed his arms over his chest and settled his weight onto his back leg. Calm, collected, seeming to not be battling longing the likes of which he'd never endured before.

All from a kiss.

Stars above, the power this woman could wield over him if she knew…

What could he say that would be safe? "How can you not know you're beautiful?"

She snorted in derision and rolled her eyes. "Oh please, because every man wants a deformed woman."

A frown pinched his forehead. "Deformed? In what way?"

She pushed away from the table and began checking the frames. "Don't play stupid with me. You aren't blind."

Mason had never considered himself a slow man. He was smart, usually a quick learner and not many people fooled him when it came to their true personality. While no, he didn't have the Gen-Heir talent Sean had as a Sympath, he prided himself on being able to spot fake words from genuine ones. Why then, hadn't he been able to spot that Jessi's shell went beyond her fear of physical boundaries, to actual shame in her body itself?

Sure, she'd tugged on the tank top all day, but he figured it was the same reason most women did. Tight clothing tended to bunch in unflattering, and often uncomfortable, ways. Yet, he realized, when she rolled her shoulders forward, it hadn't been the soft curve of her stomach or hips she'd been trying to avoid him seeing, but rather the crisscross of scars along her shoulders, neck and upper arms.

The scabbed over scrapes from a couple days ago looked good, healing nicely. Mason stopped himself from reaching to investigate how well her skin was recovering by fisting his hands and tightening his arms across his chest. "You think I'm bothered by a few scars?"

She whipped around so fast her hair flew. "A *few*?"

Mason shrugged. "What do you want me to say? You have a lot? I have a lot too. Scars don't say anything about who you are, just what you've been through. They don't *change* you unless you let them, or you want them to."

Her hands rubbed up and down her thighs. She glanced at his body, uncertainty flickering across her flushed face. "You have scars too?"

"Who doesn't have one or two?" he asked, and then held up his hand when she opened her mouth. "Yes, I'm very aware you have more than one or two. I'm simply saying, they're a part of life. And yes, I have many. Some worse than others."

She twisted the hem of her top between her fingers, her gaze skittering over him. "Can I... can I see them?"

Mason almost said yes. Then he noticed the thin, faint white mark curving over her shoulder near her collar bone. Only one or two scars seemed to carry over, all the rest were on her back. He wanted to know why, and how bad they truly were. He took a deep breath. "When you're ready to show me yours, I'll share mine."

Jessi recoiled as if she'd been physically hit, missing the collection bucket behind her by a narrow twist of her feet. "That will never happen."

Keeping distance between them, Mason unfolded his arms and peered curiously into a bucket. The rich amber contents reached a quarter mark. "You sure have a lot of nevers in your life."

"You sure have a way of pushing me towards them." She went to the wall of jars and pulled an armload down. "I can't believe you'd ask me that."

Mason clasped his hands behind his back. "Why?"

She started again, her green eyes wide. "Why? What do you mean *why*?"

"I mean just that. Why do you find it so hard to believe I'd wish to see you? All of you?"

The way she looked at him made him think he must have sprouted a second head on his shoulders. When she spoke, her voice was little more than a squeak. "A-all of me? N-naked?"

All the color drained from her face. Mason knew he treaded on dangerous ground. Yes, he'd love nothing more than to see this woman naked. Would he say as much? Nope. "Those words never left my mouth, did they?"

She took a shaky breath. "How then, do you plan on seeing *all* of me?"

Mason went to the door. With his hand on the handle, he looked at her. "I'm going to check on Wilson. Come get me for the next set."

"You aren't going to tell me?"

Mason couldn't help being pleased at the thread of genuine curiosity in her voice. "How I'll see all of you?"

She nodded.

"That's easy. The same way you're letting me touch you. One piece at a time."

8

ONE PIECE AT A TIME.

Mason's words still echoed in Jessi's mind the following afternoon on their journey to town. She'd done everything to avoid looking at him. She managed yesterday, and this morning. But now, with nothing around them but tall trees and dancing light and shadows, he was the only thing to look at unless she wanted to watch Mildred's big horse butt clopping down the uneven wagon trail.

Jars rattled gently in the back, intermingled with crates of corn and other extra produce she had to sell on the way to and in town. Everything in the wagon was for sale to anyone they encountered. A lot of the families on the outskirts appreciated her stopping by and offering honey for purchase, saving them a trip when they learned of a delivery.

In the dappled, shifting light, Jessi took the time to really look Mason over. The reins rested comfortably in his large hands. The sleeves of his navy shirt were rolled halfway up his thick forearms. A dusting of dark hair accented the visible corded muscle. Thin scars broke up the olive tint of his skin, familiar in what they were. Old knife wounds. A knot formed in her gut, but she kept going. The fabric of his shirt stretched over his large biceps and shoulders.

He'd pulled the sides of his hair into a small braid, leaving the rest to flow freely down his back. The edges and ends fluttered with the wisps floating around, making him have to sweep a stray strand away every now and again. The tan fabric of his pants pulled taut over his muscular thighs and fell to cover the tops of his dark brown boots. Big boots. She supposed she shouldn't be surprised, everything about Mason seemed large.

When he glimpsed her way, the light caught his inquiring pale eyes just right so they seemed to be made of actual silver. Jessi looked back to the road, a little embarrassed at having been caught staring. She swore his lips twitched. Would she ever see him smile? She wanted to ask, but knew what the answer would be. What did he have to smile about? At one point in her life, she'd been there, she understood. She wouldn't draw more attention to his miserable state of mind.

Though, giving him a sideways glance, she had the urge to catch him in a smile, to be able to do that much for him. The revelation startled her. Why should she care about his happiness?

Because in the few days he'd been in her life, he'd changed everything.

For the first time, Jessi felt desirable. Wanted. And the emotions weren't merely for her, but within as well. Never in her life did she think she'd be able to look at a man and wish to spend more than conversation time in his presence. Mason made her imagine and long for an intimacy she'd only read about and seen in one other couple, her parents. A beacon of normal, safe love she'd been snatched from. He made her remember there was something different than pain, and blood and silent screams…

Needing something to focus on, she asked, "How did you get your scars?"

He swept a quick glance her way before focusing on the road again. "Many, many different ways. Some by being stupid as a kid, others by not paying attention as an adult."

Jessi shifted on the seat until she faced him. The gentle bounce of the wagon made her wrap her arm around the back of the bench for balance. "Tell me about one."

He scratched at his beard under his chin. "All right. I have a rather nasty one on my shin from an ice skate slicing me open when I was nine and playing ice ball. Do they play that here?"

"They did in Uconn, but it doesn't get cold enough for long enough down here to have much of a season. But for the few weeks we do have a hard enough freeze, so they usually place ice wicket."

"Ah, well that's fun too."

Jessi couldn't help but give a short laugh. "Not violent enough for you?"

Mason shrugged. "My grandmother enjoyed ice wicket. It's even civilized enough for my mother to play."

"I've seen some old ladies take their wicket game seriously. If you hit their puck, be warned, they'll send you flying across the ice so far away from the next wicket you'll never recover."

"Trust me, I know all about how fast a game can go south when women are involved. Don't stand between a woman and her chance at winning *that* game. I still haven't figured it out yet." He shook his head and sighed.

"Bragging rights. Only one person can win. There's no second or third. It's over when the first person clears the last placed wicket. It's one of the only games where strength doesn't matter. Only finesse." Jessi smiled at the memory of the first time she'd won. "I was twelve when I won my first game. We'd played with another family in my mother's apartment building. My father was visiting and we'd convinced him to come outside to play. I was so excited. Not only did I beat two kids, but three adults too."

Mason shook his head again. "I don't think I've ever won that game."

"Really?"

He gave her droll stare. "I've only ever played against other women and kids. Once I was old enough and my mother could no longer force me to play, I stopped."

Jessi laughed. "I see. I promise if we play together, I'll go easy on you."

"Yeah, right."

She grinned, couldn't help it. Being playful with him was nice. "No really, I will. I'll even teach you something maybe."

"That's what Cora said the last time I attempted to play. Then she smacked my puck so hard it landed in three feet of snow off in the woods somewhere. I was still searching for it when she won the game."

"Did you ever find it?"

He smiled, a quick flash of straight, white teeth that transformed him from handsome to devastating, softening his eyes and the angles of his face. Jessi's heart skipped. "Yeah, in the spring."

Jessi laughed and wanted to help him hang on to the fun event. But she knew the good memory would soon serve as a reminder there would be no more, not with his sister. So she took a deep breath and changed the subject before the darkness could creep back in and take over. "What about an adult scar?"

"What age do you consider adult?"

Jessi looked over the jars rattling in the back thoughtfully. "Eighteen? Nineteen?"

"I probably earned my worst scars when I was training at nineteen with a Wolvenguard team. I hadn't been placed yet as I'd just graduated academia. I was doing all the formal training for the different Guardian team positions I could potentially fill as a strategist. On Wolvenguard teams, it doesn't matter if you'll be a supporting role or not, everyone has to help in a prisoner escape. They use trains mostly to start since the only way in or out of a prison is via rail, and then they jump off when a trail is found."

Jessi stared at him in disbelief. "Off a train? Are they crazy?"

"Yes." He stated the word with a fixed stare. "Completely crazy. I think they're all adrenaline junkies."

"What happened?"

"I missed the team queue for when to safely jump. The dogs had corralled the prisoner and speed was essential. If you leave the wolves too long with their target, they can injure or even kill someone, so it's vital to get there in time and help take command of the situation. I ended up jumping into a bad thicket, sliding along feet of thorns. They had to cut me free to get to me and I spent two nights in a hospital having thorns surgically removed from all over my body. My left side took the brunt of the impact, I swear my skin feels like sandpaper. Needless to say, I did *not* get invited to join a Wolvenguard team."

Jessi covered her mouth to keep from laughing. His left side was away from her, which she figured was good, or she'd be tugging up his shirt to see the evidence of his folly. At which point, she'd be obligated to reveal *her* left side. No thank you. Yet she couldn't help but wonder, was his worst as bad as hers? "They really don't bother you?"

His thumb rubbed along the leather rein, his wide chest expanding on a long inhale, as if he were carefully weighing his answer. "No. They're proof I survived something that could have otherwise killed me. Or, if not kill me, wound me enough to teach a valuable lesson. Even the ones from an enemy taught me I let them get too close."

A tingle slithered up her spine and she couldn't help but rub her hand along her bare neck and down beneath her shirt. The faint raised lines marring her back greeted her fingertips. *Proof I survived...* They were definitely that for her.

She glanced at the road and then gasped. She'd been so wrapped up in conversation, she hadn't been paying attention to where they were on the route. "Oh, turn left there, in that drive. It's the first house I stop at to offer honey."

Mason slowed Mildred and directed her onto the narrow, deeply rutted wagon path that led to a small, single story wood framed house. One corner of the roof was caving in, both the front windows sagged from the uneven foundation. In a few years, if the brothers who owned the house didn't do some critical maintenance, the whole place was going to fall around them. No one came out in greeting from either the house, or the small barn behind it.

Mason brought Mildred to a stop. The mare shook her head and snorted, but otherwise obeyed. "Do you think anyone is home?"

Jessi shrugged and jumped down. "Maybe. They have some fields, so they may be working them. I'll go check."

"Wait." Mason leapt down, his dark hair flying out around his shoulders. "Who lives here?"

At the back of the wagon, Jessi unhinged the tailgate. She pulled a crate of honey forward. "Three brothers. They lost their mother about two years ago."

With his fists pressed into his sides above his hips, Mason surveyed the dumpy grounds around the house. "How old are they?"

Jessi tried to ignore the effect his tall, muscular presence, standing strong and powerful, had on her. As if the very ground he stood on would obey if he said so. She hadn't seen this side of him. She glanced around, wondering what had him on edge. "I'm not sure. My age?"

He looked over his shoulder at her. "Are they triplets?"

Shaking her head, she laughed. "No, I'm just saying

they're close to being around my age, I'm sure a few years spread between them, older and younger."

"And you always come here alone?"

The thought of going anywhere alone made Jessi shudder. "No, Wilson and Sesay are always with me."

Mason's shoulders drooped and he shook his head. "Great, a wolf and an old man."

Jessi pulled forward a crate of produce. "Actually, that wolf keeps everyone away. I wish I had him now."

They'd made the joint decision to leave Sesay with Wilson. The dog loved going off to town with Jessi, his tongue flapping in the wind of the ride. But her self-appointed guardian needed the protection and limited help more than she and Mason did.

Mason searched around again, for what Jessi wished she knew. She opened her mouth to ask him when he shook his head and sighed. "Where are the fields? I'll go look, you can stay here with the cart."

"You're a stranger. You're likely to get shot if you just walk up on them."

"That doesn't make me feel better."

"Why are you nervous at all? I've been delivering goods here for years."

He rubbed the back of his neck. "I don't know. Call me cynical. I've traveled the world dealing with the worst in humanity. We both know that's what brought me to you."

Brought me to you. Like he was *hers.* Jessi's heart clenched. Why, oh why, did she suddenly, almost desperate in the wish, want him to be? Yeah, because he'd want a woman who panicked at the mere thought of being intimately touched, let alone actually allowing it. Sighing, she headed towards the fields.

"Stay here, I'll be right back."

"Are you worried someone may take something?"

She turned and walked backward. "Maybe, I mean, worst in humanity and all that, right?"

He made a motion to follow and she shook her head. "No, I'll be fine. I'm going to check, that's all. If I see them working, I'll call out and return, they'll hopefully follow. If not, we'll leave and go to the next house."

At first she thought he'd argue again. Then he gave a curt nod, which she returned before twirling forward and almost skipping to the fields. She hadn't felt this carefree in years, maybe ever.

The faintest of movements when she went around the back of the house told her she wasn't alone. Jessi froze. Anyone sitting out back would have heard Mildred ride up. On a deep inhale, she turned, a sliver of alarm racing along her senses. The three brothers lounged on the low back porch. Jake, who Jessi figured as the youngest, leaned against a post. Mitch sat on the edge, while the oldest looking brother, Ray, sprawled in a rickety chair.

Ray shifted, a faint thread of movement. "Hey there, Jes. Is the old man with you?"

Jessi took a half step, lining up for a clear run to the front of the house if she needed. "No, not this trip."

Mitch stood. "I don't see the dog either."

The youngest, Jake, smiled slowly. "You left them both back home, did you? Old man's about worthless now, huh?"

A quick assessment revealed no guns. That didn't mean they didn't have knives. Of course their fists would work plenty well against her. "I stopped by like I always do, but if you're busy or uninterested, I'll be leaving now."

She turned on her heel, dirt sliding under her shoe.

Jake jumped from the porch, all lean muscle, his young face set in hard lines. "We're definitely interested, been waiting almost three months for that load of liquid gold to come around."

Jessi didn't wait for further explanation; they'd made

themselves clear enough. She launched into an all-out sprint, screaming Mason's name as she fled. She only made it a few feet before someone slammed hard into her back and sent her flying. Dirt, grass and small rocks flew into her face and bit into her palms.

A heavy body landed on her, pinning her to the ground. Dark fear clouded her vision and sent her into a panic. Strong fingers wrapped around her mouth, cutting off her screams. His hips pressed her further into the ground, keeping her from being able to buck or kick. The hard point of his elbow dug between her shoulder blades.

He yanked her head back, his pelvis pushed lower and harder. Old memories of terror and pain flared to life. The weight of a man along her body made her stiffen. Air seized in her lungs. "Just hold still and you'll be fine. We just want the honey."

The heaviness of his body vanished. Grunts and a curse sounded. What seemed like seconds later, she was hauled up to her knees. Trembling, Jessi tried to focus, but everything swam and she couldn't breathe.

Mason's strong arms enfolded her, hauling her onto his lap. *Mason.* Not anyone else. Mason, who was safe. With a finger under her chin, he forced her eyes to meet his. Somehow, she managed to focus on him, to register the protection of his body around her.

"Hey, here, look here, at me. You're going to be fine, nothing happened," he said.

She nodded. Hot tears coursed down her cheeks. Stupid flashbacks. If she had been in danger, she'd have just laid there and... No. She couldn't think about that. Her fingers clutched at the loose cotton of his shirt. "Okay... I'm okay."

"You sure?"

She nodded again, and then leaned over and vomited.

. . .

MASON BARELY CAUGHT HER HAIR BEFORE JESSI LOST HER SHORT-lived battle with composure. Not that he blamed her. After he'd taken quick care of the two young men determined to steal the honey, he found Jessi pinned, her skin white with terror. Mason's vision had turned red. He glanced at the man sprawled unconscious on the ground a few feet away. The scab didn't move. Mason wasn't even sure if the guy was breathing, nor did he care.

Jessi shook so badly, he knew she wouldn't be able to walk to the cart. Tears still worked a trail down her dirt-streaked cheeks. Before she could launch a protest, Mason stood with her in his arms and carried her. The moment her feet touched the wagon, she shifted from his arms onto the seat, not meeting his gaze. Mason ignored her discomfort and fumbled around in a bag near her feet. He removed a jar of water and handed it to her.

"It's the best I can do for now. We can get you a toothbrush in town."

"Thanks." Her voice was rough. The water sloshed from the jar when she took off the lid, her hands shaky.

Mason grasped the jar, and her hands, between his. He held tight until she met his stare. "You're okay."

"I know." She sniffled, pulling her hands free. "Thank you."

"I won't let anything happen to you." And he meant every word.

Tears still shimmered in her eyes, but had stopped falling. "You won't always be around, will you?"

"I can be," he said softly. Then pushed away before she could turn him down. Again. "We aren't stopping at any other houses. If the store you supply in town doesn't buy it all, I'll make up for the lost revenue. It's clear people have made the connection between Wilson's illness and your being vulnerable on your own. I'm not chancing someone else thinking they can take advantage."

He did a quick check of Mildred's hooves and leads before jumping back into the seat. They rode the rest of the way into town in silence, except when Jessi gave direction. In between mutters or hand gestures, she nursed the jar of water. Mason missed their light banter from earlier. Anger washed through him again. A woman without a past like Jessi's would have struggled with the attack. Mason imagined she'd relived some, if not all, of the horror of her captivity in the one single, selfish moment the man had attempted.

Mason took a deep breath to calm his nerves to keep from doing or saying something foolish. She wasn't to blame for the attempted robbery. At some point, she'd found the young men to be trustworthy. The betrayal had to hurt on multiple levels.

The city she brought them to was different than the one he'd found to give him directions to their house. This one was larger, more organized, with brick paved roads and apartment homes intermixed around the stores and businesses. They even appeared to have a small trolley line that ran through the center of the wide roads.

Mason took in the busy streets and sidewalks. "What city is this?"

"Old Charleston. If you keep following this road, you'll eventually hit the ocean." She set the jar of water between them. "I have around five stores who take my honey. I don't usually have enough for all of them. They'll be happy to have their fill this trip."

Mason fell into the leisurely flow of traffic on the inside lane. A mixture of horse and rider, wagons, carriages, and even a few Ariots - small vehicles run by magnetic engines harnessing the power of positive and negative attraction. Ariots were expensive, due to a shortage of resources to make them, so they were sparse among the means of transport. Those who needed to turn or pull off in front of a storefront moved into the outside lane. Different colored bricks served to differentiate between the lanes. The ones in their lane were a rich, vibrant red. The brick in the next lane was a soothing cream, with a different texture.

"Is this the only city you supply?"

"Yes. One of the shops has several smaller stores in other towns. It's up to the owner whether he supplies his other stores or not. He's my first stop since he always buys more than anyone else."

Mason took in the warm colored buildings on either side of the wide thoroughfare. Some were brick, others were painted. Most were three stories or taller. Women in both gowns and pants like Jessi's strolled the streets with bags or crates, their children chasing behind. Some had men with them, most were alone, clearly feeling safe and comfortable. Haven City was similar, only certain areas were considered unsafe to venture into for the average person.

Businessmen and merchants wove their way through the crowds, busy to get to their next destination. Street vendors called out their wares to those passing by. Mason had to strain to hear Jessi's directions above the noise of everything around them. Twenty minutes later, he slowed Mildred to a gentle stop on a quiet side street in front of a two-story shop. Jessi leapt down and went inside with a quick mumble about returning shortly. Mason took his time, surveying the small collection of storefronts and street merchants.

A flutter of fabric caught his attention. A dark-skinned young man sat beside a cart overflowing with a rainbow selection of sheer scarves and shawls. Silver rimmed glasses glinted in the mid-afternoon sun. Nose buried in a book, he fought a stiff breeze that swept through the narrow street, holding the pages down.

Mason lifted his hand when he approached the cart, letting one of the silky scarves brush across his palm. "How much?"

Surprised, big brown eyes stared at Mason behind the

glasses. "Oh." The book snapped closed in the young man's lap. "Hello."

A remarkable green slip of silk woven with silver threads caught Mason's attention. He pulled the fabric free and held it out for the merchant. "I'd like this one."

"Oh, of course." He cleared his throat and stood. "We're having a special today."

Mason listened, looked at the hopeful young man when he finished, and then on a sigh pulled down two additional random scarves. He needed souvenirs for his mother, didn't he? Sure, because what she wanted when he'd gone to learn about how her daughter had been brutally murdered was for him to show up with *scarves*. Idiot. He paid for the merchandise, thanked the man, and went back to the cart.

Jessi was pulling crates full of honey forward. Beside her a tall, older man with thick silver hair cut short and neatly combed grasped one, hefting it into his arms. Mason slid forward, taking one from Jessi when she went to lift it. Startled, she looked up at him with wide, green eyes the same remarkable shade as the scarf he'd just purchased.

"I... I didn't see you when we came out. Sorry." She grabbed another crate, hefting it into her arms that he'd learned earlier today were stronger than they looked. She'd slung crates full of honey and produce without complaint into the wagon. Her livelihood demanded she do so, and usually without any help.

"I was over there." Mason nodded at the merchant.

Jessi stood on her toes, then turned her attention back to the crate. "We shouldn't be long."

Frowning, Mason followed behind her and who he assumed to be the shop owner. She seemed reserved, careful to keep any and all emotion locked in so all she appeared to be was a boring woman dropping off some goods. He had to wonder as they entered the store, lit only by the wide windows in the front, and passed by rows of tidy stocked shelves, if she always acted this way or if the event from earlier prompted the behavior.

The shop owner straightened after setting a crate down and held out his hand. "Bishop Hantley."

Mason accepted the man's hand and shook firmly, introducing himself. Jessi seemed to ignore the exchange, removing jars of honey and shelving them.

The older gentleman crossed his arms over his narrow chest and looked Mason over. "You're not from around here, are you?"

Mason lifted a brow at the inspection. "No, I'm from Sziveria."

"Ah. Can't see what someone from there would want from here. Unless there's trouble? Seems Sziverian's only show up to do some rescuing."

Since he dealt mostly in the shadowy underworld, limiting exposure to those around him to keep from being easily recognized, Mason had no idea how the average human viewed his country. "We're champions, are we?"

"Well sure, I mean of course you know about that situation a couple weeks ago, no I guess it'd be months now, at least two, with those outlaws and that pretty young girl. Sziverians swept right in, took out the group and rescued the woman. All without a single loss of innocent life."

Mason tried to recall the event. "If I remember, the young woman in question was Sziverian."

The shop owner nodded. "Yes, but what other country sweeps in and rescues its damsel in distress?"

Jessi stood with empty crates. "Did you need any additional jars?"

Hantley blinked his dark brown eyes, almost as if Jessi had materialized in front of him. "Oh, of honey?"

She shifted the crates onto her hip, both hands braced on them. "Yes."

"I suppose I should, how many do you have to spare?"

"However many you want."

Mason narrowed his gaze on Jessi's taut face. Every muscle in her body practically vibrated with discomfort.

Hantley rubbed his chin in thought. "I'll take two additional crates. No, make that three, then I can send some away."

She nodded stiffly and turned to leave. Mason followed, noting the owner stayed behind this time.

At the cart, he stacked the full crates to carry all at once. "What's going on with you?"

A stray lock of shimmery red hair swept across her face. She tucked it behind her ear while adjusting objects in the back of the cart. "Nothing."

Mason glanced around the mostly deserted street, but knew even without an audience, now wasn't the time to find out what had her on edge. "Wait here, in the cart. I'll be right back. Has he paid you?"

She shook her head.

"How much will he owe, and is that negotiable?"

"As in more?"

"As in he can't make me think you always accept less."

Understanding lit her smoky green eyes. "Ah. No, what I charge isn't negotiable. But he knows and he won't try to steal. No one else sells honey in this area."

Satisfied, Mason returned inside, the crates loaded in his arms. Her lack of argument about staying at the cart confirmed his suspicions. Something was off. After the delivery and payment, he'd find out what. Hantley was still at the shelves where Jessi had neatly arranged her product. He set the boxes down and stepped away. Jessi might do the man's job for him, but Mason sure wasn't.

Hantley rose on his toes and searched over Mason's shoulder. Mason didn't pretend not to know what the man searched for. "She's back with the cart."

"Are you staying long? In Carolina?"

"As long as I need to."

"With Jessi and the old man?"

While Mason didn't want to have a conversation with Hantley, he *did* want to know why Jessi was so uneasy around the shop owner. "Yes, I'm renting a room."

The man shifted on his feet somewhat and Mason looked him over. A few buttons at the bottom of his untucked shirt were undone. His trousers had skipped a button, leaving an odd folded gap in the center. Surely in the minutes he'd left Jessi to deal with business on her own something hadn't happened… Mason breathed away the anger. No. It wasn't possible, he wouldn't consider it. The few moments after she'd been thrown to the ground, she'd lost her mind. She wouldn't have stocked shelves, upset yet calm, *if* she'd been attacked by the store owner.

A woman bustled in from the back. Annoyance pinched at the corners of her thin mouth. At some point her dark hair had been bound in a neat bun atop her head, but now flopped in a sad state to one side. She tossed a long card of some sort behind the check-out counter.

"I'm outta here, Bishop. I need that…" Her words died when her gaze settled on Mason. She licked her lips and patted at her hair. Mason didn't miss the way she adjusted the top of her gown either, which had also somehow been pushed to one side. "Oh, um, I need the uh, extra…"

A dark red flush spread across Hantley's face. "I will discuss that with you later."

"I don't have later," she snapped, her dark eyes flashing. "You said I'd get it today, and I need it today." Her long fingers waved at the crates. "If you don't have the tinnies now, I'll take one of those jars."

Hantley hesitated, his face still brilliant red. Mason had gathered since the confrontation with the brothers, honey was a valuable commodity. If the number written on the shelf was any indication, the jars were worth their weight in Westican currency.

The woman crossed her arms over her chest. "I can get it from the till myself, or I can come by your house tonight."

Eyes wide, Hantley grabbed a jar and handed it to her. "Here. Now go."

She sashayed to the front. "See you in a few days." Using her hip, she opened the door and shook the jar with a wink. "Thanks for this. Maybe next time I'll do something a little extra for you, too."

Hantley cleared his throat and ran a shaky hand through his thick white hair. "Women, like to get whatever they can from us, huh?"

Mason flattened his mouth. "We need to be going, Jessi said you know what you're to pay her."

"Ah, yes of course, this way." Hantley patted his back pocket and frowned. He shook his head and swept the sleeve of his shirt across his forehead.

Mason followed the shop owner through a set of double doors into the back of the store. A small sorting table was just beyond the entrance. An open bottle of oil was perched on the edge, the lid on the floor. Beside the lid was a discarded handkerchief. Realization sank into Mason. He paused, deciding he didn't want to go any further. Hantley returned with a small, sealed wooden box.

"It's all there." He shook the box, coins rattled within. "Including the amount for the three additional crates."

Mason accepted the payment with a nod. Back at the cart, he handed what he was sure amounted to a small fortune in tin coins to Jessi. She set the box in her lap, on top of the scarves he'd purchased earlier.

Taking the reins, he glanced at her. "So, didn't like what you walked into, did you?"

9

SHOCKED, JESSI SNAPPED HER ATTENTION TO MASON, THE HEAVY box full of tinnies forgotten. She decided playing ignorant might be her only way out of a conversation she really didn't want to have. Especially with him. "I don't know what you're talking about."

The gentle clop of Mildred's hooves on brick filled in his silence. He didn't bring them back out onto the busy main street, but guided the mare through narrower, quieter side streets. Jessi fidgeted with the silky, colorful heap of fabric in her lap. She'd found them tucked up under the seat. Never in her life had she held anything so soft, or beautiful. Like solid water in her hand, the fabric flowed across her skin and between her fingers. One was a stunning shade of green woven with glistening silver, another brilliant purple and the third one flowed from yellow to rich orange.

"She wasn't unwilling," he finally stated, but still didn't look at her.

Jessi breathed deep. No, the woman had not been forced. She'd only gripped the edges of the table with white knuckles, her skirts pushed up to her hips, legs open, while Hantley grunted and thrust, working for something he didn't seem to care he alone wanted. The woman stared over his shoulder, vacant, her bottom lip drawn into her mouth. His large hand kneaded the woman's exposed breast in time with his working hips.

The coupling had been so... emotionless.

Jessi had stood frozen, wanting the floor to swallow her whole. The little tinker of the bell hadn't alerted them to her presence. And when Hantley changed from grunting to some-thing higher pitched, his thrusts almost desperate, Jessi spun away, not wanting to be more a voyeur than she'd already unwittingly found herself. Knowing she was bright red from root to toe, she'd returned to the front of the shop and whacked the bell with all her might.

"I know that." Somehow the silk had become a tether, comforting her raw nerves.

He slowed Mildred to a stop. Jessi looked around and saw not one person on the street. Mostly apartments or small homes rose up on either side to shade them from the late afternoon sun.

"Talk to me, honey," he urged, shifting on the seat until he faced her.

Heat bloomed across her cheeks. She tucked her chin into her chest to keep from meeting his eyes. "There's nothing to talk about."

"Obviously what you saw upset you."

"And like I'd talk about that with you?" Mortified, Jessi swallowed. Mason was the *last* person she wanted to discuss sex with. Already he'd seen more of her shame in one day than she ever wanted him to know.

"What else are you going to do? Keep it pent up? Sit there and wonder if what you saw was all there is between consenting adults?"

Surprised by his guess, and forthright attitude, Jessi stared at him. "I'm not—"

"Look." He leaned forward, resting his elbows on his

knees, hands clasped. "I'm not going to lie, *most* of the time sex is… selfish. A pursuit of self-pleasure that's usually better than what one can achieve on their own."

Jessi blinked. "On their own?"

Grimacing, he straightened, rubbing the back of his neck. "Yeah. I mean, didn't your parents, or some vulgar female friend talk to you? You know… about how things work?"

A smile twitched at her lips. "Vulgar friend? Does everyone have one?"

Mason sighed. "I think it's like a female rule or something. My sister *was* that friend."

Curious now, enough to set aside her embarrassment, Jessi regarded him. "So is sex either forced or endured? Is that all there is to it?"

Palms out, he held up his hands and shook his head. "No, jeez no. I wasn't trying to imply… damn I'm not very good at this."

"I'm sorry." Jessi quickly looked back at the scarves, picking at the swaths. "I didn't want to talk about it to start with, so we can stop."

"No, I want you understand, between the right two people, coming together is an amazing experience."

A peculiar tightening happened in her chest, compelling her to meet his gaze once again. Had he had amazing sex with someone? Under her lashes she looked him over, at the solid set of his firm jaw, at the way his breathing was a little too labored. Somehow, she couldn't imagine Mason being emotionless when it came to sex. Startled by her thoughts, she couldn't believe she imagined Mason in that role period. "Why are you telling me this?"

Shifting to the front, he shrugged. "I don't know, I just don't like the idea of you being afraid again."

A sliver of jealousy mixed with a dose of interest had her asking the question before she could stop herself, "Have you had this wonderful experience yourself then?"

He urged Mildred back into a light canter. "No, not really. But my three closest friends have something special with their spouses. You don't get that something special by enduring, you get that by *enjoying*."

Jessi didn't know how to take that. She chewed her bottom lip. "You don't…" What was the expression he'd used earlier? "Try to have something better than what you can do on your own?"

"I won't die if I keep from temptation, or accidently take those I love out with me. A few minutes of meaningless sex isn't worth the cost of my life, or anyone else's. If sex is going to kill me, I'd rather die because it was that damn amazing my head explodes or some nonsense."

"Human Rabies Syndrome."

Mason nodded. "Had a friend die from it. He killed his wife and two young daughters before he succumbed himself. After that I… I couldn't."

Jessi squeezed his forearm. "I'm sorry."

"Is it bad here?"

She released his arm, confused by how reluctant she was to do so. The sensation of his muscles moving under fingers was hypnotic, and pleasant. "I don't think so, but I don't know for sure. I think they like to keep it quiet, when a case happens."

"I've always been fascinated by how societies handle the illness. Some don't care, where others don't wish to see their nation annihilated by something capable of wiping them off the map if they aren't careful."

"Has that happened?"

"Two countries that I know of have areas that are on the brink. Our country is forbidden to travel to them, and at least three other nations have a lax view on at least attempting to keep their citizens responsible. Of course, that doesn't stop the occasional ship, with the always stupid young soldier, who takes the bet from his friends to test his luck. They call it zombie jumping."

Jessi's eyes widened. "Oh."

"Yeah, stupidity at its finest. To be that young and dumb. Plus, you don't actually know if the person is infected or not, until you get sick. Such a terrible risk, and waste of life when it happens."

Jessi angled in her seat, careful to keep the scarves on her knees from floating away. "You're really passionate about this."

"You would be too, if one of your closest friends tore his family apart all because he couldn't keep it in his pants for the one week." He lifted his index finger. "*One single week*, he was away from his wife."

They turned down another road and Jessi noted the next store she'd need to sell at up ahead. Once again, only the echo clop of hooves broke the silence between them.

"I always thought," he said, speaking so low she almost missed the words. He shook his head, sending a strand of dark hair over his shoulder. "I always thought *that* would be how I lost her. To her own insatiable desire to seduce any man she could."

Jessi didn't have to ask of whom he spoke. The anguish on his handsome face told her. Cora. He pulled to a stop in front of the store, and this time he went inside with her. They both announced their presence with loud shouts of greeting. Thankfully, the owner was arranging shelves, and nothing humiliating had to happen. Again. Jessi wrapped up business quickly and they moved on to the next shops.

By the time they made it back to the house, night had fully settled. Sesay waited on the porch, barking, but couldn't be bothered to amble down in greeting. All the better Jessi figured, since Mildred never did care for the huge dog. Mason unhitched the mare for Jessi to lead her into the stall and care for her.

She'd finished up and was hanging the tack when Mason entered the barn, Sesay at his heels. The smooth, fluid way he seemed to sweep across the distance left her mesmerized. All long legs and rolling strength. Strands of black hair flowed out behind him, dancing from the motion and a gentle evening breeze. No man had a right to look so good. Shaking her head, she sighed and finished her task.

Heavy shadows from the sole lamp near the barn entrance accented his high cheekbones and muscled frame as he stopped near the stall, resting his forearm on the half wall. "Wilson is sleeping. He liked the cane I found him at the last store we stopped at."

"Oh good." A breath of thanksgiving rushed from her lungs. "I was worried he'd say he wouldn't need one."

"No, I think the incident in the kitchen was enough. He doesn't want a repeat. He said he used the thick stick I'd found for him before we left all day. The functional cane will be much better."

"Thank you for getting it for him."

"I'll finish hanging the fence tomorrow morning too."

Jessi closed the stall. "I can do that, or at least help."

"If you're up in time, you can help." He pushed away from the wall when she walked past.

"If I'm up? What time do you wake?"

"Around four-thirty."

Jessi stopped and blinked up at him. "Why in the inhabited world do you get up so early?"

Even in the dim light she could make out a twinkling of humor in his eyes as he opened his arms. "You don't think I look like this by standing around, do you?"

Words failed her when she looked him over, from his wide shoulders, to the visible strength of his thighs through his pants. All too well she recalled the way all that muscle had felt wrapping her in security. Not used against her, but used to comfort. She swallowed and cleared her throat. "I hadn't thought… about that."

At the back door, he reached into his pocket and withdrew a handful of colorful silk. "I bought these for you."

Stunned, Jessi accepted the gift. "Why?"

He sat with a shrug on the short, single step that led to the kitchen. "I don't know. Your day hadn't been great to that point, thought maybe some color would brighten it."

Jessi let the silken fabric flow across her hands. "Actually, my day had been great until, well, the brothers decided they weren't very neighborly anymore."

"Do you think they'll retaliate?"

"They'd have to know where we live. Wilson never allowed Sesay to let anyone come farther than the walkway. I'm actually surprised you made it all the way to us."

"I knew the right words to say." In the faint light of the moon, he gazed down at his hands and sighed. Jessi felt more than saw a sense of tension rise in him. "I want you to consider something, seriously."

Jessi frowned and sat beside him. "Why do I have a feeling I'm not going to like this consideration?"

"Probably because you won't. But… I want you to hear me out, okay?"

Jessi nodded. "All right."

He reached out, grasping a floating strand of green silk. "Wilson doesn't have much longer, you know that, right?"

A knot formed in her chest. She didn't want to talk about, let alone acknowledge, losing her guardian, or what that meant for her future. "He'll be okay. This isn't the first time he's been sick, or weak."

"Surely you know this is different."

Jessi plucked at the silk, arranging it in a colorful heap on her thighs. The scarf Mason held fluttered between them. "I know he's getting old, and with age comes some… difficulties."

"All right, so say he gets better, but in six months is worse again and when he passes, you'll be all alone here. What are you going to do?"

The knot tightened in her chest. He'd came right out and spoke her biggest fears aloud. She licked her dry lips. "I'm not sure. I'll figure it out."

His hand slipped across until his fingers found hers within the silk. "I know you don't want to go back to Sziveria with me, honey. But you need to consider how you'll handle this place, and yourself, on your own. Eventually you'll have to ask someone here to care for the house. You can't reroof, or do large improvements to your greenhouses, or even the barn. You could take the chance and find an honest man like Wilson to share the house with, but you won't know for sure if you can trust him. And would you be able to?"

"You were a stranger, and I did," she felt compelled to point out, rather proud of herself at the realization. Every aspect of her life that Mason touched seemed to unfurl into a potential blossom. She couldn't help but glance at him sideways and secretly wonder what else he could help her discover and allow to bloom.

"Yes, but..." His fingers slid away on a sigh. "I can't stay."

The loss of his touch left an ache Jessi didn't understand. Staring down at the mass of silk, barely visible in the silvery moonlight, she frowned. "And what would I do in a foreign land? No place to live, no means of providing for myself? Not to mention, making myself a possible target for whoever seemed to wish me dead? I don't see how that's a better situation for me than taking my chances here. At least I have my bees to provide, and a house."

His cool fingers brushed under her chin, forcing her to search out his shadowed gaze. The flutter of his lips across hers took her by surprise and she gasped. He took advantage and slipped his tongue inside. In maddening slowness, he teased her mouth. He explored, tasted, and demanded, all in unhurried strokes. His beard tickled her chin and nose. Before she could stop herself, she slid her fingers along the soft bristles and right to where her hands always seemed want to go; his hair.

Soft as the silk in her lap, the strands flowed along her wrists and forearms. Her fingers fisted into the mass, wanting... something. More, yes more. Mason didn't disappoint, taking the kiss from gentle to passionate with a growl that sent heat straight to her core. The space between them disappeared. His arms wrapped low across her back, pressing her chest to his. Her breasts grew sensitive, and she realized with a little shock, she wouldn't stop him if he tried to touch them. She *wanted* to know how his hands would feel on her skin.

A little stunned by the inner revelation, Jessi pulled away. Her breath fell in heavy pants, mixing with his. He pressed another, lingering kiss to her mouth, his hands gripping her hips. Jessi squeezed her eyes shut and her thighs together, anything to stop the urge to climb on his lap and get closer, until only the fabric of their clothes separated them.

"Do you still want to know what you'll do if you come with me?" he asked on a whisper against her lips.

Jessi leaned into his words. Her mouth brushed along his, knowing she was completely seduced by his actions and not caring. "What?"

He kissed her again, long, wet, breathtaking and heart pounding. And when he broke the embrace, his words forced the rest of the air from her lungs. "You'll marry me."

10

"I'M SORRY, I'LL DO WHAT NOW?" JESSI PULLED AWAY, HER fingers sliding from his hair, and blinked. She must have misunderstood him.

His hands however, didn't leave her hips. In fact, his grip tightened enough to let her know he was uncertain of her response. "If you went home with me, I'd provide everything you need. Clothes, a home, food, all of it. But I can't do that unless you're viewed as my wife. I refuse to have anyone see you as anything less."

"Anything less?" She considered the words for a moment, and then pressed her lips together in understanding. "Ah, you mean as a paid companion. Would it really matter? I won't see any of those people again, would I?"

"You are more than that."

His words, spoken softly and with conviction, made her heart turn over in her chest. How could she possibly be more than that? And why would he care how others perceived her? They hardly knew each other... right? Yet, as she stared at him, she realized he seemed to know her better than anyone else in her life ever had.

Jessi took a deep breath and stood. Everything he

suggested was impossible. "Mason, I am the nobody daughter of an accountant and likely a businessman from Sziveria. From what Wilson said about you, your family sounds like royalty."

He chuckled and shook his head. "Definitely not royalty. Just an old line my mother is far too proud of."

"Then she certainly wouldn't appreciate you showing up at home with me." She grasped the doorknob, pausing before turning it. "Besides... I have nothing to offer you... as a wife."

"Actually," he stood with a groan and faced her before continuing, "you'll be offering me a whole lot. A chance to possibly learn more about my sister's death, and almost an entire year where my mother can't attempt to marry me off to someone I have no attraction to, let alone any desire to be stuck with for any length of time."

"A year? And you'd *want* to be stuck with... me? Really?"

In the dim, gray darkness, he was nothing more than a looming shadow that drew near, bracing his forearms on the frame and door behind her. The crisp, woodsy scent of him and sunshine enveloped her. Jessi pressed into the solid wood, unable to see his eyes, but searching all the same. Her lips still felt swollen and tender from his kisses, and oh if she were honest, she'd admit she wanted a repeat. But she was afraid. With each kiss, a little more of the invisible wall she'd erected around herself began to crumble, until she had to admit to the stirrings he evoked. Since she wasn't willing to see where those stirrings would lead, she had no business kissing him.

"I can't imagine wanting to be *stuck* with anyone else," he whispered, his warm breath teasing across her lips. Her stomach fluttered. He was *so* deliciously close.

How could his words be filled with such sensual promise? Maybe it wasn't the words so much as the delivery. Unsure, Jessi tried to focus on something else, because she'd never be able to explore the possibilities he offered. His nearness made coherent thought impossible. "But I can't... I won't..." Darn it! Cheeks burning with embarrassment, she swallowed and tried again. "We won't um, you know..."

Somehow, he could see better than her, because when his mouth met hers, there was no mistake. His lips brushed and coaxed until she opened for him without protest. Her eyes fluttered closed, and her fingers gripped the knob digging into her back to keep from giving in to the urge to press her hips forward and seek him out. His mouth moved over hers, his tongue explored and made a whole new set of promises, until her knees shook and desire throbbed between her legs.

She wanted him.

No doubts, no questions.

Except, would he hurt her? She didn't have much time to contemplate the thought when he pulled away.

"If all I ever get is to kiss you, that'll be enough." His large hands smoothed along her jaw, to the hair bound at the back of her neck in a sweet, intimate caress. "Your body is yours to command, and that includes when you have a husband."

Would any other husband feel that way? Jessi realized with painful clarity, Mason was giving her an opportunity as well. One where she could safely explore a relationship without demands or fear. Like all little girls, she'd once dreamed of love, marriage, kids and the bonds of family. All those dreams had shattered in the midst of rape and torture. Who would want her, let alone deal with the trauma she endured, at times on a nightly basis?

Jessi pushed his hands away and twisted the knob. The door fell open behind her weight and she almost stumbled. "You don't know me well enough to know what you're asking."

"I want to know you."

Jessi shook her head, hating the sting of tears. "No, you don't." She took a deep breath. "If you knew, you'd have to face all over again what happened to your sister. I won't make you go through that. I won't marry you, I can't. I'm sorry."

She fled inside before he could stop her, or say something, anything actually, that would make her change her mind. Deep within her heart, she knew the effort on his part would need to be minimal. Desperately, she *wanted* what he offered. A chance to experience a sense of normalcy. To pretend, for however long he offered, she wasn't broken beyond repair.

Behind her, Sesay whined and Mason soothed, but she couldn't tell if he followed or not. Nor did she dare to look. She raced up the stairs, holding tight to the rail as she took them two at a time. While Jessi didn't consider herself a coward in most circumstances, she fully admitted to the failing now. A second before she reached her door, his voice sounded behind her. How had she missed his footfalls on the stairs? He was so much larger, she should have *felt* them.

"Honey, wait," he called when she reached the landing.

If she were quick enough, she could be in her room and close the door before he could attempt to change her mind. However, his legs were longer than hers and by the time her fingers brushed her doorknob, he stood behind her. Steeling herself against the confrontation, she turned and met his stare. His *amused* stare. What?

A riot of colorful silk spilled from his hand, held out toward her. "You left these. Again."

Jessi stared at the scarves, not quite comprehending he'd followed her to deliver them and not to discuss his plan. "Thanks. What am I supposed to do with them?"

"Do with them?"

Her fingers curled around the soft fabric. "Yes. I use thick wool ones, but I've never owned anything like this. Are they different?"

A layer slid free from her grasp. Then he was close enough to once again surround her in his sharp, woodsy scent, and heat. Every muscle in her body froze as his arms wrapped around her, yet never touched. A soft weight slid around her waist and settled on her hips. Startled, Jessi glanced down. Masons impossibly large hands worked smoothly to tie the purple scarf in a loose knot at her left hip. Then the yellow one glided free, and he repeated the action around her neck.

Only the green and silvery one remained in Jessi's hand. Slowly, he pulled it free, his eyes on hers. He wrapped it under her hair and around her head behind her ears.

"This reminded me of the color of your eyes," he said softly. Much to her regret, he stepped away when he finished, his arms dropping to his sides. "There. Beautiful."

Jessi touched a hand to the scarf at her waist, and on her head. "That's all? You're not going to try to talk me into... your crazy plan?" She couldn't bring herself to say *into being your wife*.

"Nope. You know my offer, it's open until I leave. Even then, I'll give you my address and a radio number to reach me should you decide in my favor."

Her stomach jumped in alarm. "You're leaving?"

"Probably soon, yes. I have responsibilities at home, I can't leave them for much longer."

Jessi fiddled with the silk at her hip. When he'd arrived, she couldn't imagine life with someone else around. Now the thought of life without him seemed... empty. Wrong. "How soon?"

He shrugged. "I told you I'd help with a few more things, then I'll go."

The silk fluttered from her fingers. "That's not necessary. I've handled things on my own before you, and I'll continue after you're gone."

"So you've said. While I'm not certain of the exact day I'll leave, I do want to make you aware I will be."

She raised a brow. "I've known you wouldn't stay forever. Is making me think about you going away your means of trying to get me to change my mind?"

"No. But I do want you to seriously consider life here alone. How difficult, and possibly dangerous, it'd be for you." He shifted to put more space between them.

A small thread of disappointment tugged at her. She wanted him close again. Near enough to sense, to smell, to touch if she found the courage to do so. Instead, she pressed into the wall beside her door, touching the chipped paint surface next to her thighs to ground her wayward thoughts.

"I'll be fine."

Shadowed emotion swept through his eyes, his attention going to the stairs when a ragged cough echoed from below. "Please promise me you'll honestly think about my offer, not shove it aside as something I asked only for my benefit. I don't want anything to happen to you."

Jessi's breath caught. All she could do was nod.

"Good. Thank you." Attention still down the stairs, he asked, "Do you think he'll be okay on his own tonight?"

"I'm going to cook, and make sure Sesay has gone out. We'll be fine." She smiled to try to help prove her point. "Routine night for us."

Some thought seemed to be distracting him, negative by the frown on his face. Jessi wanted to ask what was wrong, but wasn't sure she wanted the answer. Especially if the shadow still lingering in his beautiful silver eyes had anything to do with her. She didn't want to be the cause of any distress for him. Alleviating what she figured to be the issue wasn't an option either.

On a sigh she slipped back downstairs. Sesay met her at the bottom. He sniffed lightly at the scarf tied to her hips. The soft brush of silk made her feel feminine. Smiling, she checked in on Wilson. He arched fluffy gray brows at her colorful presence, but said nothing about the additions.

Setting aside the paper he'd been holding, he eased to the edge of the chair. "How did it go today?"

Jessi sat in the chair next to him. "I'm glad Mason came

along. Those brothers up the road would have..." She swallowed and tried again. "They would have stolen all the honey."

The wrinkles on his face deepened with a grimace. "And you likely wouldn't have returned home at all. Doubt I could have stopped them, either. Yes, it was a very good thing that young man was with you." He sighed and shook his head. "I'm too old to take proper care of you anymore."

She opened her mouth to deny his role in her life, she was responsible for herself, but she snapped her jaw closed on a frown. Like a mythical hero, he'd shown up when her captor had stepped out, untying her from the bed she'd been strapped to. Wilson had scooped her up in his arms and they'd fled, stopping long enough two days later for her to heal somewhere no one would demand answers. He'd never asked her to leave, and she'd never offered. Accepting the shelter and the care he gave, like a child starved for a parent. Which she supposed at the time, she had been.

"I'm old enough to care for myself now. Lots of young women live on their own."

Wilson shook his head. "No, they don't. Even in the big cities they live together, two or three to an apartment, or with a relative, like you do now." He sighed and sagged in his seat, suddenly looking all of his years. "You need to start thinking about plans. You can't stay here alone. You must know that."

Anger, and if she were honest, a small amount of fear, rose within her. "Did Mason tell you to say that to me? Has he spoken to you?"

His forehead crinkled. "No, why would he have? Has he spoken to *you* about something important?"

Jessi took a deep breath. For a moment she considered keeping Mason's offer personal, but Wilson deserved better than secrecy. "He asked me to go to Sziveria with him, and tonight he asked again, but that I go as his... wife."

Wilson's watery eyes narrowed on her. "His wife? Why?"

"Because he said if I arrive and stay in his home people will think..." She shrugged. "I don't know, he seemed to believe they'd think less of me."

"And that bothered him?"

"Yes."

Wilson eased back in his chair. "Why does he wish for you to return with him at all?"

With a start, Jessi realized she hadn't sat down and talked to Wilson since Mason's arrival, nor had the men seemed to converse about anything private. They must have been discussing mundane safe topics, like the weather, whenever she saw them together. Jessi explained what Mason had told her. She tried to stay emotionless during the conversation. To push dark memories far into the recess of her mind, where they always lingered, threatening to surface at even a hint of permission, such as the mention of anything to do with her captivity.

"Seems logical," Wilson muttered when she'd finished, scratching at the white stubble on his chin. "But he has nothing but your name."

"I think he's hoping that'll be enough, or I'll remember something useful once I'm there." Jessi huffed. "He hasn't really explained his plan."

"It's a good offer, girly. You won't have a better one. And he's a good man."

The fear returned, sharp and breathtaking in its strength. Tears threatened to gather and she took a slow, deep inhale. "I-I would make a terrible wife."

Deep, heartfelt sadness filled Wilson's gaze. "Jes, you have no idea what kind of wife you'd be, or what he even expects of one. Have you spoken with him?"

"No, he asked me tonight and I've already told him no."

"And did he accept your answer?"

She sniffled and resisted the urge to wipe her forearm under her nose. "Yes, of course he did."

"As final?"

"Well no, not exactly that. He respected my decision."

Wilson gave a pointed stare. "And I trust he'd respect *every* decision you make, concerning marriage to him."

Her heart suddenly beat a little too forceful. She didn't pretend not to understand him. "He said as much, yes."

"Good." Wilson reached for the cane braced against the wall. "Then sleep on it, I really want you to consider his offer."

"I can't leave you." This time she didn't stop the threatening tears. "I can't. And I know you won't go with me."

"There are homes—"

"I'm not sticking you in an end-stage home!" Jessi's hands fisted in the silk draped across her thigh. "How could you ask that of me?"

Wilson let the cane fall back to the wall and instead reached for her. She took his hands without delay. Wispy dry, cold skin greeted hers, the bones within a little too fragile for her liking. His gaze searched hers, still holding on to lingering sorrow. "If Mason leaves before I pass, and he likely will, you can't handle that on your own. What will you do with me? Burn the house down around my carcass?"

Jessi gasped at the distressed image his words conjured in her mind. She snatched her hands free and stood. "I'm not talking about this."

"We have to talk about it. Just because you don't like it doesn't make the situation any less real."

She waved a hand and strode to the kitchen. "Well, I'm not discussing it now."

The soft *click, click, click* of Sesay's claws on the hardwood followed close behind. In the kitchen she busied herself making food, despite a nonexistent appetite. Jessi couldn't remember such a stressful day in a long time. Even being tangled in barbed wire had been preferable.

Now she seemed to have some very difficult choices to

make, concerning not only her future, but her guardians as well. When did that happen? When did she come to be the one who solely had to care for him? Her shoulders sagged and she fought a losing battle with anguish.

Gripping the knife handle, she took a second to let the rush of emotion pass before continuing. They'd be okay... everything would be fine. She'd make the right choices for them both.

Wouldn't she?

11

Over the next five days Jessi ignored Mason's offer and Wilson's acceptance of his impending death. She threw herself into the only thing she knew. Their account books and her bees.

Mason however, seemed determined to remind her in subtle ways her *no* wasn't the answer he wanted. At every opportunity he touched her in little ways. His hand brushing along hers. A soft tug on her hair, or caress across her hip when he passed by, usually trailing the silk sash she'd taken to wearing daily until the long strand fluttered to return to rest at her thigh.

The intimacy wasn't lost on her. Despite only touching where she'd given permission, he made those small areas of her body familiar with him, comfortable. He hadn't kissed her again though, and Jessi found herself imagining all the ways she could take him unawares with one of her own. Wouldn't that be shocking? Her thoughts alone were rather surprising to her.

No matter how much she fantasized about a future with Mason, one in which he thought he knew what he'd be getting into with her, she couldn't bring herself to sit down and have the difficult talk. Ignoring him seemed to be out of the question, though. At every turn he was *there*, helping, talking about nothing and yet, everything, keeping her thoughts from straying to the dark places they liked to wander to when she was alone.

How was she going to live without this man?

Forcing the annoying thought away, she busied herself in her ledger books. She'd left food on the table, choosing to sequester herself with work rather than possible conversation... or temptation. While he hadn't mentioned his offer again, the words were always at the front of her mind. Along with the strong desire to agree. Disgusted by her lack of resolve, Jessi groaned and dropped her head on the book laying open before her. Rows of numbers usually calmed her. Right now they all blurred together into incoherent symbols.

A soft knock sounded on her open bedroom door. Not bothering to lift her head, she turned her cheek, knowing it was Mason since Wilson couldn't navigate the stairs. She waited for irritation to flare at the disruption, but none came. Only a strange sense of relief of him being in her doorway, waiting for permission to enter her space. Hours had passed since she'd last seen him and she realized with a quick blink, she'd missed him.

Oh sweet sunlight, she was in trouble.

"May I sit?" he asked, stepping into the room.

Soft wind from the open bedroom window fluttered the loose navy cotton shirt at his torso, and unbound strands of hair around his face. His dirt crusted boots disappeared underneath the legs of dusty tan pants. Whatever he'd done in the last couple hours had left him unkempt. Not that she minded, since dust-covered seemed to be her perpetual state of existence as well.

Instantly her room shrank by at least half. Jessi straightened and glanced around at the remaining space. The only place to sit, beside the rickety old spindle chair she occupied, was her equally rickety bed. Mason, on her bed, seemed a dangerous combination. She ignored the delicious tremors of yearning, a warning if she ever had one, and nodded. While she could wish and want, she'd never act, so what was the harm?

The springs creaked and the old wooden frame groaned under his weight. He tested it before settling completely. "This bed is bigger than mine."

Jessi looked the bed over, a warm flush spreading across her cheeks. "Yes, I considered switching rooms when Wilson allowed you to stay, but I didn't figure you'd want to deal with my invading your room daily for my things."

He leaned forward, bracing his elbows on his knees. "What are you doing?"

"Our ledgers." She sighed. "But I can't seem to focus."

Mason shook his head and equaled her sigh. "Who can ever focus on ledgers to begin with? Terrible chore."

Jessi couldn't help but laugh. "I enjoy the task. Numbers… I don't know, they make sense, they help me to feel, grounded, settled. At least they usually do."

"Is there anything I can help with?"

She flipped the pen she'd be holding between her fingers and gave another short bark of laughter. "Is there anything you *haven't* helped with? I'm beginning to fear a dependency issue if you don't start letting me do things on my own again."

Indecision played across his face as he took in a deep breath, opened his mouth to speak, shook his head and tried again. "What do you need to feel settled from?"

Besides you? Jessi turned her attention back to the rows of numbers, only half finished from her sales and purchases days ago. "Wilson is trying to convince me to take him to an end-stage home."

"A tough request."

She rolled the pen along the book, frowning. "One he has accepted."

"That you cannot."

Anger tore through her over the situation. Flexing her jaw, she snapped, "No, doesn't appear I can."

"Did you know Wilson, before?"

Jessi glanced over her shoulder at him. Curiosity reflected in his pale gray eyes. A sudden urge to bury her fingers into his long mane, settle on his lap and cry made Jessi look away. She knew he'd hold her, let her access her grief without judgement. He'd be strong while her broken heart struggled to accept the looming loss of her guardian. Their relationship was already on shaky enough ground, she didn't need to add to the confusion by giving into a moment of weakness. Ignoring the impulse, she focused back on the rows of numbers.

"No. He told me someone sent him, but never said who. I was to hurt to question, and once I was well, he refused to say. He's old enough to be my grandfather, and never treated me as anything more than the child he rescued."

"And you trusted—trust—him." The words were a statement, a fact, not a question.

Jessi nodded, still rolling the pen around. "Yes. He never touched me, despite my injuries. Someone else, always a woman, handled them, someone I assumed he trusted. It took me two months to heal enough to travel here, and another three before I could be useful around the house and farm. Not once in all that time did he pressure me to get better before I felt I was. I owe him..." Her voice cracked and she took a deep, sniffling breath. "Everything."

When Mason remained silent, Jessi chanced a look. Shoulders slumped, he stared down at the floor, his hands clasped so tightly between his knees his knuckles were white. Without asking, she knew what he was thinking. Why hadn't anyone miraculously shown up and saved his twin? A man of his power, not only of person, but she knew he had the same strength of soul, seemed dwarfed by the enormity of grief.

Drawn by his pain, Jessi couldn't stop from joining him on the bed. She sat slowly and waited to see if he'd deny her presence. At first he didn't seem to notice. The faint stiffening of his frame and slow exhale let her know the moment he became aware.

Frowning, Jessi sighed. "This is what I meant. Why I can't return with you, or marry you. My past is tied directly to your tragedy. The two don't mix. Every time you think of what I've gone through, you'll remember how you lost your sister."

There were other reasons she had to refuse. Reasons she was too cowardly to come forward with, or even acknowledge beyond what they already had. Playing with the scarf edges now dangling between her legs, Jessi wished she were stronger. Strong enough to be open about her fears, and ask the hard questions. To show him physical scars and speak about the invisible ones. Maybe then he'd see how wrong he was to consider life with her, regardless of how short they'd be together.

"I remember how I lost her without your help," he whispered. "Every time I just *stop*, I remember. The words in the death report describing her broken body. The stupid yellow piece of paper that told me she was dead. The look on my mother's face when I somehow choked out telling her the daughter she'd birthed was never coming home. You have nothing to do with any of that."

He turned his head to look at her, his hair falling like a curtain over his shoulder. "In fact, you provide some much needed, and much appreciated, distraction. I can at least breathe when I'm around you."

Jessi's heart both broke and swelled at the same time. She

didn't think such a thing was possible. Tears burned behind her eyes. Enough. He had to know. Licking her lips, she stood and went to the door. Carefully, even though she didn't think Wilson could hear, she latched it closed with a faint *click*. She faced him and her nerves threatened to abandon her when he looked her over in confusion.

"Why did you close the door?"

"Habit I guess. I know Wilson can't traverse the stairs, but I still feel the need for privacy," she admitted. "Silly as that may seem."

"Why?"

She took a deep, bracing breath, ignoring the pounding of her heart and encroaching anxiety attack. She could do this. She *had* to do this. "Because you aren't going to let taking me with you, or your marriage offer, go. You'll ask again, at least once, and you'll think you know what you're doing, but you don't. I need you to see why. I'm not going to say yes, not ever. And after..."

Jessi didn't want to think about after. About the disgust, or his rejection, or the pain she knew would be inadvertently inflicted on him. The physical manifestation of his sister's torture, though healed, no less evident. The reminder of suffering both women endured. One who survived, and one who hadn't.

Acid burned in her stomach. Her nerves were so jumbled, she couldn't stop the tremble of her fingers as she reached for the buttons on the loose pale peach shirt she wore. Mason spine went straight the second he realized her intent, his eyes wide.

Still, he asked, "What are you doing?"

"You've said you don't care, but I do. You can't ask me to be to your wife and not know, not see."

Jessi licked her dry lips and somehow managed to undo another button. In an effort to gain courage she closed her eyes, turned her back to Mason, and pretended she was alone. She ignored the faint creak of the bed springs and rustle of fabric. Before she could slip another button free, strong arms banded around her, pulling her close to the warmth and steel of his chest.

"Jessalyn, stop," he whispered into her ear.

Jessi waited for the panic to arrive from a man at her back. But none came. Only a curious flush and a strong desire to curl her fingers around his muscled forearms. Instead, she took hold of the silk. "I have to."

"No, you don't. Your discomfort doesn't change how I feel, or what I want. Neither will whatever you believe I need to see concerning your body."

While Jessi knew she'd never accept his offer, a small part of her heart clung to the chance he provided. If she were ever brave enough to go to him as his wife, she didn't want his reaction to be part of the experience. No matter what he said, he'd have one. And if he were to reject her because of it, she'd rather that happen now, before any chance at a relationship could even be born.

With her eyes still squeezed shut she managed to make her voice work. "I... have to."

"Then you'll let me."

Shock left her frozen. His arms fell from around her. The silk scarf loosened from her hips and then slid around her neck, and she realized he was serious. Slowly, his fingers edged along the opening of her shirt, brushing her skin, leaving a fiery trail to the next button.

"Say yes," he breathed into her ear.

He caressed up to her collar bone, his touch fluttering from her navel, between her breasts and then back down again. A delicious pulse grew at her center. She pressed her thighs together to try to quell it, but that only seemed to make things worse. At his next pass, he spread his fingers enough to graze the swell of her breasts and her breath caught at the sensation.

"O-okay," she somehow managed to say.

The warmth of his presence shifted and a soft tug on her shirt made her jump.

"Step back," he ordered.

She obeyed, taking slow backward steps, his arms still around her, her back to his chest. Unable to stop herself, she watched with a thrill dancing in her stomach as he undid each button until her shirt hung open, baring the flesh of her stomach. His fingers explored the tender skin between her hips at the edge of her pants. Jessi's breathing increased, matching the crazy rhythm of her heart. Mason's excited breathing in her ear made her want to lean back, bury her hands in his hair and kiss him. But she didn't. She stood on dangerous enough ground as it was.

The sleeves of her shirt slipped down her arms and fell free of her hands, leaving her bare. Silk fluttered across her breasts. Jessi realized he'd done so on purpose, giving her a means to cover herself, and she did, arranging the soft fabric over chest. The silken length caressed her nipples and made her gasp. An action that deepened when his fingers fanned around her hips to her back.

The reaction she'd expected never arrived. There was no deep inhale of aversion. He didn't throw her shirt back up onto her shoulders, or twist her around so he didn't have to see the damage anymore. Instead, the springs of her mattress squeaked and his arms banded around her waist. His whiskers touched her back a moment before his entire cheek rested against her scarred flesh. He held her so close his chest pressed into her buttocks and upper thighs, her hips fit into his shoulders.

He was hugging her.

Tears slipped down Jessi's cheeks before she could stop

them. She rested her hands on his arms and took slow, grounding breaths. "You aren't... disgusted?"

"If I am, it's only by what has been done to you." A shaky breath blew across her skin and Jessi shivered. He whispered something so softly she couldn't make the words out.

"What?"

Mason's arms squeezed tighter around her until she almost lost her balance. "Why did he do it?"

"Mason..."

"Tell me."

His beard nuzzled across her back again in a sweet, caring caress. His lips pressed kisses with each sweep. Odd sensation followed the trail. From shivering numbness to overwhelming intensity, the damaged nerves struggled to make sense of the intimate journey he mapped across her skin. Everything he did was so completely unexpected, Jessi almost sobbed with the strength of the emotions swirling within her. Confusion, hope, joy, acceptance, longing. Mason created them all.

"Please tell me," he asked again.

The reminder helped her focus on something besides the onslaught of unfamiliar emotions. Her fingers tightened around his arms, drawing strength from his touch, his presence. "Blood excited him, so he'd... he'd cut me, b-before—"

"Shh, I'm sorry," he breathed into her back. "You don't have to say more."

Her head fell back on a sigh and she couldn't stop from allowing some of her weight to sink into him. More hot tears ran wet paths down her cheeks. "I thought I'd bleed to death. I was so sure I would. But I lived, night after night, tied to the bed by my wrists on my stomach. Naked, covered in blood, and sweat, and..."

Bile rose in her throat, she couldn't bring herself to say *and him*. After the first slice of a blade across her skin, he'd become aroused. A few painful inflictions later and he was forcing himself inside her or pleasuring himself however he saw fit. After the fourth day, she'd run out tears and screams. She'd become nothing more than a lump lying face down on a filthy, thin mattress. No longer even caring about the myriad of suffering playing through her mind from the torment and torture forever trapped in the bedding. Over time the memories of his other victims had thankfully faded, but not her own.

She took a ragged breath. "Anyway, infection arrived before blood loss could kill me. Then Wilson's rescue, and I didn't die after all."

"And he only hurt your back?"

"Yes, he always kept me on my stomach." She softened her hold on him and turned her head, wishing she could see him. "You said your sister was different?"

In a sudden lurch, she fell onto the bed with no time to react. One moment she was standing, the next the mattress bounced beneath their weight and his body wrapped around hers. Every muscle in her tensed. His arms shifted until he cupped her left breast and right hip in his large hands, while his thighs curled into hers. He hugged her so tightly to his chest the hard thump of his heart pounded against her ribs. Yet, when his head came to rest in crook of her neck and he breathed in, slow controlled gasps, shoulders trembling against hers, she realized nothing about the hold was sexual. The hot slide of tears rolled from her neck to her shoulder blade, and her heart broke with the surprise of Mason crying.

Jessi wrapped her arms around the one gripping her chest and held tight. She wondered if he'd cried before now. *Really* cried. If he'd allowed himself the perceived weakness of giving in to grief. Despite being half-naked, she provided what she could, remaining silent, allowing him to use her as the anchor he seemed to need.

Time slid away until only the blue haze of twilight filled her room. The embrace he held her in never lessened. She thought maybe he'd fallen asleep, but when she attempted to move, his arms tightened, as did his hands. Awareness slid through her and her body responded in an unexpected and wholly female way. To keep from arching her back into him and turning so his hand would slide from her hip to between her legs she stayed perfectly still.

What was wrong with her? For the second time she found herself mired in the foreign need of desire. How had this man churned up such emotions in her? Never in her life did she think she'd ever allow a man to hold her as he did, let alone wish for so much more.

"I'll be twenty-nine tomorrow," he whispered, startling her from her musings. "And she'll forever remain twenty-eight."

Shoving aside caution, Jessi twisted in his arms. He didn't stop her, allowing her to face him, but he didn't give any more space. Her bare chest pressed tightly to his clothed one, her knee slid between his so their legs tangled. Fresh tears glistened in his pale eyes. In the dying light she could make out his face. She traced the frown lines, from his brow to his lips. His sadness hurt her heart so much she didn't ignore the urge to kiss the pain away. She brushed a soft kiss across his unresponsive lips.

Mason pressed his forehead to hers, eyes closed. His hands fisted in her hair and a tremor ran the length of his large frame. "What if... what if I can't get through tomorrow?"

Jessi caressed his damp bearded cheek and jaw until she reached his hair. Slowly, she stroked her fingers through the silken mass in gentle sweeps. "You will, because what is the alternative? Even if you have to lay in bed all day and grieve for her, you'll wake up the next day and you'll be twenty-nine. A new day. And next year on the same day, you'll figure out the best way to deal again."

"I don't want to deal. I just..." He took a ragged, tear-filled breath. "I just want her back."

"I know," she whispered, and held him close when another wave of grief swept him under.

A SOFT SIGH AND EVEN SOFTER BODY AWOKE MASON FROM FITFUL sleep. The sigh turned into a jolted whimper and a thrash and Mason tightened his arms. She quieted. He blinked in the darkness, trying to remember. His eyes were gritty, like sand filled them. An ache scratched in his throat.

Jessalyn, her scarred back exposed to him in a fragile moment of trust. Grief the likes of which had never assailed him before, both for his lost twin and for her lost innocence. All of it rushed forward in a wave of memory that left his jaw clenched. And through the mess of his tears, she'd held him, without judgement or pity. An anchor in his turbulent storm.

Warm, bare skin under his fingers made him shift and glance down. In the dull, colorless light filtering in from the window he managed to make out the elegant curves of Jessi's naked torso. She stirred again, a faint slide of her body along his. A mild breeze toyed with silk draped over her, fluttering between her breasts and sliding the edges across her belly.

When he'd bought the scrap of silk, he had no idea he'd get to see it in such a remarkable setting. Mason couldn't stop his fingers from following, tracing along the edge of the scarf to the gentle arch of her hip, up her ribs, to the full curve of her breast. A husky, sleepy moan escaped her parted lips. In a lazy stretch, she shifted until she lay with her hips pressed to his, her shoulders on the mattress. Muted shadows played over the gentle lines of her body, teasing and tempting. On a growl, he surrendered, lowering his mouth to her breast, licking the swell to her nipple.

She responded exactly how he'd imagined she would. With a breathless gasp, her torso rose, her fingers slid into his hair. Mason grasped her hip, kneading the supple flesh while he pushed his growing erection against her pliant body. She didn't shy away, or panic as his other arm wrapped around to her back, holding her close to better suck and lick at her beautiful bounty.

A delicious shudder raced down her form. Her leg hooked over his thigh, changing the way they fit together. Mason knew if he moved his hand between them, slid past the barrier of fabric, he'd find her wet, ready. The thought sent him into full arousal. It'd be so easy to take her now, in the sleepy haze of desire, before she realized what they were doing. To push her pants down her hips, caress her into a full frenzy until she flew apart in his arms, and then…

Mason released her nipple and drew a ragged breath, resting his cheek between the pillow softness of her breasts. She smoothed his hair away from his face and over his shoulder. Her hips moved along his, sending a shaft of pleasure straight to his toes that he knew she shared when another gasp sounded in the stillness.

"Why did you stop?" she whispered.

Mason squeezed his eyes closed and somehow managed to pull forward control from the deepest recesses of his person. "You aren't mine to have."

Her touch continued to sweep through the long length of his hair. Gentle, trusting, all the things she shouldn't be toward him in that moment. "What if I want to be?"

Mason moved until she was forced to lay completely on her back, his stomach over hers. He braced his elbows on either side of her chest and rested his chin on his palms. Despite the pale light, he could make out her beautiful face and eyes. A soft flush darkened her cheeks. Everything in him needed to claim her.

"You want to be my wife?"

She licked her lips, leaving behind a glossy sheen. "Would I need to be… for you to…" She touched her tongue to her bottom lip again and he almost groaned. "For you to keep going?"

"Yes."

"Oh."

Mason braced his forearms on the mattress beside her, lowering his head until his hair swept along either side of her chest, and licked the valley between her breasts. "See the problem is," he whispered into the side of her breast and brushed his bearded chin along the sensitive flesh, feeling more than hearing the shudder of her breath, "I won't be able to walk away from you. I have to know you'll be mine, for however long I can have you, but mine all the same."

"What if all I can give is one night? Tonight?"

He blazed a wet trail from her breast to her collarbone and up under her chin to her mouth. Her breath fell in heavy pants before he captured her mouth in a searing, possessive kiss. She moaned and lifted her hips to press against his thigh between her legs. Mason held her close, crushing her chest to his, wishing with everything he could cast aside his standards and accept the one night she offered.

But she meant more to him than that, and he knew the moment he lost himself in her body, he'd never walk away. He'd give up everything he and his family had worked centuries for and stay in Westica, if that's what it took to keep her.

Dragging his mouth away, he shook his head. "It's all or nothing. If you can't give me more, I won't take less."

Her fingers fisted in his hair as she took a long, shaky breath. "I've never wanted anyone before."

"I know."

"It feels..." She took another bracing inhale. "It feels really good."

Mason couldn't help but smile, nor could he stop the sliver of pride at her words. Pride in her for acknowledging her body's response, and himself for developing the desire within her. "Honey, it is good, very good. And I promise, it only gets better."

Her back arched, forcing every inch of her closer to him in a move he wouldn't have thought her capable of. "Show me."

Mason's hand slid down her back and he caught himself a second before he'd have pushed her pants down. Instead, he caressed the smooth skin at her hip, sliding his fingers just under the band and then back up again. "Marry me."

She lifted into his touch. "I think I'd agree to about anything right now, but I'm scared."

"Of what?" he asked, looking down the length of her body, at the way she trembled with desire, all for him. "The fears you've had you are proving you can overcome."

"And when your society sees who you've brought home?"

"I don't care what they think."

"I do." She sniffled and shook her head.

Mason sighed and rolled onto his back. "Then we'll stop until you are ready, and I somehow manage to show you the only people who will ever matter in our relationship are the two of us."

Amazingly, she rolled with him, draping her arm over his chest, laying her head in the hallow of his shoulder. "The two of us, I like the idea of that."

For a moment Mason hesitated, worried in his current raging need touching her again would ignite a fire he'd burn from the inside out over if he didn't find release. Then she sighed, her warm breath fluttering the fabric of his shirt over his heart. He wasn't an animal and he wouldn't act like one no matter how deep his desire ran.

And for her, it ran all the way to his bones.

Still, she trusted him, trusted his restraint, and his words. When she was his, and only his, he'd allow himself to indulge in whatever she'd permit. Until then, he'd take what he could, and that meant nothing more than holding her.

Wrapping his arms around her, he hugged her close and

pressed a kiss to the top of her head. "Perhaps you'll like the idea enough to finally say yes."

She murmured something and relaxed into his side, all loose limbs and soft curves. A new, intense pang of need slammed through him, causing his muscles to tense and his pants to be far too restricting. Squeezing his eyes shut, Mason tried to slow the rapid pulse pounding through him, but the effort was useless. While the woman he wanted more than anything in the inhabited world fell back asleep in his arms, he'd be edgy, unfulfilled and chaotic in thought. At least he mused, it was better than the alternative, which was dark, bottomless depression.

In the short time he'd known her, the fractured, but not shattered, woman known as Jessalyn Silverna, had given him a gift of peace. Mason realized with a little start, he was falling in love with her. Though if the emotion were true, or his fervent need to feel *anything* other than anguish, he didn't know, and really didn't care to examine. She was funny, and passionate when she gave herself permission, and cared more deeply than any woman he'd ever met. He wanted her heart as much as he wanted her body, and he wouldn't take one without the other.

On a sigh of resignation, Mason slipped out from under her. She grasped a pillow and wrapped around it with a sexy little moan. Slowly he tugged the scarf free, enfolding the fluttering length around his neck. He inhaled her sweet honeyed scent lingering on the silk. He stared down at her sleeping length, at the delicate swell of her breast pressed into the pillow, the soft definition of her bicep, her slender fingers curled around the edge. The mild summer breeze from the open window tugged at the loose curls around her neck. The silver light of the moon accented the tantalizing slope of her waist into her hip. Mason's fingers twitched to draw her in this perfect moment. A woman, fully her own.

The urge shocked him. He hadn't wanted to draw since

Cora's death. Now he did. Deciding the fleeting moment may be all he had, he quietly went and retrieved his pencil case and pad from his backpack. When he returned, she still lay motionless, the soft rise and fall of her chest even in sleep. Sitting on the edge of the bed with the moonlight over his pad, he lost himself in his art. The sharp scratch and sweep of his pencil mingled with the rustle of fabric.

Gray light brightened the room when Mason added the last detailed shadows to her pants and skin. He'd drawn her from the front, facing him, though he did add the hint of scars still visible at her waist and upper shoulders. Part of her history, and the future she forged despite the cruelty bestowed on her. When he'd told her scars were moments survived, he'd meant the words. Nothing about her could make him burn less hot. Even now he resisted the urge to trace some of the larger marks with his fingers, and keep going, right around to the beauty that continued to form her body.

When he smudged the last shadow with his pinky, the sweep of her curves indented into the mattress, he simply stared at her. His woman, if she'd but take the chance. A pang shot through his clenched heart and he took a deep breath. Ignoring the crossroads he currently found himself at would be unwise. Either he stayed, and worked hard to convince her of the life they *could* have and hoped he had a ranked Guardianship and a home to return to, or he went home to the family he left behind, and the responsibilities he'd sworn to uphold.

While he knew she'd be worth every moment spent pursuing, he couldn't hold out forever. Eventually he'd give in to the pull of their sensual attraction, and she'd convince herself it was enough. Heart still in his throat, Mason wrote words meant only for her along the bottom. He left her room on quiet steps, and then gathered together the few possessions he'd dispersed around the room he'd been renting.

Downstairs, Sesay met him with a soft whine, as if sensing his imminent departure. Kneeling, he patted the dog's large head, his fingers sinking into soft, thick fur. "You take good care of them, okay? Especially Jessalyn. *Custrazva*, all right? Keep her safe for me."

The wolf licked at Mason's face. Mason smiled and scratched between his ears. When he stood, the dog protested on a soft yip and pushed the side of his body into Mason's legs to keep him in place.

"Sorry, buddy, I have to go. But, don't worry, I'm sure I'll see you again. Hopefully soon."

Mason edged around the irritated wolf into the kitchen. He set the folded drawing, a signed marriage contract, a letter, and an intricate silver bracelet he'd picked up from Cora's room, in the center of the table. The bracelet was the only possession of Cora's he's taken into his personal care. Everything else he'd sent home. At the time he had no idea why having the bracelet was so important. Now he did. If Jessalyn accepted his offer, she'd wear it as his promise to her.

A long, slow exhale left his lungs. She only had a few weeks to decide, or have to delay until spring of the next year when the ocean thawed. While he'd wait for her, Mason didn't want to think about her spending winter alone. He didn't want to leave without her period. But the choice had to be hers, made without fear or coercion. When she came to him, he wanted her to trust in the future they'd build together.

Hefting his pack over his shoulder, he slipped out the side door. Over the last couple mornings, he'd worked on a bicycle he'd found hidden under a tarp. Wilson had waved away his asking if he could buy it, saying he'd done more than his fair share to earn the old bike. Thankfully the small amount of mechanical skill he'd acquired over the years served him. Only the chain and one of the pedals needed adjusting. He'd get wet if it rained, but he could deal with that.

Mason slid onto the seat and threw his pack onto his shoulders. He popped up the break stand and balanced on the bike. After one last look at the house that had served to heal more wounds than he'd known he'd arrived with, Mason rode away, into the bright rise of dawn on his twenty-ninth year of life.

12

A HAPPY TRILLING SONG ROUSED JESSI FROM SLEEP. WITH A curling smile she stretched, her hand reaching for the warm strength of Mason. Memories of his mouth, hot and wet on her breasts and skin, sent tendrils of desire pulsing through her entire body. In the darkness she'd found a hidden woman waiting to be released. And with him, unleashing her had been easy.

Her hand met with cold empty space and on a gasp, she shot up. She grasped at her throat when nothing, not even her scarf, fluttered around her naked chest. Wrapping her arms around herself, Jessi slid from the bed and picked up her discarded shirt from the day before. With trembling fingers, she did the buttons, crossing the short distance to Mason's room.

An empty room greeted her.

No.

Mason wasn't gone. He couldn't be. She rushed inside, searching every corner, every drawer. Nothing except a pouch of tinnies on top of the small chest under the window. Everything had vanished, including the man who'd occupied the space. Hoping she was overreacting, Jessi ran down the stairs.

She knew she wouldn't find him in the house, he was never inside so early in the morning.

A glint of sun reflected on the kitchen table. She stopped and took a step back. A bracelet rested on top of a stack of papers. Tears burned Jessi's eyes as she tumbled onto a chair, reaching for the band. Three hammered silver strands formed a cuff bracelet. In the center an infinity knot looped around the strands, seeming to hold them together. The jewelry was beautiful in its simplicity, elegant in design. Jessi wrapped her hand around it and reached for the top folded piece of paper.

She gasped as a strong surge of desire and affection flickered across her senses before the impression of Mason, hunched over an artist pad on the edge of her bed, his hand working feverishly to convey what he saw, swam across her vision. Taking a deep breath, she slowly unfolded the page and revealed a stunning, half naked, sleeping woman. Under the woman, written in quick, masculine cursive was: *Jessalyn Silverna. How I see you, how I'll always see you. Sexy and beautiful.*

Jessi's gaze moved back to the woman. This was *her*? If she hadn't experienced the memory locked in the paper itself, she'd have rejected the words. Yet, the truth was in the emotion, in the flash of images she couldn't deny. She blinked in disbelief. Lush curves formed her visible thigh, hip and breast. A soft bend created her waist. Full pouty lips complimented a perfectly sculpted face, with rounded cheeks and a cute nose. Not even her hair looked crazy out of control, but sensual, falling in curls around her naked shoulder.

Another tear raced down Jessi's cheek. She hadn't even known he could draw, let alone create something so detailed and beautiful. Carefully, she refolded the page on the seam he'd already put in place to preserve the art. She pulled the next piece of paper to her and gasped when she read the heading. An actual marriage contract. Post-dated to a month ago, and signed by Mason. He'd left a small note in the same scratchy script at the bottom on a torn piece of paper.

Jessalyn, I post-dated the contract to make it easier for you, eleven true months instead of twelve. The bracelet I've left as my promise to you, to always respect your body, your mind, and your heart. To always see you as beautiful as you truly are. If you decide in my favor, a jeweler in Old Charleston will have your ring. I already miss you. Love, Mason

Under his signature he'd left the name and address of the jeweler along with four transmission numbers to reach him by. Jessi read the basic contract over, heart pounding. Here it was, a future she never in her life thought she'd be holding. And the man offering it had left without a word. Though she couldn't really blame him. She'd said no hours ago, and still he held out hope she'd change her mind.

The creak of wood and clop of a cane hitting the floor made Jessi dash the fallen tears from her cheeks with the back of her hands. She needed to focus on something besides the empty loneliness Mason's departure left behind.

Wilson ambled through the archway, his silver hair sticking up in various directions. Sesay stayed close to his side, tongue lolling from his open mouth. Wilson sniffled and then sighed. With a frown he took in the small collection on the table, and then Jessi. "So he left."

Jessi didn't figure a small pile of papers gave away Mason leaving, rather her puffy eyes and a sadness she knew she wouldn't shake for a good long while. "Appears he did."

Wilson sat heavily in a chair across from her. The legs skidded along the floor and the seat creaked. He heaved another sigh once he settled. With a groaning yawn, the dog sat next to the chair, eyes bright. "Well, what are you going to do about it?"

Jessi slid the paper back and forth in front of her. "There's nothing *to* do. I can't leave you, and accepting would mean going to an entirely new country, where I don't know anyone, or their customs."

"You would meet people, and you would learn." He turned his face away and coughed, his thin frame shaking with each strenuous exhale. When the episode passed, he took deep, gasping breaths.

In an effort to find normalcy, Jessi stood to make herself busy preparing food. She pulled out pans, bowls and ingredients for pancakes. "I'm sure I would."

"I want to go look at the home tomorrow."

Jessi froze in cracking an egg. "No."

"Jes…"

"No!" She turned, clenching her teeth. "I just lost Mason, I'm not going to even think about losing you too."

"You haven't lost him. And if you have, then it's your choice. I won't be able to travel for much longer, and you don't have the strength to get me into the back of the cart on your own. We must do this while I can." He paused to catch his breath before continuing. "You can't ignore reality any longer. Each day I struggle to get out of bed. Breathing takes effort. Please. Let me go somewhere I know I'll be handled with dignity when I die. Where I know *you* won't have to deal with it."

Jessi turned her back to him again and dumped ingredients with enough force to send puffs of flour into the air. "You aren't something I deal with, Wilson. You're important to me."

"And I'm thankful for that. Now prove how important and honor my request."

A fresh tear coursed down her cheek and she swept it away, growling in annoyance. "I'll think about it."

"No." A heavy thump made her flinch and glance over her shoulder. He gripped his cane in both hands, knuckles white. "If you won't take me, then I'll figure out a way to hitch that old mare myself. I won't get stuck in bed having you care for me in ways you have no business caring for me, and then dying on you. I've told you this before."

Pain blossomed in her chest. Jessi braced her palms on the counter and took a deep, grounding breath. "Fine, j-just give me today to get used to it."

"I wasn't asking to leave today. I have to pack a few things."

Jessi nodded. "I guess I do too."

"You'll stay with me? In the city?"

Jessi turned and braced her back against the counter, meeting his solemn stare. "Of course I will, I'm your granddaughter, aren't I? They won't know any better, and besides you know I'd never leave you."

"My granddaughter, huh?" He waved a gnarled, wrinkled hand and scoffed. "Nah, that makes me feel old. My grandniece. I like that better."

A choked sob, half laughter, half heartache at the absurdity of his words erupted from her. "Fine, grandniece I am then."

PACKING THEIR BELONGINGS TOOK MORE THAN THE DAY WILSON had allotted. Jessi didn't complain. Daily he changed his mind about what he wanted in the single crate he'd designated for himself. Making her switch things out with what he wanted stored, for if she ever returned to the house to sell or keep, whatever she decided.

Jessi didn't have many belongings, and she found the only items of true importance were the two remaining scarves from Mason, his drawing, and the bracelet she'd been compelled to slip onto her wrist. She tried to convince herself it wasn't an agreement, since she hadn't signed anything. But the promise he'd attached to the object settled in her heart.

The only promise missing had been of love.

At the near idea of Mason loving her, Jessi's heart had

about pounded free of her ribs. She knew the notion was fool-ish. At no time had he made claim to the emotion. Except his whispered *I won't be able to walk away from you.* Making her wonder, if she'd succeeded in breaking the iron resolve he seemed to possess, would he have stayed?

On a long breath, Jessi dropped a well-worn book into Wilson's box and shook her head. No, because he was perhaps the only man in the inhabited world who wouldn't let her use herself for base pleasure, either hers *or* his. Deep in her heart though, Jessi knew the pleasure would have been anything but surface. Somewhere along the way, Mason had done the impossible. He'd made Jessi long to be part of a rela-tionship.

"Well," Wilson muttered, glancing around the small space he'd get to call his own, "it'll do I suppose."

Jessi set the box down on the slender bed pushed against a drab, brown wall and followed his examination. A narrow four drawer dresser, a little table under a slit that somehow was considered a window, and rod with a few wire hangers made up the space. "The gardens are very nice, and they have a huge greenhouse. The woman who gave the tour said it was almost a full acre."

Wilson growled, rivaling any of Sesay's, and waved his hand. "Like I'll be attempting to walk a garden path. I'll land on my face."

Sniffling a little, Jessi pulled a few books out of the box. "That's where I'll be every day, and Sesay too. They said as long as he stays with me, he can visit and even lay around while I work in the greenhouse."

They'd made a deal with the house to cut the cost of the room by half if Jessi helped maintain the conservatory grounds. She was beyond thankful. Losing not only the farm, but her bees, had been a difficult blow. No way could she sit in the small room she'd rented from a widow down the street day after day, visiting Wilson for a few hours while waiting for him to pass. She'd go insane.

Another provision concerning Sesay had also been made. Since she'd be working on the property, the dog could stay with Wilson, or with her, for the duration of her shift. She'd had to prove he wasn't aggressive, was indoor trained, and could obey orders.

Jessi set the books on the dresser, only a step away. The room was so small, Sesay sat in the doorway. "What are you going to do? Sit in here all the time?"

"They have a gathering room, with games and food."

Yes, the communal end-stage home had a room for games, for dining, for sewing, for reading, for... just about anything the residents would desire. A beautiful summer walking trail outside, and a greenhouse for the rest of the year, complete with benches, birdbaths and pottery art. Despite all the amenities, and the excellent care, the entire establishment seemed depressing. Sadness weighed heavy regardless of where Jessi roamed. And she'd committed herself to the location daily. She glanced over her shoulder. For Wilson.

"I'm going to help you outside at least every other day. You need sun, and fresh air."

"And you need to radio that man of yours." He eased himself onto the thin mattress, his cane gripped tight in his old hands. "They have one here you know. The cost of making calls is part of our payment."

"I didn't know." She unpacked the clothing into the dresser. "But I doubt his ship has arrived yet."

"But you could leave the number for here, and he'd know how to reach you, too."

Jessi took a deep breath. "I'll think about it."

He scoffed, his cane scraping the floor with a rough squeal. "Thinking, thinking, always *thinking*. You're going to think yourself right out of an opportunity if you keep it up."

Her fingers touched the bracelet on her wrist, tracing over the individual bands to the knot at the center. "I was thinking of going to the jeweler tomorrow, you know, to see what he left for me."

Wilson's eyes twinkled with the first signs of a smile she'd seen in a long time. "I think that's an excellent idea."

THE JEWELER, A SHORT, ROUND, HYPER MAN WHO COULDN'T SEEM to stay still for longer than two seconds, was overjoyed when Jessi found her nerve to enter the shop a week later. For five days, she'd walked as far as the sidewalk in front of the door, only to lose her courage and quickly turn around. He pulled out a small beautiful, high-polished chestnut box and placed it reverently on the glass counter before her.

"Wonderful choice. Your husband knows what a marriage means. Few men take the leap with their feelings. Truly refreshing when one does," the man rattled off so fast Jessi blinked, trying to process the words.

Then he was gone, off to see what other customers needed while she stood alone with the box. Heart pounding, Jessi pulled the case forward. Nerves made her fingers tremble as she lifted the hinged lid. Inside a simple, yet stunning, ring rested. Three thin, pounded silver bands formed an infinity knot, similar to her bracelet. Unlike her bracelet, which appeared held together by the knot, the ring flowed. No beginning, no end. The design and execution were nothing short of remarkable.

Of their own accord, Jessi's fingers slipped the ring on. A flurry of Mason's emotions skittered through her mind. Happiness, nerves, a touch of fear. Over what, she wished she knew. The brief glimpse of his emotions, of being able to *feel* him again, made her heart squeeze. Light glinted off the three slender strands of metal, each a varying shade of rich silver, as if they were made from three different white metals.

Perhaps they were, Jessi knew nothing of metallurgy. The infinity knot itself was a rich silver, flashing the color of Mason's eyes as she inspected the ring on her hand.

"Ah, very good, very good, perfect fit!" the jeweler chortled with a wide smile, displaying white, but crooked teeth.

Before she could sputter a protest, he affixed two slender sliver chains from the ring to the promise band, symbolizing the connection of promises made to the commitment of marriage, a Westican tradition. "Your husband said he wanted tradition met."

Somehow, Jessi found her voice. "Does my husband have his ring?"

The jeweler gave another toothy grin. "He said you'd handle that for him."

"I see." Out of her element, Jessi searched the glass counters. "And where would the men's rings be?"

"This way, this way." He motioned for her to follow with a sweep of his arm and far too hurried steps.

Jessi brushed along other perusing customers, excusing herself when she bumped a plump lady's backside when she bent over as Jessi tried to slip behind her. The merchant patted a long glass case and then he was off again, raising his hand and chin in acknowledgement to another customer.

Sighing, Jessi blew a lock of hair from her eyes and leaned forward. Rows of masculine rings glittered in the natural and created light streaming around the store. Some gold, some silver, some a paler, almost white metal, and others a coppery bronze shade made choices difficult. Jessi glanced at her bridal ensemble and decided something silver to match hers. The choice narrowed down her options considerably.

Searching through the various designs, she spotted one made with several strands of silver, and wound around a thread or two throughout was a thinner piece, giving the ring an almost… she smiled… wired appearance. Yes. All the band was missing were the little barbs. Close enough in design to hers, people would assume the bands were a set. Jessi would know they symbolized how she and Mason had met. She wondered if he'd see the resemblance.

When the jeweler returned, he made happy noises at her selection and disappeared into the back of the store for the size she'd need, which he said he had on file. Jessi pressed a hand to her fluttering stomach. How many women chose to marry their men apart from them? That she was able to even consider the union was nothing short of amazing, and a testament to the man she'd come to know in Mason. She missed him so much.

She accepted the ring, and all the paperwork that went with it. Out on the sidewalk she stood for a moment, frozen. The documentation fluttered in her hand, the little paper bag with the boxes swayed from a strong breeze. Last night she'd signed the contract, a formality that wouldn't be official until it was delivered to the Sziverian Records Department. Still, signature to paper, a ring on her finger and one for the man to be her husband… Jessi was married.

And she hadn't told her husband the news yet.

After swinging by the house she'd rented a room from to drop off the items from the jewelry store and to check on Sesay, she walked the short distance to the end-stage home. The sun hung low in the sky. Long shadows and amber bands of light stretched along the street. Leaves skittered and floated from trees and across the bricked walk and streetways. The days were rapidly shortening. If she didn't book passage to Sziveria soon, the travel season would be closed until the first spring thaw.

Wilson was asleep on his narrow bed, so Jessi let him be. He slept most days and had stopped eating except for a bowl of broth a day. The staff assured Jessi it was normal and to let him consume what he felt comfortable consuming at this point. Jessi wanted to argue, to take a stand against the impending loss, but she was helpless to do more than provide comfort, which everyone promised her was enough.

The radio room was a small space with a table large enough to seat three people. Outside the door were waiting chairs in case someone was making a call. Since the door was open, Jessi peeked inside and found the radio available. With a sigh of relief, she closed herself off for privacy. If she'd had to wait, she was positive her nerves would fail. The large radio was bolted into the wall with instructions for use. After steeling against the jumble of memories attached to the unit, some bright and some agonizingly sad, Jessi followed the directions, using the first set of numbers and channel Mason had left.

A faint crackle and hum whispered across the line while she waited. She'd never made a call before, so wasn't sure the length of time to wait until she gave up. Nervous energy had her biting her lip and tapping an uneven thrum on the table. What seemed like forever, but in likelihood had only been seconds, a masculine voice finally spoke.

"Residence of Primary Guardian Wintersfall, who is on the other end? Over."

Jessi's spine straightened and she cleared her throat before holding down the transmit bar to answer. "My name is Jessi. I was given this number to reach Mason Dandridge." When silence answered she flushed in embarrassment and added, "Over."

"One moment, please. Over."

Another burst of anxiety fluttered in her stomach. She pressed the back of her hand to her hot cheek. The constant hum on the line kept her hyper aware of the wait. Had he changed his mind about her? She glanced at the ring connected to the promise band and drew a deep breath. No, he hadn't. He wouldn't.

"Hey honey, I was wondering when I'd hear from you."

Jessi's heart soared. Tears gathered in her eyes. She tilted her head back and sniffled to compose herself. Wow. She hadn't realized just how much she'd missed him until the sound of his voice filled the space.

"Hi," she somehow managed to get out. "I um, I picked up my ring. Yours too. I thought you'd like to know."

There was another long silence. Jessi fidgeted in the seat. Her fingers brushed along the smooth expanse of the transmit bar.

"That's great. How are things?"

"They're…" Jessi considered how to best answer. With the depressing truth, or a watered-down version of acceptable. "Okay. Wilson is happy in the home we found. I'm not sure if, um, if I'll be able to make the crossing before the freeze happens."

"I understand. I'm really glad you decided in my favor."

Jessi smiled. "Yeah, me too."

"I'm also glad you radioed to tell me. We're about to leave on assignment, so if you're able to make it before travel closes, you'll be staying with Kevin's wife, Raina. Are you okay with that?"

"I suppose I'll have to be. Or I'll just wait."

"She can help you learn our culture. Plus, she's pregnant. Kevin will feel better knowing she isn't alone while he's gone. You'd actually be doing us a huge favor, if you're able to make it."

"I'll think about it."

"Great, thanks. If we're ever able to radio, I'll be able to talk with you too, if you're at their house."

Jessi agreed that was definitely in the positive category. "She'll be okay with Sesay?"

"I know that dog goes everywhere you do, of course she'll be fine with him." There was a brief crackle before he came back on. "I have to go, Sean needs the radio. I really miss you."

Jessi's heart contracted. She touched the radio. She didn't

know who this Sean person was, but at the moment she didn't much care for him. "I miss you a lot, too."

Then with a silent *snick*, he was gone. Fresh tears stung behind Jessi's eyes and she breathed them away. She wished he'd stayed. While Sesay provided a sense of security at night and provided something to hold onto when the nightmares became unbearable, the loss of Wilson would be more difficult than warm doggy fur could comfort, she was sure. She needed Mason's strong arms around her.

Knowing if she spent much more time alone she'd sink into a dark void she'd struggle to emerge from, Jessi forced herself to rise. Her difficulties were far from over. Allowing them to rule her wasn't an option. She brushed her fingers along the promise band and her marriage ring. Either weeks or months, she'd be seeing Mason again. For now, the knowledge would have to be enough to get her through.

Besides a few shopping expeditions and a theatre show or two, the woman never left the Raiventon compound.

Tamina couldn't blame her.

A nobody in Haven City, even a nobody married to a Primary Guardian, wouldn't be all that welcome. At best she'd be treated like Primary Guardian Wintersfall's wife, a social oddity everyone wanted to view as though looking through a cage at the zoo. Tamina snickered and accepted the help from her Ariot, painted in a pretty deep red. The outrageously expensive vehicle was a smoother, faster ride than a horse drawn carriage. Plus, she liked being in control of the harnessed magnetic power. Anyone who saw her in it knew she came from money. Exactly how she liked things. Holding onto the vision of the new Mrs. Dandridge as little more than a curiosity, she tapped the file against the full skirt of her dress.

The dowager Guardianess waited at the top of the wide stone stairs leading to the front of the house. Potted roses bloomed in vibrant shades of red and pink lined each stair, bringing additional color to the dark brick of the two-story mansion. The bold colors added to the elegant air of the noble woman garbed in vivid blue silk. A sash of satin cream and silver draped from her shoulder and wrapped around her slim waist to cascade from the opposite hip. The setting sun cast golden glimmers into the silver hair styled in a graceful knot atop her head. Sapphires sparkled in the warm light from her ears, neck, fingers, and wrists.

The Dowager Guardianess Kynhaven liked to remind everyone her money was old and to be respected. A careful resting expression left Tamina to wonder what mood the aging woman could be found in this evening.

Out of respect due, Tamina dropped into a swift curtsy. "Dowager Kynhaven, I hope I've not interrupted anything this evening."

Eleanor waved a dignified hand and scoffed. "Come child,

if I'd be annoyed by you, I'd not have chosen you for a daughter-in-law, would I? What brings you to my doors?"

The thrill of recognition made Tamina smile as she held out the file. Yes, *she* was the chosen bride, not some unknown commoner from another country. "I've brought news from Haven City."

Raising a perfectly sculpted black brow, Eleanor accepted the folder. "Oh? Must be important."

Tamina waited, taking in the manicured lawns and gardens beyond view. Down a sloping hill, greenhouses were clustered as far as she could see to the horizon. The Dandridge fortune wasn't built on Guardian finances and shrewd investment decisions alone, but on an empire of soap making and distribution. An empire Tamina had every intention of running soon.

The dowager slowly closed the file and smiled. "I see. Let's go inside and discuss this very interesting news, indeed."

14

———

Master Guardian Raiventon's Residence
   Haven City, Sziveria

"Oh summer sun, if this baby doesn't pop out in the next day or two, I'm refusing to get out of bed."

Jessi glanced up from the ledger she'd been poring over for Raina Merrick as the very pregnant woman sank with a grimace into the chair in front of the desk. Muted light poured in from a wall of windows giving a beautiful view of a well-maintained greenhouse garden. Months ago, Jessi had been set up in the spacious music room, the only other area that hadn't been claimed for office space downstairs. Sitting around staring out windows hadn't worked for Jessi. So she'd begged, pleaded and basically acted very non-Sziverian. Raina had taken pity on her and handed over ledgers her assistant never seemed to have time to manage. Sesay lifted his head and whined softly in greeting before settling back at Jessi's feet.

"I don't see how the baby has any room left." Jessi set her pen down and smiled at her friend. *Her friend.*

161

Over the months of Raina training Jessi in Sziverian culture, shopping for Sziverian fashion and missing their men, the two women had bonded. Raina had helped Jessi through her grief of losing Wilson, something she'd been forced to realize she'd held inside, hurting her further. Sorrow stabbed at her heart. She still missed him, and wished he were around for her to share her journey. He would laugh at some of the more absurd customs she had to learn about.

Raina rubbed the tight navy cotton fabric over her belly with a sigh. "They weren't supposed to be gone this long, you know. Three, maybe four months at the most."

"Do you think it's the weather?"

"No." Raina frowned and shifted before she settled again. "I think things didn't go as planned and they're still sorting through whatever it is they're doing wherever they are."

Jessi rolled the pen in thought. "Will they be able to tell us when they're heading back?"

Raina shrugged, fidgeting again in the seat. "I don't know. This is the first time I've been able to talk to Kevin when he's away. It's been wonderful, I won't lie."

Despite the few conversations Jessi had also been able to have with Mason, she had to agree, hearing his voice, even if for only a few seconds, had been nice. "Hopefully it's soon then."

"I didn't think I'd have to handle the nursery alone. Thanks for all the help with that again. Between you and Patricia, we did pretty well on our own. But I can't fathom having this baby without him, no matter how much I'm ready to not be pregnant anymore. He needs to get home."

Jessi sighed and decided not to comment further on the topic of their absent husbands. She'd learned quickly Raina either cried or became hot-tempered when emotional situations weren't in her control. Which here lately, seemed to be *all* the time. Between months of separation from her spouse, and the impending birth, Jessi knew Raina Merrick held herself together most days by deep breathing alone.

The situation wasn't the pregnant woman's fault by any means, she was after all, growing another human. Dealing with the emotional hormone fallout simply wasn't something Jessi cared much for. She was a no drama kind of a person, something that had been cultivated in her basic lifestyle with Wilson. Sziveria was proving to be anything but calm.

Jessi admired and felt sorry for the woman in equal measure. She couldn't imagine going through pregnancy alone, not to mention the actual birth. The *almost* night sprang to Jessi's mind. Had Mason not had the self-restraint, she may have found herself in the same situation. At the rate things were going, Jessi would spend all her married life, well, single.

"Are they normally gone this long?"

Raina stood and paced the space in front of the desk, hands pressed low into her back. "I have no concept of how long they're gone for. Kevin and I were married for four years before he was allowed to spend any length of time home."

Jessi's eyes widened. "Mason wrote our contract for one year."

"If you want to remain his wife at the end of the year, write a new one. That's the normal way things are done. If you decide being married to a Guardian isn't what you want…" Raina shrugged, rubbing the fullness of her stomach.

For a moment Jessi considered reminding the woman of the reason for her marriage. When she'd arrived, she'd been greeted with enthusiasm, as the *real* wife of Mason Dandridge, not a decoy or means for information. She'd liked it. A little too much if she were honest. Then she'd realized everyone around her had to believe their farce of a relationship. Which meant Jessi did too.

"We'll see," Jessi said, picking up her pen as a means of distraction. "How long is yours for?"

"Our contract?" Raina grimaced on a deep inhale, her fingers reaching to steady her against the desk. "Forever. Our entire lives."

"Wow. You decided that after a year?"

Raina grinned and shook her head. "No, I decided that before I even met him."

Jessi tried to wrap her mind around marrying a complete stranger for life. "But… why? I mean, contracts can't be broken, right? That's the reason for the year limit, isn't it? What if he was a terrible husband?"

"No, contracts can't be broken, that's why the length limits yes, so a couple can make sure they want to be married for longer if they choose at renewal. If not, they do nothing, go their separate ways. Unless a child is born of course, then it's an automatic eighteen-year renewal."

At the information, Jessi frowned. "So, a baby means eighteen years, no matter what?"

"There are exceptions, like a crime either committed by or against the spouse. But they have to be proven by the accuser same as every misconduct here in Sziveria. Sziveria doesn't force anyone to stay married to a criminal. And of course, any exceptions written into the contract."

"You can add some?"

"Of course. The only exception I added to ours was infidelity. If either of us are unfaithful, the contract is void."

Jessi's attention settled on Raina's round belly. "Even now?"

"Well, not now, we're stuck together for eighteen years no matter what either of us do."

If the whimsical expression on the woman's pixie-ish face were any indication, Raina didn't mind being *stuck* with her husband. "And you really weren't worried when you signed for life?"

"No, I wasn't. I'm still not. Best decision I ever made…

well second best." She grinned again and rubbed her stomach.

Light caught the silver of Jessi's ring. Contemplating all that Raina had said, Jessi twisted it as far as the chain would allow. When this was all said and finished, would she feel the same about her decision toward Mason?

Raina's groan of frustration pulled Jessi's thoughts away. She regarded the overly pregnant woman. "Do you want to go for a walk in the greenhouse?"

"Yes, please. I haven't been able to get comfortable today no matter what I do."

Jessi patted her thigh when she stood. Sesay gave a wide, whining dog yawn, stretched with paws out front and then ambled beside her. The door to the conservatory was in the room with them, off to the right of a huge gleaming black piano. She traced her fingers along the smooth edge as they walked past.

Raina had mentioned her husband played, but only for her. The shy confession had reminded Jessi of the sensual drawing Mason had done, though she wasn't sure if she'd been the only one to receive such from him. The thought served to remind her that while her heart seemed content in what was known of her husband, her mind still lacked information. Important things. She knew he'd never loved anyone else with his heart, but somehow she couldn't see him never having loved someone with his body. And why did she even care? The almost violent jealous response of the thought of anyone else touching him, bringing him pleasure, made Jessi want to hurt someone. It was irrational, even for her.

Especially for her.

She had no business being jealous over something she wasn't willing to give. Walking into the damp, warm interior of the conservatory she chewed her lip. Or was she? The thought had been plaguing her nearly as much as the memories of his hands and mouth on her skin. She'd come so close to begging for whatever he'd give her that night. Despite six months of separation, Jessi couldn't imagine she'd desire him any less the next time she *did* see him.

They walked in peaceful silence. Sesay had free rein in the open space, and made quick work of exploring, bounding off with a soft *woof*. Small birds chirped and fluttered from high open windows, where beams of light cut through the medium growth of trees. Even in the coldest of winters, the green-house provided a warm, stable growth environment. A necessity in the much cooler year-round climate of Sziveria. For now, the weather was temperate, at least until the sun set. Jessi had learned quickly not to be caught outdoors after dark, the temperature plummeting into freezing within moments of the last rays disappearing over the horizon.

To break the silence, Raina quizzed Jessi on Sziverian culture and etiquette. As the daughter of an Arch Guardian, she'd been raised in the sort of high-society Jessi's mother had avoided like the rabies syndrome. Jessi understood why. While the answers were easy to give, living them out would be a different matter entirely. A *lady* Jessi was not.

She swished the long, navy silk skirt around her ankles. An equally light weight, comfortable long sleeved cream button up top with navy accents completed the simple, yet refined outfit. The moment Jessi stepped off the ship, Raina had sent for her stylist and they went shopping before arriving at her house. The Master Guardianess had a near panic attack at the thought of Primary Guardian Kynhaven's wife showing up at her house wearing pants and a man's shirt.

The harried shopping experience nearly sent Jessi running for a return ship to Westica. But she'd committed, and the idea of another long voyage with a sea-sick dog wasn't something Jessi wanted to experience again. Ever.

One and a half laps around and Raina came to a sudden stop. Jessi reached for her, concerned when she noted Raina gripped her stomach. Raina's pale brown eyes met Jessi's, wide and terrified.

"Uh oh," Raina whispered.

Jessi looked her over. "What?"

"I think my water just broke."

JESSI CONSIDERED HERSELF A PATIENT PERSON. AFTER MEETING Ryan Voklane, her self-assessment changed. The team liaison personified calm and collected in a manner Jessi had never before experienced. At this point, Jessi would have left the screaming, desperate woman in labor on her own.

Raina's head, hair damp around her perspiring face, rested on Jessi's lap. In gentle sweeps, Jessi smoothed her fingers through Raina's tresses in what she hoped were comforting motions. Rose Hildbrand, a Women's and Infant Medical Scientist, was a sweet, older woman who was all plump curves and soothing smiles. She positioned pillows and blankets around Raina while humming a calming tune. Krista Eastridge, a youthful blonde with pale green eyes whispered words of encouragement as Raina's birthing coach. Jessi's job was to make sure Raina didn't suddenly make a lurch for the radio Voklane stood near, which she'd attempted at least six times already.

"Where is he?" Raina sobbed, trying to sit up.

The birthing coach laid a gentle hand on Raina's chest. "Hush, your stress is the baby's stress. Be calm."

"I am being calm!" Raina snapped, her teeth clicking together. "I want my husband, and I want him *now*."

Jessi shot a desperate glance to Voklane. He gave a barely perceivable head shake and shoulder hunch. He'd been tuning the unit for hours trying to reach Kevin Merrick from a list of frequencies. Trying to ease some discomfort from sitting on the floor, Jessi shifted her hips. Outside Raina's office windows the sun was a low, burning orange ball on the horizon line of other houses.

"Please let Ryan carry you upstairs to your room," Jessi attempted to convince for what felt like the hundredth time.

"No. I'm not going anywhere until I hear from my husband. If this baby is born on my office floor, so be it." Raina's jaw clenched and her eyes squeezed shut.

"Breathe my dear," Krista crooned and then proceeded to lead in deep breathing exercises.

A tear slid down Raina's cheek. "He promised me, Ryan."

"I know," the man said with a sigh. "But your father had no way of knowing how bad the situation really was. They've been trying for six weeks to get out. The infrastructure isn't there. No trains, the roads are blocked near the harbors. Dandridge is doing his best to find a way home. Last I heard, they had a plan, they were just waiting for approval."

Raina's eyes flew open and she glared. "How long has my father kept them waiting?"

"He didn't. I may have implied if they had a way, take it."

"When was this?"

"Three, four days ago?"

She tried to sit up again. When Krista kept her down, Raina turned her glare on the young woman, who gave a graceful smile. Raina ignored her. "In that red binder is a list of all the known ships, arranged by country, and if they have a radio on board, the frequency."

"Raina, the country isn't—"

"*Check it.*"

Jessi stirred, shifting out from under Raina's head. Krista swept into the vacated place with an ease that spoke of doing the maneuver often.

"I'll check," Jessi offered, holding her hand out.

Ryan handed her the dark red binder. "The country is Buratun."

The book flopped open in her hands and she tried to

maneuver the pages to the B section. "I've never heard of them before."

"That's because they aren't recognized, yet. They've been three names in the past hundred years, all under tyrannical regimes."

Ah, okay then. Jessi let lose a long exhale and glanced at Raina, still grimacing through a contraction. Thankfully Buratun did have a page, along with two ships listed. Neither was designated passenger, but Jessi figured that little fact wouldn't stop the Guardian team from hitching a ride. She set the book down next to the radio for Voklane. The first ship didn't respond. The second claimed to have no paying passengers onboard.

Ryan's messaged the ship again, his face relaxed. "Come in, *Wave Orchid*." The ship responded over a crackle and hiss through the airwaves. "I'm aware the passengers I seek may have paid an additional fee to keep their journey private, however, *if* a man by the name of Kevin Merrick happens to be on-board, please inform him his wife has gone into labor. Over."

Silence. Ryan seemed to be counting, his fingers tapping in a set rhythm.

"Who is this? Over." a man's garbled bark said over the waves.

"Voklane. Merrick or Blackbain? Over."

"Blackbain. Emergency code, please."

Jessi gaped when Ryan recited the longest alpha-numerical code she'd ever heard from memory. A choked cry sounded behind her. Jessi glanced over her shoulder. The birthing coach grasped both Raina's hands, whispering into her ear while the Medical Scientist knelt between Raina's legs, her feet positioned on the woman's thighs.

"Won't be long now," Rose stated, giving them both a look of warning.

Ryan picked up the heavy radio unit and carried it across

the distance to the corner of Raina's desk. Noting the yellow power display, Jessi cranked the magnetic charge to ensure the conversation wouldn't be cut short.

There were no pleasantries when the radio exchanged hands. No *thanks* or *you're welcomes*. Desperation hung in the air. Jessi knew nothing of birthing babies. The two experienced women seemed to have everything under control. Even Voklane, a single man, didn't balk when Raina grabbed his pant leg and yanked, taking his wrist when he hit the ground. She sobbed into the radio receiver while her husband spoke soothing words of love and endearment that broke Jessi's heart. These two should not be apart for such a momentous occasion. Yet they were, and they were handling it the best way they could.

Jessi slipped silently into the hall, closing the door behind her. Raina's struggled cries still sounded in the quiet interior. Mrs. Taft, the Head Housekeeper, appeared in the doorway to the breakfast room at the end of the long corridor from Raina's office.

"How is she?" the round, gray-haired woman asked.

"I was told any time now she'll begin."

Mrs. Taft nodded. She wiped her hands on a towel. "My Tabby had her daughter a couple weeks ago. I can't wait to see these two little ones running around this house."

Tabby was Raina's stylist, who like her mother, stayed in the house for her employer daily unless they weren't needed. The two younger women were closer to friends in relationship. Jessi nodded and smiled. She didn't know where she'd be when those little babies were old enough to walk, so she couldn't feel excitement at the idea.

"I'll be in here, if anyone needs me."

Mrs. Taft blinked. The rag paused. "Oh, I thought… you aren't going to go back in and help?"

"No, I don't know anything about," Jessi waved a hand

towards the door, "all of that. I'd probably start screaming and crying with Raina when things became *really* intense."

The older housekeeper shifted from one foot to the other. Jessi paused in the door to the music room. "If you like, you can knock and see if they need help. I'm sure Mr. Voklane won't mind."

"Yes, maybe I… maybe I will." Mrs. Taft's smile wobbled. "I sort of see our pretty little Guardianess like a second daughter. I was part of the Arch Guardian's staff when his wife died. When Raina married and moved here, I came with. The girls grew up together, you know."

The woman continued to prattle. Jessi didn't know how to be respectful and walk away. So she eased into the music room until the woman slid from view. Exhaling, Jessi pressed a hand to her quivering stomach.

She missed her simple home with simple chores. She missed Wilson and her bees. Eventually the waves of home-sickness would end, but like now, she had no control over when they came. A short yip drew her attention to the glass doors leading to the greenhouse. Happy, if not a little desper-ate, golden eyes stared at her. In the chaos of Raina's labor, the poor dog had been left to his own devices outside.

Jessi sank to the floor when she let him in. Her fingers glided into his thick, warm fur, easing away all her heartache. Sesay hadn't left her side, even at night when she slept, for six months. Without him, she knew the adjustment would have been near unbearable. His spongy moist tongue licked at her jaw, pulling forth a smile.

"You and me, huh boy?" She scratched at the coarser fur along the back of his neck. Ever obedient, his tongue lay flopped out, breathing doggy breath all over her shoulder in patient stillness until her anxiety eased enough for her to stand.

He settled at her feet while she worked at the little desk.

Hour logs, invoices and books lay open, taking up every inch of space. Lost in the task, Jessi failed to notice the door open.

"Young woman," a sharp female voice cut through the silence.

Jessi gasped and jumped. The pen in her hand flipped and clattered to the floor next to Sesay. The dog leapt up, attuned to her distress, and gave a short growl.

An older woman stared at her with emotionless dark eyes. Black hair laced with thick strands of gray was piled in an elegant knot atop her head. Small tendrils fell around her shoulders, an unsuccessful attempt to soften her otherwise stern features. Looking over her thin-lipped frown, a patrician nose lifted enough to give the impression she looked *down* at people regardless of their height, and the void of her gaze, Jessi wondered if the woman even knew how to smile. Nothing anyone did would make her appear less severe. The dark crimson gown, with a sash of rich, golden yellow only added to an appearance that the very air around her wasn't to be encroached upon.

The woman's eyes grazed the visible parts of Jessi until she wanted to crawl under the table, disapproval evident in the woman's increased frown. "Jessalyn?"

"Yes, can I help you? I'm afraid if you need Guardianess Raiventon, it may be a couple weeks now, she—"

Long fingers with manicured nails flicked out in annoyance, silencing Jessi. "No. I care not about Guardianess Raiventon. I'm here for you. Get your things, you're leaving with me."

Jessi blinked. "Excuse me? Who are you?"

"Eleanor Dandridge, the Dowager Kynhaven." Jessi didn't think it was possible for Eleanor's nose to raise higher and still allow the woman to see. She'd been mistaken. "I believe you and my son were quite disrespectful and married without my knowledge or approval."

Oh great. Her mother-in-law. "I don't think your grown son thought he'd need your approval."

Eleanor raised a sharp black brow. "Oh? You think you know how our family handles its private affairs?"

"Well, he married me, so…" Jessi picked up the pen. "He told me stay here until he returns to the country as well."

If fire could ignite in someone's gaze, Eleanor's would be leaping. Her jaw tensed, along with her shoulders. "You will not remain in this city continuing to bring gossip and accusations to our good name. I'll not suffer some ignorant *Westican* to slander what I've worked so hard to build. I'm not asking, I'm demanding as Dowager that you return to Kyn Manor with me."

Somewhere in the tirade Jessi knew was something important. However, she couldn't quite get beyond the demeaning way in which her heritage had been choked out. Like she was garbage, less than, not worth the clothes on her body. Palms flat on the table, Jessi rose to her full height. "I am not ignorant. Yes, I am Westican. It's a beautiful country, where citizens are encouraged to follow their passions, not stuck in some slot that needs to be filled. When my husband tells me I can go somewhere else, I'll gladly leave with you. Until then, I remain here."

Fury turned the Dowager's cheeks red. Small tremors danced along her arms and shivered the fabric along her legs. Then with a shallow inhale, calm settled around the woman in an impressive blanket. In a flurry of silk, she turned and strode from the room.

"And goodbye," Jessi muttered and sat back down.

Her relief didn't last long. Mason's mother returned, with a trembling young blonde woman behind her. Eleanor waved a hand toward Jessi. "Tell the Westican. Go on."

Garbed in the simple green and light gray the house staff wore, the woman inched forward. She brushed her fingers along the edge of her apron, focused on the floor. "The d-dowager would like me to inf-form you that refusing her is n-not allowed."

Jessi frowned, unable to keep from looking at the smug Dowager. "What do you mean, not allowed?"

The staff member eased forward and spoke softly. "To refuse her, Guardianess, is to dishonor your husband. As the elder Dandridge, and former Primary Guardianess Kynhaven, she commands respect in all things."

Eleanor had served for the family as the Primary Guardian, not Mason's father. Belatedly, Jessi recalled Raina's lesson on older generations. They were respected. Adored by a nation who saw their knowledge and years as blessings to be honored. In one act of defiance, Jessi had dishonored Mason and insulted a former Guardianess. Somehow, she didn't think anyone would be impressed with her newfound skill. "I see."

"Should I pack for you?" the young woman asked.

"Yes, please."

The blonde fled, edging past the Dowager to get to the door like poison flowed from her skirts. Probably did. When Jessi rounded the desk, Sesay followed.

"Is that beast yours?" Eleanor asked.

"Yes, he's my guard dog."

"You'll have no need of a guard dog at my house. Kyn Manor is the safest place for you."

Jessi took a deep breath and tried to remain calm. "He goes everywhere with me. We've been together for almost six years. Sesay belonged to my... uncle."

"No." Eleanor didn't wait for further argument. She turned on her heel and left the room.

Tears burned behind Jessi's eyes. She glanced down at Sesay. The dog turned his head in question and lifted his paw, scratching at the air before settling back on his rear. How could she leave him? Worse, how could she survive without him at her side? Deep inside Jessi wanted to believe Mason would fix everything when he returned home. But they'd never spoken of his mother, at least if they did, Jessi couldn't recall. For all she knew, he venerated the ground Eleanor walked on and anything she said became law.

For the first time, Jessi questioned her decision. Sesay belonged with her. He was *her* responsibility, not someone else's, and he didn't deserve to wonder why he'd been abandoned. While he was a smart dog, he was still an animal. She couldn't exactly explain that in four or five months, she'd return for him.

Sinking her fingers into the soft fur between his ears, she headed to Raina's office. Sesay kept in perfect step with her. She rapped softly on the door and waited. While now wasn't the time to interrupt, she couldn't leave Sesay in the music room without explaining, or without knowing what would happen to him. On the other side of the door Raina's muffled cry of exertion sounded through the door. The door cracked open. Ryan's head poked out. Fatigue lined his face.

"Yes?"

Jessi hoped she could speak without bursting into tears. The poor man didn't need another female to comfort. "The Dowager Kynhaven is here."

His pale blue eyes widened. A curse hissed from his mouth. His gaze fell to Sesay. "Let me guess, you can't take the wolf."

"No," she barely managed to whisper.

He slid his hand down his face on a sigh. "Leave him in the greenhouse, I'll take care of him."

"But—"

"Jessalyn, he can't go with you. If the Dowager has spoken, you can't disobey her, not right now, not without your husband. Leave him in the greenhouse. When Dandridge returns I'll fill him in and make sure he gets the dog back for you." He reached out and grasped her free hand. "He'll be safe and well cared for, I promise."

"It's a stupid rule you all have."

Ryan smiled weakly. "Only when it's abused."

Raina let loose another heavy grunting scream and Ryan disappeared, the door closing with a faint click. Jessi guided Sesay back toward the music room to lead him out to the greenhouse. Behind her the sudden tiny, yet loud cry of a new, precious life echoed. The tears she'd been denying broke free.

15

NINE DAYS LATER
  Haven City, Sziveria
  MagnaRail Station

THE HISS AND POP OF THE MAGNARAIL TRAIN COMING TO A STOP made Mason reach for the bracing bar in front of the passenger seat. The car rumbled, trembled faintly before the delicate sensation of falling moved through the cabin. Mumbled delight swelled as the passengers acknowledged the feeling along with the safe arrival of the train.

Beside him, Kevin didn't bother to wait for the conductor to give the all safe signal for passengers to rise and collect their possessions. He stood, reached into the overhead bin and yanked down his bag. Mason glanced across the aisle to Sean, who regarded his wife with interest. Katria sighed and nudged her husband. On a puff of air, Sean rose and collected their gear, tossing Kat her things, which she caught with a glare of annoyance.

"What?" Sean asked when she continued to frown at him.

"You want to keep him from getting in trouble, we *all* have to be at the door. That means we move. Quick."

Once they were clear of the aisle, Mason grabbed his bag and joined them. The idea was, while one man could be reprimanded for disobeying the directive to stay seated until the all safe signal, a group would simply be frowned upon. Mason noted several additional passengers had taken their lead. Even better.

Beyond the train, a crowd seemed to breathe and sway as though one. Loud conversation attempted to rise above the cacophony of merchants, cargo trains roaring through ten rails away, and messengers clamoring to gain the attention of their assignments. A huge metal and glass awning kept the rain and snow away, but not the wind or biting cold of late winter. Mason took a long, slow breath. Damp air, the bite of wet cement, and the competing scents of humanity filled him. Home.

Normally after a long mission away he'd head to his mansion in the city. But that'd mean confronting a house once full of life, laughter, and the infuriating madness only a sibling could bring. The house was empty of all that now. Mason's heart clenched. He still couldn't bring himself to set foot in the home Cora had taken over and made into her own. A skeleton staff remained on site to keep squatters, looters and non-human vermin away. The mansion would swallow him like the tomb it'd become.

An attendant who'd been watching the open doors stepped aside with a motion to exit. The depressing reminder of loss was no longer all that awaited Mason. Jessalyn, his wife. He still struggled to believe it was real. He still replayed the radio conversation in his mind when she'd told him the news. With a small smile he jumped off the final step to the loading platform between the rails and followed the line of passengers to the crossing point.

Ahead of him the rest of the team did the same. At the

juncture where the path split leading to the main station or baggage retrieval, a small collection of people loitered. Some held signs, others searched the flowing crowd. One man stood out amongst them all, his fair skin, ice-blond hair, and pale blue eyes immediately recognizable. Ryan Voklane.

Mason increased his speed. Ryan never met them at arrival, instead sending a messenger if they were needed at his office. Kevin paused when he reached Ryan's side and was nodded away after a quick word. The tall interceptor wasted no time, rushing into the flow of pedestrian traffic with ease, his only concern getting home to his newborn son, and wife. Sean and Kat were given the same treatment, a cursory comment and waved off. Which meant... Mason took a deep breath and ignored the rush of anxiety. If anything bad had happened to Jessi, the ship would have been contacted again. Unless it happened when they made port a day ago in Port Tabria...

Ryan fell in step beside him instead of them carrying on a conversation with listeners. Mason's fingers clenched around the handles of his bag. "What's going on?"

Hands clasped behind his back, Ryan kept his focus on the crowd shifting ahead of them. "The Dowager Kynhaven arrived at the Merrick residence."

Mason grimaced and resisted the urge to speak a string of foul words. "How did she learn Jessalyn was there?"

"I have no idea. The women shopped quite a bit. It's likely someone overheard something."

"No newspaper announcement?"

Ryan shook his head. "No, Delanee Ralston kept her end of the bargain."

"You sound surprised."

As if dislodging an unhappy thought, Ryan shook his head again. "She will expect a meeting."

"She'll get it. Now what happened with my mother?"

"Your wife is safe at Kyn Manor, where her presence was *requested* by the Dowager. Her wolf was not allowed to go."

The information made Mason stop and stare. Oh, not good. "Where is he?"

Ryan motioned with his head to continue forward. "With Arch Guardian Wolvenguard."

Mason swallowed a groan. "At this point the amount of favors I'm going to owe the Ralston family will be never ending. Why couldn't you keep him?"

"Do I look like someone who can care for a Ruthenarc Wolf? I don't even speak their command language."

"I thought everyone at the FIO could work with a Wolvenguard team?"

"No. Those of us behind a desk don't."

Mason looked over the team liaison for Arch Guardian Synintel, the leader of the First Intelligence Office special teams. If Ryan had an inch of fat on him from lounging behind a desk all day, he hid it well. "I see. Well thank you, for taking him somewhere safe."

Ryan frowned, stopping near a lot where bicycles and Ariot's were parked. Along a sidewalk in front of the station hired horse drawn carriages waited for fares. "She was… very distressed."

Mason scrubbed his free hand down his face. "Yeah, the wolf is her, I don't know, safety harness. He makes her feel in control of her surroundings. Damn it, this is not good."

"Do you know where the Arch Guardian lives?"

"Yes, thanks."

"I'll be waiting for my invitation to Kyn Manor. Don't make any major plans without my knowledge."

Mason raised a brow. "You mean approval?"

"No, knowledge. We're back to the unknown players on the board. I can't approve when I don't know who all is ultimately involved."

Ryan headed into the lot and Mason heaved out a sigh. As

a Primary Guardian, he technically couldn't show up at an Arch Guardians unannounced. He should state his need and be invited. But he needed that wolf and he needed to get to Kyn Manor. Social criteria mattered little to him at the moment.

In a play for authority, a desire found only in those who'd previously held a modicum of power, Eleanor Dandridge, his oh so lovely mother, had emotionally crippled his wife. To fix it meant showing up with the dog and yanking the proverbial cloak of power off his mother's shoulders. Mason wasn't sure what the Dowager had been thinking, or hoping to accomplish. He wasn't sure he if he even wanted to know.

Taking a hired coach to the area known by locals as Arch District. Three hundred years ago, when Sziveria was an infant and the rankings were established, they'd wanted all the Arch Guardians in one huge compound. The powers that be at the time however, pushed back. They each had a specific role to fill. Some required more social aspects, where others were filled by the decade, not the generation. A compromise was met. They wouldn't share a house, they'd share an entire section of the city. Taking up six blocks, six structures were assigned to a Guardian whose sole purpose was to run their assigned section of administration.

Arch Guardian Wolvenguard ran all the Wolvenguard teams in the nation, keeping the worst of the worst off the streets and in their prison cells. The job was dangerous, and meant to be occupied ten to fifteen years, *if* the Guardian survived that long. The position was relatively new, created within the last sixty years or so, since so far only someone of Ruthenian heritage could inherit Beast Master Gen-Heir abilities. Not to mention Ruthenia would only allow one of their own to acquire a Ruthenarc Wolf. Begging the question again, how did Wilson get a hold of one? Deklan Ralston, the current holder of the Arch Guardian Wolvenguard rank, was number fourteen. Dangerous position indeed.

The hired coach stopped at the entry street to the District. Mason paid his fare. There were no guards, but an unspoken agreement with the citizens of Haven City kept the uninvited out. *If you don't enter unsolicited, we won't shoot you on sight.* Mason would take his chances. He needed his dog back. He didn't have time to play the *Oh I'm sorry, I didn't notice your message* game.

No carriages drove down the wide brick street. No Ariot's whished past. The street appeared deserted. Bag gripped tight in his hand, Mason kept a free hand visible and headed down the street. A dusting of snow and ice coated the sidewalk and settled in the cracks between the bricks. Large dirty brown piles gathered along the curbs and lawn edges. Naked tree branches scratched and creaked in the heavy upper drafts.

Mason walked past Synintel's house. The looming wrought iron gate was closed. No one stood guard on the property, which likely meant the Arch Guardian wasn't in residence. If he were being a decent father, he'd be at his daughter's house, holding his new grandbaby and getting into the good graces of the son-in-law he'd let down. The reality – the man was likely at his office at the FIO, working.

At the end of the street a three-story brick mansion towered. The roof slanted at a steep angle, forming an almost steeple at the top. The copper had long ago turned a beautiful green, a vivid contrast with the rich red brick. Decorative wooden arches over each window provided an elegance that attempted to soften the harsh angles. A gloomy sky and lack of anything living around the house caused the effect to fail.

Three wide cement steps led to a large, recessed front door. Two massive copper snarling wolf sculptures flanked the first set of stairs, leaving no mistake as to who resided on the property. Streaks of copper wash flowed from the base of each oxidized monument, adding to the creep factor of the place. Mason took a deep breath and wondered where

Wolvenguard had hidden a warning sign. Enter at Your Own Risk seemed most appropriate.

Mason took the stairs to the front door, which opened before his foot hit the final one. A lanky young man with dark brown hair a little too long tracked Mason's progress with emotionless gray-blue eyes. Shoulders square, feet braced far enough apart of launch into an attack, the boy kept his body between Mason and the interior. Mason had to give the younger man credit, he didn't flinch when Mason's full height, and weight cast a shadow over him.

"Your business?" the young man asked.

No point in dragging out nonexistent formalities. "Wolvenguard has my dog."

The boy's expression remained guarded. "Wolvenguard has lots of dogs, I wasn't aware any had a different owner."

Mason resisted the urge to both sigh in frustration, and grab the front of the boy's too big gray shirt and throw him away from the door he guarded. "The wolf was brought to him a little over a week ago to care for until I returned to the country."

"This isn't a kennel."

Mason gritted his teeth. "I'm aware of that, thank you. Can I get my dog?"

"Name."

"Mason Dandridge, Primary Guardian Kynhaven."

The door closed in his face. Seconds later it opened to reveal a tall, beautiful woman with pale brown skin and dancing golden eyes. The long crimson flowing skirt she wore and loose flower print blouse did little to conceal a figure much too thin for the society she constantly attempted to dazzle into revealing all their lurid secrets. Crossing her arms over her near flat chest, she looked him up and down. "Primary Kynhaven, you return safe and alive. Still married?"

"If I get my dog, I will be."

Her full lips parted into a stunning smile. Delanee Ralston

had always given Cora a run for her talent in writing, and in allure. While Cora had been classically beautiful, Delanee was exotic, willowy, yet not fragile. One didn't look at Delanee and think delicate. Her long legs carried her lithe frame with a dancer's grace, hips swaying in a rhythm all her own as she beckoned him to follow. With a shake of his head, Mason wondered how many men had followed that same gesture to disaster.

"Deklan is finishing up a report, but he told me to take you to the conservatory where the dogs are right now." She swept her fingers through long, very dark red hair with a hint of curl at the ends.

Mason set his bag down next to the door before following Delanee into a spacious entry way. Wide marble stairs dominated the area, rising to the second floor, where they split in a sweeping curve to carry on to the third story. "This house is…"

Delanee waved a slender hand. "Yeah, something else. The first Wolvenguard had much to prove and put all his resources into the house. I think it's some sort of mixture of Ruthenian and Sziverian styles between the outside and inside. Deklan isn't fond of it."

Rooms upon rooms lined the yawning space on either side of the stairs as they ventured deeper into the manor. At the very end, Delanee opened wide double doors, revealing a bare room the size of most houses in the country. Not even a piano sat collecting dust in a corner.

"I take it he doesn't entertain much," Mason commented as they made their way to a wall of glass with five sets of doors.

Delanee let out a very unladylike snort. "My brother? Have you met him?"

"No, not yet. I wasn't home when he was endowed with the rank and honored."

"Ah, well, that was a huge event, I don't think he remembers most of that night, except maybe our youngest sister Dyna, hissing at Arch Guardian Immetana." She paused at the center door, her hip braced on the handle and rolled her eyes in a dramatic fashion. "*That* was embarrassing."

"Hissing, like a cat?" Mason accepted the weight of the door as she stepped out onto a wide stone patio with a fire pit and plush covered furniture.

"Yes, she's in her association phase." Delanee sighed. "It's a really annoying phase where she mimics the animal she'll be able to connect with someday, especially since it co-mingles with all things teenage angst and lasts until her first bonding."

"She's a Beast Master, too?"

Delanee stopped where the patio met a stone laid trail, her hand shielding her eyes from a bright path of sun poking through thick clouds, intensified by the layer of glass three stories above. "Looking to be."

Mason followed her attention down the vegetation lined walkway, but saw nothing. "Are they in here?"

"This greenhouse takes up the remaining footprint of the block. It's huge. They're in here, just wait."

Distant barking echoed through the thick overgrowth of trees, vines and ferns. "Why does it look like a jungle in here?"

"Training. Provides a more realistic setting if it's natural and not landscaped," a deep voice answered behind them.

Mason glanced over his shoulder. An impossibly tall man rivaling him in size sauntered through the still open door from the ballroom. The sides of his shoulder length dark auburn hair were pulled back into a knot at the crown of his head. Slender streaks of silver shot through the rich color, a testament to the harsh life chasing criminals. Teal eyes surveyed the scene before him, contrasting vividly against his golden skin. A cotton maroon sweater with the sleeves rolled up his forearms left little doubt to his strength, pulling tight across his chest, shoulders and biceps with each movement. Black pants, and boots meant for running in any weather condition completed the not-high-society look the rest of the inhabitants on the street must snarl at whenever he walked by.

Mason held out his hand. "Kynhaven."

Deklan accepted without hesitation. "Deklan Ralston."

Mason looked at him in question.

Deklan smiled, releasing from their shake. "I feel like *Wolvenguard* is some sort of curse. If I don't address myself as such, maybe I won't die on the next run."

"I would prefer that," Delanee weighed in.

Mason resisted the urge to rub a sudden sore spot in the vicinity of his heart. Change of subject needed. He returned to surveying the greenhouse, the echo of frantic barking getting closer. "So, my dog. Thank you for keeping him."

Deklan scratched at day old stubble along his jaw. "Yeah, interesting situation. He hasn't eaten much and has only interacted with my wolves. Of course he's too old to bond with anyone but his owner, who Voklane told me is Westican?"

"I don't know about his owner, but when Wilson passed, my wife took ownership, and she's Westican, yes." *His wife.* He still wanted to shake his head and make sure he wasn't dreaming when he spoke of Jessalyn being his.

"He must have bonded to her. She calls him *Sesay*?"

Mason couldn't help but smile. "Yes."

"I checked his marking, do you want to know his name?"

"Will he respond to it?"

Deklan shrugged. "He might. Then again, it won't matter since he isn't on a team."

Four massive wolves burst through the vegetation. Two were rich gray, like Sesay, one was almost completely white with pale blue eyes and another golden brown. Their furry ears were upright, tails swishing in excitement.

"His name is Wulf."

Mason couldn't help but laugh. "Figures, I'd been calling him wolf."

"Did he respond?"

"Who knows, I usually followed it with a group command."

Deklan crossed his arms over his chest as the pack came to an excited stop before him. "He's nine. There isn't any owner information on his marking, so I don't know anything beyond that."

Mason crouched down. Time to test the new name. "Ready to go see your Jessalyn again, Wulf? I know she misses you."

"Oh good," Delanee began with a sardonic roll of her eyes at her brother. "You aren't the only crazy who talks to dogs."

Deklan made a face and waved to the gathered wolves. "They have ears, they can hear, so yes, I speak to them."

Wulf padded forward and sat before Mason, lifting a large paw. His golden eyes twinkled, but he didn't act as excited as the others in the group, whining and spinning, doing whatever they could to get Deklan's attention. At least, Mason figured, the dog seemed to recognize him still.

"I'll get you a lead," Deklan said, turning. When the horde of mongrels followed, he pointed and barked, "*Sesay Osat'yi.*"

They made pitiful sounds. One flopped on its belly, another stretched, back legs twitching, while the third sat heavily, tongue lolling out the side of its mouth. Wulf stiffened in front of Mason. Deklan sighed and shook his head, disappearing into the house.

Delanee chuckled. "He lost his alpha a couple weeks ago. These are all still puppies in Ruthenarc wolf years. Without the alpha to help guide them, their conditioning has fallen completely to him."

Mason reached out and sank his fingers into Wulf's thick fur. "That must have been painful."

"Yeah, he took it pretty hard." Delanee sat with a sigh of her own, crossing her legs in an elegant sweep of limbs. "So, are you heading to Kyn Manor when you leave here?"

"Yes."

She lifted a dark sculpted brow. The toe of her shoe peeked out from under her skirt with every flick of her ankle. "No one knows for certain what's going on where your wife is concerned, if you were wondering. *The Havener* has received some tidbits, but not enough to do anything with. Yet. I know they're sitting on it until they have a bit more confirmed, but I don't know how much longer they'll wait. Not much is happening in the city right now, and they need something scintillating for their readers."

"And *Haven City Chronicle* doesn't?"

She gave a little sniff and raised her chin. "We pride ourselves on actual reporting, not gossip, for our social pages. Our readers expect the truth, not rumors."

"Of course they do."

"Anyway, this doesn't change the fact that your marriage has been filed, but no official announcement has been made. I'm shocked *Havener* hasn't been printing the speculation alone, it's been very... creative."

Mason rose. "You mean everyone has been talking about my marriage for the past six months?"

"No, just the past two weeks. Since the Dowager Kynhaven arrived and practically dragged your wife down the Merrick's driveway. *Havener* did run a brief paragraph about that on their gossip page. I convinced my editor to wait until I could speak to you before we printed anything."

"How kind of you," Mason said neutrally. He didn't appreciate the visual of his mother manhandling his wife.

Delanee glanced at her buffed nails. "Well, we did have an agreement. When should I be expected at the manor?"

"Give me a day to smooth things over as much as I can, then arrive. But our original agreement still stands. I approve everything before you send it off. I agreed to this to help strategically get information about my marriage out to society."

She waved a hand. "Of course, of course. Having an exclusive at the manor is making my editor giddy with anticipation. He doesn't need to know any of the details about our arrangement. That I've made one is enough." She sighed and straightened. "I miss her too, you know. Whatever I can do to help, I'm going to."

The knot in his chest from earlier returned and this time he did rub a fist over it, grimacing. He'd found in the previous months if he failed to latch on to the thought of being a single child now, instead of a twin, he'd make it another day without feeling like sanity slipped through his fingers. The key was not dwelling, or even acknowledging, his only-child status. Moments like this, where he was faced with the reminder head on, made the task difficult. He wasn't looking forward to his arrival at Kyn Manor. "Thank you."

Deklan returned with a long strap of leather entwined between his fingers. He held it out to Mason. "Loop this around his neck, it stops before a choke, so don't worry about that. Voklane said he traveled well."

Mason slid the lead onto Wulf, thankful he didn't reject the tether. "I'd imagine he does, after the long trip from Westica."

Deklan tsked and shook his head. "*Zhaktu* shame he's someone's pet. He would have made a great alpha. Wish I knew more about his previous Master."

Mason glanced at Wulf and considered the old man, who'd been well past his prime for leading a team. "You think he had one?"

"Wolf that well behaved? Yeah, he definitely had one."

"His previous owner, an old man, rescued a woman from an abductor. Do you think he was maybe used for interception missions?"

Deklan stared at the dog in thought. "I've never heard of a Beast Master being utilized that way, but perhaps. I'll talk to my father about it, I'm curious now. Was the man Ruthenian?"

"If he was, his accent was long gone." Mason wound the leather strap around his hand until only a short length remained.

Wulf bumped into his side, his luminous eyes curious when he looked up. Mason tugged the lead with a short pull and headed for the door, thanking Deklan once more.

Outside the house, with his bag in one hand and the leash to his dog in the other, Mason headed down the street, his focus on the upcoming reunion. Jessalyn had been the one bright spot whenever he thought of returning home. The only thing worth stepping back onto the shores of Sziveria if he were honest. And his mother had likely made her regret the decision. Now he had to wonder if he were too late, if she'd be happy to see him, or begging to return to Westica.

16

———

THE TOO REAL SENSATION OF A KNIFE EDGE SLICING FROM HER shoulder blade to her hip ripped Jessi from sleep on a scream. Trembling, she fisted her hands in the soft sheets tangled around her legs and waist. Hot tears flowed down her cheeks as she squeezed her eyes shut and tried to breathe through the thick press of pain in her chest.

A nightmare, nothing more.

She was safe, far away from a captor who was dead. He'd never kill, let alone hurt, again. All these things she whispered to herself in the dark, and still the fragments of horror spent in cruel hands flashed through her mind. Jessi allowed herself one choked sob before scrubbing her shaking hands down her face.

How many more nights immersed in memories of torture and rape could she take? Biting her lip and trying to grasp onto threads of sanity, she knew not much longer. She needed Sesay... or more, she needed Mason. At this point, she didn't care which of them showed up, either meant safety, comfort.

Slamming her hands down in disgust, she kicked the sheets away. Could she be any more pathetic? Needing a man, or a dog, to get through a night without nightmares? If the last ten nights were any indication, then yes. One more night of pain and fear and she was liable to sink into a corner and remain no matter who arrived to remove her from her room. And she *hated* to admit as much. Jessi despised the power her abductor still held over her, in her own wretched mind.

Like all the other mornings, she dragged herself to the shower, every muscle shaking. The filth of his touch lingered on her skin. The burning sting of his knife ached along her back. A heady rush of adrenaline and fear pounded like a drum in her ears. Only the warm slide of soap and water helped her feel somewhat human again, allowed her to wash away the troubling dream.

After brushing her teeth, and combing her hair, Jessi slipped into a flowing dark purple flower print skirt and a soft lavender tunic style top. The shirt complimented her frame, hugging her breasts and flaring over the skirt at her hips. She'd take confidence anyway she could. Using her fingers to scrunch her hair, she slipped her feet into dark brown leather ankle boots. While spring wasn't far, a chill still hung in the air. Snow stuck stubbornly to the shadows and ice slickened exterior surfaces until the sun burned it away.

No candles or lamps lit the dark, silent hall. Kyn Manor was a two story behemoth, shaped in a square. The center of the house formed a bricked in courtyard garden with a tall glass ceiling, which meant all the corridors eventually led in a circle around the house. The interior corridor windows overlooked the garden, but little dawn light penetrated through the glass ceiling to the windows below. Even in noon sun, the hallways still required lamps for full visibility.

Jessi eased her way through the darkness by memory. Thankfully chairs and tables were in recessed alcoves and in no danger of being ran into. At the wide stairs leading to the ground floor, she used the railing for balance. The soles of her boots on the gray marble steps echoed in the empty foyer. All the doors were closed to the library and study across from the stairs, an indication from the household staff the rooms had been cleaned recently. The doors to the breakfast room and dining hall were open to the left. Somewhere on the ground floor was also a grand ballroom, a gaming room, a formal sitting room, and a banquet room for when large crowds gathered and buffet style meals were served. Since those rooms didn't matter, Jessi hadn't paid much attention on the tour.

The mansion was a study in dark and light. Pale gray marble floors, dark mahogany doors, split walls of cream and navy. All of it shouted wealth and generations of attention to detail. Small marble statues, huge oil paintings of still life, and potted trees completed the *look don't touch* feel. Every morning Jessi missed the small, broken-down two-story shack she'd made into a home with Wilson. She missed the warmth, the knowledge of belonging she'd taken for granted when she'd had it.

Using the banister for leverage, Jessi swung her body around toward the wide corridor leading to the kitchens and the backdoor to the area the locals referred to as Glass City, a collection of close to fifty huge greenhouses that grew herbs and other necessary ingredients for the family enterprise. Three more houses were the process of being built. Along with all the outbuildings, the area resembled a very clean, well-organized city. And the aptly named expanse of stone footpaths, wood and glass, had become Jessi's refuge.

The kitchen bustled with activity. Pots clanged, water ran, fists pounded dough on counter tops, something sizzled in a pan. Lamps hanging from the ceiling bathed the huge room in brilliant light. The head cook, Anthony Saldina, whom everyone called Sal, was the first to notice her. His warm brown eyes brightened and he lifted a ladle he'd been using into the air.

"Ah! Jess, my girl! I made your favorite. At least I think

it's your favorite. You made noises you don't make with my other food." He carried his large frame over to the farthest counter in the kitchen where all the prepared dishes waited to be served at the appropriate time and picked up a single plate.

Jessi met him half way, holding out her hands to accept whatever delicious treat he'd made for her this time. Sal seemed intent on making Jessi feel welcome through food. Since the day of her arrival, he'd lavished one decadent dish after another on her. Sometimes in front of Eleanor and Tamina, others, like now, when everyone else slept. Or when the huge house closed in on her and Jessi couldn't stand being alone, so she'd wander into the busy kitchen. Jessi wasn't sure if he showed her special treatment because eventually his boss would return and Jessi would sing his praises, or because he genuinely had a concern for her. Moments like now, when a still warm slice of blueberry lemon tart coated with a fine dusting of powdered sugar slid into her hand, she didn't care.

"Sal, if you keep feeding me this kind of stuff, they're going to have to roll me back to Westica." Jessi slipped onto the nearest barstool next to a woman vigorously whipping something pink in a large wooden bowl. With a grin, Jessi set the plate on the slate tiled countertop.

He waved his ladle on the way to the dish he'd been overseeing at the massive nine burner stove. "I feed you so you are beautiful for Primary Kynhaven on his return. Not that you aren't already, but you have hidden curves, I'm finding them for your husband. He will thank me."

"Ah, is that what you're doing?" Jessi laughed and tore a piece of the tart free, its flaky butter saturated crust crumbling at her fingertips.

"Yes, then this talk of Westica will go away. He will get lost in your beauty and remain contracted to you."

Jessi paused with the bite almost to her mouth. "He did ask me to marry him while I looked like this, you know."

The twinkle in his eyes danced with amusement. "Yes, I know. But the Dowager keeps throwing it in our faces that you're only here for another couple months. With my help, he'll agree to another five years. You'll see. Five years and then a baby, and you'll have him however long you want him."

Startled by his proclamation, Jessi stared. The piece of tart dropped from her fingers to the plate with a *plop*. "A baby to make something last? I mean, I know the eighteen-year rule, but most couples actually decide *not* to get married that long on their own?"

Sal shrugged and stirred the large steaming pot he loomed over. "It's the way of things. Very rare for a couple to decide beyond three to five years. Starting a family decides for them. So, eat. Fill in those curves and make him want to make babies, hmm?"

Beside her, the woman giggled. Others in the room offered praise, and some not-so-subtle ways to accomplish the task the moment Mason arrived home. The staff had learned quick Jessi was nothing like Eleanor, or Tamina Peyton for that matter. The dark-haired beauty was proper to the point of painful with the staff and guests. Around Jessi, everyone could be themselves, and they'd made use of the luxury the instant they'd realized.

A baby. The idea both excited and terrified Jessi. For a baby to happen, she'd first have to allow Mason into her bed, something she'd been debating on over the past six months, sure. But being faced with it, by practical strangers, made the decision somehow more real. They already assumed such was the case, of course. Only the next time her husband frequented her bed, a fruitful union was the goal. Or so everyone teasingly bantered.

The lovely little square of tangy sweetness lost its appeal.

Jessi tried to ignore the good-natured advice floating around her. Early in the months spent with Raina she'd learned pregnancy, and children, were highly prized. The staff cared enough about her to want to see the next generation be part of her union with their Guardian.

And Mason was literally *their* Guardian, something that had come as a bit of a shock. As his wife, in his absence, Jessi should have taken over the responsibilities of the, home, township and business, but Eleanor had made it clear Jessi wasn't welcome to the task. No, Miss Tamina Peyton, as a Sziverian born and bred socialite, was helping the Dowager with the duty. Since Jessi knew nothing about how to deal with *that* specific insult, nor how to run a small city and all the issues guaranteed to be included, she let it ride. The Kyn Manor staff took the offense for her, and had been spoiling her since.

"Eat, eat!" Sal waved in her direction before wiping his hands on his bright red apron.

A bowl of fresh fruit was pushed across the counter to her by another cook walking by, followed by honey sweetened peppermint tea. Despite her appetite vanishing, Jessi ate, not wanting to offend the chipper chef. He'd not allow her to leave his kitchen anyway if she didn't finish the little meal he'd prepared for her. Jessi savored the delicate tart and fruit, and sipped at her tea until everything was gone.

On her way out the door to Glass City, Sal lifted an opaque white glass dish covering. Chopped boiled egg whites, thin slices of cucumber and a swipe of creamy cheese adorned a plate. "What do you think for Miss Peyton's breakfast?"

"I think she's going to be starving in thirty minutes."

Sal pondered her words, easing the covering back over the plate. "Well, she will be disappointed, my staff is on break until lunch after we serve breakfast."

"No morning tea?"

He motioned at a completed dish with little cheese and vegetable rolls. Three per saucer sized dish. "Already finished."

Jessi couldn't help but laugh. "You are being very mean."

Sal shrugged. "She said my cooking wasn't helping her keep her beautiful figure and she wanted more of what I've been putting in front of you."

Perplexed, Jessi stared at him.

"And she's not my Guardian, or even his wife," Sal said with another shrug.

But the little witch had implied she was, or soon would be, which had offended the head cook enough to do the opposite of Tamina's wishes. The entire situation baffled Jessi. "You don't know me, and yet you care that she would attempt to assume my position. Why?"

Several kitchen staff froze, expressions stunned. Jessi shifted on her feet, hand on the doorknob. Sal turned to face her, all the fun light fading from his warm brown eyes, replaced with a grim seriousness Jessi wasn't sure she cared for.

"Primary Guardian Kynhaven chose you. You wear his promises. You wear his ring. You bear his name." He flicked a finger toward the silver adornment on Jessi's left wrist and hand. Without thought, her fingers brushed the bracelet. "He's away right now, serving our great country. How is he repaid for this? By another woman coming into his home and making demands of his staff while his very mother shuns the woman he chose? The Dowager we must obey, to a degree. The power hungry hyena? Not so much.

"You are a good woman. Sad too often, but good. In his place, we must care for you. It's our duty, and our honor." At the end of his words, the kitchen moved as unit in a swift executed bow.

Jessi kept from stumbling back in shock. Never in her life would she have imagined people bowing before her... like she was special, worthy of such an action. Of which she was neither.

If only they knew the true reason for Mason's desire to marry her.

Would they be so loyal? Perhaps. The Kyn Manor crew seemed to miss the female twin as much as the male. They spoke of her often, and with enough enthusiasm, Jessi forgot the woman wouldn't come walking through the door any day. Their love for their Guardian and his deceased sister had bolstered Jessi's resolve to stay in Sziveria. To help Mason fulfill his self-proclaimed oath to find whoever wanted his sister dead. Authority alone didn't produce such devotion. Only good people did so. And now they'd pulled her into their sphere.

"Thank you," was all Jessi could think to say. She offered a small smile and slipped outside before anyone could say anything more.

Muted gray pink light toyed with the frost covered landscape, sparkling and glinting off grass blades and flower petals. Ice-tipped leaves shivered in a faint breeze. Jessi wrapped her arms around her waist to ward off the cold, keeping to the brick path leading to Glass City. The quiet stillness only early morning provided added to the silvery wonderland. Nothing, not even birds, stirred yet.

Like city blocks, glass houses occupied acre after acre of land with paths winding between and around them. In front of each house, a neat carved wooden sign told what plants were grown within. Kyn Manor employed two Gen-Heir Botanists, who created the perfect artificial environments from cedar forests, to the sub-tropical requirements of vanilla orchids. Walking into each conservatory was a journey in fragrance. The sweet perfume of jasmine and roses, the earthy aromas of sandalwood and patchouli, the spicy bite of cloves and cinnamon, she loved all the various combinations when she walked through the doors. Today she'd be helping plant lavender. An entire greenhouse full of the highly scented herb. Yesterday they'd planted black chamomile and peppermint.

A warm, humid burst of air hit Jessi as she opened the door into the greenhouse. The scent of earth and manure hung thick in the moisture rich environment. Set in little clay pots on shelves, the baby lavender plants waited to be transplanted into their forever dirt. Jessi donned a long canvas apron, tying it behind her back. Once she was sure her clothing was protected, she pulled a tray full of seedlings and went to work.

Hours later other workers filed in, bringing laughter and camaraderie to the stillness. Over a week ago they'd balked at the idea of their Guardianess digging in the dirt beside them, but Jessi changed their minds. She couldn't sit all day in the house, staring out a window, dwelling on the flickers of memory so close to the surface. She'd go insane. Like the household staff, they'd thankfully decided to take her under wing.

Mid-morning sun climbed high into the sky, warming the glass house until someone propped open all the doors, allowing a fresh cool breeze in. During the summer months, the ground level panes could swing open for plants that needed more moderate temperatures. A soft hush fell across the workers and Jessi glanced at the door where everyone's attention seemed to focus, curious. Had Eleanor finally decided to put a stop to her daily routine?

The silhouette of a tall man shimmered from the narrow path between the row greenhouses. In front of him a large dog trotted and danced. As he moved closer, long strands of dark hair caught by wind became visible. Jessi's heart leapt into her throat. She was up and whispering his name before she even realized her intention. Her shoe caught in the edge of her skirt. She yanked, not caring when fabric tore as she rushed forward.

People moved out of the way without her having to speak a word. Something must have shown on her face. She could only imagine... desperation, hope, probably even the desire she seemed intent to hide from herself. All of it warred within her.

Mason was here.

Steps away.

She just needed to make it to him without landing on her face. Erratic, almost howls of excitement rent the air. An eager mountain of fluffy gray fur barreled down the brick in her direction. Sesay pranced and yipped in high pitch barks around her legs, catching the long folds of her skirt on his tail. Happy as she was to see him, nothing compared to the elation of finding herself swept into Mason's strong arms.

Jessi barely had time to wrap her arms around his shoulders before her feet left the ground and her chest crushed to his. She gasped as his mouth closed over hers and all she could do was hang on. Her fingers tangled in the long length of his midnight hair, burying deep. Not caring how likely inappropriate it was for her to open her mouth and accept every bone-melting stroke his tongue offered. Let them watch if they wanted.

He tasted how she remembered, of man and passionate promises he alone could deliver.

"I missed you," he managed, pulling at her lips with long, breathless kisses between each word.

Through the haze he wove around her, Jessi was able to form a single coherent, "Yes."

A sigh fluttered across her lips to her ear as he pressed his cheek to hers. "If I don't stop, I'm not going to be able to walk for a bit without embarrassing myself."

Jessi blinked and pulled back. He slowly slid her down his body. The unmistakable beginning of his thickening erection pressed into the softness of her belly. Jessi flushed. Her fingers slid through his hair to his shoulders. His silver eyes danced and he flashed her a grin. Perhaps *embarrassed* wasn't exactly what he meant.

And sweet summer sun, if every cell in her body didn't thrum with desire. Leaning back, she took him in. He looked different, good enough to climb into his arms again. Gone was the bushy beard hiding the strong lines of his face, replaced with a short-cropped strap defining his strong jaw that met a moustache and outlined his sinfully sexy mouth. His tan was deeper, bringing out the rich olive undertones of his skin. A contrast to the pale gray sweater he wore rolled up to his elbows, with the top two of five buttons at his neck undone. Black slacks hugged the muscles of his thighs. If he'd cut his hair, she doubted if she would have recognized him except for the light gray of his eyes. The thought made her clench her fingers into the long, silky strands.

Sesay wasn't to be ignored. He continued to yip and pounce in circles, determined to gain her attention. Jessi released her hold on her husband with a reluctant sigh. Mason let her slip from his arms, though his fingers trailed down her arm to her hand, as if to remind himself he really had been touching her. She knew the feeling, she wanted to lean into his legs to keep some sort of physical connection. Which was, she admitted, both insane with a mild touch of pathetic.

Their marriage was a set-up. A means to lure whatever enemy lurked in shadows that somehow connected them. Yet here they were, acting like whatever was between was *real*. And he'd admitted to missing her. Jessi took a long, slow breath to ease the flutter in her chest, brushing her fingers into Sesay's thick coat around his neck.

"He feels a little thin," she commented with a frown, the bones of his shoulders prominent under her hands.

Mason crouched down beside her, petting the now blissfully happy dog between his furry ears. "He wasn't eating. I learned his name, if you want to know it."

"Oh, that's right, I remember you telling me what I called him was some sort of a command?"

"A group command, for all the wolves under a unit," he clarified.

"How did you learn his name?"

"It's actually tattooed inside one of his ears. He was taken to Arch Guardian Wolvenguard for safe keeping. Since Wolvenguard has his own team, he knew where to look."

So many things about Mason's country confused her. She knew an Arch Guardian was important, but not what they did in any specific capacity. Now wasn't the time to learn either. "Okay, what is it?"

He smiled at her sideways. "Wulf."

Jessi couldn't help but laugh. "Seriously?"

"Yes. If he responds, he's bonded to you."

"And if he doesn't?"

Mason shrugged. "Then we keep calling him *Sesay*."

The dog's hot breath panted in Jessi's face, content to sit now and be loved on. His golden eyes took in the surroundings with lazy curiosity. Did she want to test her bond to the animal who'd saved her life so many years ago? Sesay, well Wulf, had always been Wilson's dog and Jessi's personal guardian. While she had zero doubts about *her* connection to him, she wasn't sure about the other way around.

"How exactly do they bond to people?"

"I'm not sure how it works. I'm not a Beast Master."

Jessi rose, caressing up one of Wulf's ears. "Are the commands the same?"

"Yes, you just say his name in place of the group command."

"Should we test his name, so I know what to call the beast?"

His fingers threaded between hers. He looked up at her, his other hand still stroking between the wolf's ears. "You don't have to, you know. I doubt he or you will ever be around other wolves to make it a concern. If you're comfortable with Sesay, he responds, it's enough."

Jessi looked between Mason and the large dog, who was the same height as Mason crouched. She didn't want to check their bond. In her mind, Sesay was hers now, fully. With the death of Wilson, she'd taken over his care. She didn't want to think the thread was only present because of a command long ago given to guard her, and reinforced regularly. Yes, he knew her, enough to continue eating apparently, but would he respond if she used his Beast Master name?

Jessi curled her fingers into her palm and tightened her hand around Mason's. "Okay, I think… I'm going to wait a little bit longer."

Mason stood, squeezing her hand. "Then we'll wait." He glanced over his shoulder at the small crowd. "Now, tell me why my wife was working in the greenhouses."

17

Hands clasped behind his back, Mason gazed out the window over the gleaming glass angles of Glass City. The setting sun burned golden along every metal edge and ninety-degree pane. Kyn Manor. Neither he nor Cora made a habit of coming home. The display of wealth, the nagging of their mother, and in his case the responsibility of an entire population of civilians, had kept them away. Allowing the township to elect a voice that wrote to him whenever he or she couldn't handle disputes had worked out well. Now home though, the duty would default back to him, with the elected official in an advisory role.

The loudest voice of dissension belonged not to his mother, or even his wife, but some woman who seemed to think he cared about her grievances. Apparently, she'd been handling the Dandridge accounts for several months, and if Mason's assumptions were correct, had been being groomed to be the next Guardianess Kynhaven.

And what a disappointment it must have been when Mason arrived from Westica, contracted. Word in the hallways was, Eleanor Dandridge didn't let that stop her future plans. Too bad Mason had decided the moment Jessi flew into his arms without hesitation, his beautiful bride wasn't going anywhere if he had any say in the matter.

The young woman's words droned on, reminding him he was supposed to be paying attention. "… and just this morning my breakfast was nothing more than pieces of chopped egg and cucumber. I ask you, how am I supposed to put rational thought to the estates accounts if I'm starving?

"Not to mention, I don't think anyone has bothered to change my sheets in three weeks. Now, I'm not trying to get anyone in trouble, and Dowager Kynhaven has assured me each morning it would be handled, but someone is getting paid for a job they aren't doing. As your accountant, I'd be more than happy to remedy pay for such grievances. Ele—, I mean, the Dowager, has assured me I'm authorized to make such decisions once I have your approval."

Mason rubbed his forehead and turned away from the window. "You want to decrease the pay for one of my staff?"

She fidgeted in her seat. Glossy brown curls bobbed around a pretty, round face. Sky blue eyes stared through silver wire rim glasses in expectation. "Yes, of course. Why would you continue to pay someone who isn't doing their job? Perhaps they should be moved to another staff position on the property if nothing else."

A small ache began to pulse behind his right eye. "I'm sorry, who are you again?"

She blinked, a rosy tinge blossomed across her cheeks. Her fingers brushed the embroidered pink floral skirt covering her all the way to the floor. "Tamina Peyton, my father was Shield Guardian Rosenthall."

Mason tried to recall the man and the position. Shield Guardians held local law enforcement positions within the three major cities of Sziveria. Rosenthall, if Mason remembered correctly, oversaw the import and export offices of the Haven City rail lines. His daughter would certainly be considered a catch if she were a Gen-Heir. Too bad he didn't care for social ladders. "I was sorry to hear of his death."

She lowered her long, dark brown lashes. "Thank you."

"You've been living here since then?"

"The Dowager has been most kind. Since I was overseeing all the accounts for the Kynhaven estate and business, she felt it would be easier if I took up residence as a staff member here at Kyn Manor. I still spend time in Haven City with my mother, of course."

"Of course." Mason turned to face the desk and tapped on an open ledger. "Now that I'm home, I can oversee the accounts. I'll speak to housekeeping and make sure your rooms are taken care of. As for the kitchen staff, I'd like to hear from my head cook personally. My wife spoke very highly of him, so I can't imagine he's neglecting his duties."

Her mouth worked like a fish trying to suck water from air. "I-I... b-but th-that's... I couldn't possibly hand over such... such menial work to you. Surely you have better things to do with your time than waste it overlooking numbers?"

Mason waved a hand. "Non-sense. I need to see how the accounts are anyway. It's been far too long since I put any effort into that part of my estates. I appreciate you overseeing it. Also, you no longer need to feel obligated to remain in residence."

The pink of her cheeks blazed to red. Her fingers fisted in the satin over her lap. "I've never felt obligated, I assure you, Primary Guardian Kynhaven."

Mason offered a shallow smile. "All the same, I know how difficult staying away from your mother must be."

Tamina worked her pouty bottom lip between her teeth. Mason resisted the predatory smile he wanted to release. Right about now she was figuring out he had realized the angle she and the Dowager were playing, and he wanted nothing to do with it. Something which would come as no shock to his mother. He thought at this point, after her many failed attempts to engineer a relationship for him, she'd know better.

Clearly, Mason was mistaken.

The desk he stood behind had become Tamina's work station. Ledgers, writing utensils, discarded pieces of jewelry, and even little cosmetic cases littered the surface. The kind of personal clutter someone comfortable in their space created. Which made him mad enough to want to swipe the entire mess right into her face. The conniving manipulation of the two women wouldn't end here he knew, and getting furious about it would fix nothing. Not yet.

So he sat. Forced himself to maintain a sense of calm. He braced his elbows on the surface and steepled his fingertips. Waited for the denial she was carefully wording in her mind before speaking out loud.

"The work I've been doing here is important, my mother knows that. I'll stay for a few days, make sure you don't have any questions. My system isn't conventional, so I'm sure you'll need some help making sense of it."

"That's entirely up to you." Mason wouldn't bother to look at her system except to compare. As she fidgeted again, her gaze skimming over the open books, he didn't need Sean's Sympath abilities to know either she, or his mother, had hidden something within the logs.

A shallow, uncomfortable smile scrunched up her face. "Great. I'll speak to Dowager Kynhaven and let her know." She paused halfway to standing up, her bright blue eyes focused on him. "I'm glad you're home safe."

"My wife is too."

A new flush spread across her cheeks. She looked away. "Yes of course, I'm sure she is. Especially since she's not taken well to our social standards. I fear she's out of her element, the unfortunate dear."

Tamina said *the unfortunate dear* like she'd say *isn't she beautiful dressed in all that garbage*? Insincere with an edge of condescension. When he opened his mouth to correct her assumption, she pressed forward, raising a hand in surrender. "I'm only saying as much as a friend of the family. I wouldn't want her, or your family name, to be the source of gossip columns because she didn't know better."

Mason remained composed. "Thank you, Miss Peyton, but it's not your concern."

She nodded and then fled. Mason watched the empty doorway for a bit in thought before gathering up all her work books. He didn't want to leave them where she, or his mother, could change a single line.

"WELL, THIS IS UNFORTUNATE."

Tamina clutched at her warm cup of tea and took a sip. The Dowager had *no* idea. Spicy cinnamon and soothing honey slid down her throat, but did little to ease the bundle of nerves playing havoc in Tamina's stomach.

In a manner eerily similar to her son, the matriarch stood at the floor to ceiling windows in her personal sitting room, elegant hands clasped behind her back as she surveyed her domain. And yes, Tamina had no doubt the woman still saw every square mile as *hers*. When the current Primary Guardian happened to be in residence, Eleanor took a step to the side, but never fully handed over control. All too soon he'd leave again, the Dowager would sweep back into power.

Tamina wasn't stupid. Hand-picked by Eleanor, the woman would have assured she remained in her role of authority, for Tamina would never dare question or seize control of what Eleanor considered hers. Mason's current wife seemed to have an independent streak. In a manner Tamina grudgingly envied, the young woman refused to be cowed. Tamina couldn't afford the luxury of individuality. She'd be exactly who Dowager Kynhaven expected and wanted.

"I told him I'd stay for a few days, to help oversee the ledgers."

Eleanor waved a hand and scoffed. "Silly child, you'll stay because I say so."

Relief tore through Tamina, but she remained poised. Regal. Shoulders back, spine straight, hands folded on her lap. The picture of refinement for a woman who valued the impression of perfect appearance. "How can I help you?"

Eleanor patted at the hair behind her neck, despite not one strand being out of place. "Mason is my genetic heir, did you know that?"

"No, Dowager, I didn't."

"Yes, he's brilliant. While I helped strategize for the Hall of Laws, he's taken our gift a step higher, helping facilitate government take overs, rescues, negotiations, and who knows what else. Which means, my clever son knew exactly what I'd done the moment he took in your desk. He has whacked my ice ball off its course."

The confession made Tamina wonder what the other twin had inherited. But bringing up Cora Dandridge was a mistake she wouldn't make again. The elder Kynhaven refused to acknowledge her daughter's death. In fact, she refused to speak of her at all. Tamina's job wasn't to help the family heal, rather to become part of the household for as long as she could. She remained silent and waited for Eleanor to divulge her new plan.

"Now it's my turn to take a hit at his. He didn't marry the Westican because he loves her. She's not pregnant, but that doesn't mean she told him differently. Of course, now he'd know, and yet, he seems insistent on maintaining the farce that is surely their marriage."

Tamina couldn't help herself. She'd heard about the welcome Mason had given his wife. A welcome she herself had once dreamed of a husband bestowing on her. "What if he really cares about her?"

"My dear, you of all people know love and marriage for ranked Guardians must be carefully cultivated. This is especially true for *this* house. If Mason doesn't marry a fourth generation or longer Gen-Heir, we risk losing our status if his children are born gen-common."

On paper, Tamina's genetics looked more than perfect for any ranked Guardian house to marry. In reality, well, she shifted uncomfortably, her family tree wasn't as it appeared. *That* little secret was hers to keep. Along with a few others. "I understand, Dowager."

"I know you do. Your mother was very decisive about who she married, and she couldn't have chosen better than your father."

Tamina smiled.

"All right, a new plan." Eleanor clapped her hands together in a show of drama. "I hope you don't mind being a bit more conniving than we have been."

Tamina narrowed her eyes and drew her brows together. "Define *more*."

A sinister smile toyed at the Dowagers thin lips. "If I can't get my son to see you as the reasonable choice, I'll just have to prove to him how unacceptable his current wife is. By *any* means necessary."

18

———

The echo of something falling in the kitchens made Mason pause halfway up the stairs. He'd thought everyone had long ago gone to bed. Jessi had checked on him where he'd been meticulously packing away every scrap of paper in Tamina Peyton's former office space. Their previous excitement at having seen each other after six months had cooled in the face of spectators. One of them being his very disapproving mother. Once in the house, Jessi all but disappeared. Having found him occupied, she'd slipped away before he could stop her.

Darkness made the hall a shadowed void. A faint glow at the end broke through the gloom. Mason eased down, listening. Another clatter followed a soft mutter. Mason pushed on the left side of the double swinging doors. Jessi froze, a small pan halfway to the stove.

The light from a single candle next to the stove shimmered in the golden red of her hair. Earlier, the unruly curls had been pulled back. Now they framed her face, falling past her shoulders. She straightened, setting the pan on the nearest burner, while tugging at the thin navy silk tank top she wore.

Loose cotton pants hung from her slender hips, the tie dangled from the front, undone.

Mason tried to ignore the way the silk hugged every curve of her torso, leaving nothing to the imagination. If he touched her, the fabric would be as warm as her skin. He shoved his hands into his pockets and leaned against the counter opposite the stove.

"What are you doing?"

She tucked hair behind her ear. "I wanted a skillet fried cheese sandwich."

"What is that?"

A loaf of bread landed on the counter next to him, along with a block of yellow cheese. "You've never had one?"

Mason turned and leaned onto the counter, his weight braced on his forearms. "No, I don't think so. Why didn't you ask Sal to make you one?"

She shrugged, cutting even slices from the bread and then the cheese. "I've cooked for myself all these years, asking someone else to do it seems... lazy. I'm not going to wake him up at ten at night because I want a hot sandwich I'm capable of making myself."

"Huh, didn't know I'd been lazy my whole life." Her smoky green eyes widened, her jaw shifted. Mason laughed and bumped his hip against hers. "I'm teasing. I don't cook. Never have, never care to. But Kevin does, he's the same way as you. If he wants it, he makes it."

"I guess this means you don't know where to find anything in here then." The knife in her hand slid through the block of cheese twice.

"What do you need?"

"Butter, or oil, whichever one isn't a solid at the moment."

Mason tapped his fingers on the stone counter and glanced around the heavily shadowed room. He pushed away and went in search of the elusive butter. After much lid lifting and jar opening, he found some. Jessi slathered the rich yellow cream onto four slices of bread. Seconds later, two sandwiches were sizzling in a hot pan. She flipped and patted them with a spatula, humming in appreciation. Mason watched, curious.

Using the handle for leverage, Jessi tilted the pan and slid the cooked sandwiches onto two plates. She set the pan to side and leaned across the distance, placing a plate in front of Mason. He stared down at the crusty golden bread.

The bread crunched when Jessi bit into it. She made a sound that left him staring, wanting to consume her mouth the way she devoured the food.

She motioned with greasy fingertips. "Try it."

Somehow he kept himself from saying *I'd rather try you* and tasted the sandwich. Rich buttery flakes and savory melted cheese burst with flavor in his mouth. He stared down at the sandwich while he chewed, looking it over. So simple. Amazing.

"Good?" she asked after taking another bite.

He nodded. "Very good."

"It's even better with tomato soup or left-over heated pasta sauce to dip it in. It's very old from what my mom used to say when she made it for us. Pre-cataclysm."

"Not many non-basic foods can claim that distinction."

"Nope. She said this and chicken and dumplings. Best comfort foods ever."

And after today, or rather the past six months if he were honest, Jessi would crave a comforting food. When nothing but crumbs remained on his plate, Mason settled his back against the counter and crossed his arms. Jessi jumped to sit on the counter next to him, her bare feet kicking as she finished off the rest of hers.

"Why were you working in the greenhouse this morning?" he asked.

She dropped a piece of crust on the plate. "I couldn't sit around doing nothing. I like working, you know that."

"I'm surprised they let you. It's not socially acceptable for the Guardians spouse to do labor jobs."

Her fingers wrapped around the edge of the counter as she shrugged. "They didn't at first. I found greenhouses without anyone and worked alone. There's task sheets in every one, I just went off those."

"I know about the sheets. I implemented them to cut down on wasted time trying to figure out daily responsibilities."

"Yes, well, when someone found me working alone, they felt bad and invited me to join them. I was thankful. I miss Wilson. I miss my bees. I missed Sesay. I missed you. I've been alone for almost six months."

Mason tamped down guilt that rose thick and uncomfortable in his stomach. "I'm sorry about that. I'd hoped Raina would help."

"Raina is part of your society. She did her best, and I'm thankful for her too, but... there was little for us to talk about."

Mason tilted his head and regarded her. "I'm from the same social standards, you don't have trouble talking to me."

"I don't know, you're... different from her. Maybe your job has changed how you see people."

Mason didn't like to think Raina had somehow viewed Jessi as less than. The woman didn't seem the type to look down on others. "She didn't treat you as an equal?"

"Yes, she did," Jessi assured, holding up her hand. "She's the most polite person I've ever met. She became my friend, and helped me learn everything I could, but she's still the daughter of an Arch Guardian, and I'm still the daughter of a nobody Westican. We didn't always know how to act around each other, and I certainly couldn't go with her to any functions except a few plays. I buried myself in helping with whatever I could for her to keep busy."

The memory Jessi painted of her time in Sziveria left Mason frowning. "I can't believe you stayed."

"Every time I was able to speak to you on the radio, you said you were trying to make it back. It was enough." Her words were soft. "What did I have to go back to? At least by staying I could still help you, like we agreed."

Mason shook his head. Why did he want her reason to be more than the arrangement they'd made? "I should have been here, not off—"

"Doing your job? Serving your country?" She heaved a sigh, her fingers knotting together on her lap. "Mason, really. I'm a big girl, I was fine. Did it suck, yeah, it did, but no more than living alone out in the middle of nowhere would have. At least I had something to look forward to."

Her beautiful green eyes met his stare. The soft flickers from the candle danced across the smooth planes of her face. Mason wanted slide between her legs, wrap her around him and taste her. Everywhere. He drew in a shaky breath and pushed away from the temptation. If, and it was a big *if*, she ever allowed him to do more than kiss her, it wouldn't be on a kitchen counter.

At least not tonight.

Dragging his fingers through the long length of his hair, he took another step away. "I better go finish packing up that office. I don't trust my mother, or that woman."

"Does she really work for you?"

"She works for my mother." Mason didn't want to divulge the plans he expected his mother had for Miss Tamina Peyton.

"Oh." Jessi slipped down from the counter. The silk of her shirt whispered along the stone, her feet padded softly to the tile floor. "Can I use the courtyard greenhouse for Ses...Wul..." She sighed. "My dog?"

"Of course. This is your house too, you can do whatever you need. And you can still call him Sesay."

She shook her head and gave a sheepish smile. "It seems, I

don't know, wrong, now that I know he has an actual name. I'm working on getting used to it."

Mason let her slip by with sheer force of will. The light caught the full mounds of her breasts through the silk and he almost groaned. Yep, throwing useless junk in boxes was just the distraction he needed.

HOURS LATER, WITH EXHAUSTION FROM OVER A WEEKS' WORTH OF traveling finally catching up to him, Mason piled the last box in one of the third-floor rooms. With low ceilings slanting toward the floor level windows, the rooms were only used in overflow situations. The room he'd chosen specifically had once been his art studio, with a door only he had a key to. Once all the original documents were in his hands, he'd begin the arduous task of seeing if his suspicions were right concerning Tamina and his mother. Mason made sure to lock both the room door and the door at the bottom of the stairs leading to the third floor.

He was halfway down the hall when a muffled cry and soft scratching sound made him stop. The scratching intensified with a whine. The cry shifted into a desperate shout. Mason squinted in the near black corridor. What pale gray light did manage to filter through the glass ceiling two stories above didn't provide enough light to make out much more than the glint of the occasional doorknob.

Mason eased along the thick carpeted hall, focused on the noise. A door vibrated. The whining scratches grew louder. He slid his palm along cool wood and waited. Nothing. He went to the next door. Another strenuous cry wailed through the darkened corridor. The wood shuddered against his fingertips. He doubted some nightmare creature kicked at the door while simultaneously torturing whoever was within the room. Which meant…

Jessalyn.

Mason snatched the door open. A gray flurry of chaos spun in desperate yips, jumping between him and the bed nestled between two windows on the other side of the room. Moonlight speared across the darkness. Shadowed shapes fell into focus as Mason moved deeper into the room, his fingers held out for Wulf. The dog's wet nose touched and then he was off again in a prance of motion. He stopped at the edge of bed and whined in desperation.

Tangled in sheets, and from what he could see from the meager moonlight, drenched in sweat, Jessi fought an imaginary struggle, very real in her mind. The pajama pants she'd been wearing earlier were in a heap on the floor. Dark silk strained across her breasts, her back arching on a cry. Above her head her arms flexed, like someone held them pinned.

Every instinct in Mason urged him to wake her. To jump on the bed and snatch her from whatever nightmare held her captive. But he knew doing so would result in nothing except a scream, a fight, a worse situation altogether.

He kicked off his shoes, undid his belt and removed his pants, and knelt onto the bed. Moving slowly, he whispered as he lowered himself beside her. He brushed her thigh. She whimpered, jerked, rolled in on herself. Mason didn't let the action stop him. In slow movements, meant to comfort, he kept a gentle pressure from her thigh to her hip, and on to her ribs. All the while he moved close, speaking her name in shushed tones.

The mattress lurched under the weight of Wulf. The dog shimmied along the blankets, forcing his muzzle under Jessi's hands. Jessi's reaction, and the wolf's shift to move nearer, spoke of a trained response. Wulf had been taught when Jessi needed him, and tonight, nothing the canine had done worked. Mason kept from pulling Jessi tightly to him in a need to feel her safe in his arms.

Every muscle in her body tense, she rolled in on herself again with another whimper. Mason caressed a hand to her hip, stroked in gentle, soothing motions. His jaw clenched until his teeth ground together. Had Cora become a survivor like Jessi, this would have been her future. Nights spent a prisoner to memories no one should have had to endure, awake or asleep. Would she have spent them alone, only screams to keep her company, with no one to help release her from their vicious grip? They'd never know.

But Jessi wasn't alone. Mason whispered soothing words into her ear, encouraged her to leave the terror behind.

Breath by ragged breath, she calmed. Her tear-streaked cheeks turned to the ceiling, but her eyes remained closed. Mason laid on the pillow beside her, his palm on the soft silk covering her flat stomach. Wulf's fur brushed along the tips of his fingers as he settled into Jessi's side. A body length shudder wracked her frame. Both dog and man shifted closer, securing her between them.

Mason stroked his fingers through her damp hair. "Your guardians are here," he whispered against her temple. "Sleep. You're safe."

19

A SPEAR OF LIGHT FORCED JESSI FROM LANGUID SLEEP. SHE groaned on a stretch. Her hip and shoulder brushed something solid, warm. Jessi froze. Hazy memories from the middle of the night surfaced. Fear, pain, the remnants of time spent in terror. Ses… no *Wulf*'s fur in her hands. Softly spoken words against her temple, her cheek, her neck. A sense of comfort. Taking a breath, Jessi glanced over her shoulder.

Half covered by a sheet, in a white cotton short sleeved shirt, Mason lay sound asleep on his back. Long strands of hair blanketed his pillow, shoulders and the mattress under his back. Jessi's fingers twitched to gather them together and let them flow across her hand. Her gaze ventured lower, over his wide chest, flat stomach, and… Gasping, she yanked the sheet and rose until her back hit the headboard. The wood reverberated with a loud clap against the wall. She flinched as Mason stirred, the sheet drawing taut across his thighs and hips, making her heart pound. For reasons she knew, and others she didn't understand…

Mason breathed in deep through his nose, flexed his muscular arms above his head on a stretch and muttered, "What is it?"

The action did little to hide what was happening below his hips. Jessi knew what was going on *there*. And when Mason made no effort to do anything but lay relaxed, half asleep, Jessi wondered why. The last time a man with an erection was near her, he couldn't stop himself from using it.

Mason opened his eyes on a frown, his focus on her. She swallowed, her gaze flickering to the skewed sheet and back to him.

He sniffled and scratched his stomach below his navel. "It's a morning guy thing, honey. Nothing I can do about it. How are you feeling?"

Somehow Jessi forced her attention to his face. In the bright morning sun, the shadow of a beard looked at odds with the neatly groomed section lining his jaw and mouth. "Feeling?"

He folded his arms behind his head, his cheek resting against his defined bicep. "Yeah. You weren't doing all that great when I came in here early this morning."

Jessi rubbed the soft top sheet between her fingers and frowned. "I had a nightmare."

"Yes."

And he'd laid beside her. All night. Without doing anything more than wrapping her in his strength and security. Jessi let that information sit for a moment, continuing to ignore the erect mass beneath the sheet. "Where's Wulf?"

"I put him out in the courtyard just before sunrise." He lifted his head, shifting his shoulders until his hair no longer pulled beneath his arms. "I think Deklan, the man who was keeping him, let them out around that time. He seemed a bit surprised when no other dogs were there to greet him."

Worried, Jessi bit her lip. "Do you think he misses them?"

"No. I think he missed you more even if he does."

Despite every attempt to keep her attention anywhere else, Jessi couldn't seem to help looking at the sign of his arousal still on display. A gentle flutter started in her chest and worked south. Her fingers twisted in the sheet. "Um, how long do you stay like that... exactly?"

He removed one arm from behind his head and set it on his chest with a shrug. "I don't know, I don't normally count the minutes. Do you want me to leave?"

"No, I just..." She took a deep breath.

What did she want?

Feel free to explore any part of me you find curious. I won't stop you.

Mason's words, spoken what seemed like so long ago, in a kitchen she'd never see again, made Jessi's heart race. Would he let her? Jessi shifted, angling closer to him. Her eyes met his as she gathered courage. Her stomach flipped in a riot of nerves, yet her hand slid along her thigh, closer to him.

"I was wondering..." She licked at her suddenly dry lips. They were completely alone, with no threat of interruption. At least none that she knew of. He was safe. All she had to say was no, and she *knew* he'd never do more than she was willing. "Is the offer still open? To, you know, explore you?"

Something flashed in his eyes and he stilled. When he didn't say a word, only flexed his jaw and stared at her, Jessi fidgeted. Maybe asking to touch him hadn't been such a great idea.

"I'm sorry." She took a deep breath and looked away.

Whatever had been holding him captive seemed to break. He blinked, rubbed a hand down his face, and exhaled in a heavy puff. "No, I'm sorry, I just, I wasn't expecting... you know." When she nodded, he met her gaze. The pale gray of his irises seemed liquid silver in the shaft of light crossing over the bed. "My body is yours, honey. Always."

The declaration made her heart ache. Jessi wanted to give the same to him, but fear stopped her. Deep inside, she knew Mason would never hurt her. However, the scars on her back and the ones no one could see, made her nod in silence.

"Come here," he whispered, wrapping an arm around her hips.

He pulled her close, until her hip rested in his side. The sheet slid away, replaced by his touch along the exposed length of her thigh. In nothing more than a thin silk tank top and shorts so short they were closer to underwear, Jessi *should* have felt exposed. Instead, the scraps of fabric seemed too much against the rapid flush along her skin. His shoulder lifted, a quick flex of muscle that sent her leaning over his chest. Before she could contemplate much, his mouth flitted across hers.

The gentle kiss flared the desire hidden beneath the surface of her confusion. She closed her eyes and smoothed her hand down his warm, solid chest, to his stomach, where she slipped under his shirt. Muscles contracted beneath her touch and the faintest shift of his hips told her he *wanted* her to keep going. But he did nothing, except brush his lips to hers in soft, non-aggressive flutters.

Jessi was the one to touch her tongue to his lips. She was the one to slide inside his mouth, take the kiss deeper, harder. More. At the edge of the sheet, she hesitated. By the pulse of excitement rising within her, if she touched him, she wouldn't want to stop.

His fingers clenched her upper leg, forced her closer until she either laid across chest, her pelvis to his hip, or slid lower, hugging his thigh with her legs. Since she wanted to be as close as she could feasibly get without crawling into his skin, she slid her body along his, gathered courage, and continued her quest south. Her mouth slanted over his, pulling him further into a haze of passion with her.

Jessi didn't want anything between her touch and his skin, so when she encountered boxers, she growled in frustration. The deep rumble of his laugh shook his chest and exited in her mouth. She smiled and then gasped when he shifted in a quick jerking motion and then took her hand and guided her fingers around his heavy, rigid length. Her eyes flew open and she froze. Pulling her mouth free, she found herself staring into his eyes. Amusement danced within them, but the tension in his cheeks and along his jaw spoke of his restraint to remain motionless, like her.

"Well?" he asked with a side smile.

Jessi tried to remember to breathe. Her heart pounded heavily, competing with his against her chest and, yes, wow, in the thick vein right under her palm. She squeezed, she couldn't seem to help it, and was rewarded by a shudder from him.

"Keep doing that, and you'll have a mess on your hand," he breathed into her ear.

A delicious shiver raced from her toes straight to her center. She slid her hand along his satiny length, marveling in the way he responded. How the simple, seduction motion made her *feel*. Sexy. Wanted. All woman, and *all* his. The realization burst inside her, like a lock snapping open.

She released him and straddled his stomach, her mouth finding his in a hot, open-mouthed kiss. His hands kneaded her rear, making motions to slide under the fabric of her shorts, only to stop and move back. Disappointment left her anxious for his denied touch. She tore her mouth free, her fingers digging into the long length of hair at his temples. If she didn't tell him exactly what she needed, what she *wanted*, he'd do nothing. The knowledge made her bold.

Jessi kissed a trail from the corner of his mouth to his ear. "I want you." She shifted her hips back, pressing against his hard length until his entire frame shook under her. "Please."

"How?" he breathed, kissing the sensitive skin where her neck met her shoulders, licking a trail along her collar bone. "Like this?"

She breathed in the clean, woodsy scent of him and closed her eyes. While she'd always figured she'd want to be in charge if she ever found herself in this moment, her lack of a positive sexual experience made her realize she wanted him to lead. Jessi needed him to show her how good they could be. "No, not like this."

Mason didn't waste time. He rolled them, rising onto his arms as his hips settled between her legs. Jessi drew her knees in, ignored the flicker of panic as he pushed his pelvis to hers and his arousal pressed against her. He lifted and reached between them, helped her remove her shorts. But instead of immediately driving into her like she anticipated, he caressed his hands up her hips, to her sides, forcing the silk top she wore up until her breasts were exposed. His chest settled on her stomach as he licked a wet trail up to her breasts.

Breath caught in Jessi's throat. His tongue swirled her nipple before sucking it into his mouth. A shaft of pleasure blossomed from her breast. On instinct, her hips lifted. He shifted his attention to her other breast while reaching between them. His fingers slipped along her slick, tender flesh with ease, forcing another shocked gasp from her. A sharp, intense yearning followed his touch, driving some hidden force deep inside her. She whimpered, twisted, needing more.

Mason worked her into a state of near frenzy, until moisture coated her skin and something, she didn't know what, hovered outside her grasp. She writhed and begged, tugging at his damp hair and ran her feet along his sweat slickened thighs. Only then did he finally push into her, and much to her shock, she lifted her hips to meet him, to take him deeper.

He rose above her and pressed his damp forehead to hers. "Talk to me."

Jessi slid her hands under his shirt, her fingers digging into the muscles flexing along his back. "What... am I..." His hips dipped, shifting his angle. An unexpected ripple of pleasure careened through her body. She squeezed her eyes shut on a throaty moan and desperately sought the sensation again. "Oh wow... supposed to say?"

Mason dropped his head to beside hers on the pillow. His fingers tangled in the hair at her shoulder. Short, frantic pants brushed by her ear, increasing her excitement. "Faster? Slower?"

"I don't..." Her teeth clenched as she neared a precipice. "I don't know."

He moved faster, harder. Pulled her further into the sensations of *them*. Of skin, sweat, hot breath and even hotter desire. Every nerve in Jessi's body cried for relief. Every muscle bunched, strained, urged and begged, until finally something yielded and she crashed over the edge, crying out a sound she'd never made before. In the myriad of passions coursing through her veins, she registered his hard thrust and tension filled body. The muffled exhale of his release.

For a moment neither of them moved. Then he made to pull free and Jessi locked her ankles over his tailbone and hugged his back. The thought of him leaving her empty, of his weight gone, made her want to cry.

"No, please, not yet," she somehow said.

"Honey, I'm too heavy to stay on you," he whispered, and brushed his lips near her ear.

"Please."

He sighed, dropping his weight to one side as much as possible. And then, locked in her, still filling her, he began to move in slow, easy circles.

"Oh, oh," she breathed, lifting her hips, taking him deeper. Little tendrils from her climax still pulsed at her center, made more intense by his movement. "What are you doing?"

"I can't be in you and not move."

He flipped his hair over his shoulder with a heavy toss of his head and then kissed her neck. His tongue traced the delicate skin from her ear to her shoulder and she moaned, turning her head and giving him better access. The intensity at her center grew, dragged her back into the bottomless void of need, where only Mason seemed to exist. Still he moved slow, unhurried, shallow, dragging each thrust to the point of madness. Jessi twisted, screamed as a wave more powerful than the first burst through her body.

Spent, and lost in amazement, Jessi stared at the shadows playing across the ceiling. She wanted to cry with relief, and laugh with joy. "So… that's sex."

"No." He shifted, settling his weight on his elbows and cupped her face, forcing her to meet his eyes. His cheeks were flushed, sweat ran in small drops from his temples. "No, Jessalyn, that was making love. I could never just have sex with you."

She covered his hand and lifted her chin. For the first time in five years, her name didn't make her want to curl in on herself, reminding her of what she'd lost. Now he'd given her something so much more, something incredible, and special. She knew he saw the tears his words brought, but she didn't care. He gave her a sweet, tender, full kiss. She wanted to ask if making love meant he loved her, but she didn't dare. She wasn't ready to admit the truth of her own heart. Doing so meant he had a piece of her no one else had been able to break yet.

"Thank you," she whispered, kissing him again.

He rubbed his thumb along her chin and smiled. "Come on, let's go get a shower. I'll show you how fun that can be now."

20

HAVEN CITY
   Haven City Enforcement Services
   East Street Division

JONATHON HUNTER TAPPED THE THICK, HANDMADE PAPER invitation delivered to his office against the edge of his desk. Across from him Primary Guardian Wintersfall stared in question. Of course, while in a professional capacity, the Guardian was simply Sean Blackbain. Jonathon had a different rank as well, one of Master Tribunii, embroidered in golden letters on his Enforcement jacket.

That rank didn't matter right now either.

The invitation, he knew, was a double-edged sword. His professional services were needed by his personal friends. Again.

This time however, he didn't mind so much. Because this time it involved a violent murder he was unable to have any part in solving, and no means of finding closure, even for himself. He still had to keep from thinking too hard about

Cora Dandridge no longer being part of the world. Part of his life.

The invitation in question was to a Guardianship ascension celebration party. The rank had been approved to pass from father to son. Since the ranking was of a Shield position, those lower than Master and not a personal family friend, weren't usually invited. As Key Guardian Asherwick, Jonathon's lower rank left him somewhat on the fringe of social hierarchy. Not that he minded all that much. He investigated enough of them to know *Guardian* was a relative term in their mind.

Jonathon sighed and tossed the invitation onto the stack of documents he was too annoyed to sift through. "Why do you need me to go to this party?"

"All of us will be at Kyn Manor for the huge marriage celebration Dandridge's mother is hosting. It's something ridiculous like a month long event. Or maybe it's six weeks. Anyway, I know you've declined to attend…"

"I can't be gone from my position for six weeks," Jonathon felt the need to point out.

"Right, and Merrick won't be in Haven City to attend this event, which has some big names who we've learned have already confirmed. By then, news of Mason's marriage to Jessalyn Silverna should be common enough knowledge to see if it's making anyone nervous."

Now it was Jonathon's turn to stare. "You want me to listen for… gossip?"

"Isn't rumor chasing part of your job?" Before Jonathon could bristle at the question, Sean added, "I know it's part of mine. Rumors can lead to a thread, and right now…" He sighed, pulled his fingers through his too long hair. "We really need something. Anything. We were gone for too long."

Jonathon shrugged. "That may be a good thing, who knows. They're comfortable again."

"So will you go?"

"Yes, I'll go. But you know I may not hear anything useful."

"I understand. What about the name check?"

Jonathon opened the middle drawer to his desk and pulled out a file. "Everything public about every Silverna in Haven City. I have no means of gathering intel country wide, you'll need a SNID operative for that."

Sean accepted the folder. "*That* wouldn't raise any flags."

"Haven't made any friends over there yet?"

Sean frowned and tapped the folder against his thigh. "Does Silverna seem familiar to you?"

"I was thinking it did actually, yes. But I can't place it, and I've tried," Jonathon admitted with a frown of his own.

"Me either, which bothers me." He sighed and shook his head. "Maybe it'll come to one of us."

"Did you see Phipps Greier was removed from his rank as Shield Guardian Enbrackon?"

Sean nodded, a small smile playing at his lips. "I did read about that. Who is the new First Prefect for HCES?"

"We don't have one assigned yet. Wade Kenrick is the interim."

Surprise flitted across Sean's face. "He's younger, and not even ranked."

"If you'll recall, his mother is Arch Guardian Eslainte."

"Interesting."

"Extremely."

"Anymore murders ruled as suicides?" Sean asked.

Jonathon couldn't help but let a sarcastic laugh free. "I don't know. I'm not given anything that isn't immediately recognizable as a violent crime. I see so much blood in a day I've almost decided to become a vegetarian."

"An escalation in violence in the last six months?"

Jonathon wiped a weary hand down his face. "Violence, suicide, overdoses, rapes, kidnappings, thefts, human trafficking, all of it. Without a leader, a lot of Enforcers were either bought, or chose to ignore what didn't immediately affect their street. Less work that way."

Sean leaned forward, his brows pinched. "And the son of Arch Guardian Eslainte, the Guardian over all the Medical Scientists, myself and those who work here included, has been named the interim of Haven City's Enforcers. Either this is very good, or very bad."

Jonathon smoothed his hands across his desk. "Or very neutral. I'm trying not to read too much into things right now. I don't know anything about Kenrick other than he flew through the Enforcement ranks, on his own, quickly. He has an exemplary investigation record, an excellent leadership record, and an excellent record of being able to honestly supply burden of proof for convictions."

"Sounds like someone else on the Enforcement Services team."

Jonathon sighed and shook his head. "I'm good. I don't have any desire to be anywhere but where I'm at."

Sean's expression changed, he focused on Jonathon with an intensity that made him want to squirm. "How are you doing?"

The grief he'd kept carefully locked away threatened to rise. For a split second, Jonathon considered lying, to pretend to misunderstand the nature of Sean's question. However, the effort would be useless. As a Sympath, the man would know his lie the second it left his lips. "Better than Dandridge, I'm sure."

"Everyone is better than Dandridge. But that's not what I asked."

A shaft of anger pierced through Jonathon's stomach, making his teeth clench. "You aren't my Medical Scientist, Wintersfall. I don't need you to look after me."

"I know, I'm asking as a friend. We were all friends with her." Compassion softened the edges of his features as he met

Jonathon's stare. "Some of us were more, or had been more, at one time."

More. Yes, the wicked woman had wanted more. More than he could give. More than he was willing. And now he had none. No more sultry laughter, playful teasing, her sexy smiles and shameless flirting. All gone, because he wasn't willing to give her a reason to stay. He wasn't able to give her the *more* she desperately wanted from him.

Jonathon took a grounding breath. "I'm fine. She was a friend, an informant when she felt like it, but a friend all the same."

Sean stood, his amber eyes filled with concern. "If you keep this bottled in, you're going to lose it, and it's not going to be pretty. You'll end up having to apologize to someone."

"Thanks for the warning."

Sean left after a curt nod, folder in hand. Jonathon leaned back in his chair, locking his hands behind his head. Every day he dealt with loss, pain, violent ends and heartache. When it came to Cora's case, he had nothing to offer except a few bits of information to something he didn't understand yet. None of it would bring her back. Nothing would change what he hadn't considered important at the time.

Scrubbing a hand down his face, Jonathon pulled forward the latest file to land on his desk and lost himself in something he *could* control.

21

Kyn Manor

WRAPPED IN A TOWEL, JESSI RESTED HER ELBOW ON HER KNEE, chin propped in her hand, and observed her very naked husband drying his hair. She'd helped him run a comb through the length while conditioner softened the collection of knots their active morning had created. Jessi smiled, shifting on the mattress. The action drew attention to parts of her body that were sore for all the right reasons, instead of all the wrong ones. All thanks to the gloriously nude man wandering around her bedroom.

"I'm going to have to bring some clothes in here," he muttered, toeing at his discarded pants near the end of the bed.

Flutters danced in her stomach. "You're going to stay with me?"

His hand paused mid dry and he stared at her. "Where else would I be?"

"I don't know, your room?"

"Which is on the other side of the house." He frowned and

glanced around as if noticing her space for the first time. "Why are you over here anyway? This is a guest quarters, not a family suite."

Jessi leaned back on her elbows. "This is where your mother put me."

His attention shifted to her. "Would you rather I be in my own room?"

"Not if you want to be here with me."

Before she could do much more than squeal out a laugh, Mason's huge form dropped over her on the bed. His weight rested on the edge of the mattress at his hips, between her legs, his arms boxed her in. The towel he'd been holding flew away. Damp tendrils of hair brushed across the exposed skin of her chest and up to her jaw as he rose over her.

"I think I've established how much I *want*," he whispered along her cheek. "And now that I know my mother saw fit to give a little message concerning you, I'll make sure we have this entire corridor to ourselves when her guests arrive."

Jessi smoothed the long, wet lengths of his hair away from his face and behind his ears. "I don't mind that she put me here. I was able to have my nightmares in—"

His lips on hers silenced her words. "We'll stay right here, I'll rename the hallway Primary Guardian Kynhaven's Personal Quarters, if I have to. I want all the privacy we can have. When you scream, it won't be in fear, but in passion, and I don't want anyone to hear it but me."

Desire swelled in Jessi's heart. She smiled, smoothing her thumbs along his cheekbones. "You can't promise that, but I appreciate the determination."

He nuzzled her neck. "Mm, determination, that's an interesting thought, isn't it?"

A delicate shiver raced along Jessi's spine. "If you show anymore this morning, they're going to send a search party to come look for us."

"Trust me, everyone finds our disappearance this morning

perfectly normal. A newly married couple separated for six months? They won't blink an eye if we don't leave this room for a week."

Jessi laughed and hugged him. "A week? Surely not."

He licked a trail to her collarbone. "Oh yes. Would you complain?"

"Would I be fed?" She gasped when he bit gently where her shoulder met her neck, turning her head to give him better access. The pulsing need he'd stroked to life with almost embarrassing ease all morning had her legs parting to better accept his shifting weight.

"Who needs food?" He groaned when she lifted her hips, the towel around her body trapped between them.

Another laugh rippled from Jessi's chest. She wrapped her legs around his hips and hugged him close. The words *I love you* almost slipped from her lips. Almost.

She sighed and pushed at his chest, unwinding from his body. Real life waited for them beyond the little cocoon they'd enclosed themselves in. "I need food, silly man. And I don't see your mother allowing you to stay much longer locked away with me in here. I'd rather not have *that* interruption."

Mason echoed her sigh and rose. With a frown of disappointment, he rolled and fell to the bed next to her. Rising on her elbows, she brushed curls from her face.

"You're going to stay right there while I get clothes on." When he went to reach for her, she leapt up on a screech, dancing away from his grasp. "No! I'm serious. I'm hungry, I know my dog is wondering where I am, and so is the rest of the house."

"Fine," he grumbled, grabbing at her discarded towel and throwing it over his waist. "I'll be good."

Jessi looked him over. The towel may have covered some of him, but he was still temptation in muscled flesh and eyes that looked at her with heated promise. Later. Yes, later she'd explore. She'd gather the nerve to touch him in all the ways he'd touched her this morning. He'd encouraged, but she'd been too caught up in how he'd made her *feel* to do much more than stare at the beauty that was his body. And oh when he moved… all fluid grace and restrained control. She quickly looked away.

Later.

She turned from him, pressing a hand to her aching chest. Her husband. Hers to bring pleasure to in the same way he did for her. Hers to *love.* But for how long? She swallowed the lump in her throat. Made her feet move to the dresser. Their length of time together didn't matter, couldn't. However long they had, she'd make use.

Silk billowed around her ankles as she stepped into a pale peach skirt. When she rose from pulling the skirt to her hips, the odd awareness of something tracing along her back made her freeze. From her right hip to her left shoulder, Mason trailed what must have been the longest visible scar. She didn't know, she'd never been brave enough to even try to look at what had become of her after every knife slice had healed. Jessi trembled, from the caress, and from the prickly numbness of her mutilated flesh.

The tender brush of his lips on her shoulder made her eyes close. His hands slipped around her waist and pulled her tight to his chest. Jessi rested her fingers over his, and let her weight fall back. Wisps of his drying hair fell over her shoulder, caressed in soft silky waves to her breast as he pressed a kiss to her temple.

"You are so brave, and I am… humbled that you let me love your beautiful body." He splayed his palms over her stomach, his fingers tangling with hers.

Jessi didn't fight the tears spilling from between her lashes. "You're the only man who could."

Forcing her eyes open, she reached for the top drawer. She pulled out the small bag with his ring, holding it by the strings on her index finger. He took the bag, but didn't step from her, didn't allow any space between their bodies.

A man stood at her back, skin to skin, and no panic welled within her. The realization made her blink in wonder. She wanted to turn, to wrap herself around Mason, to shout the victory of the moment. Trust was an amazing thing, she grasped, and Mason had hers completely, without question.

Silver glinted in the bright sunlight streaming into the room. The bag fell to the floor forgotten.

"Will you put it on me?" He rested his right hand back on her stomach, the ring resting on his left palm.

Jessi licked her lips and took the ring with trembling fingers. "I'm afraid," she admitted, more to herself than to him. "That once I put this on you, I'll want you to wear it forever."

He hugged her tighter, dropping a cheek to her head. "I will wear it forever. You're my wife, always."

"For another five months," she corrected, slipping the ring over his knuckles.

"No," he whispered into her hair. "Always."

22

———

"WHY IS YOUR HAIR SO LONG?"

Mason flipped pages over in the ledger book he was trying to focus on, lines blurring together. "What?"

Jessi gathered the length of hair from his shoulders to his back, the weight falling in flutters between his shoulders. When had she left the couch by the window to stand behind him? Mason braced his forearms on the edge of the desk and tried to glance over his shoulder, but her hold on his hair stopped the movement.

"What..." He tried again and she released enough pressure to at least let him lean back and meet her curious jade green stare. "What are you doing?"

"You kept tossing your head, like your hair was bothering you, I'm pulling it back."

Honestly, he rarely noticed when his hair became annoying anymore. Usually he kept the mass pulled back in some manner, but the morning had escaped him. For rather pleasing reasons all around. "Oh. Well, thank you."

She kissed his temple and then secured his hair into a ponytail. "My pleasure." She let the tresses flow through her fingers before settling the weight of her hip on the desk next to him. "Are you going to answer my question?"

"What was it again?"

A smile teased her lips. "Why do you keep your hair long?"

A knot formed in his chest. Mason redirected his attention back to the ledger. Little doodles ran along the edges, of a mouth curved into a sensual smile, of eyes sparkling with laughter and the promise of passion, made him blink. When had he done all that?

Mason dropped the pencil and rubbed his face with both his hands. "I am losing my mind."

Jessi's forehead creased. She leaned closer to the ledger. "Who is that? Well, who are the pieces?"

Mason leaned back in the seat and fixed her with a stare. "You're joking, right?"

"What do you mean?"

He clasped her hips and pulled. She squealed, tumbling onto his lap. "It's you, wife." He brushed curls away from her neck and kissed the exposed skin. "Apparently I can't stop thinking about you."

She wrapped her arms around his shoulders. "Why are you ignoring my question?"

On a sigh, he rested his forehead against her temple. "It's..." *Hard. The answer hurts. It makes me remember what I've lost, what I'll never get back.* "Silly."

"I doubt that."

Mason wrapped one of her loose, vivid red curls around his index finger. His heart squeezed. "When we were little, I'm talking three or four, my mother had my hair cut very short, in one of those little boy cuts. At the time, Cora's was, I don't know, longer, I don't remember how long. Anyway, when we came home she took one look at me and had a fit. A couple hours later, Sal found her on the kitchen floor with a pair of his kitchen shears. She'd sliced all her hair off, right down to her scalp."

"No!" Jessi gasped.

Mason couldn't help but laugh at the memory. "Oh yes. She told my mother we were *twins*, and twins were the same, no matter what. My mother acquiesced. I didn't get my hair cut short again for five years. Cora did the exact same thing. Mother decided she'd rather have a longer haired boy than a short haired girl. I tried to cut my hair again when I went into training with the Wolvenguard team."

Jessi's eyes glittered. "She cut it again."

He nodded. "Yep, up past her ears. She looked ridiculous. Cora didn't have one of those faces that does well with short hair. So." He waved a hand at his head. "Long hair."

She pulled the weight of the ponytail over his shoulder, toying with the ends. "I love your hair. I'm glad your sister made you keep it long."

"That's good," he said, surprised when his voice didn't crack from the tightness in his throat. "Because I don't know if I'll ever be able to cut it again."

Her lips brushed gently to his. "I don't ever want you to. Except, you know, to keep from going wild on me. Maybe a trim every couple years or so?"

Mason laughed against her mouth, her soft hair wrapping around his fist as he held her closer. "Sure, I don't think I'll let it get much longer."

She shifted on his lap to face the desk. Mason relaxed in the chair, letting his fingers glide down to exposed skin of her neck, to her shoulder and back. Distracted, she let him, but angled her head to give him better access. He smiled, his heart constricting in his chest. His wife. In every way imaginable now. He'd claimed her by name, and she'd claimed him by body. The urge to reach around, caress her hips, her breasts, to lift up her skirt and touch her in all the ways he'd learned she loved, had him taking a deep resisting breath. Anyone could walk in, since they hadn't locked the door.

"I can help you with this, you know," she said, tucking hair behind her ear. "If you'd like. There's something…" Her hands hovered over the edge of the ledger and she shook her head. "I don't know. Maybe nothing. I'd like to help, though."

Mason wrapped his arms around her waist and dropped his chin on her shoulder. "I want to say yes. Badly. However, you'll have to deal with Miss Peyton, and I don't think that's such a great idea."

"Don't think I can handle my own?"

Mason's mouth twitched with a smile. "I know you can. I'm more worried about how she'll behave and in turn speak about you. Defending against rumors is impossible."

Jessi shifted until she could look at him. "And you think she'll stay silent if I don't work with her?" She shook her head and sighed. "I don't think so. If she and your mother have decided to make me the anti-thesis to your society, nothing I do will make it any worse. Or better."

Of course, she was correct. As was her assessment of the situation. Eleanor Dandridge was determined to see Tamina Peyton painted in a light that made her a social beacon for their family name. While in turn, Jessi's Westican heritage would likely serve as a reminder of why all good mothers of ranked Sziverian's needed to look to their homeland to find suitable spouses.

Mason dropped his head to Jessi's back. "I'm so sorry I dragged you into such a mess."

Her chuckle shook her shoulders and rumbled in her back. "I'm not. I don't care. They don't know me, they don't know why I'm here, or how important it is. Does your mother even know? Would it change anything if she did?"

The subtle reminder for the true reason for Jessi being in Sziveria rubbed him wrong, just as it had days before. Had only a few days passed since she'd run from a greenhouse to see him? And here he'd been hoping their time together, in and out of sheets, would help her realize he wanted more from her than answers. If he were honest with himself, since the moment he'd met her. Despite everything she'd been through, she still managed to be light in darkness. Sunshine breaking through his misery. Somehow he needed to… what? Tell her? Would she even believe him?

"I doubt it." The words echoed his thoughts, but answered her question all the same. He leaned back and rubbed his hand across his brow. Jessi twisted until she sat sideways again, able to look at him. "Mother hasn't really acknowledged Cora's gone, yet."

"Isn't that… bad?"

"I don't know. I don't know much about dealing with grief," he admitted. "She lost her daughter, she didn't get to see the body. She and Cora were never close. To be unmarried and nearing thirty is unheard of in our country. To be from a ranked family and unmarried… it doesn't happen. If Cora visited, there were always suitors as guests waiting. Whenever mother visited Haven City, a parade of men came through the house as well to meet with my sister."

"But you were unmarried."

"I know, and again, rare." He picked up her hand and kissed her palm. "But now I'm married."

A wicked gleam danced in Jessi's eyes. "And your mother doesn't know how to cope."

Mason threw back his head and laughed. "No, she doesn't."

"Will you be all right dealing with Miss Peyton if I do the ledgers for you and have questions?" Her finger tapped against her chin. A frown pinched between her brows. "Though, I'm not sure I'm okay with that. I mean, she is technically competition in this strange world of yours, yes?"

"If we were only promised, yes." He pressed his lips to

her palm again. "But, we're *very* much husband and wife. You have nothing to fear of Tamina Peyton."

Pink flushed across her cheeks. Her chest rose in a heavy breath. "Well, good, then… I guess we've decided that."

Mason grinned and held her hand to his chest. "Look at us, solving problems as a married couple."

"Not the problem we need to be solving though." With a frown she slid from his lap.

Disappointment flared inside Mason. "Honey, I'm not—"

A hard knock disrupted his words. Before he could tell whoever was at the door to go away, it opened. Sean strode into the room, a folder in hand. Katria entered behind, her expression mimicking the somber attitude of her husband. She closed and locked the door.

Sean crossed the distance to the desk, his stern features softening some as he took in Jessi. He held out his hand. "Sean Blackbain, Primary Guardian Wintersfall. I'm Mason's team leader. You must be Jessalyn Silverna."

"Dandridge," Mason corrected.

A smile flickered across Sean's mouth and in his amber eyes. "Yes, of course. Dandridge. Guardianess Kynhaven, pleasure to finally meet you."

Jessi glanced in uncertainty at Mason before accepting Sean's extended hand. "Thank you."

Katria sat on the couch Jessi had occupied earlier in front of the window. A smile he wasn't used to seeing toyed on Kat's lips. "I know how overwhelming suddenly being a Guardianess can be. Let me know if you need any help adjusting."

Sean's attention shifted to his wife. "You haven't adjusted. You just ignore all social functions and niceties. If someone annoys you, you walk away." He made a turning motion with his fingers. "Just turn your back and… go."

Fire ignited in her brilliant blue eyes. She sat forward and held up her index finger. "I did that *one* time, Sean. *One*. You know what the alternative would have been. I told you what he said to me."

"How many times have we talked about this? Because you walked away, he continued to say it, and think it, and believe you were considering the offer, didn't he? I had a mess to handle and I wanted to kill the man myself." Sean dragged a hand through his shaggy hair and sighed. "You are stunning, Kat. I know when I walk in a room with you what men see."

She flicked her wrist toward him. "And I know what women see. This is why we should stay home!"

Mason rested his forearms on the desk and regarded the agitated couple. "You two have been home for what, five days? There's six weeks of events scheduled. Is someone going to die if they anger one of you? Do I need to make a timeout room?"

"Work out room, you mean?" Sean asked.

"Sure, I have one of those too."

Kat eased back on the couch, a different sort of smile toying at her lips. "Told you he was back."

Mason stared at his teammate. "What do you mean, I'm back?"

Sean tossed the folder on the desk with a grin. "You haven't been yourself for a long, long time." He held up his hands in defense when Mason scowled. "I understand, trust me. But we weren't sure how six weeks of happily married was supposed to look like if you weren't, well, happy."

"And you were going to… what?" Mason held his palms open in question. "Help make me happy if I wasn't?"

"No," Katria began, perching on the end of the couch as Sean joined her. "We were going to suggest you and your pretty bride figure out how to fake it. I mean, we fake enough that you should be a pro by now."

Sean tugged at the long braid hanging down Katria's back, his eyes filled with laughter. "I don't fake anything. Is there something you want to tell me?"

Katria slid her hand up Sean's forearm, a teasing smile playing at her lips. "Lie to you? Impossible."

Sean's body jerked and he snatched his arm away. Katria threw her head back and laughed.

Mason shook his head and sighed. He wondered when the couple would find an equilibrium, if ever. Then again, the playful nature they'd developed was something he admired in their relationship. "Do the two of you have a room yet?"

Amusement still bubbled from Katria. "Why, do you think we need one already?"

"Providing you aren't planning a repeat of six months ago," Mason said, casting her a look he hoped conveyed there would be no sneaky escapades while under his roof.

"Hey, that was our room, you could have knocked!" Kat defended.

Sean cleared his throat and leaned closer to her. "That was Kevin, love. Mason's talking about the library at the Barton's."

Red flared across Kat's pale cheeks. "Oh, right." She folded her hands in her lap, her smile considerably weaker than her previous one. "I promise, I'll be good at your house, Mason."

"Did you tell her to say that?" Mason asked, looking at Sean.

"No, I told her the Dowager doesn't need more ammunition. Which she'd have if we caused a scandal."

"And a reason to take away support from you," Katria added softly.

Jessi brushed a hand along his shoulder. Mason grasped her fingers in his and pulled her closer. The entire exchange with his teammates must have left her feeling like an outsider. Though he appreciated Sean and Kat behaving in their normal manner, as though Jessi were one of them. Which now she was, whether she realized it or not.

"About lack of support," Mason said with a long exhale.

Mason explained about Tamina Peyton, adding his suspicions. Jessi remained quiet through it all. Even from the distance of nearly the entire room, Sean seemed to sense her unease, watching her closely.

"Don't take this personally," Sean said to Jessi when Mason finished.

Jessi's fingers tightened around Mason's hand. "Hard not to."

"I understand. However, Sziverian culture and history are fiercely protected by our elder generation. They're not quite as bad as the Ruthenian's, but it's a close second. The Dowager feels her ancestral name will only be honored by marrying her son to another high-ranking Guardian family. To accept anything less would make her look weak to a society that holds family connections above all else.

"Eleanor Dandridge knows *nothing* about you, your family, how many generations, if any, Gen-Heir traits have passed on to." Sean shifted his focus to Mason. "It's driving her insane. You'd do well to remember, on top of losing her daughter, she's defending this house from every formerly ranked Sziverian in the country. Be somewhat kind to your mother."

Mason sat back heavily, the chair shifting with a squeak from the force. "I hate it when you do that."

Sean shrugged. "I know, but sometimes we don't look at everything from the correct perspective. Is your mother being nastier than necessary? Probably. Do you still need to be cognizant of her emotional state? Yes."

With a growl of frustration, Mason waved his hand in annoyance. "Be an adult and everything."

Sean laughed. "Yeah, because the life and death decisions you make as a Guardian are easier than dealing with your mother."

"Actually," Mason said with a depressing sigh. "I think they are."

. . .

JESSI CLOSED HER EYES AND LET OUT A SIGH OF RELIEF AS SHE strode down the dim corridor to the greenhouse entry. Far away from the study and the strangers who'd arrived and thrown her short lived little happy world back into chaos. She'd always known the passionate nights and days spent in quite companionship they'd had over the past three days would come to an end. Though she'd hoped they'd have had a bit longer. Three days for six months apart didn't seem quite fair. Then again, life never was, why should anything change now?

She reached for the glass door to the courtyard. On the other side, Wulf's big golden hope filled eyes stared at her. Warm air swirled around her as she pulled.

"Jessalyn!" a somewhat harried female voice called. "Wait!"

Jessi stopped with the door cracked enough to keep her dog from rushing inside. Not that his manners were so terrible, but being left behind when Eleanor collected her from the Merrick's, had given him some separation anxiety she was having to work through. He yipped and jumped in place, doing everything in his power to get her attention to return.

The stunning woman with long, glossy black hair and eyes a shade of blue Jessi hadn't known existed in humans, walked at a clipped pace down the narrow corridor. The plain black dress she wore didn't hinder her movements in the least. The skirt swayed around her ankles without getting tangled, while the bodice clung to her fit frame for freedom of motion. Her pale skin stood out in the near darkness, a soft porcelain to Jessi's warm ivory. Jessi didn't want to compare herself to this woman. With her striking looks and enviable confidence, how could she not?

The woman stopped, a small smile toying on her full lips.

"We weren't properly introduced. I'm Katria Blackbain, Sean's wife."

Jessi returned the shallow smile and nodded. "Yes, I gathered that. Is something wrong?"

If the forthright words stunned Katria, she didn't let it show. "Sean brought a list of names with him from Haven City. We were hoping you'd look them over, see if you recognized anyone."

Glancing at her desperate dog, Jessi opened the door and made a sweeping *enter* motion with her index finger. He rushed in as if he expected her to change her mind and then sat next to her.

Katria took a quick step back with a gasp. "What is that?"

"My dog, Se—, I mean Wulf. Mason told me he's a Ruthenarc Wolf."

"I heard my father talk about them, but… I've never seen one. Is he nice?" Katria took a tentative step forward.

"Yes, of course. Here, like this." Jessi held her palm out, fingers down to Wulf. The dry skin of his nose touched to her hand and then waited, expectantly, for her pat between his ears.

Katria repeated the process, a grin spreading across her pretty face as her fingers sank into the thick fur of Wulf's head. "Wow, he's so soft."

The dog sat, content to be loved on while Jessi tried to figure out if the woman had an angle for catching her alone, or if she'd simply come to ask Jessi to return. For a few quiet moments, Katria smoothed her fingers over Wulf's head and down the back to his neck with a small smile.

"I don't want you to think Sean was trying to belittle you by what he told Mason concerning the Dowager," Katria said softly, her too blue eyes rising to meet Jessi's stare. "Sean is a Sympath. He's constantly having to remind those of us who don't understand emotion like he does that others actually have them."

Katria chuckled quietly and shook her head. "Actually, sometimes he has to remind me I have them, too."

A lie formed on Jessi's tongue before she could stop. "I wasn't bothered."

Katria raised a brow. "Really?"

Not wanting Katria to see the sudden heat in her cheeks, Jessi stepped away from the light of the door. "I don't know anything about your culture, or this family. I met Eleanor Dandridge thirteen days ago. She hasn't spoken to me since ordering me to leave Raina's house."

"It's not *my* culture. I'm a first generation Sziverian. My parents were from Ruthenia and lived a quiet, solitary life. I didn't know much about Guardians until I joined the First Intelligence Office, and even less about rankings until I found myself married to Sean."

They fell in step side by side. Wulf ambled between them, the tips of his claws clicking on the hardwood. Worry nagged at Jessi. The half-opened door to the study loomed ahead and she slowed to a stop.

"Will Mason really become a social outcast if he stays married to me?" Jessi asked, hugging an arm around her waist.

"I don't know." Katria angled her body to meet Jessi's stare. "But I don't think he cares. Neither Mason nor Cora were bothered by societal standards. They forged their own paths, and I have no reason to believe that's changed for him."

Jessi chewed on her bottom lip. When he'd asked, she hadn't known the full ramifications of his decision. Would it have mattered if she had? After all, it was his society and he was a grown man. However, the idea of a life spent defending her, and their marriage, didn't seem an exciting future. What if he regretted the choice? Jessi took a deep breath. She was getting ahead of herself. They only had five more months.

Despite his talk of *always*, he'd made no indication of changing the parameters of their original contract.

A new knot formed in her chest. Five months didn't seem near long enough. What would happen to her after? She took a deep breath and exhaled away the anxiety. Thoughts for another time.

"Nothing happened when your husband married you?"

Katria chuckled and started back toward the study. "Our situation wasn't the same. Sean's family… they aren't old like Mason's, nor as respected. Traditional Sziverian Guardian families have a different set of rules I'm learning. At least for themselves. It's all very…" She waved her hand and sighed. "Outdated, I feel. Kevin's wife would be able to answer all this better than I can."

Jessi made Wulf wait until both she and Katria walked through the door before she allowed him to follow. Mason still sat behind the desk, a folder opened in front of him. Sean had moved to one of the plush chairs situated in front of the fireplace, turned to face the desk.

Katria crossed the distance to her husband, whose eyes tracked her progress with a faint amber glow. Sean accepted his wife's weight on his lap with a smile and an intimate ease that made Jessi turn away from the private moment. A twinge of envy spiked in her chest. Would she and Mason have the time to reach such a comfortable state? Did she even want them to? If she had to walk away, she'd be leaving so much more behind. Then again, what could be worse than leaving while he owned her heart?

Shaking her head, she chastised herself. She *had* to stop thinking about the future. Or more importantly, a future without Mason. Each day spent loving him had to be enough.

Wulf ambled up to Mason, setting his big head on Mason's thigh. Somewhere between Haven City and Kyn Manor, the two had bonded. If their connection was obedience worthy, Jessi didn't know. Mason hadn't attempted to use the dog's name yet with an order. Wulf's tongue lolled out, bright pink against the black fabric of Mason's pants. Mason obliged, his fingers working a soothing stroke down the back of Wulf's head.

Jessi rested her hip on the desk and pointed at the open folder. "Is that what Katria came to get me for?"

"Yes." He rose and motioned to the chair. "Here, have a look."

She laughed and shook her head, turning the papers her direction. "I'm fine where I am, it doesn't look like much."

Neat rows of names, addresses and other bits of information were written in clean, masculine penmanship. All the names were male, all the addresses were in Haven City. Jessi frowned. "I don't know where my father lived. Couldn't he have lived anywhere?"

Mason returned to the seat. Wulf returned to his petting position. "Yes. Haven City is the best place to start though, since it's the densest population center in the country."

Jessi glanced over the list and frowned. Something nagged in the deep recesses of her mind, something important. She chewed on her bottom lip, the names blurring together. "I don't..." She sighed and rubbed at an ache in the center of her forehead.

The warmth and pressure of Mason's hand on her thigh brought her attention to him. He gazed at her in concern. "Are you okay?"

Slowly she closed the folder. "I don't think I have my father's last name."

"Why do you believe that?" Sean asked, his tone and demeanor calm.

Jessi tried to recall what she could from her childhood and the snippets of conversation she'd managed to catch between her parents. "When my mother refused to go to Szi... come here to live, my father worried about our safety. My mother said she wasn't concerned because we didn't carry his name."

"Do you know any of his name?" Mason asked, drawing the folder back to him.

"His first name was Howell, I know that much."

Mason glanced at Sean, who shrugged. "I don't know enough people by a first name basis. You?"

Mason shook his head and looked back at Jessi. "You're sure he isn't Howell Silverna?"

"Not if what my mother said is true."

"Nothing changes," Sean said. "Whoever knew of her, knew her name, last name and all, and her likely association with her father. The article on your marriage ran this morning in the *Haven City Chronicle*. *The Havener* will likely run with it tomorrow."

"Delanee Ralston will be here for the exclusive content any day now," Mason informed him. "She's supposed to keep us current on the society page. Something must have waylaid her. I told her she could arrive yesterday."

"Excellent. Has your mother shared the guest list with you yet?"

Mason opened a drawer and pulled out a sheet. "Yes, I've added a few from the original suspect list that are in our ranking class. Will be interesting to see if they accept."

Katria rose and took the paper from Mason. Jessi tried to ignore the roll of unease through her stomach. All along, putting her out there to see who took the bait had been the plan. Now with everything beginning to move, she questioned the sanity of her decision. Being the center of attention had never been something she desired, especially after her abduction.

Sean looked the list over and rose. "I want to add two as well, and I don't see Voklane."

"He said he's going to attend as he's able, unless we need him sooner or for a specific reason." Mason had a pencil ready for Sean when he reached the desk.

"HRS threats?" Sean scribbled on the paper.

Sighing, Mason ran his hand over his face. "I thought about hiring security." He met Katria's curious stare. "But I knew Miss *bacer* over there would be offended."

Katria's shoulders straightened and she flexed her jaw. "I would not."

Mason cast her a droll stare. "Oh really? You'd be fine with my handing the safety of the house over to someone else?"

Jessi fought a smile as the woman bristled, pink staining her pale cheeks and wondered why Katria cared at all. Mason had told her very little about his team, the topic of them hadn't come up much.

"It's your house, and I can't exactly carry my rifle slung over my back everywhere I go," Katria said with a flippant wave of her hand. "Doesn't go well with a formal gown, I've been told."

Jessi lifted her eyebrows at the offhand comment. "I'm sorry, formal gown?"

"Yes," Mason answered instead of Katria. "Mother has at least two dances and three formal dinners planned for here at the manor, and one formal theater performance scheduled in town. She's managed to book a traveling acting company. The town will be invited to attend as well."

When Raina had taken Jessi shopping in Haven City, she'd mentioned formal gowns and the need for a stylist. Jessi had ignored her. No way was anyone going to see her without her clothes on except her husband. Raina let the situation go, and Jessi hadn't thought to bring it up with Mason. Not once in her life did the need for a gown of any sort arise. Her simple life hadn't called for one, let alone someone to help her dress.

Anxiety pinched in her chest and made her palms grow damp. Jessi straightened from the desk and took a deep breath. "Can I talk to you for a moment, Mason?"

Surprise flashed in his pale gray eyes, but he nodded. "Here, or…?"

"Wherever."

"All right." He glanced down at Wulf and pointed to the floor. "Wulf, *Osat'yi*."

The dog yawned, wide and long. Sharp canines flashed and then he shook his head. He settled onto the floor near the desk chair. Jessi blinked. Well, that answered the question on the bonding issue.

Mason grasped her elbow and led her from the room. They went two doors down. The room was dark, the curtains having been drawn. Mason left her near the door and crossed the room without bumping into anything. Light spilled into the small, narrow room. Three round tables covered in green felt and framed by six gleaming dark brown chairs were arranged artfully in the room. Dark cream and green striped paper and gilded framed paintings of cards and gaming pieces hung from the walls. The opulence of Kyn Manor never failed to surprise Jessi when she encountered something new.

She brushed a hand along the soft covering of the table nearest to her. "What is this room?"

"The card room. It'll be used nightly when we have guests, along with the billiard room and gaming room, I'm sure."

"There are three rooms just for games?"

"Of course. Everyone prefers something different, or to go between them. Games are fun, and the house was built during the height of Guardians expecting to entertain not only their fellow protectors during the winter months, but the town as well."

Jessi frowned. "The winter months? You mean people would stay here all winter?"

"Sometimes. When I was young, we'd only have winter guests from out of country. My mother served on our seat at the Hall of Laws. Entertaining foreign dignitaries was an honor for her."

Looking around, Jessi tried to imagine the room full of guests, with her mingling between tables, a gracious, elegant host. The idea was so preposterous, she almost snorted. She shook the phantom images away. The light from the window framed Mason as he headed to the center table, pulling a chair out. He motioned for her to join him. After closing the door, she did.

He braced his forearms on the edge of the table, his gaze searching. "What's wrong?"

Taking a deep breath, she met his stare. "I don't think I can do this."

23

———

The declaration didn't shock Mason. In fact, he'd been expecting her doubts to manifest sooner. He tapped his fingers on the table top in a random rhythm and nodded. "Okay."

Jessi snapped back and blinked. "Okay?"

"Yes, okay."

Confusion clouded her pretty jade green eyes. "Do you want to know why?"

"Do you want me to?" He sighed and turned to face her when she remained silent. "Look, I'm not going to force you to do anything. You know that. If you say you can't do this, we'll find another way. Your name is in the paper, it's been seen. I'll talk to Delanee and we'll figure it out."

"And your mother?"

"What about her?"

Jessi motioned all around the room. "She has so much planned, and our marriage is part of those plans. Showing you off." She frowned, her hands dropping to her lap. "Or rather, showcasing how unfit I am to be your wife."

Mason wanted to strangle Sean. He gathered her hands into his and waited until she met his eyes again. "I know they say when you marry, you marry the family too. But you didn't marry my mother, you married me." She glanced away and he squeezed her hands. "Hey, look at me, honey."

After a deep breath, she brought her focus back.

"Good. Now, if I was worried about how we'd look to everyone here, I wouldn't have married you. You are beautiful, smart, and funny. Everyone will see that. However, you are important to me. If being paraded in front of society is too much for you, we'll return to Haven City. Mother can throw her party, I don't care."

"You'd do that for me?"

He squeezed her fingers again. "Yes."

"What about the gowns?" she asked so softly he almost didn't catch the whisper.

"Gowns?"

"Yes, formal gowns. I can't put them on by myself." A faint tremble danced through her hands.

Mason rubbed his thumbs along the back of her hands. "And you're worried."

"I don't want…" She took another slow, deep breath. A bright pink flush spread up her neck and to her cheeks. "I don't want some stranger to see me, or to talk about what they see. And that's even assuming someone would agree to work with me."

The concern was a valid one, to a point. With Delanee Ralston in residence, guests would be looking to gossip to the journalist in hopes of making a named appearance in her articles. While Mason could control the pretty young writer to a degree, she was intrepid and looking to build a name for herself. She'd only ignore information within reason. Inviting her was a gamble, one he needed to take, which meant all information passed her way had to be carefully cultivated. He didn't need his wife worrying about her reputation, or her secrets being dragged into the light for the sake of someone's career.

Mason flexed his jaw in thought. "Any stylist elite worth her salt would stand in line to work with you. You're a Primary Guardianess of a dynasty family. The talking however, yes, that's a worry regardless. Everyone has to worry about their privacy staying private. If I find you someone I trust, will you let them help you?"

Anxiety pinched her features and shone in her eyes. Mason resisted the urge to drag her onto his lap and hug her.

"Will you be there the first time someone sees me?" she asked.

Mason nodded. "Of course I'll be there. I'll get ready in the same room with you every night too, if you need me to."

"All right."

He reached down and pulled her chair closer until their knees touched. "And you'll never be alone once guests arrive. But you have to promise me you'll take that seriously. If you want to go for a walk, you find me or one of my team mates to go with you."

"I have Wulf."

"And he's great, but I still want one of us to go along. If these people are who we suspect, they don't play games."

A small smile tugged at her lips and she lifted her attention to the ceiling. "You're playing a dangerous game though. Flaunting me in front of them, hoping they're paying attention enough to see who I am, and then hoping they don't react too quickly."

Mason inhaled sharply and grimaced. "Yes, I suppose that's true."

"Listening to you in there, I can't help think your sister and I... we were pieces to be eliminated, but for different reasons. I want to know why."

Mason caressed a knuckle down her soft cheek. She closed her eyes and pressed into his touch. "You aren't some piece to be used, Jessalyn."

Her eyes flared open. "Why do you insist on calling me that?"

"Why do you insist on letting some scab steal from you what your parents gave to you in love? He didn't take anything but what you're willing to let him have. You are still *you*."

Unshed tears threatened to spill over her lashes. She grasped his hand, holding it in place against her cheek. "You can't possibly understand the pain, the humiliation or the fear. I don't want to be *her*. They kidnapped *Jessalyn*, fed her to some monster, and hoped she'd die beneath him."

To the arctic with it. Mason surrendered to the urge to have her near and pulled her across his thighs until she straddled him. He claimed her face between his hands, forcing her to meet his stare. "You didn't die. They didn't win, and neither did he."

Mason pressed a hand to her chest, over her pounding heart. He leaned in close, his mouth a whisper from hers. "You are very much alive, full of fire, courage and endurance. I will honor what you wish, but you will always be Jessalyn to me. The woman I sketched, unashamed of her beauty, baring her scars to help a broken man heal."

Her eyes fluttered closed. A silvery tear tracked down her cheek and over his fingers. "Oh sweet sunlight, the things you make me *feel*. I never thought them possible."

Emotion constricted in his chest like a fist. Closing his eyes, Mason pressed his forehead to hers. He knew if spilled the words *I love you* clogging in his throat, she'd wonder if he meant them, or if they were being used to convince her. "I don't want you to do anything you don't want. I mean it."

Her hands wrapped around his wrists. The warmth of her breath brushed across his lips in a sweet caress. "I know. And I won't lie, I'm scared. Everything here is different, and I don't understand half of your culture. What we're attempting is dangerous. But... I'll try. For you."

"Thank you." The words were inadequate for what he felt, what he *really* wanted to say. "And I'm sorry if I—"

"No." She took a short inhale. "I'm grateful. Over-whelmed, but grateful all the same."

"I'm sorry, we can—"

She pressed her lips to his, cutting off his words again. "Mason."

"Yes?"

"Stop trying to apologize," she whispered into his mouth.

Mason slid his fingers into her soft hair, pulling her closer. "Okay, honey. I'll try."

The curve of her smile teased his lips. "I'm almost scared to ask, but why do you call me *honey*?"

Mason pulled back until he could see her curious gaze. "Do you mind?"

She shook her head, sending her red curls dancing across his wrists and forearms.

"Good." He brushed his thumb along her bottom lip. A sigh parted her mouth and her eyes drifted closed. Desire stirred in his belly, low and deep. "You taste like honey. Even away from your farm, it still lingers, like it's in your blood."

"Really?" She leaned closer.

An intimate awareness rushed through him as her breasts pressed into his chest and her hips shifted. Every thought process not associated with Jessi shut down. Only she managed to make him forget where he was, what he was supposed to be doing with little more than a touch. Strad-dling his lap, all woman and all *his*, hopeless wasn't quite a strong enough word for his situation.

Mason caressed from her face to her thigh. He pushed away the fabric of her skirt until he found warm, bare skin. She shifted on a gasp, sending a sliver of pleasure through his growing erection. The soft edges of her silk underwear brushed his questing fingers and he slipped under them. A shiver raced through her body, her mouth locking to his.

Over the past three days, Jessi had become increasingly bold, and he urged her on. Opening his mouth, he waited for her to explore, to take things further. To let him know *she* wanted more. She didn't disappoint. Sweeping her tongue inside, she lifted from his lap. Her arms encircled his shoulders while she grasped fistfuls of his hair.

Mason needed no other urging. The tips of his fingers found her damp. Her faint whimper followed his touch and he groaned, delving deeper, finding her ready. Quickly his mind worked to calculate how long they'd need before they were truly missed. Jessi's mouth slanted over his, her pelvis moved in an unspoken plea for his touch. Mason pulled on the thin scrap of fabric, intent on removing it when a sharp knock vibrated the door.

They froze. Well, that answered his question concerning when their disappearance would be noticed.

"Oh no, no," Jessi breathed and fled from his lap, adjusting her skirt.

Mason grabbed her hands, forcing her to stop and meet his stare. "It's okay, we weren't doing anything wrong."

Pink bloomed across her cheeks. "What will they think?"

Mason released her hand and laughed. "The same thing I thought when I accidently found Sean and Kat in a host's library. They loved each other too much to wait."

Her mouth fell open and she stared at him. Before she could speak, he stood, adjusting his pants as he made his way to the door. A stern younger woman, with sandy streaks in her brown hair frowned up at him with dark blue eyes.

"Primary Guardian Kynhaven," she said in a solemn voice, presenting him with the top of her bun as she bowed her head. She adjusted the front of her crimson blouse. "Visitors have arrived and wish to speak with you."

The Attendant Elite for Kyn Manor, Claire Miggins, took her job seriously. Disapproval flowed off her in waves as she took in his disheveled appearance. Mason yanked the useless cord from his hair and ran his fingers through the long length. "Thank you, Miss Miggins."

She clicked her shoes on the hardwood to acknowledge his courtesy. "Shall I show them to the study or the sitting room?"

"Who is it?"

A clipboard he hadn't noticed appeared at her hip. "Masters Raiventon and a Miss Ralston."

"The study please."

A click echoed and she disappeared around the corner to the foyer. Mason turned, fingers still in his hair. The flush had left Jessi's cheeks, and her clothes were back in perfect order. She'd even managed to tame the playful mess he'd caused to her curls. A sigh slipped past her kiss swollen lips.

"We messed up your hair," she said and took the tie from him.

Mason grinned. "Worth it."

Jessi shook her head and laughed. "Turn around, I'll fix it." Mason did as instructed. The soft tug of her fingers had his chest tightening. "You really aren't embarrassed someone *knew* what we were doing in here?"

"What, talking?"

She pulled on a strand. "No, definitely *not* talking."

The weight of a ponytail fell between his shoulders. He turned and took her hands in his. "No, I'm not embarrassed at all. You're my wife. If we choose to disappear into any room, we can. It's my house." He squeezed her fingers. "Now come on, Kevin and Raina are here, and I want to meet the baby."

Excitement brightened her eyes. Mason smiled, keeping hold of her hand, and led her back to the study. Her steps faltered when they walked through the door and her gaze landed on the incredibly tall interceptor.

"That's Raina's husband?" she whispered, her other hand wrapping around his forearm.

"Yes."

The woman in question beamed at all the onlookers for the tiny bundle held in Kevin's strong arms. Raina rested her head against Kevin's bicep, her fingers pulling at the knitted yellow blanket around the baby's face. When Raina spotted them, her smile grew.

"Jessi!" Raina motioned them closer.

Jessi glanced up at Mason, as if suddenly unsure of her place among his people. He let go of her hand and nudged her gently when she made no effort to move closer. "I'm right here."

Kevin's pride-filled gaze met Mason's and he smiled. The baby let out a short, shaky cry, the sound of new life. Mason's chest constricted as he looked down into the tiny scrunched up face created by his closest friend. Little fingers fisted and shook, grasping at air.

"My son," Kevin said softly. "Tanis Merrick."

Chatter and comfortable laughter muffled behind the door as Jessi slipped from the study with a sigh. The blissful silence of the foyer welcomed her. Wulf brushed past her skirt and waited, licking his muzzle. She paused to see if anyone noticed her absence. When no one came to collect her, she let loose a breath of relief.

Gatherings had always overwhelmed her, and Mason's group was no exception. Everyone seemed relaxed together, while she didn't fit into the dynamic. Even the pretty journalist, with milk-in-tea skin and a smile that made everyone want to stare, had settled into the camaraderie.

Pushing from the closed door, Jessi had to acknowledge she wasn't being perfectly honest with herself. The conversation from the card room kept swimming through her mind. Mason's passion, both in words and action, slipped into her thoughts any chance she allowed, leaving her foolishly staring into nothing. By the third time, she'd been so embarrassed she took the first chance to escape unnoticed.

With Mason's request to not be alone, Jessi opted for the courtyard greenhouse to take a secluded walk. The interior garden didn't count as even leaving the house. She held the glass door open for Wulf, breathing in the damp, musty scent of soil and greenery. He sniffed, found a big leaf plant to pee on, and then smelled some more. Jessi motioned for him to romp around. Let loose, he galloped away, tearing through dirt and vegetation.

Jessi meandered the pebbled path until she found a wrought iron bench situated in front of a large flowing fountain. The water gurgled and frothed over the top of a tall slate rectangle, flowing along the solid length in a wall of water to a square basin below. Birds twittered and fluttered on branches, disturbing leaves. She glanced up, squinting in the bright light streaming from above, and noted four open glass roof panels.

Across the courtyard a short bark of annoyance joined the gentle cascade of water and bird song. Jessi set her palms on her thighs and relaxed into the peaceful solitude. The gentle ripple of silvery water over dark stone held her mesmerized.

In her mind a battle waged. Mason's words crept in. *They loved each other too much to wait.* She argued with herself. The sentiment didn't apply to them. Or if it did, he only meant them instead of the crude words he could have spoken. But what if he meant what he said? What if he… Jessi took a deep breath and kneaded her thighs as tingles danced across her skin.

Loved her.

Could she hope for so much? Could she afford to have that dream? The fountain didn't answer. Groaning, Jessi dropped her face into her hands.

A sudden pressure on her neck forced her headfirst, off the bench. Before her knees could hit the ground, a firm hand bit into her bicep and snatched her upward. Jessi's feet twisted, kicking up pebbles. Fabric tangled between her ankles. She barely had time to register someone pushing her forward before her hip slammed into the edge of the fountain and water rushed to meet her torso. Fiery pain blossomed down her side. She tried to reach out, to stop the inevitable, but only air greeted her fingers. Fear penetrated her confusion as liquid enveloped her in a cold rush, stealing any breath she'd managed to save.

Jessi thrashed. The top of her shoes, her elbows, and knees met the slick bottom of the shallow pool. Her skirt swirled and floated around her. If she could get her feet under her... She turned, braced her feet and pushed. Her head broke the surface and she sucked in a lungful of air. Behind her, the assailant applied pressure to her shoulders, using brute strength to force her back under.

Water flooded into her mouth and nose. Jessi reached over her head, searching for anything and found fabric. Digging her nails in, she yanked. The material tore away, sliding her further into the water. She released her hold and tried again. Only the soft swish of her struggle and muted burble of flowing water broke the deafening cocoon of silence. The pressure between her shoulders increased, joined by another lower on her torso, preventing her from rising again.

Panic birthed desperation. Her lungs burned. She flailed, pressing her mouth closed to keep from drawing water in, knowing if she did, she'd kill herself before he— whoever he was— had a chance. Willpower fueled her and she tried to move deeper into the water, hoping to break his hold. Every cell in her body screamed for air.

No!

She hadn't survived a crazed lunatic all those years ago to die in a fountain now. Curling into herself, she used her knees for leverage. The attacker's grip tightened between her shoulders, pressed harder on her spine. Her knees ground into the hard cement bottom. The meager remnants of air rushed from her on a scream of pain. Then she simply floated, suspended in the quiet depth. She didn't immediately recognize her freedom until someone grasped the back of her shirt and hauled her up.

Chaos reigned as she choked and gasped, trying to pull oxygen into her starving lungs.

"I've got her, go!" someone shouted. "Kat, upstairs, now, facing the back of the house!"

A heavy cough tore through her throat and she vomited water.

"I can command the Ruthenarc," a woman said.

Jessi was yanked hard over the lip of the fountain. Water flowed in a rush from her clothing, soaking dark brown boots and adding to the puddle already gathered on the brick.

Wulf's frantic barking echoed through the distortion of conversations happening around her. "Do it, but be careful. If something happens to you, your brother can literally destroy me. Kevin—"

Mason, she thought maybe Mason spoke.

"On it."

Another intense cough seized her chest in a violent spasm and she gagged.

"*Sesay, Straes'ya!*" the same female voice commanded.

Someone pounded on her back, pressing her ribs into the cement edge. Sean's blurry face entered her field of vision, pinched with concern. Leaves rustled and branches cracked. Wulf's barking grew distant.

"Can you stand?" Sean asked.

Jessi tried, but her legs failed to work. Her throat burned from the coughing she couldn't seem to control. Too weak to stop herself, she slid back into the fountain. Strong hands grasped her biceps and in a single pull, the water released her on a surge, drenching the ground and her rescuer. She landed in an ungraceful heap on top of a solid male frame.

"Look at me, honey," Mason urged softly, his large hands smoothing sodden hair from her face.

Her gaze locked with his as a warm hand surrounded her left forearm, pulling it free from where it was pinned between them. Blinking, Jessi followed her arms journey, confused.

Sean smiled, his fingers pressed into her wrist. "Breathing easier?"

At his words a small cough moved through her throat, but she nodded. For some reason, her voice refused to work.

"Good." Sean attention shifted to Mason. His words seemed muffled, as if he spoke through a door. "You need to get her upstairs, wet clothes off, and get her in a hot shower. Don't panic if she doesn't seem responsive. She's shocked, and very cold. I'll check on her in an hour."

"If they catch the guy…"

"I'll come get you."

24

———

WATER DRIPPED IN A CONSTANT TRAIL DOWN MASON'S LEGS AND along the floor as he carried Jessi to her room. She trembled, her pale hands fisted in his shirt. A faint blue ring lined her lips, pressed together in a frown. Every few seconds a short, barking cough would erupt from her, shaking her entire body.

He'd almost lost her.

Had Kat not noticed she was missing. Had Mason not rushed to the courtyard. Had Kevin not burst through the clearing to the fountain, knocking the assailant over. Had Sean not snatched her from the water without a second to spare, he would have.

Yet, somehow, despite an interceptor and a Ruthenarc Wolf, the man evaded capture. Although, he had to consider who they were dealing with. And apparently, they'd underestimated them. Again.

Frustrated, Mason used his foot to push open the bedroom door. Jessi's teeth chattered.

"Almost there, honey," he whispered into her wet hair.

He leaned into the door to close it. The outer curtains on the windows were open, letting muted light in through gauzy cream fabric. A quiet, resting feel permeated the room. A house attendant had made the bed, and tidied the space. Not that Jessi allowed her room to become disorganized. If he left something on floor or out, she'd pick it up when she walked by. Jessi's shivering form in his arms didn't allow him to dwell on the domestic routine they'd developed over the past few days.

In the spacious bathroom, he set her on the dressing table chair. While the water ran from cold to hot in the open shower, he made quick work of her wet, clinging clothes. The fabric ended up in a drenched pile at her feet. He added to the pile with his own, then scooped her up. Her cold skin against his chest sent a shiver racing along his spine.

Steaming water fell in a cascade onto the rich dark blue tile of the shower floor. Mason stepped over a shallow lip, and then sat cross-legged in the center of the spray. Jessi curled into him, shaking, still chilled to his touch. He wrapped her in his arms, more for his benefit than hers. A confirmation she was with him, safe, secure.

Slowly, as the water pounded over them, Jessi ceased to shake. Her breathing steadied, and when Mason shifted enough to see her face, he found her asleep. More out of a rush of anxiety than any real rationality, Mason pressed his fingers into her neck. Her pulse beat a steady thrum. She was breathing, so of course her heart functioned, but his fear didn't ease until the proof tapped against his fingertips.

Mason hugged her close, taking comfort in the now warm slide of her wet skin along his. After several still minutes, when most of the anxiety of losing her faded to a simmer, Mason rose with his precious cargo in his arms. Water ran in rivulets down his thighs as he carried her to the bed, leaving damp footprints in the plush beige carpet.

When he leaned over to lay her down, she awoke on a long, panicked inhale and sank her nails into his shoulders. Mason grimaced in pain and sank his knees onto the mattress.

He grasped her hands, pulling them free. "Hey, you're safe, it's okay."

Her long lashes fluttered open. Green eyes clouded with confusion and fear looked at him, then around the room, down at herself, and back to him. "W-what happened? Why am I naked?" Then she blinked, leaned back and looked at him again. "And you?"

Mason yanked the blankets back and settled her onto the soft sheets. "You were freezing, I held you under the shower."

She glanced into the bathroom, where the water still ran and tendrils of steam escaped through the wide entryway. "Oh." She accepted the sheet when he billowed it over the top of her. "Who attacked me? In the fountain?"

"We don't know, yet," he admitted on a sigh. "Hopefully Delanee and Kevin were able to track him down with Wulf's help."

Wet curls stuck to the side of her face, her shoulders and back. She swiped them away with an annoyed flick of her hand. "He came out of nowhere. I didn't even hear or see him."

Mason frowned and held his hands out. "Hold that thought, let me get something dry on, and something for you to wear, too."

"Maybe a towel?"

"Sure."

He retrieved a stack of towels, handing her two. He wrapped one around his waist. On the way to the dresser, he used the other to dry his hair. "What do you want to wear?"

"Is anyone going to come in and see me?"

"Sean will, to check and see how you're feeling." Mason opened the top drawer, where all things silk underthings were kept. He brushed his fingers along the enticing fabric. "But, you can just wear a robe, if you feel comfortable with that."

"A robe and my pajamas. The shorts and small top ones, will be good, I think."

Mason took a grounding breath. He remembered very well the clothes she wanted. How the thin silk clung to every curve of her body. Or better, how the scant articles felt under his hands, and how easily they came off. Ignoring the memory of their first morning together, Mason gathered what she asked for, along with what he needed.

Jessi tucked a strand of wet curls behind her ear, exposing harsh red lines running down her forearm to her elbow. His heart constricted at the fresh physical evidence of violence against her. Mason crossed the distance in three long strides. He knelt on the bed and grasped her hand. Her palm was equally scratched.

"Where else are you hurt?" he asked, the clothes falling forgotten as he reached for her other hand.

"I'm fine, Mason. They're only scrapes."

Mason sank onto the mattress and gently pulled at the sheet. She let the covering fall away without a fight. Angry pink abrasions covered her knees. A bruise formed along the length of her right hip, puffed and red, from the joint to her upper thigh. Guilt and fury warred within him. This was *his* house. Of all the places in Sziveria, she should have been safe under his roof.

In a delicate caress, he trailed his finger along the center of her palm, avoiding the scratches. He moved down her forearm, stopping before her elbow. Sighing, he leaned over and pressed a kiss below her knee. "I am so sorry."

She shifted enough to reach for him. Her fingers toyed in the damp length of hair at his shoulder. "Why?"

He wrapped his hand around the warm, supple muscle of her calf and pulled her leg straight until he could kiss her lower thigh. "You're supposed to be protected here."

A soft gasp escaped her as he glided his tongue along the

inside of her leg. "Those who mean to harm don't exactly play by any rules."

"I know." Mason moved up her body, purposefully skimming over the thatch of her dark red curls to her smooth stomach. That way led to distractions he didn't have time to explore. He kissed between the soft curves of her hips. "Still shouldn't have happened."

Her breathing hitched. She parted her legs to accept his weight over her. The heat of her center at his stomach forced a groan free. His eyes closed to find the inner restraint he used to have before he knew exactly how good she felt.

"Do you know where I was when I was abducted?" she asked, her fingers burying into the wet hair at his scalp.

Mason rested his chin on her chest below her breasts and met her eyes. "No."

Her torso lifted enough to meet his palm as he skimmed over one soft globe, her beaded nipple brushing his palm. "My bed. My father was home too. I couldn't have been safer." She pulled a hand free and made a fluttering motion. "Just whoosh, disappeared with me into the night."

Mason caught her hand. There was no fear in her. No shadows darkened her eyes as she recalled, for his benefit, the start of the most horrific event of her life. He pressed delicate kisses to her fingertips. How could this amazing woman be his?

"I love you." The words tumbled free before he could stop them. But really, as he looked at her, his beautiful brave wife, he didn't want to hold them in anymore.

Pink flushed across her cheeks. Tears gathered in her eyes, and her mouth opened on a deep inhale. A sharp knock sounded on the door. Her gaze shot past him. Mason sighed, lifted onto his arms and pressed a quick kiss to her lips.

"Hurry and put the robe on, I'll see who it is. If its Sean, I'll make sure he waits until you're comfortably dressed."

She nodded, the glisten of tears still shining in her smoky green eyes. For a moment, Mason considered ignoring the knock. He wanted to gather Jessi in his arms, kiss away the fright of her attack, for both of them. More importantly though, he needed her to understand how much she meant to him. Not as a means to an answer, but as his friend, his lover, his wife.

The visitor wasn't in the waiting mood, however. Another round of knocks, louder and more insistent, rattled the door.

Mason made sure the towel was still secure around his waist and swung the other over his shoulder. He opened the door, prepared to tell Sean to wait a second, and froze. Large blue eyes stared in shock at him through glasses. Bright red bloomed across Tamina's cheeks and down her neck. Her eyes wandered down his bare chest, to the towel wrapped around his hips, and then shot back to his face. A flash of awareness widened her eyes. She must have realized he was naked. Well, almost. Mason bit back a groan.

"I heard the Guardianess had an accident in the courtyard fountain. I was coming to check on her," Tamina said, bracing one hand on her hip, an action that brought attention to her hour-glass figure.

"How thoughtful of you," Mason managed.

Tamina beamed. "Thank you. Does she need anything? Do you? No one told me you had to fish her out of the water."

"Who told you anything at all?" Mason asked with a forced calm.

Tamina shrugged and adjusted her spectacles, her gaze flickering to his chest on a flash of glass. "I was concerned when I heard the fountain may be unsafe, so I asked a groundskeeper to specify. I offered to send someone to check the brick and make sure it didn't need a proper cleaning. I do know how slippery they can get when moss builds up on them. I know you don't want any of the upcoming guests to have a similar accident."

Mason wrapped his hand around the towel laying over

his shoulder. The curious stare she offered made him wonder how much truth she spoke, or if she were trying for more information. "There's nothing wrong with the fountain, though I appreciate your concern for the safety of the manors visitors."

Another brilliant smile brightened her face, shadowing a flicker of disappointment. "I'm at the Dandridge family's disposal. *Whatever* their needs may be."

Mason raised a brow. Since he stood in his wife's room, nearly naked, *whatever* he needed was obviously being handled. He cleared his throat, and decided the best way to deal with her vague offer was to ignore it. "Is there anything else you need?"

The flush of her cheeks deepened, but her gaze remained fixed on him. "Actually, I was to find you next. How nice to manage two at once."

Indeed. Mason waited.

She made a soft conciliatory noise and smiled. "Yes, well, your mother would like you to join her for dinner, in the private family dining room."

Normally the task of ensuring Mason arrived to dine with the Dowager would fall to Claire, as the manors Attendant Elite. By asking Tamina to do so, his mother had cast her approval to the woman for the staff to see. Mason kept his face carefully neutral. Inside he seethed.

"What shall I tell her?"

Mason smiled. "To add additional place settings."

He closed the door before she could respond. Behind him fabric rustled. He glanced over his shoulder and frowned. Jessi's feet touched the floor. The robe swirled around her ankles, the tie laid undone at her hips. She clutched the edges together between her breasts.

"What are you doing?" he asked, closing the distance between them on quick strides when she swayed.

"I'm going to that dinner with you." Her gaze met his, her

chin lifted in a challenge. "Unless you'd rather go without me."

"No, your place is at my side. However, someone just attempted to kill you. I don't think a power struggle with my mother is what you need right now."

Jessi's shoulders squared and her chin raised higher. "Maybe it's what she needs."

25

———

Jessi didn't know what she'd been thinking. Sure, she wanted to show Eleanor Dandridge she wasn't some simpering weakling. But sitting across from Tamina Peyton, who glowed in a stunning pale blue and silver evening gown, Jessi had to admit she couldn't hold a candle to the daughter born of Sziveria.

In contrast, Jessi wore what she managed to pull over her head without hitting the floor face first. A simple green cotton gown and a flowing sheer ivory overlay. The combination helped her feel feminine, which she enjoyed when in the presence of her husband, who had professed to love her not even two hours ago.

The man who'd attacked her had escaped. Even Wulf hadn't been able to track him, something that had not only seemed to bother the beautiful journalist who'd run him, but offended her.

Emotionally, Jessi was a walking time bomb. If she processed her afternoon, she'd crack. Deep inside she knew she should have stayed away, but pride was a funny thing.

So here she sat. Every muscle in her body ached. Holding the fork to push food around her plate, because putting it in her mouth took too much effort, was a monumental task. Beside her, Sean frowned. She knew he wanted to check her pulse again. For the hundredth time.

Ornate bronze candelabras, expensive porcelain flatware, and an intricate embroidered cream satin table cloth covered the rectangular surface. The family dining room was still meant to impress whomever occupied the room. Jessi wondered as she lifted her crystal glass filled with water if there was another, far less formal, more comfortable, family room to eat in. Nine of the twelve tall backed chairs were in use. Jessi contemplated how ridiculous it would have been to utilize the room with only two or three people.

Eleanor sat at the head of the table, her back to a large window. The encompassing amber glow of the setting sun cast her in a halo of light. A faint musical note broke the silence as her fork tines bit into the porcelain. She presented a gracious smile to all her guests, her dark eyes twinkling. Yes, the Dowager was in her element, even if the moment had been unplanned on her part.

Jessi somehow managed to set her glass down without sloshing the contents all over the expensive table cloth. With a quiet exhale of relief, she folded her hands in her lap. Mason brushed his fingers over hers.

"Are you all right?" he whispered.

Across the table, Tamina placed her fork with a tiny cut of meat on her tongue in a show of elegance. No tremble of her hand. Every dark hair was perfectly in place in a lovely upswept style at the crown of her head, very similar to Eleanor's. A healthy glow infused her skin.

Jessi wanted to throw something at her.

Anything to mess up the vision of perfection.

Instead, she nodded. "I'm fine."

"Are you sure, dear? You're looking quite pale," Eleanor asked, concern laced in her voice. "We wouldn't want you to tax yourself after such a dreadful accident."

Tamina's smug smile had Jessi resisting to glare. Another micro bite slid between Tamina's full, colored lips.

Jessi picked up her fork. "Yes, I'm sure, thank you."

Mason squeezed her thigh. Katria leaned over, her curtain of black hair almost landing in the gravy threatening to drip from her plate.

"I think you look lovely, Guardianess Kynhaven." Katria grasped the crystal stem of her glass and lifted it. "To us, stuck at this marvelous dinner. I can't remember the last time I was at such a *welcoming* table. Can you, my love?"

Sean choked. Katria frowned and set her glass down. She patted her husband's back. He waved her hand away with a cloth napkin.

"I appreciate you allowing us to dine with you," Raina commented, a sweet smile warming her pixie face. "From my understanding you were only expecting your son. We've missed him and appreciate the chance to share a meal."

Eleanor dabbed at her mouth with a napkin. "My pleasure. I don't get to entertain much anymore, I'm thankful for the joyous event that has allowed me to indulge. Of course you're always welcome at my table, Guardianess Raiventon. How is your father?"

"He is well," Raina answered.

"He is busy," Kevin answered at the same time. Raina sent him a sideways glance. "Very busy."

The table fell into another long silence. Jessi chanced a glance back at Tamina and found the woman staring at Mason. An inquisitive light shone in her blue eyes.

Tamina's fork touched the plate with a delicate *tink*. Her gaze remained transfixed on Mason. "Now that you've returned home for an extended stay, will you cut your hair to more fashionable standards? I mean only Beast Master's wear it so long, and let's all be honest, they match their nature. Everyone expects them to look like their uncivilized Ruthenian ancestors."

No… oh no she did not. Jessi stared at her in disbelief.

Everyone responded as though they'd been physically slapped. An uncomfortable stillness settled over the room. At the end of the table, Delanee's fork dropped to her plate with a loud clatter. Eleanor carefully laid her napkin down and then rose. Without looking at anyone, head held high, she left the room. Mason cursed and shoved his chair back. Jessi tried to reach for him, but he was around the table and out of her grasp before she could make her hand obey.

Jessi shot a glare at Tamina. "I should be thanking you for that, but I know how much pain you just caused them."

Behind her glasses, Tamina blinked. "Over what? His hair? How ridiculous."

"No more ridiculous than you considering my heritage to be uncivilized," Delanee chimed in, tossing her napkin on the table as she stood. "I'm sure my Arch Guardian brother will be thrilled to know he's maintaining his animalistic reputation."

The color left Tamina's face. Delanee strode from the room.

"Well," Katria chimed, a grin on her face. "This has been fun." She pointed her fork at Tamina. "I want to go to more dinners with you. Normally I'm the one to make a fool of myself, but wow, I don't…" She looked at her husband and shook her head. He mirrored the gesture. "Yeah, I don't think I've ever done anything quite that bad."

"No, you haven't," Sean agreed.

Katria's grin grew. "Yay for me."

Jessi wanted to chase after Mason. She knew he was making sure his mother was okay, but the words had to have punched him too. Raina nodded, first toward Jessi, then at Tamina. A knot formed in her stomach. Despite being weak, sore, confused and now angry, she held the house title. Raina was reminding her of the importance of that position.

Jessi rose. "I think we can safely assume this meal is over.

If anyone is still hungry, feel free to remain, or to take your plates back to your rooms."

Raina stood, an approving smile in her eyes, though it didn't reach her mouth. "Thank you, Guardianess Kynhaven."

Kevin joined her, hand low on his wife's back. His stormy gaze locked onto Tamina. "Perhaps next time, you should learn the family's history before you open your mouth."

"Being the daughter of a former Shield Guardian, I thought you'd know better," Raina said so softly, Jessi almost didn't hear her.

Tamina's color returned on a rush of pink. "How was I supposed to know something as simple as suggesting a hair cut would be a sensitive topic?"

No sympathy registered on Raina's face. Her chin lifted and she looked down at Tamina. In the blink of an eye, the sweet woman morphed into a regal lady. "This family suffered a horrific tragedy less than a year ago. Safe subjects in the presence of others include the weather, the season, the family business or position, menu options, and what's currently playing at theatres and music arenas. Common etiquette taught to every ranked Guardian child. Recall your training, Miss Peyton."

Tamina's jaw flexed. She inclined her head. "Yes, Guardianess Raiventon, I will do so, thank you."

"Are you ready, princess?" Kevin asked, kissing the top of her head.

Raina looked up at her husband, touched his cheek and smiled. "Yes."

Sean and Katria silently exited behind the other couple, leaving Jessi alone with Tamina. Jessi smoothed her hands on the table cloth between plates, unsure what to do, or say.

"Well," Tamina said, breaking their uncomfortable silence. "I don't suppose you'd be willing to enlighten me about what all the fuss is about."

Petty dislike wormed its way into Jessi. She wanted to tell the woman to figure their reaction out on her own. The hole Tamina found herself in wasn't dug by Jessi, and she had no desire to help the woman out. However, the Dowager would be gleeful at Jessi showing her lack of high breeding by taking the low route.

Too fatigued to continue standing, Jessi eased back to the chair. "Mason shared a special bond with his twin sister. They never cut their hair short."

Something flickered in her eyes. "I see. And he told you this?"

Jessi stared at the woman. "Yes. I know it may be shocking, but he talks to me. I'm his wife."

Tamina waved a well-groomed hand. "I didn't mean to imply otherwise." She settled back in her seat, her hands disappearing beneath the table, and leveled a serious gaze on Jessi. "I was hoping I guess, things hadn't become so serious between you two. He was only in Westica for a short time, and then you arrived without him. I figured the marriage was a mistake on his part. Something to help him get over his sister."

I love you. Mason's words echoed in Jessi's mind. A rope to cling to in the rocky situation she found herself in. Some of Tamina's words were dangerously accurate. Mason *had* married Jessi to help him get over Cora, in a sense. In another, Jessi believed they shared something special enough for Mason to ask. And if not, things had changed since.

Jessi kept her expression impartial as she took on the woman she now knew without a doubt had become an opponent. "We married because we love each other. Guardianess Raiventon informed me the concept is sadly lost among most of Sziverian society. I was told to expect opposition to the idea."

A less than civil smile curved Tamina's lips and glimmered in her eyes. "You will *never* be accepted by the

Dowager Kynhaven. You are a nobody. Useless to your husband. You can never hope to be the Guardianess he'll require at his side."

"Maybe not now," Jessi admitted, running her fingers along the smooth edge of the butter knife resting beside her plate. Too bad she never learned how to throw one. "But I'll learn."

"I don't have any requirements for my Guardianess," Mason deep voice rumbled from the doorway. Jessi gasped and snapped her attention to him. His silvery eyes shone with intensity as they took her in. "But she's definitely the Guardianess I *need*."

26

"I AM SO SORRY YOU WERE LEFT ALONE WITH HER," MASON SAID, the door to her room closing softly behind them. "I wouldn't have chased after my mother if I'd known everyone would abandon you."

Jessi dropped onto the bed with a sigh of relief. Exhaustion washed over her. She wanted to curl up into the soft sheets with Wulf on one side and Mason on the other and sleep for a week. "I'm not made of porcelain you know. I'm not fragile. I handled her fine on my own."

"I know you aren't fragile." He joined her on the bed. Gently, he gathered her into his arms until her weight rested against his chest. "You are the least fragile woman I know, besides Kat."

His cheek rested on top of her head, sending a cascade of black silk over her shoulder. Jessi smiled and reached up, tangling her fingers into the length. On an intimate embrace, he hugged her close. His legs folded around her, cocooning her in his strength. The sharp, clean scent of him made her close her eyes, leaving no part of her untouched by his presence.

"So why are you upset?" Jessi asked, her words faint even to her.

"Because you're my wife, and I'm a big strong alpha male who doesn't like you to be challenged."

Jessi opened her eyes and tipped her head back, laughing. "A big strong alpha male, huh?"

He squeezed her gently. "Yep. Bet you didn't know that when you signed my contract, did you?"

Concern shone in his eyes and Jessi touched his cheek, her smile fading. "What's really wrong?"

He caught her hand and held it to his face. "Kat is sending her stylist elite. Both she and Sean trust Rebeka. The woman has seen Kat through poisoning, a knife wound, and I'm told a rather nasty fall from training a couple months ago with Kevin. She has kept their life private for them, they expect her to do the same for you. And she's agreed to take you on as a client while they're here."

Jessi tried to pull her hand free, but all Mason let her do was lower it, lacing his fingers through hers. "Okay."

"I think," he pressed a kiss to the back of her hand, his gaze locked on her, "it would be best if she met you and addressed your concerns before the first time she has to help you into a gown."

Understanding dawned on Jessi. "And you want to do this soon."

"Yes, if you're up for it, she'll be here in a few minutes probably."

He didn't try to keep her hand when she tugged on it again. She swallowed to try to ease the dryness in her throat. If she had to have an absolutely awful day, why not have it all at once? "All right."

"Are you sure you're okay with this?"

Jessi pushed free from his hold and stood. Anxiety flitted around inside her, making her agitated. "Yes. I agree seeing first is a good idea. I'm sure I'm rather shocking."

Before she noticed him move, he was off the bed and in front her. He captured her face between his hands and forced her gaze to meet his. "You are beautiful. *All* of you."

A soft knock disrupted the moment. Jessi shied away and reached for the cotton robe he'd handed her earlier. She disappeared into the bathroom on the tail of hushed voices coming from the door. After making her efforts to undress swiftly so she didn't change her mind, Jessi shrugged into the robe with a bracing breath. She'd kept her underwear on, positive the woman didn't need to see her *completely* naked.

Rebeka, who appeared to be Jessi's age, with pretty brown curls piled atop her head and kind hazel eyes, smiled and nodded at something Mason said. They noticed her at the same time and fell silent. Jessi clutched the fabric between her breasts and willed her feet forward.

"Thank you for asking me to be your stylist while you're at Kyn Manor. I'm so excited to be working with two Primary Guardianesses." Genuine delight shone in her warm gaze.

"No, I thank you. Katria assured us you'd not spread rumors."

Rebeka's eyes widened. "As a Stylist Elite, I've taken an oath. To breach it would cost my certification, not to mention, breaking confidence is wrong, in all ways."

"Money can be a large enough motivator for many," Mason said quietly.

Rebeka nodded, her expression sober. "Yes, I understand. I promise you, I'm trustworthy."

Since no single moment would be better than another, Jessi took another long breath and turned her back to the woman. Mason held up his hands and stepped away.

"Wait a minute for me, please?"

Jessi stared at him. What in the inhabited world was he doing? He smiled and then went to the dresser. Long purple silk fluttered from the top drawer. One of the scarves he'd bought for her in Westica. The one she'd actually been wearing the day he came home. His gaze locked with hers, remaining fixed as he stopped before her. The light fabric slid past her shoulders and settled. The weight of his hold on both sides a fixed pressure at the base of her neck.

Like she'd done so many months ago with the silk, he provided a sense of shelter for the vulnerable moment. He nodded faintly, a small show of encouragement. Jessi released the edges of the robe and let them fall away. The soft cotton slid off her shoulders, over her back and pooled at her feet on the floor.

Mason's gentle smile grounded her. His hands slid down the silk, sweeping past her nipples on the way to her stomach, where the back of his fingers caressed the skin near her hips. A tremble raced along Jessi's spine, from his touch or nerves, she didn't know. But Mason's eyes never left hers, and the spark of heat in his gaze shifted her awareness from the situation to him alone. If Rebeka made a sound at her exposed back, Jessi failed to notice.

Mason leaned forward. His lips brushed a kiss across hers. "Thank you."

Jessi slid her hands up his thick forearms. "For what?"

His words were soft, meant only for her. "You didn't know you'd be needing someone to help you dress. Or be forced to be compared to another woman. You didn't know you have to smile and pretend to be happy to be my wife for dozens of strangers to see, and thousands to read about."

Her fingers squeezed into his muscles. "I am happy, or I wouldn't still be here. You know that, right?"

A sigh fluttered along her lips as he pressed his forehead to hers. "Why are you so amazing?"

Jessi laughed, she couldn't help it. "I'm not."

Before he could argue, Rebeka cleared her throat.

"Guardianess?" she asked hesitantly.

Jessi tilted her head. "Yes?"

"May I ask some personal questions?"

Jessi stiffened, her gaze once again meeting Masons. He frowned, but didn't intervene. The choice was completely up to her. "About?"

"Fabric and such. Anything that causes you pain or discomfort?"

"No, not that I'm aware of."

"Any style you aren't comfortable wearing?" Rebeka asked.

Jessi gave Mason a droll stare. Really? He winked. "Nothing with an open back, or exposed shoulders."

Rebeka chittered. "Of course, how silly of me." The fabric of the robe brushed along Jessi's calves for a moment. "Here, let me help you back into this."

Soon, the woman's job would be to assist Jessi into whatever clothing she'd need to wear for an evening, or a day, to wherever the Dowager insisted they go or do. Taking a deep breath, Jessi released Mason's arms and held out her hands. First one sleeve, then the other slipped over her arms, glided up her back and settled on her shoulders. Mason pulled the edges together while Jessi handled the belt. Rebeka came into her field of vision. The stylists pretty hazel eyes looked Jessi over.

"Definitely greens, silvers, dark grays and shades of peach for your colors. For events where you're the sole focus, I'll be sure you're in Kynhaven colors. All the others, what suits you and makes you shine." Rebeka clapped her hands together, eyes shining. Not a hint of trepidation or disgust on her pretty face. "I can't wait."

Rebeka held up two fingers. "Two!" She pointed at herself. "Me! I'm not even a genetic heir, I'm gen-common and I get be the stylist for two, yes *two* Primary Guardianesses." She did a punch in the air and a little hopping turn. "Take that you nay-sayers!"

Mason laughed. Jessi stared, unsure how to respond. She was excited over the woman's enthusiasm, but what genetics had to do with it she wasn't sure. At some point Mason had tried to explain his country's fascination with inherited abilities, but Jessi still didn't understand.

A gentle flush spread across Rebeka's cheeks. "Sorry." She executed a short bow. "Thank you for the opportunity, I won't disappoint."

"We know," Mason assured her, still smiling.

Rebeka left on a grin, the door closing with a faint click behind her.

Mason pulled Jessi into a hug. Sighing, she wrapped her arms around his waist and rested her cheek on his chest. He caressed her back in soothing strokes.

"Feel better?" he asked.

"About?"

"Someone helping you dress."

Jessi leaned back and met his gaze. "Yes." She pressed her fingers into the solid muscle of his back and rose onto her toes. Her lips brushed across his. The soft, trimmed hair of his beard tickled her upper lip and chin. "I was hoping you were asking if I felt better for a different reason."

He quirked a brow. "Oh?"

Jessi smiled and kissed him again.

"Oh." Mason grinned. His hands slipped under her butt and hefted her upward with an ease she still hadn't managed to get used to. On a laugh Jessi wrapped her legs around his waist and her arms around his neck. "Want to see how much better I can *really* make you feel?"

Jessi answered with a passionate kiss.

27

Jessi brushed her fingers along the neckline of the formal gown Rebeka had helped her into. Sheer red silk allowed the golden satin beneath to be seen, shimmering in the bright light of her dressing room. Navy satin petals formed a belt at her natural waist and dispersed like an explosion along the bodice and down the flowing skirt. Little crystal beads twinkled within each leaf shape, giving the gown a fairytale quality Jessi couldn't believe she wore.

The Kynhaven colors were bold and elegant. The neckline went all the way up her back, swooped at her collar bone, exposing a hint of her breasts. The hem swept along the floor, the folds of the skirt billowing behind her with each step. A gleaming necklace of rubies and diamonds graced Jessi's throat, and a matching bracelet at her wrist. Little sapphire and diamond pins were pushed into the intricate braided style atop her head. Cosmetics made the woman staring back at her in the mirror a near stranger, defining the soft curves of Jessi's cheeks, lips, and the smoky green of her eyes.

Despite the transformation, Jessi was still a nobody from Westica. No matter how hard she tried, the square of her shoulders and tilt of her jaw was nowhere near as regal as

Raina Merrick had tried to drill into her. Somehow, she was supposed to convince guests, and a journalist, Mason's choice in a wife suited not only his house, but his rank. Maybe if she kept her mouth shut, the ruse could be pulled off. Jessi rolled her eyes and sighed. Mason accepted her role in his life, Jessi needed to do the same. If he didn't care about everyone's opinion, she shouldn't either.

Except, staring at her foreign reflection, left alone in her dressing room, doubts filtered in. For the past week Jessi had barely seen her husband. He slid between the sheets late into the night, too exhausted to do more than wrap around her and fall asleep. When she awoke the next morning, he'd already be gone. There hadn't been time for conversation. Touching the silken fabric of her skirt, she offered a half smile, knowing if extra time had presented itself, they wouldn't have spent it talking anyway.

With a bracing breath, Jessi left her room. Other guests milled about, either leaving their quarters for the gathering or returning to finish getting ready. Claire had given Jessi the time to arrive for the event. Jessi assumed Mason would meet her before they entered together, since he hadn't dressed with her.

At least a hundred guests had arrived over the week. Having been given little instruction as to her role, Jessi had sequestered herself into the study and reviewed the Dandridge accounts and logbooks. She'd made some disturbing discoveries. Since Mason was busy being the host of his rather large estate, Jessi hadn't been able to bring up her concerns. She was hoping they could leave the event early tonight and spend some time together.

Claire met her at the bottom of the stairs. The ever-present clipboard was cradled in the crook of her arm. She touched a finger to her ear, and after a nearly imperceivable nod, smiled at Jessi. "Right on time, Guardianess. The receiving line just formed."

The stiff fabric of the attendant's straight black skirt and light gray blouse barely moved with her clipped steps. Jessi followed her down the brightly lit corridor to the back of the house. Two sets of double doors spilled more light into the hall. Festive music and the hum of conversation floated in the air. Claire stopped outside the door and motioned for Jessi to continue.

"Enjoy your evening," the woman said with a faint bow and then disappeared.

Jessi peered into the bustling room. A riot of colors swayed and bobbed through the crowded space. A couple brushed past her, waving in merriment to a group gathered to the left of the double entryway. The inner glass wall to the huge L shaped room was lifted, opening into the courtyard, giving the space a lush, airy atmosphere. The large receiving line Claire had spoken of followed the curve of the room, growing with each moment as people tried to decide where in the process they should stand.

A soft flutter at her inner elbow made Jessi jump. She glanced to her left. Eleanor lifted her chin and met Jessi's confused stare.

Her dark, cold gaze flitted over Jessi's gown, unimpressed. "You and I will be walking the receiving line."

Jessi's spine stiffened. "This is for mine and Mason's marriage, though."

"Yes." Her bony, chilled fingers wrapped around Jessi's forearm in a leading hold. "And by my walking you, I'm showing my approval of the union."

Unease slithered along Jessi's spine. "Who will Mason be walking with, then?"

Eleanor leaned in close, until their heads nearly touched. "Look at them," she whispered, pointing a slender finger. "So beautiful together."

Jessi's gaze found Kevin first, the tallest man in the room by almost a head. Not far from him, Mason stood, his long, braided hair fell down his back against a navy jacket and matching pants. He turned, laughing, the sparkling chandeliers above catching the soft gray of his shirt, setting off his pale eyes. Tamina smiled coyly on his arm in a stunning maroon satin gown adorned with a golden floral beadwork pattern. Together they made the Kynhaven colors.

Tamina, chin raised on a smile, laughed. Her eyes twinkled behind her wire-rimmed glasses. She brushed a hand on Mason's jacketed arm. Everything about her, from her posture, to her expression, to the ease in which she conversed with those around her, said *I belong here.*

"Why are you doing this?" Jessi asked, ignoring the knot in her stomach. Her pride wouldn't allow her to show any outward betrayal.

Eleanor walked them along the line of guests, greeting with a nod and a smile. "Because you will never amount to even half of what she is already. Tamina was born into this life, trained from birth to be the wife of a Guardian. She was unable to take her father's Shield seat, which was a shame, but she's her mother's genetic heir for accounting. Accounting isn't a Guardian role. As the fifth generation to carry a genetic inheritance, she and Mason would produce offspring guaranteed to be heirs."

Interesting, since only hours ago Jessi had found some very disturbing discrepancies in Tamina's so-called Gen-Heir accounting logs. "Unless they all carry the accounting gene, then what will you do?"

"And what is your genetic ability, dear?"

Jessi wanted to gloat in her victory. *Didn't like that question, did you?* "I don't know," she lied. "Westica doesn't care about such things."

"And your Sziverian father didn't either?"

Jessi shrugged. "I guess not since he never spoke of it."

The din of conversation grew louder the closer they moved to the musicians playing on the upper-level balcony near the bend of the room. Eleanor leaned closer. The stones clipped into her braided crown brushed against Jessi's temple. "Producing a genetically common child could cost my son everything our family has spent hundreds of years building. Would you really do that to him?"

Jessi caught sight of Mason again, being led in a different direction by Tamina, who'd glanced briefly their way. "I think," she mused, willing her husband to notice them. "Whatever goals *he* sets for his future are the ones we'll make together."

Eleanor patted Jessi's wrist. "That's so sweet of you, child, to assume he'll stay with you past the year obligation."

For a split second, Jessi wondered why she was putting up with this old crone's abuse. She didn't need to prove herself to any of these people, least of all the woman forcing her around the room, showing off how *unsuitable* Jessi happened to be. She hadn't even decided if *she* wanted to remain after their year was up. Yes, Mason had professed love, and if she were honest, she'd admit the same. The hard truth remained however, Jessi would never be what passed for a ranked Guardian's spouse. Nor did she know if she wanted him to remain with a disfigured wife. Even though he made every effort to let her know her scars didn't bother him, the secret would always have to be kept. Eventually they'd have to hope to be lucky enough to find a woman like Rebeka. Jessi hated that she had to deal with the reminders of her past. She didn't need the scorn if others were to find out.

Lifting her chin, Jessi met the gaze of each curious guest. All she needed to do was be seen, and notice if a flicker of recognition flashed in anyone's eyes. Once she made the journey around the room, she could disappear.

A striking, tall woman sashayed through the crowd. The rich satin of her gown slid along the delicate curves of her lithe frame, bringing out her golden irises. Delanee smiled and nodded to people she passed. The tight coils of her dark red curls bobbed along her shoulders. When she stopped before Jessi, a champagne flute poised regally in her long fingers, the sparkling liquid a few shades lighter than her eyes, Jessi resisted the urge to take the glass of mind-numbing liquid from the woman.

"Guardianess Kynhaven," Delanee said with a genuine smile. "You look stunning in your house colors this evening." She turned her gaze to Eleanor. "As do you, Dowager."

Eleanor tilted her head. "Thank you, Miss Ralston."

A glitter of amusement tilted at the journalist's full lips. "Master Guardian Raiventon asked me to inform you they're ready for the announcement when you are."

Surprise spread across the older woman's face, bringing attention to the wrinkles on her forehead. "What announcement?"

Delanee finished taking a sip of her drink. "Of their son, of course. That *is* what tonight is about."

Eleanor opened her mouth, but the crowd made a collective noise of approval, forcing them to turn toward the entrance. At some point Kevin had disappeared, because now he made a dramatic entrance with his precious son nestled in his large arms. Jessi glanced around. How had he managed that? Raina appeared at her husband's side, glowing with love and pride as she looked at them both. Unconcerned about the throng of witnesses, Kevin leaned down and brushed a tender kiss on his wife's lips. A roar of approval and applause rolled through the room.

Eleanor fled to their side, a wide smile on her face. Her dark ruby dress swayed around her noble form, drawing the eyes of everyone around. Jessi let a sigh of relief rush from her mouth and then quickly covered the action, her cheeks warming.

Delanee bumped her hip to Jessi's. "I won't tell anyone, don't worry."

Jessi chuckled. "Thank you. Were the events really mixed up?"

"Absolutely not. Claire Miggins is an Elite after all. She will likely have to find somewhere very isolated and scream when she learns her schedule was compromised tonight." Delanee lifted a finger from the flute and motioned. "As bad as I feel for the woman, *that* sight is completely worth it."

Jessi followed Delanee's line of vision. Mason disengaged Tamina from his arm. The woman's cheeks were brilliant red, her jaw set in a harsh clamp. She glared at the couple still caught at the door with their beautiful new infant being showcased.

"What happened?" Jessi asked, trying to keep her voice even as Mason's gaze fixed on her from across the room and didn't leave.

"Kynhaven noticed what his mother did and glanced at Kevin, who simply said," Delanee cleared her throat and dropped her voice an octave, "'Raina and I know how to catch a cat'."

Jessi frowned in confusion. "What does that mean?"

"I don't know. Both the Guardians Wintersfall laughed. And then Kevin vanishes, just," she waved her glass around in the air, "gone. Raina smiles at Mason, who looks at me and asks if I'd mind reminding his mother she has a duty to announce a birth." Delanee touched her temple. "A match flared in my head as I realized they changed the importance of the evening with little more than smiles and cryptic words."

A smile curled Jessi's lips. Mason drew closer, the crowd parting around him. "Sneaky."

Delanee sipped her champagne. "Brilliant."

Slivers of awareness raced along Jessi's spine. Mason stopped in front of her. His hands brushed the gauzy fabric at her shoulders and slid down her arms on a whispery touch to her fingers. He brought her knuckles to his mouth, feathering a kiss along them. The pale gray of his eyes danced with a smile and a promise only she understood.

"You look amazing," he whispered against her fingers.

"Thank you." The heat in his eyes sent a warm flush along her skin. How was it he could send her thoughts scattering with a look?

"I apologize for my mother."

"She's persistent."

Mason lowered her hands, but kept hold of one, wrapping her fingers around his forearm. He set a leisure pace toward the Merrick's. "She is making me forget I'm to respect her wishes as an elder in all things."

"Why did you agree to walk with Miss Peyton tonight?"

"I didn't. She arrived, wrapped herself around my arm, and said my mother asked her to keep me company until you arrived." A frown distorted his handsome face. "It won't happen again."

Jessi sighed. Unease and guilt warring inside her. "Mason—"

"Don't," he snapped with an edge she'd never heard before on his voice. His jaw flexed and he leaned down at brushed a kiss on her lips. "I'm sorry, just don't, okay? I know what's going on inside that pretty head of yours. Not here, not now. I love you. *You.* Understand?"

Jessi nodded, words lodged in her throat.

He pressed another quick kiss to her mouth. "Good."

"Oh you two," Delanee crooned. "Giving me all the good romantic stuff to write about. I can already see it in the article. *And he knows what she's thinking before she does.*"

Mason grinned. "I told you I'd make being here worth your time."

Delanee smirked. "Oh trust me, I haven't regretted a single moment."

28

Warm, smooth muscles glided under Jessi's palm. She breathed Mason's scent in deep, snuggling further into the shelter of his body. A hushed whine made her frown and groan. From past mornings, Jessi knew all she had do was slide her hand down and they'd shift from content holding to passion. A familiar tingle of awareness thrummed through her at the thought of Mason alive and ready under her hand. But Wulf's whine turned into a hushed woof. The dog wouldn't wait for much longer.

On a sigh, Jessi made to roll away, but a strong arm banded around her waist. Mason's breath ruffled in her hair near her neck. His muscular thigh slipped between her knees, forcing her legs apart.

"Where are you going?" his gruff voice whispered across the sensitive skin of her neck.

Jessi slid her fingers into his hair, sending messy waves over her shoulder. "Wulf needs to go out."

He kissed the pulse racing faster at her throat. "So you've decided to call him his name now?"

The firm tip of his tongue left a wet trail from her throat to her collar bone. "Yes," she breathed, as an answer and a response.

"I love the way you respond to me." His hot breath caressed the top of her breasts.

Another whine of impatience tore through the haze Mason wove around her senses. "Are you going to love the way the dog responds to not going outside?"

Mason's forehead dropped to her chest. His shoulders shook with laughter. "Probably not." He heaved a sigh and rolled away. "I'll take him out."

The mattress shifted as his weight left the frame. Naked, his muscles rolling with every step, he crossed the room. His fingers combed through his hair as he disappeared around wall into the bathroom. Jessi flopped onto her back and stared up at the dancing shadows on the ceiling. At moments like this, watching him in all his strength and power, his touch still fresh on her skin, she couldn't believe any of it was real. Couldn't believe she'd managed to capture his heart. Somehow, he saw past the torn up remains of a woman. Tears burned and she quickly breathed them away. Rubbing her face to reset her frame of mind, she sat up.

Wulf's golden eyes peered at her over the edge of the mattress. A huge, furry paw landed on the comforter. Jessi rolled closer to him and scratched between his ears. His tongue flopped out and hot doggy breath fanned across her cheeks. Jessi scrunched up her nose.

"What have you been eating?" she asked with a chuckle, and then shook her head. "Never mind, I don't want to know."

Mason returned to the bedroom, a confused frown on his handsome face. He'd combed his hair and pulled the sides back. The shadow of growth on his cheeks and neck had been shaved away, leaving the clean lines along his jaw and chin, and around his mouth. His pants were unbuttoned, hanging low on his hips. The edges of his unbuttoned shirt drifted behind him, revealing too much tempting flesh.

"Do you know what happened to my clothes?"

"You're wearing them?"

His frown increased and he shook his head. "No, not these. The ones I was keeping in your closet. I wore this last night."

"Someone took your clothes?" Jessi chewed her bottom lip in thought and then glared at the air. Only one person would dare order his possessions removed from her room. Mason let out a growl, seeming to have come to the same conclusion. "Do you think she would?"

"Oh yes, I think she definitely would, and did."

Sighing, Jessi threw the sheets off. She reached for her robe tossed on a chair in front of the nearest window. "I'll go get you clothes while you take Wulf. Unless you want to switch? You know what you need."

"No, I'm not ready for you to go out of the house, in any capacity, on your own yet."

Jessi slipped the cool silk robe over her arms. "It's been over a week and nothing else has happened, even with all the guests."

Mason snapped his fingers and pointed at the floor near his feet. Wulf pounced over, his bushy tail a blur of excited motion. He yipped in anticipation and danced around Mason's legs. "No. We can take care of the dog and then get my things together, or you get my things, and I'll take care of the dog."

The set of his jaw and shoulders told her she'd lose any argument. She glanced down at her silk top, shorts and robe. "Is this enough?"

"No one will be stirring from their beds for another two hours, at least."

Jessi raised a brow. "Must be nice."

Mason shrugged and went to the door. "They have

nowhere to be, and like at home, everything from food to clothing is handled for them, why would they get up early?"

Why indeed? Jessi wrapped the flowing robe around herself while he buttoned his pants and then his shirt, closing off her view one enticing inch at a time. Once finished, he opened the door and Wulf bounded out. Mason shook his head, following the exuberant dog on a chuckle. Jessi trailed behind them both, her bare feet sinking into the plush hall carpet. Mason held his hand behind himself and wiggled his fingers. Smiling, she picked up the pace until she reached his outstretched hand.

The calm moment grounded her, helped remind why she put up with a disapproving mother-in-law and a woman intent on taking her husband. All of the chaos was worth the memories they built.

Mason opened the door to the courtyard. Damp warmth rushed in a wave past them, ruffling the edges of Mason's hair and Jessi's robe. Wulf took off on a burst of wild energy. Leaves skittered along the brick path in his wake. Birds squawked in alarm and flew to the open windows above. Tendrils of light filtered from overhead, piercing the thick foliage in the center of the courtyard, creating soft shadowed shapes. The hush of water burbling made a knot form in Jessi's chest and she slowed, pulling on Mason's hand.

"Can we wait here for him?"

Mason glanced around. "I think he'll be fine on his own for a bit. We'll go get my things and then return for him. I'd leave him here like we have been, but some of the guests went a little crazy when he jumped out of some bushes yesterday."

Jessi laughed. "Oh no. I hadn't heard about that."

Mason held the door open for her and shrugged. "It's our home, he's our dog. I wouldn't worry about it, except I don't want anything happening to him."

A soft flutter around her heart had her rubbing her chest.

Our home. Our dog. Why was she so scared to go all in with this man? He owned her heart. Time and again he'd made himself clear about how he felt about her, and the past burdens she carried. And yet fear still clung to the edges of her conscience, whispering her faults and insecurities, reminding her she wasn't perfect, or even pleasing to the eye. Too many personal issues and not enough experience to be who he needed.

In her unpleasant pity-me session, she'd stopped moving toward the door. Mason frowned. "What's wrong?"

"Nothing." Jessi faked a smile and quickly squeezed past him into the house.

He grabbed her hand, forcing her to stop. His warm, strong fingers laced between hers. "What's wrong?"

Jessi rose onto her tiptoes and pressed a soft kiss to his mouth. She stroked the thin edge of his beard along his jaw. "Really, it's nothing. Let's go get what you need and return to Wulf. I don't want him to cause anymore issues."

Because really, her big guard dog seemed to be the cherry topper on the list of *Reasons Why Jessi Silverna Doesn't Make a Good Wife for Primary Guardian Kynhaven* to all the invited guests. Like she needed another one.

MASON OPTED NOT TO DELVE DEEPER INTO JESSI'S OBVIOUS distress. Whatever she wasn't sharing was hers to keep private. While annoyed, Mason had made his stand on where they stood, or more specifically where *he* stood. Either she believed and trusted him, or she didn't. Clasping her fingers, he tugged her into motion to the back stairs leading to the second floor. Since they were on the opposite side of the house from where his personal room was located, they'd end up walking the long way.

House staff carrying trays of food, cleaning supplies, or clean articles of clothing hurried down the long corridors connecting the house together. Jessi clutched at the edges of her maroon silk robe to keep it from opening, though no one paid them much attention. They rounded the corner leading to the family corridor and Mason almost collided with a breathless Delanee.

"There you are!" she stated, grasping his forearm. Her golden eyes were wide. A heavy flush brightened her cheeks. "I have been looking everywhere for you this morning."

Mason stopped, but gestured at his room. "It's that door there."

Jessi hesitated for a moment, but then nodded and continued on. Her fingers slipped free after a quick squeeze. Mason focused his full attention on the journalist.

"Is everything okay?"

She nodded, dark red curls swaying. Then she frowned. "I'm not sure. Maybe. It depends."

Mason moved them off to the side of the corridor, catching the tail end of silk as Jessi stepped into his room. "What is it?"

"I went to town last night."

Mason stared at her. "When? The party went until past midnight."

She waved a hand. "After that fiasco, I noticed several of the younger guests were in a hurry and I wanted to see where they were going."

"And you're already up?"

A glint shone in her gaze and she bounced on her feet. "Actually, I couldn't sleep. I would have gone to your room sooner, but no one could seem to tell me exactly where you've been sleeping."

Jessi came rushing from his room. Her lips were pressed in a tight line, her cheeks crimson. Mason waved his hand in a *get on with it* motion to Delanee. He'd deal with one issue at a time.

"Right." She shook her head. "So, last night. I followed the group to this tiny little house on the edge of town. It looked like no one had lived there for some time, but a light in the window let people know someone was indeed home. The group did some silly knock, the door opened, and there was a quick exchange."

Mason recoiled. A clandestine exchange never led to anything good.

Delanee opened her hand. A small glass bottle half full of fine pink powdered rested on her palm. Mason snatched the drug from her. Jessi leaned forward, trying to get a look at the jar, but said nothing.

"Magic lily dust?" he asked in disbelief, holding the tiny bottle closer to the lamp burning a few steps away. "In my town?"

"I think," Delanee began cautiously. "Someone brought it here just for this gathering. They knew they'd have customers."

"Yes, but they'll start peddling this crap to locals now, too." He handed the bottle back to her. Anger tightened his muscles. "Give this to Kevin, and tell him exactly where you saw the person selling."

She nodded and turned to leave. Mason touched her shoulder. "Thank you."

A big grin brightened her pretty face. "Of course. Like I said last night, this has been a great opportunity for me. I'm glad to help in any way I can, but I'm even happier about all the story information I'm gathering. To think, big city problems migrating to small towns? No one else is reporting on it."

Mason's frown intensified. "I'm not too happy about a Haven City issue finding a home here." He pointed to her fist clenched around the bottle. "You know what people are doing for that mess, don't you?"

The overly excited journalist cleared her throat, her smile fading. "I've heard rumors, yes. I'm sorry. But at least you can do something early. Other small towns may not have that opportunity if no one is saying anything."

Mason turned his attention to Jessi. "What's wrong?"

She hooked her thumb over her shoulder. "There's a situation in your bedroom I can't handle."

Ignoring the urge to sigh, Mason strode to his room. He used the heel of his hand to shove the door open. A shocked gasp sounded. Bare feet poised over the bed, Tamina froze mid motion. A sheet barely covered her naked torso, clutched to her chest by a fist, a round breast and bare hip peeking through. The smooth skin of her back and butt was exposed, confirming the fact that she was completely nude beneath the sheet. A quick glance around the room confirmed, yep, he hadn't mistaken the door to the room he'd grown up in.

"What are you doing in here?" Mason asked, refusing to give her privacy when her eyes darted to the open door.

She scooted back onto the bed, brown eyes wide. Her hair was a riot of loose dark brown curls around her shoulders. Either she'd waited in the bed all night and fell asleep, or she snuck in earlier this morning. Since she searched frantically on the side table for something and slipped her glasses onto her nose, Mason figured she'd been in his room from the night before. Jessi must have woken her.

Tamina tucked the sheet under arms and threw the blankets over her legs. "Um." She licked her lips, her face, neck and arms bright red. "The Dowager said no one was using this room. She asked if I'd mind so the room I'd been using could be given to another guest."

Mason rubbed his forehead against the headache forming between his eyes. "My mother overextended the house and decided to put you in my room? That's what you're going with?"

"It's the truth!" Her voice wobbled in conviction and a hint of despair.

"And the little fact that the spread of rumors about you

sleeping in *here* are going to be running rampant through the house by this afternoon has nothing to do with it?"

Tamina glanced between him and Jessi. "What exactly would that accomplish?"

Mason held his arms open in frustration. "I don't know, you tell me."

Jessi's gentle touch slid along his forearm. "Nothing. No one would believe you were in here with her. And even if they did, what would it matter? We know the truth."

Frustrated and annoyed, Mason pulled his hand down his face. He shook his head. "I am so sorry. You don't deserve to put up with this crap."

Jessi squeezed his arm. "Neither do you."

Mason's gaze settled on a portrait of him and Cora as children. A sharp pain pierced his heart. If Cora were here, his mother wouldn't be pulling her deceptions. And if she did, Cora would set both her *and* Tamina straight. In fact, Tamina would likely already be on her way back to Haven City. Mason swallowed the lump in his throat. Cora wasn't here. They wouldn't have the chance to rescue each other from their mother's conniving plans ever again. Nor would Cora be the hard voice of reason when he preferred diplomacy over hurt feelings.

Silent, Mason walked to the painting. He gazed at the innocent, happy faces, clueless to the tragedy of their future. Not more than seven or eight, they both had shorter hair. Cora was missing a tooth and the bow on her dress was askew, like she'd yanked it in an attempt to rip it free before the artist began.

Behind him someone made an urgent sound, but he ignored the conversation. He traced the lines of Cora's jaw, her short hair, the silly grin on her young face. Someone's arms enfolded his waist. A body pressed into his back. Mason blinked and looked down, the red silk telling him Jessi wrapped around him. He laid his hands over hers and took a deep breath.

"I'm okay."

Jessi squeezed his middle. "I know."

Mason chanced a glance at the bed. Only rumbled sheets and disheveled pillows remained. "Where did Miss Peyton go?"

Jessi kept her hold around his waist and leaned around until her cheek rested against his bicep. "I told her to leave."

"And she listened to you?"

"Yes. I might have also let slip I'd discovered her secret."

Mason frowned. Lifting his arm, he urged Jessi to move into his side. "What secret would that be?"

Her heavy sigh blew across his chest. "Are you sure you want to know now?"

"Sure, why not, can't be much worse than what I'm already dealing with this morning."

She took a deep breath and regarded him. "When I touched her books, I had odd flashes of memory, which shouldn't happen on something as mundane as a ledger. She was so nervous and excited, that some of the entries she made left behind an impression. I decided to look deeper and found discrepancies. And after her reaction, I think I can safely say she's been stealing from you."

Mason closed his eyes and tilted his head back. Jessi's fingers brushed the ends of his hair. "Do you think my mother knows?"

"I don't think so. If your mother wanted to give Miss Peyton money, why would they steal it from your account? The excitement she left behind on the books leads me to believe she'd had a plan to the theft all along."

Mason stared at the decorative square tiles of the high ceiling. "Is it from my account? How does she have access to that?"

"Actually, it's been from the business account." Her arm tightened around his stomach. "I'm so sorry."

He sighed. "I'm thinking my mother is going to be sorrier." The enormity of the con made Mason chuckle and shake his head. "Wow, she was even willing to crawl into my bed naked. She must be taking a big chunk."

The muscles in Jessi's back tightened. "I don't know the value system here yet, so I don't know if the amount is equal to what she would have taken if they were tinnies."

"It's not far off. A Sziverian raimark is only a little more valuable than a Westican tinny on the conversion scale."

She blew out a long breath. "Well, in that case, I'll know more for you after today. But, you aren't going to be happy."

"Even if she'd only taken one raimark, I'd be upset." Needing a change in topic, Mason pulled the painting down. "Do you think you'd mind if we made your room officially our room?"

She pulled away enough to meet his gaze. "No, of course not. Why?"

"I'm going to move all my things. I think if we do a little rearranging, we'll both fit."

Jessi smiled and hugged him close again. "All I need is a bed and a dresser. You can take anything else out you need to."

Mason grasped her hand and pulled her to the door. "I know I've said this before, but thank you for putting up with this mess. I asked a lot of you when you moved here."

"I wish we were making more progress. I don't think anyone recognized me last night."

Mason squeezed her fingers. "If they did, you wouldn't have noticed. These people are stealthy and good at what they're doing. Someone has considered you some sort of threat or you wouldn't have been attacked in the courtyard."

"I know." She sighed. "He hasn't tried again though, so maybe it wasn't even related."

"No one else would have need to attack you, for any reason," Mason felt compelled to point out.

Mason stopped a house attendant on their way back to their room. He ordered all his personal items moved to Jessi's room, which would now be the Guardian Kynhaven suites. The Dowager was not to interfere with the new arrangements. This was one situation where his mother's elder status wouldn't be honored.

At the door, he handed the painting to Jessi. "I'm going to go get the dog before someone panics and does something foolish when they see him."

Jessi shook her head, a smile tugging at her lips. "I still can't believe someone was scared of him."

"We know he's an amazing dog. Anyone else? All they see is a massive wolf, who has big teeth."

Jessi held the portrait out, looking it over. "Where do you want me to put this?"

"On the bed for now. I'll figure out where to hang it later."

Much later, he figured as he strode down the hall. After he dealt with his mother's meddling, the theft from his business accounts, and the drug dealing happening within his city's borders.

29

HEALTH SERVICES
  Providence Lane Division
  Haven City

THE COLD, STERILE ROOM OF THE MORGUE SEEPED INTO Jonathon's bones. Alone in the silence, with only the dead to keep him company, he rested his elbows on his knees and stared at the sheet covered corpse a few feet from him. Ashen fingertips poked free from the white covering. Strands of limp black hair fell over the edge of the metal table. Clasping his hands together, he rested his chin on his braided fingers and tried to find a sense of calm.

At half past three in the morning, the call from a radio box, located on every corner for civilians to reach enforcement in an emergency, reported the murder. The location put the violent crime in Jonathon's jurisdiction. While under typical circumstances, the investigator on duty would have handled the call. The situation turned out to be anything but normal.

Then again, Jonathon mused as he scrubbed his hands down his tired face, when was homicide ever really ordinary?

On location, the Tribunii assigned had lost the contents of his stomach. Twice. The man had operated under Jonathon for three years, and was working toward his own Master Tribunii status. Or he had been. Violence of this magnitude had never been witnessed in Haven City until today. Sure, they had their fair share of assaults and murders, domestic and crimes of convenience. But not torture.

Days' worth.

Four to be exact if the Medical Scientist Examiner had gotten her timetable right. Before today she'd never been wrong, Jonathon didn't think she'd start now.

Four days of being cut. Being tied down. Being raped.

Anger seethed through his veins. Bile burned his throat. He ignored both. The same crime had landed across his desk seven months ago. Cut for cut. Rope burn locations the same. Similar physical description. Long straight black hair. Pale skin. Full figured. Light colored eyes.

The medical report sent from Westica on Cora Dandridge, at his request.

Someone had gone through a lot of trouble to recreate her murder. Jonathon knew for a fact the psycho who'd committed the crime was long dead. Which left him with two options. Either a copycat had found the file on his desk and decided to play, which meant he'd be seeing more killings from the archives, or someone decided to send a message. Since Delanee Ralston's first article from Kyn Manor printed a week ago, Jonathon was betting on a message.

Too bad his brutalized victim couldn't speak. That was his job, to be her voice, her justice. Jonathon forced himself to stand. At the table he brushed a finger along her cold, lifeless hand. Tomorrow her parents, her husband, and the infant son she'd left behind would collect her. Like Mason, Jonathon and everyone else, they'd get no answers as to why. Why her? Why the savagery of the crime?

Why did she have to be gone?

The unfairness of it all brought Jonathon to his knees on a roar of anguish. He tilted his head back and stared at the drab gray tiles of the autopsy room. Two nights ago, he'd been here, listening to the report on the findings of a four-year-old whose mother had mistaken him for an intruder during her high on magic lily dust. Three days before that it was a man who'd been brutally assaulted at the rail station by a group of kids looking for money. The man had none to give, and he paid for it with his life.

For years he'd worked himself into exhaustion for *them*. For the voiceless. The victims. And he'd verbally sparred and flirted with a beautiful journalist who'd always been sure to remind him *they* needed him. Almost eight months he'd lived without her laughter, her teasing, the words of encouragement he'd taken for granted, like the woman delivering them. Why? Why didn't he convince Cora to stay? Why couldn't he have been the man she clearly needed him to be?

Jonathon folded in on himself, his forearms resting on the frigid cement floor. Reading of Cora's torment had been one thing. Seeing the physical manifestation of it almost killed him.

"Hunter."

His name echoed as if in a void.

"Hunter! Asherwick!"

Jonathon forced his head to turn on the cold floor and met concerned silvery blue eyes. The man's short pale blond hair gleamed in the antiseptic light of the room. He pushed on Jonathon's shoulder, helping him into a sitting position.

"Are you okay?"

Jonathon shrugged the man's hand off. "I'm fine. Thanks."

The man looked at the table and then back to Jonathon. "I can take it away, if you want."

"Take what away?" Jonathon asked, his stomach still in knots.

"The memory of this."

Jonathon stared at him, confused. "What? How?"

He shook his head. "That I can't answer. And I don't offer this often. But that," he nodded at the table, "no one should have to remember seeing, knowing what you know about the crime."

"She lived through it."

"And her pain is gone now."

Jonathon collapsed back onto his butt. He rested his arms on his bent knees and let his head hang, trying to focus on his breathing. "Those she's left behind in life are just starting. They won't get the same courtesy. I can't find her killer if I don't remember the specifics."

"Very well." The man stood and walked over to the table. He pulled the folder with the crimes specifics from the holder at the end. "Has your promised made any progress on the communications with New Columbia, Perazil or Graecily?"

"Um." Jonathon tried to wrap his head around the change of topic, thankful for the rope to grasp to pull him through the quicksand of his own mind. "I'm not sure. When we asked her, it was before… everything. I haven't followed up to be honest."

Awareness seeped into Jonathon's slow mind and he glanced up at the man still pursuing the file. "Who are you?"

The man flashed a quick smile. "Sorry, I thought you knew me. Guardian Ryan Voklane."

"Wintersfall's intel team leader?"

"Liaison," Voklane corrected, his brows pinching while he flipped a page. He muttered a curse.

"Liasion?"

"Yes, to the Arch Guardian Synintel. I don't run the team, just relay orders and information."

"The Arch Guardian is interested in this?"

Voklane glanced up. "Everyone is interested, Hunter."

"Is the case being transferred?"

"Probably."

Jonathon didn't know whether to be thankful or not. "Sziverian National Investigative Division?"

"Yes."

"Will I stay informed?"

"I'll try my best."

Jonathon forced himself to stand on protesting legs. "I suppose I'll *try* to get Sylphine, my promised, to make radio contact, too."

A smiled tugged at Voklane's lips. "Guess I deserved that. I will do what I can, I promise." His attention returned to the information in his hands. "Of course, we both know a skilled interceptor, so, guess we can stay as informed as we want in the end."

"Merely skilled?"

Voklane smiled again, but said nothing.

"Oh, by the way," Jonathon began, remembering information he'd been asked to procure. "Sean wanted me to go to an ascension celebration party and see if I could learn anything."

"And did you?" Ryan asked, flipping through pages in the file.

"I heard an odd snippet of conversation. Something about the girl needing to be dealt with before they lost their leverage. Does that mean anything to you?"

Voklane frowned. "Leverage? That can't be good."

"No, I didn't think so either."

"They could be speaking about Dandridge's wife." Ryan titled the folder toward the covered body on the table. "Or even this poor girl here. It's interesting information though, and I will pass it to them. Thank you."

Jonathon shook his head and saw himself out. He took his sleek black two-seater Ariot home, keeping his attention on the road and not on the memory of the attempt at impartiality from the medical scientist describing the autopsy. She'd choked on her own tears too many times to be effective.

Jonathon parked beside his house. Wisps of icy rain

drifted in the air. The lamps burning near the street barely cut through the darkness. Crossing his arms against the chill, Jonathon walked at a brisk pace up the walk to the front door. No one greeted him. Then again, no one ever did. His little sister Ramsey had stopped waiting up for him when his smiles had disappeared. She said she didn't need another reminder of life's tragedy. She had a mirror.

After locking the door, he took off his coat and shoes in a routine that helped bring a sense of normalcy. Not ready to face the solitude of his empty bed, Jonathon sat on the stairs leading to the bedrooms above. The soft pelt of ice hitting the windows kept the silence from crushing him.

"Jonathon?"

The delicate musical lilt of her voice made Jonathon want to drop his head in his hands. A tremble ran the length of his body.

Sylphine.

He needed her with a strength, or maybe a weakness, he couldn't afford, nor would she offer. The warmth of her body settled over him as she sat on the stair. He wanted to lean into her, feel her soft flesh press along his, take comfort in simply being held. Instead he stayed still, kept the distance she demanded of him.

"What are you doing up still?" he asked.

"I heard you come home. I want to make sure you're okay."

"Am I?"

A shuddering breath rushed from her. In the darkness he couldn't make out her features, but he imagined them to be a little distressed. As a Sympath, she knew his surface emotions before she sat beside him.

"No," she whispered.

"No," he confirmed, head bowed.

Her touch fluttered along his sleeve, but stopped before reaching the skin near his wrist. "What happened?"

"Just a really bad murder."

"There is more."

"Yes." He turned even though he couldn't see her. "But you won't even touch me, so why share what really hurts?"

A sharp inhale told him he'd struck a nerve. He was too keyed up to care. "That is not fair."

"No?" He shrugged and stood. "Maybe not."

She joined him, but pressed into the banister, keeping distance between them. "Where have you gone? You are not the man I know."

"Sorry, I'm just me. Can't be anything more right now." He reached for her. With a gasp, she shied away.

"Do not!" Sylphine cried out, fear clear in her sharp delivery.

Something snapped in Jonathon. Ugly and broken, hidden and buried too long. The fear, anger, guilt and grief tore out of him in a torrent of pain. "I am *done*."

He yanked the silver band linking them together from his wrist and threw it on the stairs. The metal bounced and clanked on the wood floor, rolling to a stop somewhere in the darkness.

"I can't do this anymore. I *need* you. I need you to accept me, to trust me, to know I'd never hurt you. But you can't. You won't. I am not whoever hurt you, and I'm damn sure *nothing* like the offender you seem to think I'll be toward you."

"I know that," she whispered.

He took a deep breath and waited. One heartbeat. Two. She stood still, not reaching, keeping the distance a gaping rift between them. "No, apparently you don't."

Jonathon turned and left her standing alone.

30

———

"Are you sure?" Mason asked, leaning forward in the seat he occupied next to Jessi at the massive desk in the library. She'd paused in her pursuit to prove the lovely Tamina Peyton a thief and shared Mason's shocked stare at Kevin.

"Yes." Kevin took his tiny son from his wife's arms. Raina sat on a plush loveseat adjacent to the desk and patted the cushion. "If I hadn't wanted to make sure he didn't know I'd been there, I would have taken the book with all his notes."

Mason braced his arms on the desk. "And Jessalyn's name was in the book specifically?"

"Name, physical description, almost hourly whereabouts. Someone definitely knows who she is." Tanis let loose a distressed mewling cry. Kevin propped his son on his shoulder, making the infant look impossibly small. He bounced lightly on his heels while rubbing Tanis' back.

Jessi shifted in her seat. The frame groaned in protest. "Wow, well that's... a little scary."

315

"Actually, this is good," Sean said from his chair in front of the desk. Kat sat curled in the chair next to him. "We wanted to know if there was a definite connection and it appears there is."

Mason tapped his fingers on the desk. On the surface he'd always known the risks to Jessi if they discovered someone was indeed after her. The reality was a little harder to accept. He didn't want her in danger. Knowing someone spied on her made frost form in his veins. After Voklane's relayed message from Jonathon Hunter, Mason's anxiety had only increased. They needed more information, and soon.

A thought took shape and he stood. He walked the three steps to the nearest bookshelf that held all the two-hundred and fifty plus volumes of the Directory of Ranked Guardians. Each for a year the Dandridge family had held their rank. His family history in hundreds of yearly editions. Prior to that, only one generation, Richard Anthony Kynhaven, had held the Primary Guardian rank named after him. Running his index finger along the leather-bound spines, he searched for the one the year of Jessi's attack.

He dropped the heavy tome beside the collection of ledgers she had spread out. He opened to the first page, Key Guardian Acherett. The page revealed the brief history of the seat, awarded to one Vincent Niels Acherett in 752 PCE. His family held the rank for two generations. Three families had since been endowed with the Guardianship. The current Acherett was a one Melissa Janine James, serving in the seat at the Hall of Laws. She'd smiled warmly for her artist rendition.

Angling the book closer to Jessi, he tapped under the woman's image. "I want you to look through this book. There is a picture of every Guardian. If your father held a rank, he'll be in here. Would you recognize his image?"

Jessi took a deep breath and pulled the book closer. "Yes, of course I would. He's my father."

Sean steepled his fingers. "You think her father is a ranked Guardian?"

"Yes. Aside from being a very powerful merchant or banker. Anyone else in power, diplomats, investigators, intelligence operatives... all ranked Guardians." Mason glanced at Raina. "We know five years ago Synintel became extremely paranoid about his daughter's safety. Makes sense if someone he knew, either personally or professionally, within the Guardian community, had lost a daughter to whoever is slinking around the underground right now."

"Synintel communicates with very few people, and certainly none lower than a Master. You can skip to Master Guardian Alterose," Kevin volunteered.

Raina sighed, rubbing their son's little belly as Kevin laid the baby on his thighs. "Even that may be a bit low, but I wouldn't narrow the options any further."

"I agree there is a sense of a power, and safety that comes with the higher ranks. We have to decide what Synintel would feel was enough of a breach of said safety to feel threatened. A Master, Shield, or another Arch Guardian?" Sean asked.

Mason considered the question. "Definitely another Arch. A Shield would probably do it, too."

"He married his daughter to a Master though, so he must have felt there was safety there as well," Sean said.

Raina shook her head. "Sadly no. He married me to Kevin because he could keep me safe with his Gen-Heir ability. I think he would have done so even if Kevin were only a Key ranking."

Sean tapped his pointed index fingers against his chin. "Still, as the rankings get more powerful, the number of assigned seats gets smaller. I also think a Master is a safe assumption if he knew the man personally."

"All right." Mason flipped to the first Master Guardian page. "Then we'll start there and work backwards if none of the others produce results. I admit it's probably unlikely he'd concern himself with a threat against a lower Guardian rank. But we can't discount it if the other search proves fruitless."

"Agreed," Sean and Kevin said in unison.

JESSI KNEW SHE WAS SUPPOSED TO BE SEARCHING THE ENDLESS pages of names and pictures for her father. But after fifty pages, she'd arrived at Master Guardian Raiventon's page. The inked image was of a young, likely teenage Kevin Merrick, and directly below his name was small type in parentheses - *Inherited rank under E&R advisement.* Jessi chewed on the inside of her cheek and flipped through a few more pages. No one else had the small notation. Curious, she read the small biography. Despite Kevin being in his twenties when the book was printed, it appeared the information only dated to the year he'd become the next generation to hold the Master Guardian rank.

Wondering about Mason, Jessi turned to his respective page. Mason's image appeared up to date for the printed year. His hair only reached to his shoulders. The picture must have been drawn two years or so after his attempt to cut his hair again. She smiled and folded her arms, reading the family history. The weight of his lineage seemed to grow with each sentence until Jessi's smile turned to a frown and she wanted to hide under the table. The Dandridge family was the only family, aside from the original Kynhaven, to hold the seat.

Six generations in, the Endowment and Revocation committee had asked if they wished for the rank to be transferred to their family name. They declined. The then Primary Guardian had stated the Dandridge family was synonymous with the Kynhaven rank and they wanted to continue honoring history. The Dandridge's were a national treasure.

In the event the line dried up, the rank would likely be retired and replaced with the Dandridge name.

Over ten generations had assured the legacy endured. Eleanor was the only child of three qualified to serve in the Hall of Laws. Her husband, a York Jonas Umberton, had married and taken the Dandridge name as required when a male, or female, married into a ranking. When the Dowager was ready to retire, she'd passed the responsibilities on to her son, who chose to serve as an Intel Guardian than in a seat.

On a groan, Jessi dropped her head onto her arms. While she managed to gain some cultural knowledge thanks to Raina and the months she'd spent in the country, she was still sorely lacking. And yes, their love mattered, but Jessi couldn't ignore he was the last hope of the Dandridge family to continue the line.

Would their children be enough for Sziveria? Jessi touched her hand to her stomach. Carrying Mason's child would be more than she ever thought she'd get to experience in life. Duty, loyalty and honor were important traits to the culture she found herself married into. And she couldn't ignore their marriage never would have happened if he hadn't lost someone so important.

Dejected, Jessi closed the book. Muffled voices sounded outside the door a second before it opened, revealing Mason. He mirrored her displeasure when he noticed the closed volume.

"Is something wrong?" he asked, closing the door with his foot.

Jessi shook her head, her chin digging into her forearm from the motion. "No, I just wasn't making any progress."

Exasperation quirked his handsome features. "That's why you keep looking."

"All the names, history and obvious sacrifices families have made for the sake of their rankings was getting to me. I figured you'd prefer if I stopped rather than convince myself to walk out your front door and find the next ship bound for Westica."

He came around the desk and dropped to his haunches before her. With a quick push, he forced the chair to swivel his direction. He dropped his folded arms onto her thighs and stared up at her. "Talk to me."

"It's stupid," she said with a sigh. Unable to resist, she smoothed her fingers into his hair, pushing the strands away from his face.

"If something is bothering you, it's not stupid. So, talk."

Jessi sighed and relaxed fully into the seat. She twisted the ends of his hair around her fingers. "How do I find out if I'm a Gen-Heir? For sure?"

"You're worried about that?"

"Yes. If none of our children inherit a ranked ability, you're it for the Kynhaven seat. Does that not concern you?"

He sighed and wrapped his arms around her waist. He rested his head on the pillow of her breasts and pulled as close to her as he was able. "No. We've held this rank a long time. They weren't necessarily set up to be this way. That's why they're named, so we remember the first of each position. We honor them. Each new family is reminded of the sacrifice of one to take on the mantle of responsibility. No one else has been able to experience that for the Kynhaven seat, except ten generations of Dandridge's. Yes, it's an honor, but the country won't suffer if I don't produce another heir for her."

Jessi caressed the soft line of beard along his jaw. "And what about you? Will you be okay if all our children are... what are they called?"

"Gen-common?" He pulled back to meet her stare, rising so they were at the same level. "They will be perfect because they come from us. The two of us. How could I not treasure them? They'll forge their own future, no matter what they inherit genetically."

A fist clenched around Jessi's heart. Her gaze dropped to his mouth. Slowly, she slid her thumb along his bottom lip. His tongue flicked along the sensitive pad. "Who would you have married if you hadn't had to go to Westica in search of a killer?"

"Probably no one. I don't get the chance to meet many eligible women, and those I do, only care about my name and rank." He pulled her thumb into his mouth. Warm heat enveloped her finger and her heart skipped a beat. A spark of awareness leapt across every nerve, igniting a need he alone built so quickly within her. He sucked and then released her thumb. "You're all for me. You're everything. I wish you could see that."

Jessi leaned forward and brushed her lips to his. Love swelled in her chest. Something she wasn't quite ready to voice, but she could no longer ignore. "I'm starting to."

He took over the kiss in a hot sweep of his tongue into her mouth. The groan deep from his throat went straight to her center, setting her further on fire for him. His lips left hers to trail down her jaw to her throat. The firm, moist tip of his tongue teased the pulse throbbing just below her skin. Jessi gasped and rolled her head to give him better access.

"I don't know if I'll get enough of you," he breathed against her neck.

Jessi dug her fingers into his scalp, holding him close. "Me either."

He pressed a kiss to her collarbone and then sighed and returned to a crouch. His fingers dug into the flesh of her hips. "But, I know we'll be interrupted. So…" The pressure of his fingers increased on a flex. "Distraction. You didn't recognize anyone?"

She sighed too, missing the sensation and intimacy of their broken embrace. "No, not yet."

Flexing his jaw in thought, he motioned for her to rise. He sat in her place and then pulled her onto his lap. "Is there anything you remember at all about him? Anything special he did? You knew he was from here, so what did he say about us?"

Jessi considered his question, her focus on the book. Warm, long hidden memories of laughter, love and belonging shimmered into her mind. Her father's soft, deep laughter. Her mother's tender, affectionate touch.

"He only visited five or six times a year, but he never missed my birthday or bringing me a gift for Wintervail celebration before the ice set in." A smile tugged at her lips as the room faded away, replaced by a montage of the moments her father would always surprise her when he visited. "For my birthday, or Wintervail, he'd bring me these beautiful little silver animals. They were encrusted with bits of sparkling glass. I'd set them up on a shelf and when the sun shone into my room at the right time of day, a rainbow would sparkle on my walls."

Mason wrapped his arms around her waist and rested his chin on her shoulder. "What else do you remember about them?"

"They fit in my hand, and they always came with a little card that told about them. Most of the animals are extinct, they were from before the Cataclysm. I guess the artist liked to create them for historical reasons. I remember this one, I would stare at it for hours. The card said it lived in the ocean once, a ferocious predator. I looked at the weird bowl-shaped top, and tiny thin wisps if silver hanging down and wondered how something so fragile could be lethal."

Mason's chin rubbed along the muscles between her neck and shoulder. "A jellyfish."

Happy remembrance made her laugh in exclamation. "Yes! That's exactly what it was."

"Sailors still swear they live. They leave nasty burn lines on skin, sometimes fatal. But one has never been caught."

"Like all sea monsters." Jessi chuckled and wrapped her

hands around his wrists. "He said the animals were special, made just for me."

His chin flexed again. "He may not have been lying. I mean, if they're what I think they are, the artist creates on order only, and only a specific number. You have to place your order early, and pay the moment the bill is sent."

"But he creates for other people the same animal?"

"Yes. Say he decides to create a leopard. He sends a card out to his loyal customers letting them know orders are open, but he's only making twenty-five. The amount of the piece is listed and the first twenty-five to send their money get to pick up their leopard. If twenty-five don't take him up on the offer, however many are left are opened to the public to place an order."

Jessi considered that. "Wow, so they're rare, but not custom."

"They're very rare. And very expensive."

"They couldn't be that much. I was only four the first time my father gifted one to me."

He didn't argue. "Keep checking the book. Only a few people would have access to that artist financially. I'm almost certain your father is a higher-ranked Guardian."

31

THE THRUM OF CONVERSATION AND DELICATE CANDLELIGHT filled the cozy theater belonging to the town of Kyn. Both locals and guests milled about waiting for the show to begin. The quaint building boasted seven private balconies, each able to seat four people comfortably. Mason, Jessi, Tamina and Eleanor shared one, while Sean, Katria, Kevin and Raina shared another across the way.

On Mason's request, Katria had stashed a rifle and pistol in their box earlier in the evening, before other guests had arrived. Mason didn't want to take any chances. A gathering this size meant any number of troubles. From the drugs he'd learned were being sourced within the town's limits, to a human rabies outbreak, he wanted a sure method of containment should the need arise.

"This is wonderful, Dowager Kynhaven," Tamina's melodious voice said from a seat offset behind Mason. "A great turnout. I think every seat will be full."

A paper fan flapped in rapid swishes in front of his mother's face. "I should think so. We don't get a performance of this caliber often. I'm pleased they accepted my offer."

In the seat beside him, Jessi remained stoically silent. She observed the crowd with an aloof awareness, her gaze shifting the stage whenever a loud bang, or wayward violin string from the orchestra pit sounded.

Mason leaned close enough to her to keep his words between them alone. "You won't ruin anything by being yourself."

A startled twitch jerked her shoulders and she snapped her attention to him. "Everyone keeps looking up here, like they expect to see some catastrophe."

"Well, my mother *is* seated behind me."

Jessi laughed, the airy musical sound turning several heads below. She tapped his arm playfully with her folded fan. "Somehow I doubt your mother has ever embarrassed herself."

"There is a first time for everything," Mason said, shrugging.

She sighed and shook her head, but did what he'd hoped. Propriety drifted away and she became his wife. Slipping her fingers between his, she drew his hand to her lap, in full view of anyone staring up at them through theatre glasses. As the musical swelled and the lamps were dimmed to a low ember glow, her hold tightened in anticipation.

"Is this your first theatre show?" Mason whispered.

She shook her head, her gaze transfixed on the thick midnight curtain opening in teasing increments to reveal an elaborately decorated stage. "No, Raina took me to a few. I'm still a little amazed by it all, though. Believe it or not, Uconn doesn't have a theatre. The closest one was in Ontaria, at one of the higher learning academies. When my father visited, my mother didn't want to spend the time with him traveling. So, if we couldn't do something in Uconnland, we didn't."

The theater fell into silence as the narrator swept onto the stage. The long tails of his black coat fluttered. The polished wood of his cane gleamed in the bright stage lights. His voice boomed through the stadium shaped room to a roaring applause as he spoke the much-anticipated title of the perfor-mance. The show, a lighthearted romantic comedy, began with laughter.

Tamina decided she wasn't afraid to die. What would panicking over her soon-to-be fate do for her anyway? Days ago when she'd been told her new task was to sacrifice herself for the greater good, she'd balked. How could everything have gone so wrong so quickly?

The answer was obvious. Jessalyn Silverna. Tamina refused to think of the low-born Westican as a Dandridge. It was a dishonor not only to the family, but to Sziveria. The bloodlines should have remained pure. Somehow the little witch had managed to seduce the heir to a nationally recognized line. The plan, infiltrate the Dandridge household and find out what Cora had learned by *any* means necessary, had failed.

Sure, Tamina had managed to secure some healthy funds for the cause. The Dowager trusted her. And why not? As the sole daughter of a respected Shield Guardian, she was a great candidate for the woman's future hopes and dreams. Too bad her son didn't share those same ideals.

The ruse was over, however. Never would Tamina have figured she'd be caught, by the very woman she scorned no less. When she'd written of yet again another failure, being told the final means for her to be useful was to die, she wasn't terribly surprised. She'd expected a visit from a shadow in the night. Instead she'd been told to make sure the curtain was left open to the corridor at the theatre. She was to allow herself to become the first victim. If she didn't, she'd be one anyway by another means. Failure wasn't rewarded. If she were wise, she'd take the immediate method.

As the theatre erupted into another round of laughter, Tamina sighed with a smile. Any moment now. Any moment.

. . .

SHARP PAIN SHOT THROUGH MASON'S SHOULDER. HE TWISTED TO figure out what caused the discomfort, when his mother practically climbed up his torso. Pale and wide-eyed, Eleanor trembled, her body pressed to his, her gaze focused on something to the left. Her fingers clutched at the fabric of his jacket.

Before he could ask what the problem was, the bloody scene unfolding had him shouting a curse and reaching for his wife. Unmoving, Tamina lay on the floor. Blood seeped beneath her in a thick dark bloom along the blue carpet. A man in a hospital gown chewed at her throat. Long-nailed fingers clutched at her shoulders.

Jessi squeaked as he yanked her from the seat by the front of her dress. Thankfully, the fabric held. He moved her behind him with his mother. The human rabies syndrome infected stopped chewing at the sudden motion. His head jerked toward the movement. Mason froze. Bloodshot eyes darted in search of prey as his fingers flexed in the pliant flesh under him.

Mason sorted through his options. Balcony to a near two-story drop below. Someone would probably break something, but they'd live. There was enough of a gap between the HRS victim in their box to reach the corridor. Jessi and his mother could likely get away while he distracted the zombified human.

The man was clearly from a containment facility, and the only one he knew of was in Haven City. Someone had to transport him. Even the fastest Ariot took hours. The man was in the final stages. At any moment he could fully give in to the virus ruling his already dead body, and he'd finally be at peace. Until then, he could do a lot of damage, cause a lot of death, with Mason's wife and mother at the forefront of the danger.

Mason put his fingers in his mouth and faced Sean and Kat's box. He let lose a shrill whistle. The noise caused the monster to rise on a twitchy jump. Blood and viscous saliva slid down his chin and dribbled onto the front of the thin pale green gown. With its attention on him, Mason shoved Eleanor and Jessi past the curtains and into the hall. Jessi screamed his name. Mason ignored her. He made a quick motion with his leg to keep the focus on him and not the precious cargo he'd jettisoned from the box.

The zombie's head snapped back. A plume of red exploded behind him. A scream echoed through the theatre. More followed, joined by the panicked rush of humans realizing they'd been much too close to becoming prey. The infected teetered for a few seconds and then fell over Tamina's motionless body.

Mason glanced across the distance. The curtain fluttered to the box the team had occupied. Mason let the bodies lie and rushed to the hall. His mother sat against the wall. Face pale with shock, she stared straight ahead.

"Where is Jessi?" he asked, searching up and down the rapidly filling corridor.

His mother remained still, silent.

Mason crouched beside her. Panic clawed to be free. He ignored the dangerous emotion and grabbed Eleanor's shoulder. "Mother, where is Jessi?"

"Miss P-peyton…" Eleanor breathed, her body shivering.

"Miss Peyton is gone. Where is my wife?"

Eleanor shook her head. Mason stood, digging his fingers into his hair. People rushed past, pushing and shoving in their haste to be free of the building. He shouted above the din for his wife. A hand grabbed his right arm. Kevin came into his field of vision.

"Jessi's missing," Mason told him. "This had to be a set up to take her."

"We'll find her."

32

JESSI STRUGGLED AGAINST AN ARM BANDED AROUND HER CHEST and a hand clamped over her mouth. The man cursed and stumbled, but kept ahead of the noisy rush approaching from behind. He ducked into a side room. The sliver of light disappeared as he kicked the door closed. Jessi had no time to figure out where she was. Darkness closed her in with her captor. They hadn't taken any stairs, or even went that far.

The man pressed her further into the room until her body collided with a solid wall. Jessi held her hands up to try to brace herself, but his weight crushed into her. He didn't stop, his form pressing deep into hers until every inch of him slid along her. His hand left her mouth to move to her neck. In a firm, almost choking grip, he forced her head back. The hold around her chest disappeared. Air rushed around her legs as her skirt shifted.

"I have been a good man," her captor breathed heavily into her ear. "I obeyed when I was told to take them. I didn't touch any of the others. What did obeying get me? A damn Verdict Council inquiry, where I was deemed guilty and stripped of my rank and property. Do you know who wants me now? No one. I'm a social outcast. Poor. If I don't succeed in this last task, I'll be a dead man."

Jessi had no idea what he was babbling about, or what his tirade had to do with her abduction. Then again, she hadn't known last time either, and her captor had spoken similar random words into her ear... She squeezed her eyes shut. His hips pushed into her butt. The hard length of his arousal behind fabric pressed between her legs. Every muscle in Jessi tensed. *No, no, no!*

"Before they get *you*, because once again another failed where I would have succeeded if they'd only listened to me, I will get what *I* want first this time. I am in control. I am the one to be feared, to be respected."

His hips jerked and the clang of a metal belt being undone echoed around her. Jessi twitched from the noise and swallowed back the bile building in her throat.

"You aren't the prettiest of the wives." His fingers dug deeper into her throat, his shoulders pressed her harder into the wall. The tip of his tongue left a long, wet trail down the exposed skin of her neck to her collarbone. "But it's dark. I can pretend you're *her*. You smell sweet enough." His free hand grabbed the inside of her thigh, under her skirt and squeezed. "And you're close in size. Yes... you'll feel very good."

Jessi struggled to breathe. If she passed out, he'd still rape her. Unconsciousness hadn't spared her before; she had no reason to think this man would be any different. Her mouth went dry. She tried to swallow, but his hand, and her nerves, made the effort futile. Tears burned her eyes. Her heart pounded a stressed rhythm in her ears. Begging wouldn't work either, so she didn't try.

Despite the dark, she closed her eyes. She pulled Mason's face to mind. His touch, his kiss. His love. What she meant to him. Everything. Her eyes opened on a growl. She forced a scream free and used all her might to push against the wall.

Not expecting her momentum, the man stumbled from her. Jessi twisted, bringing her fist out, not caring what she connected with, just that she did. When she landed the hit to something soft, she kept going, bringing in her other arm and her leg. She thrashed, screamed, kicked, punched, forcing her abductor away with each solid connection she made.

"Only. My. Husband. Can. Touch. Me!" she screamed through her tears and anxiety.

They fell under her onslaught to the floor. Jessi scrambled up, making sure her knees dug into each location she could manage. Vindication swept through her at a hard grunt and pitiful whimper.

Light blinded her as the door burst open. Jessi was swept into strong arms. The familiar sharp, clean scent of Mason surrounded her. She curled into him on a sob she couldn't hold back. She buried her face into his shoulder. Her fingers clutched at the silk of his finely woven jacket.

"Shh, it's okay honey, I have you. You're safe," he murmured, his arms holding her tighter.

The chaos of panicked voices and running feet drifted past. Sean muttered a curse and a woman gasped in shock. Confused by the disorder around her, Jessi lifted her head enough to see. Katria held the doorframe in a tight enough grip to turn her fingers white. Behind her, Raina stood pale, hugging her torso, as if she were trying to make herself smaller.

"Sean," Katria pleaded. "Please, please, *please*, let me put a bullet in him. Just one. I won't kill him. Please!"

"No," Sean snapped from inside what appeared to be an unused storage closet.

"I'll use my smallest caliber round." She dug into a bag she had dangling from her wrist. A small silver bullet appeared between her fingers. "Look, see, I even have one with me. Please, my love, please let me do this."

"No."

"But—"

Sean leaned from the room, glancing down the hall. "I said no. If I let you shoot him, then Kevin will break both his arms, and Mason will insist on something too. There will be nothing left for the FIO."

Katria clamped her mouth closed. Jessi tried to make sense of the odd conversation. She shifted in Mason's arms. He looked down at her, concern bright in his eyes.

"Are you okay?" he asked, touching his forehead to hers.

"I am now. What's going on? You know him?"

"Yes, his name is Phipps Geier. He's a former Shield Guardian who lost his ranking when he attempted to smuggle in goods by falsifying documents using Raina's logistics code. At least, that's the official report."

Jessi sniffled and wrapped her arms around his shoulders. She knew he had to be getting tired holding her, but she wasn't ready to be out of the safety of his embrace yet. "And unofficially?"

Mason sighed. "That's a long story, honey."

Jessi considered the words Phipps had whispered evilly to her. "I'm assuming I'm not the only spouse he's attempted to kidnap."

"No, you're not. You were found the quickest, however." A weak smile tugged at his lips. "Thanks to your ferocity. He didn't stick you with anything?"

Jessi shook her head.

He kissed the top of her head. "Good."

A shudder ran through her. Jessi took a calming breath and buried her face in the crook of his neck, breathing the scent of him in deep. "I want to go home," she whispered against his skin.

Tension stiffened his muscles, but he nodded. "All right." He turned enough to see the small group and said, "Sean, are you okay to handle this?"

"Yes. Kevin is dealing with the HRS victims. I have Phipps

here. I'll use the town radio and call Voklane for further instructions."

"I'll take care of Eleanor," Raina offered.

Mason inclined his head. "Thank you, I appreciate that."

Jessi remained silent as he carried her from the rapidly emptying theatre.

STEAM SWIRLED IN THE AIR, MINGLING WITH THE SOFT PATTER OF water falling onto tile in the bathroom. Mason helped Jessi out of her gown. She had an almost desperate quality to her movements as she struggled to get out of the yards of light pink satin. Once free, she stumbled into the water. The thin silk of her thigh length ivory chemise clung to her like a second skin. Her hair, still swept up in a delicate knot atop her head, drooped under the force of the spray.

Mason struggled to stay out of the water, to keep from sweeping her into his arms and assuring himself once again, she was safe. Whether she was truly unharmed, he hadn't been brave enough to ask. Her behavior left no illusions. Phipps had tried, and Mason closed his eyes and hoped the former guardian had failed to accomplish the likely end goal of rape. The man's pants hadn't been around his ankles. His shirt hadn't even been pulled free. But as Jessi grabbed the soap and began to violently scrub at her skin, Mason's heart leapt into his throat.

Unable to stand her obvious anxiety, Mason stepped into the shower, still fully clothed. He took the soap from her hand and set it back into the dish. His slick fingers slid along her jaw, forcing her to meet his gaze.

"You're okay." He kissed her tears away and met her stare once more. "You're okay, understand?"

"He..." She closed her eyes, took a deep breath. A tremor slithered along her entire body. "He tried..."

Mason's fingers tightened along her jaw. "But he didn't. Right? He didn't."

She shook her head. Dark, soaking locks tumbled to her shoulders. Pins clattered to the tile around them. Mason finished the task, combing his fingers through the thick mass, relief filling him. She rose onto her toes, her hands fisting in the wet material of his shirt. Her lips brushed to his, once, twice, light yet desperate seeking kisses. Mason met them, but didn't do anything to further the questing of her mouth or hands. Simply took comfort in the warmth of her presence, safe in his arms, in the beauty of her emerging desire.

The water sluiced over them, between their bodies and joined mouths. When her tongue sought entrance, he opened for her, unable to stop from taking over the kiss. She let him, yanking his shirt open with such force the buttons popped free. Her fingers found his bare skin, splaying across his stomach to his hips, where she curled her fingers into the edge of his pants.

"You're wearing too much," she breathed into his mouth. Her lips pulled kisses from his, while she struggled with his belt.

"Honey, I don't think—"

"I don't think, I *know*. I need you. Now." She abandoned the belt and grabbed his jaw, dragging a long kiss from him. "Please."

Mason stared into her smoky jade green eyes, sheltered from the water by his presence over her. Slowly, he undid his belt. She made quick work of the buttons fastening his pants and then shoved them down. The feather light brush of her fingers along his shaft made his breath hiss free. He stepped out of his pants and kicked the saturated pile away.

"How?" he asked, wanting to give her complete control.

"I don't care, just… now, please." She rose on her tiptoes again and captured his mouth.

Mason attempted to keep things measured, but she

pressed her hips to his and tried to climb him. "Easy, slow down honey, there's no rush."

"Yes, there is. You don't…" Her voice broke and she tried again. "You don't understand what he tried. I only want you. I only want the memory of you, and me. Of us. Just us. Please, Mason."

Mason's heart cracked. He swept her up, his arms banding around her back, pulling her close. She wrapped her legs around his waist and held tight. Her fingers delved deep into his hair, her mouth closed over his in a frantic, open-mouthed kiss he didn't dare try to change. He brought her to the wall, pressing her weight into the cold tile. She lessened her hold around his hips enough for him to reach between them, to feel she was more than ready.

The muscles of her thighs flexed as his fingers slid along her slickened flesh. When she writhed and made wild little noises for him in her throat, Mason asked, "Like this?"

"Yes," she breathed, shifting as best she could along his torso until her opening brushed his hard length.

Mason held her upper thighs. He gritted his teeth and eased into her in careful, unhurried strokes, despite every nerve in his body demanding he slam deep inside her. In a warm, wet cocoon of satin, her body accepted him. Groaning, he kept his pace easy.

Jessi cradled his head, her body pressing tightly into his and he increased his tempo, using the delicate rhythm her rocking hips set. The heavy rush of her breath brushed across his ear. Mason turned his head and found her mouth, kissing her deeply as he thrust into her. The tremors of her climax started seconds before she tore her lips away on a cry, her back arching off the wall. Mason kept his strokes even, but quick. He pulled another wave of pleasure from her before joining her on the rush.

She trembled, her ankles unlocking from around him. Slowly he eased them to the floor and held her close. She rocked her hips against his, taking advantage of his still erect state inside her. He let her, kissing her neck, urging her by supporting her hips. She came apart on another cry and collapsed against his chest.

Wrapping her entire body around his, she buried her face against his throat. Tremors wracked her and he kept her pressed tightly to his chest. The hot splash of her tears mixed with the water flowing around them. Mason rocked her, letting her cry. He knew better than to try to change anything about their position.

She leaned away enough to look at him. She smoothed her hands along his jaw, up his cheeks and traced his eyebrows. Instead of rising to kiss him, she pulled him to her. "I love you," she whispered, and then kissed him with the heat of her words between them.

Mason's chest clenched. He shifted enough to lay her down and covered her body with his. He kissed her until they both struggled for breath again. When he rose, she smoothed the wet strands of his hair from his face and over his shoulders.

"You don't want to go back home?" he asked.

Confusion twisted her beautiful face. "I am home."

"But you said..."

She smiled, her eyes warm, yet tear-filled. "Mason, *you* are my home. You have given me everything. I never thought I could have this, what we have, what we are together. Someone tried to steal that from me again tonight, and I..." She took a deep, careful breath. "I knew he couldn't, because you love me. No matter what happens, I know you'll still love me, for me, because you don't see what everyone else does. And I love you so much. I'm sorry I didn't—"

Mason kissed her. "No. No apologies. Love is enough, Jessalyn. We are enough, and anything else, we'll work out. Together."

Her legs wrapped around his waist, pulling him closer on another smile. "Together."

Much later, they lay in the warmth of their bed. Mason rested on his side, his fingers trailing a fluttering path from Jessi's breasts to her pelvis and back up. Disbelief still made him want to ask her to repeat her declaration. He loved hearing the words. Loved knowing they were meant only for him.

"I wish Cora could have met you," he said before he could stop the words from tumbling out.

Jessi shifted closer until her fingers could brush his face. "I'm not going to ask if she would have liked me. You will feel obligated to say yes. Do you think we would have managed to get along?"

He laughed. "I don't know. I think she would have liked you simply because our mother doesn't approve. Cora was always on a mission to frustrate our mother. She had a true gift for it." Sadness swept through him, dampening the euphoria from earlier. Mason shifted until he could lay his head on her stomach. He wrapped his arm around her hip and hugged her close. She stroked from his scalp to the long ends of his hair. "I miss her so much."

"I know."

"I keep thinking any day it'll hurt a little less, but it hasn't," he confessed, staring at the shadows playing across the sheets near the end of the bed. Grief threatened to choke him. "I just... I still can't imagine my life without her in it. And yet here I am, living, unable to share all the amazing parts of life I've discovered."

"So share them anyway. However you need to."

Mason shifted, until he could see her. "What do you mean?"

"Write her letters, or create a sketch journal with all the things you'd want her to see. Just because she's gone doesn't mean you stop loving her, or that you have to stop expressing that love."

Mason kissed her stomach. "I might do that."

Jessi smiled. "Good."

"I have to go to Haven City tomorrow. Will you be okay here or do you want to go with?"

Her gaze shifted to the beast curled up on the floor under the window. "Everyone is leaving now because of the attack, right?"

Most of the guests had in fact cleared out the moment they'd arrived back at the manor. Only a few remained, unable to secure a mode of transportation to return them home.

"Probably, yes."

"I should be fine here, if you think I'm safe?"

"Sean, Kat, Kevin and Raina are staying until I return, so yes, you'll be safe."

"I'll stay here. With everyone gone, Wulf can run outside again." She shifted her leg along his. "How long do you think you'll be gone?"

Mason slid between her now open thighs and kissed a trail down her abdomen. "Not too long."

33

———

THE RUSH OF TRAFFIC ON THE STREET, AND PEOPLE ON THE sidewalk, created a constant hum of noise. The skitter of leaves and occasional chirp of a bird brave enough to chance a morsel from underfoot was drowned by the urban sounds. Mason tried not to breathe in the collective scent of humanity existing in closed quarters, remembering for the first time in a long while why he enjoyed the estate house. The quiet solitude and clean air might be worth suffering through his mother. Maybe.

Mason climbed the wide stairs to the bleak, gray stone FIO headquarters. The tall building left a cold shadow that stretched across the wide street. Phipps Geier had been taken into custody late last night and Mason wanted an update. He could cross off two tasks with his visit to the city, and hopefully have some decent information to return with to Kyn Manor.

At the front desk he received a visitor's pass and directions to the office he already knew how to locate. He found his way through the maze of corridors, less chaotic than an Enforcement building, but no less filled with people. Voklane's office door was open, the room empty. The small, tidy space reflected the man. Nothing personal decorated the walls or plain wooden desk. Everything was perfectly organized. Mason wondered what the man's house looked like inside.

The little, near priceless silver figures in Mason's pants pocket clanked together softly as he sat on one of the two chairs in front of the desk. He arranged them so they didn't dig into his thigh while he waited. They'd been placed in a special keepsake box, but since Mason didn't plan on staying in the city any longer than necessary, and he didn't want to advertise his precious cargo, he'd ditched the box.

Ryan paused at the door, speaking in hushed tones to someone. When he noticed Mason, he quickly wrapped up the conversation. He closed the door before sitting behind his desk.

"Was Kevin working with your wife?" Ryan asked, picking a pen up from the desk to fiddle with.

"No, why?"

Voklane's silvery blue eyes glittered with humor. "She did a good job on Geier. I think she cracked a rib."

"She stepped on him."

"Ah. Is that why you're here?"

"Partly. I might have some information for you."

The pin flipped in an arc of blurred motion between his fingers. "As long as I have information for you, correct?"

Mason shrugged. "Sharing is important, you know."

Voklane chuckled. "So my mother used to tell me." He sighed and set the pen down. "All right. Both Tamina Peyton and Phipps Geier had a tattoo on their upper left arms. Lifted wings with flowers between them. We think nasturtiums, but we haven't had a botanist confirm if it's a close, or even perfect, representation."

Mason absorbed the news. "She was definitely working with them?"

"Yes."

"She stole from me over the months she'd been working for my mother."

Ryan sat forward and folded his arms on the desk. "How much?"

"I don't know yet. Do you want the amount once I do?"

"Yes, it's possible you aren't the only victim. Whatever they're doing, they need funds. The drug and trafficking sales must not be enough." He rapped his knuckles on the wood. "Damn."

"What are they paying for they'd need that much capitol?"

Ryan shook his head. "Nothing good."

"Anything else?"

"Yes, but it's going to be difficult to hear."

Mason shifted to the edge of his seat and clasped his hands between his knees, resting his elbows on his thighs. "What?"

Voklane sighed again and stood. He went to the window and locked his hands behind his back. The light played off the pale blond of his short-cropped hair. Mason remained patient, noting the tense line of Ryan's shoulders. The man was clearly trying to figure out how to word his awful news.

"There was a rather brutal murder. Whether it was conducted in Key Guardian Asherwick's jurisdiction, or the body was dumped, we haven't been able to learn yet," he began quietly, turning enough from the window for Mason to hear, but not see his face completely.

"Okay."

"The murder was a copycat to your sister's."

If someone had punched him in the gut, the shock wouldn't have been any different. Mason stared at Ryan's back. "Come again?"

"An exact copycat. Asherwick thinks someone stole the report sent from Westica."

Unpleasant burning churned in his stomach. Mason

ignored the sensation, and the memory of the vivid description he'd tried all these months to forget. "What do you think?"

"I think the report was easy enough for anyone to ask for. Westica doesn't know who is actually official or not to be able to verify the legitimacy of a request. Since you're convinced Cora's death was the result of something she discovered, therefore her murder was likely an assassination gone wrong, they probably had access to the record before we even knew to ask for one."

Mason reached into his pocket and pulled out one of the little figures. "I don't think my sister's murder was an assassination. I know. Just as the same people likely meant to murder Jessalyn as a means to force the cooperation of her father."

Ryan stared at the glittery artist rendition of an animal once known as a South African Penguin. Cut obsidian and diamonds sparkled in the weak light from the window.

"What is that?"

"A Gerard Bachtell original."

Ryan's brows shot up. "Really? I've never seen one in person."

Mason turned the tiny penguin. "Jessalyn's father brought her one at least once a year. He hasn't been able to give them to her for at least five years. I took a chance and went to Bachtell's shop and asked for the animals in holding for Jessalyn Silverna."

"And he had them?"

"Six, yes. Purchased, but not delivered." Mason met Ryan's gaze. "Do you want to know who paid for them?"

Ryan took a deep breath. "Am I ready to know?"

"I wasn't."

Ryan shoved his hands into his pockets and rocked on the soles of his feet. "All right, tell me."

"Arch Guardian Praekasdian."

Ryan collapsed into his seat. "You're lying."

"I wish."

Ryan scowled and cursed a long, fluent streak. "Well, now I know why Synintel lost his ever loving mind so many years ago and married Lorraina to Raiventon." He shook his head. "She's really Praekasdian's daughter? Really?"

"I'm ninety-percent sure. I'll be a hundred-percent once I open his page in the Directory."

THE RUMBLE OF WHEELS ON GRAVEL ANNOUNCED MASON'S arrival home from the city. Excitement fluttered in Jessi's chest. Somehow, she managed to remain calm and seated. Doing anything else would send the dog resting on the floor into a bundle of chaos.

The house was dark beyond the library, where Mason's team had gathered. A peaceful solitude with all the guests having fully departed. Sean sat with Katria on the couch in front of the fireplace, a newspaper spread along their laps. Kevin leaned against the shelves nearest the door, flipping randomly through a book.

Jessi continued to try to solve the mystery of Tamina Peyton's thefts. So far, what she had to share with the family wasn't positive. Wulf lounged belly up, with his front paws curled into his chest and his ears flopped to the floor. Every now and again Jessi rubbed her toes in the soft fur of his chest.

Mason entered the room without flourish, closing the door behind him. Wulf whined and flipped onto his feet in an awkward roll. He bounded around the desk on light, excited feet. Mason kept walking, patting the happy beast dancing around his legs.

"What did you find out?" Sean asked, turning and bracing his arm along the back of the couch.

"A lot," Mason replied, then sighed.

Suddenly nervous, Jessi stood. He came around the desk and grasped her hand. Holding tight, he reached into his pocket and removed a handful of sparkling objects. Carefully, he set them on the table. The gem-studded silver glittered in the low light of the room. Jessi gasped and picked one up. A brilliant array of vivid blues and greens twinkled between her fingers in the shape of bird of some kind.

"Are these the same as what your father gave you before?" Mason asked softly.

Jessi nodded, tears burning her eyes. Still holding one of her hands, he reached across the desk and pulled the *Directory of Ranked Guardians* to them. As he flipped through the back pages, the rest of the team gathered around the desk.

When Mason stopped, he turned the book to face her. "Is this your father?"

The heavy beat of her heart echoed in her ears, adding to the tense silence that descended in the room. Jessi stared at the artist's rendition of her father, staring at her from the page with the same warmth in his gaze she remembered. A tear slipped down her cheek. She brushed her index finger down the picture.

"Yes..." She took a deep steadying breath. "That's him." She looked at his name, his entire name, and whispered it to herself. "Howell Cristoff Demaine."

"Arch Guardian Praekasdian?" Sean asked in disbelief.

Kevin cursed and raked both his hands through his hair. "You can't just meet with him."

"I know," Mason said. "I've already reached out to Wolvenguard."

Sean tapped the page. "Look, he listed her as his daughter six years ago." He glanced up, his amber gaze intense. "I'm assuming Aislynn is your mother? He listed her as his wife. That's why Silverna seemed familiar."

Jessi nodded. "Yes. Why would he do that? And who is he?"

"Were they married?" Sean asked.

"In Westica, but I don't know if it was recognized here. My mother was so paranoid about being associated with him she kept her name, and gave it to me. She said he was very important and people sometimes tried to do bad things to the families of important men."

"Turns out she wasn't so paranoid after all," Katria said with a frown. "He must have felt you'd be safe in Westica. His pride in his family was greater than any fear."

Sean's expression turned grave. "I think Cora was definitely on to something concerning the uninhabited zones being explored and possibly resourced illegally."

Kevin titled his head back on a heavy sigh. "By prisoners likely. Provided by Sziveria, because they had the Arch Guardian of the penitentiary system by the throat."

Jessi tried to follow, but still wasn't sure she understood. "My father is a warden?"

Sean shook his head. "No, he's over every warden in the nation, along with the Wolvenguardsman. While we have an Arch Guardian who leads the Wolvenguardsman, the teams who go after escapees, fugitive, and violent criminals being pursued by enforcement, Praekasdian is who Wolvenguard gets most of his orders from as far as what needs to be done. Or if something needs to be changed in how the teams are handling recovery or pursuits. Your father is in an extremely powerful position."

Sean's attention shifted to Mason. "You contacted Wolvenguard, you said?"

"Yes, he's going to reach out and request a meeting, nothing specified."

Kevin rubbed his bearded jaw. "Last I heard, he's living in the Northern Boundary, within a house he had built between Cliffs Edge and Stonebreak Prisons. Very remote."

"At least it's those two, and not Northern Pointe. I don't

think they thaw out except for two months a year," Mason said with a shrug.

Kevin shook his head. "You don't understand, they're all terrible. There's a reason the correctional facilities are in the south and the max security prisons are in the north. By choosing to live in the most desolate place in our nation, he must have wanted to make sure they couldn't bother him except when absolutely necessary. Maybe you'll get lucky and Wolvenguard will say the right thing to get him to come to Haven City."

Jessi tried to imagine her father, always carefree and full of laughter and life, living anywhere considered *desolate*. "He must have been desperate. I can't imagine him agreeing to do anything illegal."

Mason squeezed her hand. "Even the most seemingly loyal can be persuaded toward a cause. Losing you was probably his."

"Along with threatening his wife," Katria surmised, leaning in close to Sean. "They take anything important."

"But if they took everything, he would have been left with nothing worth saving," Mason said. "I bet Aislynn Silverna is still alive."

An invisible fist squeezed Jessi's heart. All the years she wasted living in fear of what her parents would think, how they'd react to her abduction and assault, settled over her like a heavy stone. "I need to see him. I have to know. He has to know *I'm* still alive."

Mason pulled her into the comforting shelter of his body. "You will, I promise."

34
___

A MONTH LATER...

A DENSE FOG OBSCURED THE LOOMING HOUSES OF THE ARCH District as their carriage clattered down the bricked street. Jessi still tried to squint through the haze, wondering which house belonged to her father, when he chanced to visit the city.

Rumor abounded that he'd ventured to Haven City weeks ago, at the behest of Arch Guardian Wolvenguard, but had swiftly returned to the Northern Boundary. Jessi knew the truth. Howell Demaine had returned three days ago. The team opted to wait for their reunion to ensure no one else had guessed at the truth.

Wulf panted at the glass. His short, quick breaths puffing a circle onto the surface. The swish of his thick tail brushed Jessi's skirt. Mason rubbed between the dog's shoulder blades at his nervous whine.

"He thinks we're leaving him with Wolvenguard again," Mason told her.

Jessi understood the canine's trepidation. "Do you really think he'll be there?"

"Why wouldn't he be?"

She shrugged. Nervous flutters made her stomach dance and muscles tense. "I don't know. Maybe we've been discovered. I don't know anything about this shadow world you seem to be part of."

"I've worked closely with Wolvenguard to make sure no one figured us out. Waiting a month since our discovery will help, too." He reached across the distance and rubbed her knee. "It's going to be okay."

Jessi wanted to crawl onto his lap and be held in his assurance. Instead she heaved a long sigh and went back to trying to see through the dense, swirling mist. The carriage crawled to a stop in front of two snarling wolf statues. Their driver opened the door. Wulf bounded out and up the fog-sheltered stairs. Mason helped Jessi from the vehicle, keeping a tight hold of her hand once she was on the sidewalk.

They walked up three steps before nervousness overtook Jessi and she had to stop. She pressed a hand to her wobbly belly. "What if he's angry with me?"

Mason tugged on her hand to get her moving again. "Then he's angry with you. Neither of us can control his emotional reaction."

Of course Mason wouldn't do what she wished and lie, saying her father couldn't possibly be mad at her. She forced her feet forward once more. "All right."

The massive front door was already open when they reached the final step. The inside didn't seem any more inviting than the outside. A vast, gloomy foyer branched off into rooms too dark to see beyond the doorways. Wide stairs split at the second floor and curved in an elegant sweep to the third level. The house was the epitome of wealth and power.

Jessi had learned enough of Sziverian history to know the man who dwelled within the monolithic house wasn't the original owner. "Did the first Wolvenguard want to make sure people felt uncomfortable in his house?"

"The first Wolvenguard was considered little better than the wolves he ran," a deep, smooth voice said from the depths. "He decided to use the fabricated reputation to his advantage."

Jessi gasped and tried to find the speaker. Six-feet-five-inches of man shifted from the recesses of a door. With broad shoulders, a trim waist, and arms as big as Mason's, the man looked like coiled power in a maroon knit sweater and slate gray slacks. Dark hair fell to his shoulders. The sides were pulled away from his face in a knot at the crown of his head. Amusement danced in his blue-green eyes, an intense contrast against his bronze skin. Jessi figured he was hand-some in a feral sort of way. While clean shaven, there were rough edges to his face, as though at any moment he could break into a vicious snarl worthy of the Ruthenarc pack he controlled.

He held out a large hand. "Deklan Ralston."

Jessi placed her fingers on his. "Jessi Dandridge. Thank you for taking care of Wulf a couple months ago."

"Of course. He's a great dog. I'd be lying if I said I'm not disappointed he isn't being worked."

Jessi smiled. "I'm sure if he could agree, he would. I'm a bit attached to him though, sorry."

Deklan grinned and crossed his arms over his wide chest. "I know the feeling. Your father is waiting in the green house for you. My wolves are upstairs, so you don't have to worry about them interrupting."

"We really appreciate you doing this for us," Mason said.

"No problem. I have a huge family. I couldn't imagine not being able to see any of them for years. More than happy to help." He pointed them in the direction of the conservatory, although Mason appeared to remember the way.

Time seemed to stretch as they walked through the dim,

open space to the glass doors at the end of the house. The muffled song of birds and fluttering leaves drifted from the opening. Tendrils of humidity and the scent of fresh dirt brushed past Jessi. She tried to focus on the signs of nature. Not the crazy stressed energy zinging from one nerve to another within her.

The back of a man's head came into view. He wasn't alone, however. A woman sat next to him. Her fading red hair was swept into a messy pile atop her head. She rested her cheek on the man's shoulder. Jessi had been expecting her father. She hadn't anticipated seeing both her parents.

All the fear and hesitation faded in the reality of her family within reach. Mason's fingers slipped from hers as she ran through the door with a cry. Her parents stood. Shock registered and then they rushed to meet her, tears streaming down their cheeks. The warmth and safety of their embrace encircled her. Different from the security of Mason's, but to her inner child, no less powerful.

Howell pulled back first. His hands cupped Jessi's jaw. His green eyes, the shade she'd inherited from him, searched her face. "It's really you. We… we didn't dare hope it was true."

Her father had aged more in five years than she'd have thought possible. Heavy lines edged his eyes and creased his forehead and cheeks. The once dark brown of his hair was mostly a rich gray. The years had been kinder to Aislynn. Her golden eyes glimmered with unshed tears. Fine lines marked a life spent mostly laughing.

Aislynn brushed slender fingers across Jessi's cheek. "Our Jessalyn, a beautiful grown woman." She looked to the doorway. "And married now."

Jessi grasped their hands in hers. "My husband, Mason Dandridge, Primary Guardian Kynhaven. He found me in Westica."

"We know of him," Howell said, reaching past her to offer

Mason his hand. "We can't thank you enough, Guardian Kynhaven."

"It's not me you need to thank, but the man I'm assuming you sent to rescue her. Wilson and his Ruthenarc," Mason stated.

Jessi stared at her father. "You sent Wilson to find me? How?"

Howell shifted in discomfort. He stepped back and rubbed his hands on the front of his tan pants. "I didn't know what he'd find and I told him he could never tell me. I couldn't know if you were safe. At some point we would have accidently put you back in danger. He just needed to keep you safe."

Jessi pulled away from her mother and went to sit on one of the many chairs situated around a low wooden garden table. Beyond the glass outside, a wall of dense gray cocooned them in complete privacy. They couldn't have asked for a better day to meet in secret. Mason took the chair beside her. She sought his hand and he obliged, twining their fingers together. The simple touch helped ground her.

"Mason's team has their ideas about what may have happened," Jessi began as her parents sat across from them. "But, if you're able, I'd like to know the truth from you."

Howell leaned forward and braced his elbows on his knees. He clasped his hands and stared down at them. Jessi waited patiently. His shoulders sagged, as if they weight of what he had to say suddenly fell on him. Aislynn rubbed his back and smiled tenderly when he met her gaze.

"You know your mother refused to marry me at first." Howell took Aislynn's hand from his back and held it tightly. "A traumatic experience in her past taught her the families of men in power were targets."

"And you didn't feel that way?" Mason asked quietly.

Howell shook his head. "No. Sziveria has always been safe, except for petty crime that all nations face of course."

"We have our share of the dangerous," Mason pointed out. "Or we wouldn't need the Wolvenguard teams."

A flush bloomed across the man's cheeks. "True enough. However, to that point, nothing ever happened to ranked Guardians, especially high-ranking. I figured being married to me made her the safest she could ever be."

A sad smile turned up Aislynn's lips. "I knew better. I refused to take his name, or live in his home country. For so many happy years, he seemed to prove me wrong."

"Then I was approached and asked to betray my country. I refused, and shortly afterward you went missing," Howell said, meeting Jessi's stare. Regret and pain shimmered in his green eyes. "Since it happened when I was visiting, I knew I'd been followed. Someone had suspected my family lived in Westica. They didn't threaten you outright. Didn't even give me a chance to change my mind. You were taken right out from under us.

"Your mother didn't handle it well. She knew your disappearance had something to do with me. I tried to assure her that couldn't possibly be the case. I found out differently when I arrived back in Sziveria and was told if I didn't agree to work with them this time, Aislynn would be next."

"Did you?" Mason asked, squeezing Jessi's fingers.

"No." Howell sighed and sat back in the chair. He dug his fingers into his thick, dark hair. "Six months later, I walked downstairs to find Aislynn tied up in the middle of my foyer. A note said this was my last chance. She wouldn't survive another encounter with them, or another rejection from me. Unless I wanted her to share Jessalyn's fate, I needed to start cooperating."

"So you did," Jessi surmised.

"Yes, to my shame I did."

Mason shifted in his seat. "What did they ask of you?"

A heavy frown deepened the lines of her father's face. "Something that should have had me turning in my resignation as Arch Guardian. But I figured they'd probably figure out a way to put someone in power they could control easier."

"Do you know who they are?" Mason asked.

"No. I only receive written notes or radio transmissions. The letters only have the strange emblem of nasturtiums framed in—"

"Wings," Mason finished. "A man and woman we believe to be associated with whoever the group is had the design as a tattoo."

A glint of excitement sparked in Howell's gaze. "So you know who they are then, what they want?"

Mason shook his head. "No. It seems everyone is kept very compartmentalized. What the FIO was able to gather, the members are assigned handlers, whom they deal with specifically. We *do* know they're after some sort of change in leadership."

"What kind of leadership?"

"Elected leadership."

Howell rubbed his jaw thoughtfully. "That doesn't make sense with what they've been requiring of me."

Mason sighed. "Except, high level takeovers require a lot of money and a lot of loyalty, which money sadly buys. If they've been requiring of you what I think they have, then it makes perfect sense."

"You already figured it out?" Howell asked in shock.

"Almost a year ago. After learning you're Jessalyn's father, and who you are, it only confirmed our fears. They've been asking you for prisoners, correct?"

"Yes."

"How are they getting away with it?"

A hard swallow bobbed in Howell's throat. "Ghost transfers."

"Come again?"

"It's called a ghost transfer. I fill out paperwork like

normal to transfer prisoners from one location to another. A routine enough event when someone has proven they can be trusted at a correctional facility, or they're causing too much trouble down south and need the maximum security. Even Boundary prison transfers when two or more inmates start a war that won't end unless one of them dies. I compile the lists, set the transfer in motion." He released a long breath, looking past them both the thick foliage beyond. "Except, the prisons don't receive any information about the incoming inmates. They disappear, like ghosts. I don't know what happens to them. I only know they don't remain in Sziveria. They're loaded onto ships, usually at Port Tabria."

Jessi glanced at Mason. She hadn't learned much about the geography of the country yet. "Where is that?"

"It's the northern most port in the nation. There's an inlet sheltered by the Tabria mountain range. Beyond that, the seas get too rough for a commercial harbor, and there's too many ice drifts, except for two months of the year. Port Tabria is able to function about six months out of the year, maybe more if we're having a temperate year," Mason explained. He turned his focus to Howell. "We learned about a year ago they've been forging cargo manifests coming into Port Scarbrough. Make's sense they aren't using the same port for exporting."

"Especially considering the cargo is human in nature," Howell stated grimly.

"Have you kept records?" Mason asked.

"Yes, of course, but I can't risk anyone seeing them." His hand covered over Aislynn's. "Especially now. However, I knew at some point they'd be discovered. You can't have a growing operation go unnoticed. While I know I'll be stripped of my ranking, I want to avoid prison time if possible. I needed to keep track of all the evidence I could."

Jessi watched Mason closely, wondering what was going

through his quick, strategic mind. He rubbed his thumb along the thin strap of a beard along his jaw.

"I don't think you're in jeopardy of losing your rank just yet. I'm obviously in no position to make any promises, but if you'll meet with Synintel's liaison, I think he can," Mason said.

"Who is he?" Aislynn asked, her eyes wide with trepidation.

"His name is Ryan Voklane. He's very trustworthy. Synintel uses him to vet Guardians placed on intel teams, and as the main communicator between himself and the FIO. If you want to avoid being detected, I suggest you start there."

Howell's frown became somehow grimmer. "You're thinking he's going to somehow perform this vetting process on me?"

"I think it would be a good idea if he does. You've been coerced into what amounts to human trafficking of slave labor if we're correct in where we believe the prisoners to be going. Voklane can help you start your case process to clear your name, quietly. If you can prove you came forward the moment you were able to safely share your information, it'll go a long way."

Howell sagged further into his seat on a long exhale. "Yes, I suppose you're right." He looked at Jessi. "We won't be able to meet again for some time, it's not safe."

Aislynn stiffened and shook her head. "No. I'm not staying away from her."

"Darling," Howell implored, turning to face her. "Think of the risk."

Aislynn clutched at his hand. "I am. She can come to the Northern Boundary to visit. No one ever goes beyond the pass, you know that."

Howell glanced at Mason. A flutter of hope settled in Jessi's chest. Mason seemed to consider their words carefully.

"I have a friend who owns a house in New Hampton. I'm

sure he'd let us make use of it whenever we wish to. Neither of us can be positive it'll be completely safe, but usually the Northern Boundary thrives with isolationists. No one will give out any information if asked."

"I agree," Howell said. "It's why we decided to deal with the constant cold and bleak environment. At least we have privacy."

Tears filled Aislynn's gaze again. "You have to consider coming soon. There's someone we really want you to meet. We don't dare bring her beyond the pass. No one else knows about her."

"Who?" Jessi asked.

A joyous smile brightened her mother's face. "Your little sister, Keralynn. She'll be two next month."

Howell's features softened. "She came as quite the surprise for us."

For a brief moment, her parents looked completely happy, content in their position in life. They'd seen beauty come from a terrible situation. And couldn't Jessi understand that? Mason seemed to as well, brushing a fluttering kiss across her knuckles.

"I can't wait to meet her," Jessi said in all honesty.

Aislynn beamed. "We will make it happen, we'll make it work. Both my babies in my arms, what more could I ask for as a mother?"

35

*K*YN *M*ANOR

Three months later

J*ESSI* *WAVED* *GOODBYE* *TO* *THE* *WORKERS* *AS* *SHE* *LEFT* *THE*
greenhouse after having helped box up the latest shipment of
lavender and vanilla scented soap bound for Italyssa. She'd
discovered working the greenhouses passed the time quicker,
as it had when she'd first arrived at Kyn Manor, whenever
Mason went away. Each time he left for a mission, sometimes
only for a couple days, other times weeks, she missed him
more. Thankfully he hadn't been gone months again. Jessi
figured if that happened, she'd escape to the Northern
Boundary to stay with her parents. She could only handle so
many days in a row of Eleanor Dandridge.

Wulf trotted beside her. Dirt coated the top of his nose and
his paws. Jessi smiled down at him. "I see you've been
digging again. Hopefully not where I'll be yelled at about it
for *your* adventures."

He panted what she swore was a smile up at her. Jessi
ruffled the fur between his fuzzy ears. At the house she

slipped her work boots off at the backdoor into the kitchen. The staff greeted her warmly on her way through. They didn't stop her, since Jessi knew how Chef Sal felt about the dog in his workspace. She understood and tried her best to respect his wishes that they only ever *pass through*.

An odd bustle of activity echoed in the foyer. Jessi slowed, frowning. Claire spotted her, hesitated, and then with squared shoulders, approached.

"Miss Silverna," the attendant elite said through gritted teeth. "The Dowager wishes to speak with you."

When did she become Miss Silverna to the household? Frowning, Jessi noted several staff members carrying bags out the front door. She glimpsed the family carriage at the bottom of the steps. "Where?"

"She's outside." The woman grabbed her hand. Tears brimmed in her eyes. "I am so sorry."

Jessi didn't know how to reply, so she nodded her thanks and then patted her thigh for Wulf to follow. The dog stayed close, brushing against her skirts with each step. Eleanor stood on the bottom stair outside, surveying the loading of the carriage with the same regal air as she did when mingling in a room full of guests. The moment she spotted Jessi, she shifted enough to be able to see both her and the carriage.

"Ah, there you are. I was worried I'd have to send someone to fetch you." The Dowager waved a hand at the carriage. "You're all packed. What my son has procured for you, he will decide if you keep or not when he returns home."

Jessi blinked in confusion. Her heart did an uncomfortable turn in her chest. "I'm sorry, what?"

"Your year was up this morning." A mock expression of sympathy crossed Eleanor's face. She brushed her fingertips across her chest. "I'm sorry, did you not realize?" The compassion melted into a hard gleam. "Or did you think you could keep living here as the mistress we both know you've always been? Well, I won't stand for it. I honored the contract while it was active. But as of five this morning, you are no longer my son's wife. Or did you sign a new contract before he left?"

Jessi fisted her hands at her sides, hating the flush of heat fanning from her cheeks. "No."

The Dowager's dark eyes focused on her stomach. She flicked a well-manicured nail out. "And you aren't pregnant?"

Gritting her teeth, Jessi somehow managed to say, "No."

"Then you can take your beast and return to wherever it is he found you." With that, she swept up her long maroon skirts and went back inside without a backwards glance.

Mortified, Jessi stared at the long drive, willing Mason to suddenly arrive and save the day. She didn't know what he'd do when he arrived home to discover his mother had kicked her out. Would he be angry, or would the Dowager somehow manage to convince him signing a second contract wasn't in his, or the family's, best interest?

Taking a deep breath, Jessi shook her head. She would not allow the woman's negative actions to influence her. They had something stronger than the Dowager would ever be able to take away. Holding the thought captive in her heart, Jessi asked the driver to take her to the Raiventon house in Haven City.

The moment Mason walked into Kyn Manor he knew something wasn't right. His trepidation was confirmed when Claire Miggins pulled him aside in an urgent manner unusual for the normally composed woman. Nearly crying, she somehow managed to explain what had happened two days before he'd arrived. Mason thanked and assured the staff that had gathered during the explanation he'd handle everything. However, he couldn't guarantee he or Jessi would return.

He found his mother reading in her private sitting room.

A cup of steaming tea, and a small collection of colorful petit fours were arranged artfully on a plate on the table beside her chair. She placed a cake in her mouth before turning a page.

"I see you made it home safely." Another page turned.

Mason took a calming breath and sat in the plush seat across from her. Late evening sun cut a golden path through the windows and across the thick navy carpet. At one time, he and Cora had played together while their mother relaxed in this very same manner. A stab of nostalgia tore at his heart.

"Why did you send my wife away?" Mason asked, seeing no point in small talk.

"I didn't send your wife anywhere. You are currently unmarried." She gestured toward her desk across the room. "I have a list for you however, now that you've decided it's time to take a wife."

"Mother, I love you, I do, but Jessalyn *is* my wife. She will always be my wife. Our assignment ran over by four days. Had I known you would have pulled this trick, I would have made sure to sign our new contract before I left." Anger seethed through his veins. He took another slow, calming breath. "I never once thought you'd do this to her. Or to me."

A grimace twisted her face. "She is a Westican. She was never fit to be your wife, or carry the Primary rank with you."

"She is half Sziverian, and is more fit than anyone you could possibly find for me."

Eleanor waved her hand dismissively. "A father the paper claimed was no one special, and a mother no one has heard of."

"The paper wrote what was requested to keep her, and her father, safe," Mason ground out. "I didn't tell you because it doesn't matter to either of us, but her father is Arch Guardian Praekasdian. Her mother is the daughter of a Ruthenian diplomat."

The confectionary square she'd picked up tumbled from her fingertips. "*What?*"

"You were always so obsessed with how much higher we could climb the social ladder, you never stopped to see we're as high as we're ever going to get. I could marry a pie-maker's daughter, and no one would care. We'd still be the same renowned, recognizable rank. My children would still be respected because they carry our name." Mason jumped to his feet and clasped his hands behind his back. He stalked to the window. The dying sun set the landscape on fire in brilliant shades of orange and red. "And if I never had a genetic heir capable of carrying on the rank, we would survive."

When she remained silent, Mason glanced over his shoulder. Heaviness weighed on his heart. "If you insist on refusing to recognize my wife, you will lose another child. I will choose Jessalyn every time. I love her. Please don't make me choose."

Tears brightened Eleanor's dark eyes. She pressed a shaky hand to her mouth and looked away. "I just wanted what was best for you both. But there was too damn much of your father in each of you. Too free, too independent. I knew when I married him, I was taking a huge risk. But he came from a good, strong family. He was willing to take the Dandridge name, along with the supporting spousal role when I took the Kynhaven seat at the Hall of Laws. I never imagined both of my children would favor their father for their personalities. Especially my Gen-Heir."

Mason shoved his hands in his pockets and turned. "Nothing wrong with independence."

"Except it killed your sister, didn't it?" A tear rolled down her cheek as she met his stare.

The fist around his heart clenched tighter. "You know, I used to think that, too. But Cora didn't die because she was curious, or even independent. She died because someone decided the information she'd found was worth more than her life. It's not right, or fair, but it's what happened.

"And we can say, well what if she hadn't gone? But we

both know she would have searched with the same persistence here, and likely the same outcome. She was driven to find the truth. I miss her, more than anyone will ever understand, but she made her own choice, followed her own path, and I can't blame her, or me, anymore for the outcome of her decision."

"I think, as her mother, I can say I understand how much you miss her."

Mason shook his head. "No, you can't. She was my twin, a literal other half of me. From the moment you and father created us, we'd existed together. Even when I was away on an assignment, I *knew* I had a twin gallivanting around Sziveria, living a life of lust and intrigue. She would be here when I arrived back on these shores, ready to drive me insane with her antics, because she was the only one who could."

He rubbed his chest and took a bracing breath. "Now there's this hole, that Jessalyn has helped mend, but that I know will never fully heal. It can't, because Cora will never be in our world again. But I have to live *my* life, and I'm going to, my way, as my twin would have insisted, and expected."

36

MASON KNEW IF HE ALLOWED HIMSELF TOO MUCH TIME TO THINK about returning to the Haven City house, he wouldn't. So he sent a message, and the carriage, to Raiventon to collect his wife. He took the time waiting for her to arrive by simply existing in the tomblike silence of a house once full of life.

A full year had passed since his world had shattered in the foyer he seemed unable to move from. Every visible surface was spotless. He'd continue to employ the necessary staff to keep the dwelling functioning. Except for the silence, nothing had changed. A large woven basket overflowed with mail. Memories drifted like ghosts through his mind. Cora running down the stairs, excited to see him, or sitting at the dining table, still refusing to find them a chef because she was too disgusted with the one she'd fired, or them arguing over things too stupid to care about now.

Mason shook away the fragments and forced himself to his office, the overflowing basket of mail in his arms. No one had greeted him and he wondered if the staff somehow knew he needed the time alone to process. His space remained as cluttered as ever, yet devoid of dust. He'd never figured out how the housekeeper managed. Taking a deep breath, he set the mail on his desk and stared at all the colorful envelopes, unrolled newspapers, and advertisement cards.

Buried in the depths, notes of sympathy and condolences would attempt to offer comfort no one but his wife had ever managed. While he knew he owed all the senders some sort of acknowledgement, he wasn't up for reading any of their words today. He quickly sorted through the mess, throwing anything he didn't care about into the burn basket. At the bottom, a thick envelope with familiar handwriting waited for him. Mason's breath lodged in his throat. Carefully, almost in reverence, he lifted the package and sat down heavily in his chair. The wood groaned from the sudden weight after not having been used for over a year.

Cora's loopy cursive was a little shaky, making him wonder if she'd been nervous or scared when she'd written the address. He licked his suddenly dry lips and leaned back, letting the bundle rest on his lap. Blowing out a breath, he dug his hands into his hair and stared up at the ceiling. Finally perhaps now they'd have a reason. Answers that had been here, only he'd been too torn up to return. Not that visiting would have brought her back. Nor would the contents likely hold any kind of consolation.

Lost in thought, he heard Jessi call out for him. The echo of Wulf's bark sounded in the quiet interior. A sense of peace washed over him. They'd make new memories in this house, together, with their children. Led by his butler, Tybalt, Jessi arrived at his study and came to a full stop inside the door. She took in the chaos that was his space.

"Wow, this…" She grinned. "Is exactly how I envisioned your space when you were in Westica."

He couldn't help but return her smile, despite the heartache pounding in his chest. "Really?"

"Yes, really." She walked slowly around the room, her focus on all the sketches he'd completed of some of the exotic places he'd been on assignment. "These are amazing."

"Thank you. Now come here."

An enticing flush enhanced her cheeks. She closed the distance, picked up the unopened package on his lap and sat. "I missed you."

"I missed you, too." He pressed a gentle kiss to her lips.

She glanced down at the thick envelope. "What's this?"

"Cora sent it, from Westica."

A shaky gasp left her. "Oh. Do you want me to open it?"

Mason wrapped his arms around her and buried his face in her neck. He breathed in her sweet scent and pulled on the sense of calm she brought. "I don't know."

She wrapped a hand around his forearm and squeezed. "We can wait, if you need to."

"I shouldn't."

"But you can. It's not going anywhere." Her fingers toyed in the loose ends of his hair draped over his shoulder.

"No." He took another slow breath. "I need to know what she found that someone felt was worth her life. No one suspected she had the time to send anything, so there are likely vital clues."

Jessi glanced at the overfilled burn basket. "Or when they came to search, it was so buried underneath junk they didn't even know you'd received anything."

"Possibly. Cora knew what she was doing though, she was one of the top journalists in Haven City. She didn't get there by being foolish. If she sent it before they suspected anything, they may have believed she never had time." He rested his cheek on her shoulder and stared at his name in black ink. "Go ahead and open it."

Nervousness bunched in his stomach as Jessi tore open the seal. She pulled out scraps of paper, newspaper clippings, and hastily scrawled notes. All the research he'd expected to have been found in Cora's hotel room was inside. Cora had sent him everything. Jessi handed him a crumbled slip of what looked like hotel stationary. Fingers shaking, Mason unfolded it one handed, unable to let go of Jessi.

Mason,

They call themselves the V Alliance. They're based out of Sziveria, but are working hard to relieve inhabited countries worldwide of resources the nations don't even realize are available to them. They're using slave labor, mostly prisoners, either in secret, or by trade agreement with countries like Mark Inland, and kidnappings from Floradesol, and unsuspecting single male tourists from Monaco Sands. The income they're generating is for a purpose I haven't been able to pin down yet. Hopefully I've sent you enough to follow the thread I've found. I know these words will come as little comfort since I'm positive I've been found out and will likely not return home to you. I'm sorry, I know I should have listened. Tell Jonathon—

The note ended abruptly. Mason flipped over the page, knowing he'd find nothing, but unable to stop all the same.

Jessi sniffled. "Something must have happened to make her believe she'd run out of time and needed to send this immediately, without finishing it." She set everything on the desk and wrapped him in her arms. "I'm so sorry, Mason."

He hugged her close. "This is more than we had before. I just…"

She tightened her hold. "I know, would rather have her back than her words."

"Yeah."

"At least you know what we've discovered and what she says line up. You have answers now."

Mason set the note on top of all the other documentation. "A new place to start searching. I'll get this all to Voklane. Did you see anything?"

"Just her writing as fast as she could. She was scared," Jessi whispered.

Mason hugged her again. "Okay…" He took another centering breath. "Okay, thank you."

"Are you going to tell your mother?"

"I'm not sure. Maybe. Probably."

"You could give her the note to read," Jessi suggested.

Mason shook his head. "I think it'd upset her more than comfort. But, we'll see. I'm not too happy with her right now."

"Doesn't mean you should keep this from her."

"I know," he agreed and then slid his fingers along her jaw and tilted her head back. "We have to make this official again. You and I. If you want to."

She moved her jaw in thought. "Can we stay here?"

He brushed a soft kiss onto her lips. "Actually, I thought we'd spend a few weeks up in the Northern Boundary. It's summer, so only freezes at night. Wulf can discover ocean waves and you can finally meet your sister."

"That would be amazing." She leaned back and searched his gaze. "How long this time?"

"What do you mean?"

"How long will our contract be?"

Mason kissed her again, his mouth lingering on hers as he whispered, "Forever."

THANK YOU FOR READING!

Keep reading for a sneak peak of
ASHERWICK

ASHERWICK
CHAPTER ONE

A fine mist blanketed Haven City, covering the ground in a haze and swirling in the air. Sylphine wrapped her arms around herself, longing for sunlight, and not for the first time since leaving the warmth of Italyssa. She tried to focus on the angry driver screaming profanities and a demand for raimarks she didn't have, to pay for the journey she'd needed from the MagnaRail station to the Enforcement Services East Street Division. Jonathon Hunter, also known as Key Guardian Asherwick in his home country, worked in the building as an investigator.

Sylphine had been foolish enough to think the driver would be charitable since she'd asked to be brought to an Enforcement precinct. The livid red of his jiggling cheeks, and the spittle coating the lower half of his dark beard, revealed exactly how *benevolent* he was inclined to be with her. Hunger gnawed at her stomach, and she knew if she itched at the edges of the course gown she wore anymore, she'd bleed.

"Mister, I am very sorry, just let me go inside to my promised and he will gladly pay you."

The man pointed at the tall, bleak building. "He's in there?"

"Yes, he is a Master Tribunii with Enforcement Services, and a Key Guardian."

He looked her over, doubt narrowing his dark eyes to slits. Sylphine pulled her shoulders back and raised a brow. Despite her poor attire and filthy state, she was an heiress and she knew how to look like one.

Shaking his head, he sighed. "I go in with you."

Resigned, and knowing she had no other choice, Sylphine agreed. At least she was in Haven City, safe despite the sketchy travel means she'd endured, very near to the man who would help dig her out of a deep hole she'd found herself stuck in. Again.

The usual bustle of the division precinct was subdued in the later evening hours. Sylphine strode with purpose to the front desk, all the while aware of the suspicious glare of the driver at her back.

Under normal circumstances, she would have gone straight to the Hunter residence. But her situation was anything except ordinary, and she refused to put Jonathon's sister Ramsey, in danger. While the chances of the Cyrano's knowing she was in Sziveria right at this moment were miniscule, the risk was still present. Hopefully since Jonathon seemed to live at the East Street Division, her waking nightmare would soon be over.

Taking a deep breath, Sylphine approached the front desk. She pasted on a smile and rested her arms on the tall reception counter. A woman looked up from a word puzzle spread out before her in the newspaper. Annoyance made the creases on her face more prominent. The receptionist returned her attention to the puzzle.

"This isn't the overnight shelter. It's two blocks," she lifted her pen and pointed to the left, "that way."

Sylphine kept her shock internal and shook her head. She figured she looked terrible, but not *that* terrible. "No, I am not..."

The woman glanced up again. A sagging, gray streaked bun shifted back on the crown of her head. "Clothing distribution is on the first Friday of every month, during business hours."

Sylphine opened her hands and shook her head again. "No, I do not need…"

"Look lady," the receptionist snapped, "unless you have a crime to report, we don't have anything for charity. I'm sorry. Go to the shelter, they have everything you need."

The driver coughed. Sylphine resisted the urge to shoot him a glare. Smoothing her fingers along the polished surface of the counter, she tried again. "I need to speak with MT Hunter. Please."

"Is this concerning a case?" she asked, leaning forward, her gaze filled with suspicion.

"I'm his promised, and I need to speak with him. Now, please. You can tell me where his office is, I will get there myself."

"MT Hunter left about an hour ago." The woman returned to her puzzle. "If you're his promised, you can get to his house, can't you?"

Sylphine sensed more than saw the driver close in behind her. His frustration rebounded off her in waves. "You said you'd get my money for your fare."

"Yes, and I will," Sylphine assured. She looked back at the receptionist. "Please call MT Hunter. Please. I have no way to get to his house. I took a hired carriage here. I swear he knows me. I have had a terrible journey. I was robbed, and I fell off the pier in Port Anchor. East Street Division is closer from the rail station than Jonathon's house."

The woman stared for quiet seconds, flipping the pen idly between her fingers. She pointed it Sylphine with a glare. "If I radio him and you're lying, I will be the witness this man needs against you to put you behind bars for theft."

Anxiety curled in her chest. *Please, please don't hate me so much, Jonathon.* "Very well."

On a long-suffering sigh, the woman twisted in her seat towards the long row of radios. During normal business hours, there would an operator for each station. She retrieved a huge binder from underneath the counter and flipped through pages. Moments later, the static of an undesignated outbound signal flared. With quick skill, she designated the call. The signal chirped.

"MT Hunter, Key Guardian Asherwick," Jonathon's voice said over the line.

Sylphine almost slumped in relief.

The receptionist shot her a sideways glower. "Hello, MT, this is Gweneth at East Street Division. I have a woman here claiming to be your promised. She insisted I call."

Tense silence cracked on the line. Gweneth's stare scathed. Sylphine held her breath.

"Who?"

ASHERWICK
Available for preorder Jan. 6th, 2022
Release date June 2nd, 2022

My Dearest Reader,

Mason and Jessi's story was a hard one to write, for many reasons. The heartache of loss, a painful past, an impending loss. They made this book more of a romance than my others as two people found the beauty in allowing another to take on their hurt. To help in the recovery of a traumatic past. We often forget we don't have to live this life alone. We forget we aren't meant to. People are placed in our life for us to connect with, to rely on, to help as well.

We also, I think, forget that our past, which sometimes we really do need to confront and heal over, doesn't define who we are. Sure, our past shapes us, makes us stronger, provides wisdom (and perhaps sadly even fear), but it is not our defining factor. We are not the sum of our yesterdays. We are not the sum of the scars, healed or healing. The decisions *we* make, of our own freewill, today, are who we can choose to be. Healed or broken. Angry or at peace. Holding a grudge or willing to forgive. Making a different choice that changes the trajectory of our tomorrow. All of this is power, held in your very hand, and it's mighty indeed.

Perhaps you don't believe that. Maybe you've even been told your past is all you'll ever be. All you'll ever amount to. Don't believe such lies. Who *you* are is only for you to decide. No one else gets that power. No one else gets to speak anything else over you with any sort of impact unless they are speaking of your potential. Your beauty. Your talent. Anything else needs to flow away, like water through your fingers. This morning you woke up to a new day, embrace all that means! You're beautiful, amazing, perfect in who you are and who you've been made to be.

All my love,
Sarah

SARAH WESTILL lives in Alabama with her US Army-retired husband. They have two sons – one they've successfully raised to adulthood – the other is still a work-in-progress, navigating middle school. As a full-on creative, Sarah lives to write, paint, teach, and meet amazing people while doing portrait photography. A veteran in the publishing industry working as a cover artist under the name Elaina Lee, she has been blessed to help hundreds of authors to achieve their own publishing goals for over a decade. To learn more about Sarah as she blogs her adventures, and about her Guardians, please visit her at sarahwestill.com or follow her on Instagram @authorsarahwestill